THE FAE OF THE FOREST

THE FAE OF THE FOREST

ELLE THRASHER

The Fae of the Forest

Ebook ISBN: 979-8-9855971-8-9

Paperback ISBN: 979-8-9855971-9-6

Hardback ISBN: 979-8-9903433-0-6

For information: elle@ellethrasher.com

Cover Designer: Damonza

Editor: Aimee Vance, Revel Books

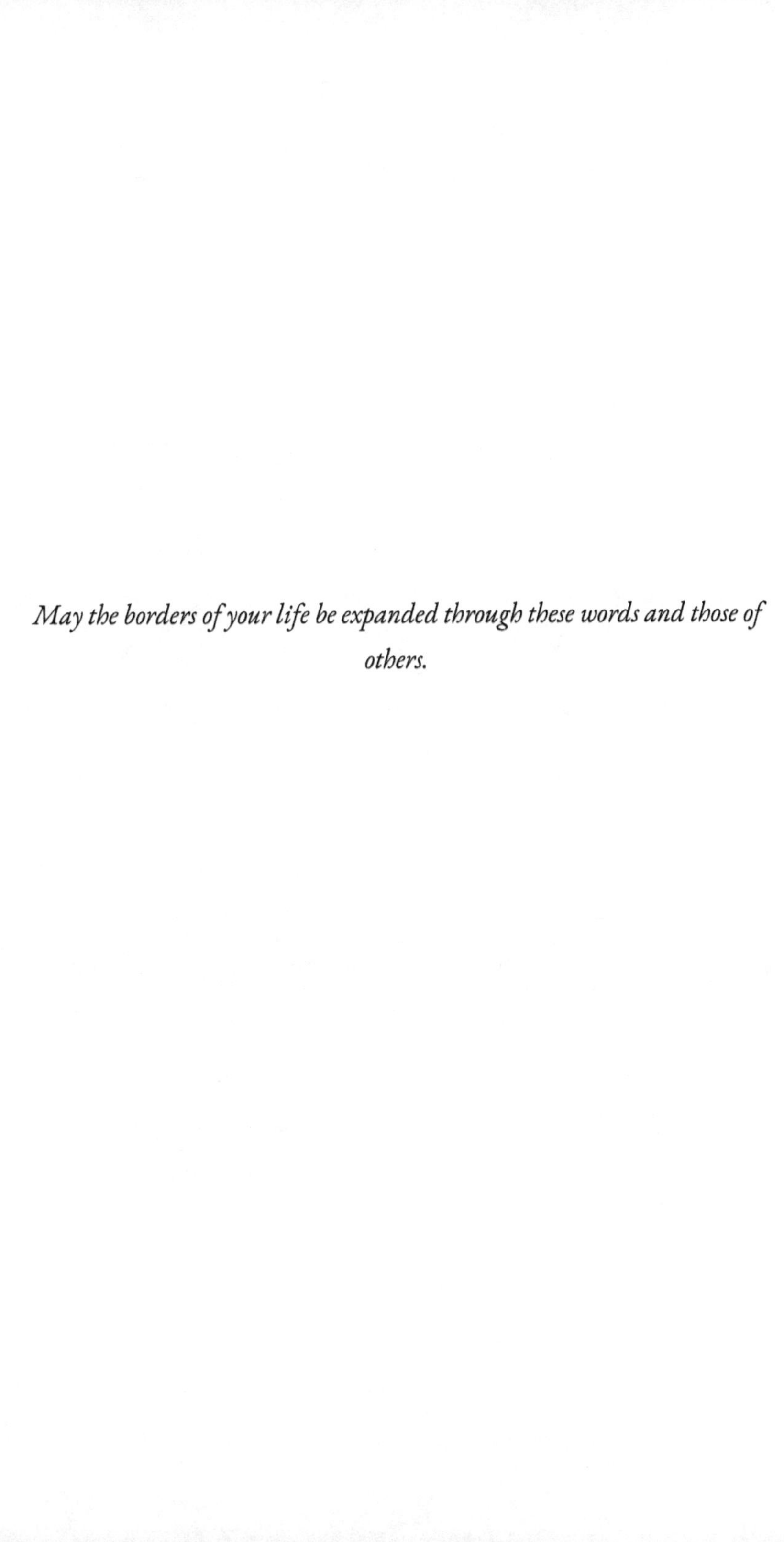

May the borders of your life be expanded through these words and those of others.

CONTENT NOTICE

The book you are about to read contains subject matter that may be difficult or unappealing to some readers. This includes, language, on-page sex, violence, minor gore, mentions loss of loved ones.

PRONUNCIATION GUIDE

Espen -- Ess-pen

Øyvin -- Oy-vihn

Alvdalen --Alv-dah-len

Balder -- Bahl-derr

Bente -- Ben-teh

Fjell -- Fyell

Freija -- Frey-ah

Gunvor -- Guun-vore

Halvar -- Hal-vahr

Kjetil -- Sheh-till

Knut-Arne -- Knewt - Ahr-neh

Leif -- Layf

Oddvar -- Odd-vahr

Reuven --Rew-ven

Skolvik -- Skoll-veek

Solveig -- Sool-vay

Torsten -- Torr-sten

Trygve -- Tryg-veh

Turi --Tuu-ree

Veigar -- Vey-gahr

Vigdis -- Vigh-diss

Wilhelm -- Vill-helm

Ylva -- Yll-vah

BEFORE YOU BEGIN...

Thank you for picking up The Fae of the Forest, book 2 in the Nordic Fae series!

If you haven't read the bridge novella, **Christmas on the Fjord,** I HIGHLY recommend doing so before diving into book 2.

There are some important plot points that will make more sense if you've read the novella ;) and it's only 90 pages long!

You can find the ebook <u>on Amazon</u>!

Best wishes,

Elle

1

LENNIE

An orb of effervescent white light no bigger than a tennis ball floated between my palms. I let out a long breath and steadied myself. This was progress from my first day of training with the light-wielding Fjell Fae, Torsten, a few weeks ago, but having magic flow from me still felt like a fever dream.

"She can do it, yes she can." Espen, dressed in his police uniform and green wool hat with wobbling pom-pom, cheered from the wintry sideline of the clearing within the forest above the fjord. I glared at him, his peppy attitude annoying this early in the morning, especially considering I'd only had one cup of coffee. Oddvar made a strong brew, but it wasn't enough for the crack of dawn on a gray, snowy day in the middle of winter in Norway.

Looking back down at the fae power gathered in my hands, I did my best to ignore the gentle breeze winding across the clearing, brushing aside the top dusting of snow. My layers and jacket shielded me from the worst of the late-January chill, but my face was still exposed to the elements. Snot slowly descended through my nostrils as a not so pleasant reminder of the cold weather. I bet I was super attractive right now. One snotty hot mess express, anyone?

"Rah, rah, goooooooo—"

"Do you mind?" I asked through gritted teeth, failing to keep my eyes from straying up to his obnoxiously handsome face. "That's not helping me concentrate."

Nothing about Espen ever helped me concentrate, but watching him do little jumping jacks and wave around invisible pom-poms was definitely not helping. With his floppy brown hair, short beard, and loving gazes at the hibernating flora, the Forest Fae looked at home in the wilderness.

"Would meditation help instead?" Espen replied, and the suggestiveness in his tone drew my attention. He brought his hands down and into prayer position in front of his chest, a smirk on his face as one dark eyebrow climbed. "Perhaps a gentle morning yoga routine?"

The glowing between my palms stuttered, but the ball of light remained as I strained to focus. "You should have let me continue my corpse pose in bed this morning."

Espen snorted. "We all know bridge pose is your new favorite."

I scoffed, but a low chuckle behind me agreed with Espen's assessment. Something in my stomach fluttered at the noise, and the orb wavered.

"You did seem fond of it," Øyvin said, his deep voice scratchy this early in the morning. I peered over at the broad-shouldered Fjord Fae with blond hair. Decked out in his signature navy-blue-colored winter gear, he perched on a boulder, keeping guard at the edge of my mini-forest-arena while I practiced using my new magic powers. Trees towered around us, blocking the view of the fjord and the town below. We didn't need anyone seeing this—including fae, because my entry-level abilities were embarrassing—nor anyone accidentally getting a ball of light to the face.

Øyvin had a few close calls with some of my magical orbs recently, and had subsequently decided to be on watch duty while Espen "coached."

"My current favorite yoga pose-meets-sex position doesn't matter right now, does it guys?"

The ball of light evaporated, and I let out an exasperated groan, my hands falling to my sides. It was hopeless. I'd inherited these new powers several months ago, but couldn't do jack shit with them other than summon a ball of light. Considering I'd been human last fall, that wasn't nothing, but we'd been at this for weeks now, and I wasn't making measurable progress. Maybe we needed to change up my training regimen?

"Focus on your breathing." Espen sidled up behind me and rubbed his hands over my shoulders in a soothing motion. The tension in my muscles diffused and a tender warmth settled over me.

I filled my lungs and angled my face toward the sky.

"And out," Espen whispered into my ear, the warmth of his words skittering across my cold cheek. He slid his hands down my arms and lifted them slightly, lining up their height with my sternum. "Breathe in," he murmured once more, and I did, the cold air tickling my lips. "Now, focus on the light again, bring that power up from your chest. Visualize it in your palms."

I focused on that new-constant, the warmth that radiated between my ribs, the something extra I'd been gifted by Halvar when Queen Freija was dying and transferred magic to him, only for it to be too much for the Fjell Fae. As the only other "vessel" in the room, I'd been the lucky one to get some of that power too, enough to turn me into a demi-fae—half-human, half-Fjell Fae.

I closed my eyes and a gentle tickle swept down my arms, pressure formed between my hands, and a glow swept across my eyelids.

"There you go," Espen said, his voice matching the church-like still-ness around us. He moved his hands to my waist and pressed his chest against my back, and I pushed my rear against the top of his thighs, reveling in the warmth he provided. "Keep breathing."

Taking another deep breath, I opened my eyes. The ball of light be-tween my palms was slightly larger than the last, more akin to a softball. I grinned, and a rumble of approval sounded from Espen as Øyvin stepped up beside us, his eyes locked on my hands.

"Push forward, not just with your hands but with your mind," Øyvin said, and demonstrated—for the twentieth time in the past few weeks—with his own palms and a ball of water. The liquid sloshed around within the confines of its shape, goading me into playing along.

Slowly pressing my hands forward on an extended exhale, I moved with the breath as Espen had taught me. The ball of light drifted forward and hovered above the snowy field, growing ever so slightly as it went. Øyvin pushed his ball of water further, passing mine and igniting that Martin Family competitive gene.

Oh, you wanna race?

I glanced over at him briefly. His eyebrow quirked high and his lips pressed firmly together in an effort not to smile.

Let's do this.

Rolling my shoulders and returning my focus to our magic orbs, I nudged mine ahead of his, only for his to zip past it two seconds later.

Grimacing, I tried again... The ball shot further across the field, and was quickly surpassed by Øyvin's. A soft chuckle emanated from Espen behind me. Øyvin's lips tilted into a lopsided smile and I faced him, careful to still keep my ball of light within the corner of my eye. He opened his mouth to say something, then stiffened and the ball of water disappeared. Mine followed swiftly thereafter as I dropped my hands, my focus drawn to the Forest Fae at my back turning and staring into the woods behind us.

The snow crunched and compacted, a rustle sounding from between the trees while someone moved among them. Their muffled footfalls audible thanks to the stillness.

The guys repositioned in front of me and turned toward the tree line where Øyvin had been stationed five minutes ago. I peered through the gap between their shoulders, all senses on high alert.

A dark-clad figure moved among the dense trunks, and worry welled inside me, unsure of what to do. Øyvin, on the other hand, with his 237 years of being a fae, knew exactly what he was doing, as did Espen at 225. Both men visibly relaxed as the figure came closer, emerging into our little clearing-slash-Lennie-training-center.

"Torsten," Øyvin greeted the Fjell Fae. Torsten nodded, his tawny hair twisted into a bun on the back of his head, his outerwear not dissimilar from what the local humans wore in the winter—a thick black jacket with a fur-lined hood and gray snow-pants.

Torsten's eyes slid to me as he tilted his head to one side. "How goes training?"

I shrugged. "Same old—"

"She just maneuvered a light ball across the field, playing chase with Øyvin," Espen interjected.

Torsten smiled, setting his hands on his hips and giving me a nod. "Well done. That's progress and control."

I gave him my best jazz hands and sighed. He was right though, it wasn't nothing. It was progress that I needed to celebrate. I gave him a more vigorous jazz hands gesture again, building up the positivity inside me and receiving low laughs from all three fae.

I brushed a stray hair off my forehead and crossed my arms. "What brings you out here this fine, cold morning?"

"Came to see how your light magic was doing and…" His features pinched together as he winced. "Halvar."

Espen and Øyvin both shuffled on the spot at the mention of the most fearsome Fjell Fae I'd met, further tamping the snow beneath their feet as a shudder ran through my body. A sense of impending doom settled over me. If Halvar had a message for us then shit was about to hit the fan… and that never ended well for me.

"What happened?" Øyvin's voice dropped to his serious tone, the one I'd heard him use around the Fjord soldiers last year when we fought against the now deceased Fjord King who'd gone on a power trip.

"Nothing," Torsten said. He raised his hands as if to say *don't kill the messenger*. "I was sent to request your presence in the throne room. Halvar wants a meeting with all three of you immediately."

Yeah, that didn't sound good at all.

Over the past two months, since the last time shit hit the proverbial fan, I'd only seen the big guy in passing. None of us had spent any time with him as he'd been busy with the Fjell Council after Freija's death. And, honestly, I couldn't blame him. Based on the moments I'd witnessed between him and the late Queen, I understood that the man needed time to quietly grieve and handle the political fallout.

"Any clues on what this meeting is about?" Espen piped up and moved to stand beside me. He slipped his hand into mine and gave it a light but reassuring squeeze. The gentle touch was enough to make my cold heart pitter-patter in the most fairytale of ways, and I felt like Snow White in the forest. Were there singing animals in these woods, too? Was this the moment they broke into song before we all walked into a mountain to face our doom? Could they go to this meeting for me?

Torsten shook his head and shrugged. "It's not my place to say. Just know that he's serious."

"I thought that was his resting state. Like Resting Bitch Face, but make it scary Viking Fae."

My guys let out long sighs, which had Torsten chuckling. "Don't worry," he said, a knowing grin forming on his face. "If Halvar wanted you dead, you'd already be six feet under."

"I know," all three of us replied simultaneously.

2

LENNIE

We traipsed up the hill on the north side of Skolvik, striding along the trail between the trees and aiming for the main entrance to the mountain, the home of the Fjell Fae. The snow on the path was downtrodden, but still crunched lightly beneath our boots.

Stepping through the main entrance, the magic washed over me as it granted us passage into the fjell's tunnels. "Any updates on the magic illusions around the entrances?" I asked.

The entrances to the mountain—magically hidden by mirages that would rebuff humans and unwanted guests—had dwindled in number since Freija's death. I didn't fully understand how it worked, but, according to Espen, the former Fjell Queen Freija's magic had been what kept the entrances hidden. When she passed, almost all of them were exposed.

"The guards' quick work on re-doing some of the mirages has been successful," Torsten replied from up ahead. His words bounced off the jagged stone walls of the tunnel. "And we don't believe any humans have noticed anything amiss."

"That's good," Espen said beside me, his gloved hand firmly wrapped around my own. "We haven't had any reports at the station."

"It is fortunate, but Halvar and his team didn't have the strength to cover every entrance. Some have been closed off with boulders and cave-ins that seal the passages for good, or at least until we find a way to restore the queen's magic and open them up again safely."

I shook my head. So much had faltered after the demise of Freija and the piece-of-shit former Fjord King, Balder. Both the fjell had weakened and, as Øyvin had mentioned, they'd had to re-erect the wall within the fjord that protected the waters from pollution. It was all a mess, but thankfully things were on the mend.

We reached a crossroads in the tunnel system and Torsten came to a stop. "I'll leave you here," he said with a smile. "Good luck."

"Do we need it?" My gut said we did, but it was worth asking.

"You know Halvar."

My shoulders slumped as the guys chuckled. Because yes, yes we did.

Traipsing through the rocky halls, we wandered into the throne room and found Halvar standing in front of the throne, hands behind his back but his posture as rigid as ever. The space behind him sat empty save for the lingering reminder of the loss that had occurred here a few short months ago. The sky-blue stone of the walls and ceiling shone thanks to the magical lanterns that were built into the wall.

Heat grew around my neck and I unzipped my jacket, pulled off my gloves and hat, and shoved them into my pockets. Even with winter in full swing outside, the temperature within the mountain was subtly warm—some sort of insulation magic keeping the residents protected from the external elements.

Halvar's eyes followed us closely as we came to a halt, the guys flanking me as they had done many times before.

"Thank you for coming." Halvar's silver hair and beard were a stark contrast to the black sweater and pants he wore. His chin tipped up as he looked over us like a general surveying his troops, and I wondered if this was what it felt like to be in the military—decorum and customs constantly on your mind in a superior's presence. How did they know when to salute or not?

I gave Halvar a quick smile, and the guys bowed their heads before straightening up to attention like his soldiers, even though they both carried the same Head Guard title as Halvar, but for their own fae factions. My slouch and shitty posture would have to be enough for Halvar though. I crossed my arms and rested my weight on my hip. "What's up, big guy?"

Halvar huffed at my casualness, taking a deep breath that made me squirm uncomfortably. "I have a task for you. The Fjell Fae Council needs to retrieve an important..." he hesitated for a second, tilting his head from one side to the other. "An individual of great importance to us."

I narrowed my eyes at him. "Have you heard of a cellphone? Fantastic technology that helps you get hold of someone," I said, then muttered under my breath, "when they remember to charge it."

Øyvin stirred beside me, probably tempted to clap his hand over my mouth. But the tension now flowing off both fae at my sides was enough to have me buzzing with curiosity.

"We tried that," Halvar replied, ignoring my sass. "Unfortunately, there was no response. So, the individual will have to be retrieved manually."

"And who is—" Espen started, just as I asked, "Why us?"

Øyvin let out a long sigh, fisting his hands at his side like he was desperate to duct-tape my mouth shut.

Halvar's jaw worked, which considering we'd only been here for a matter of minutes must have been some kind of record. I was exceptionally good at getting under people's skin quickly, and apparently that included this seemingly ancient mountain fae. "You three have been requested by the Council due to your considerable powers, and as a test of your loyalty, Lennie and Øyvin."

My brow furrowed. "Loyalty?"

"Yes, *loyalty*." Halvar focused on me and Øyvin. "Espen and the Forest Fae have proven trustworthy with our alliance over the past few decades. Aside from the assistance we had from Øyvin and some of the Fjord Fae in the battle against Balder last year, you two are untried."

Øyvin opened his mouth, but I beat him to it. "So, that's why you want him as well? You want to strengthen your new alliance with the Fjord?"

Halvar nodded and Øyvin inhaled audibly. "Understood," the Fjord Fae said.

"And I'm just here for shits and giggles?"

Halvar's eyebrows pinched together. "You are a demi-Fjell Fae. This is your opportunity to show you deserve to be one of us. To show you are worthy of the powers you now have. Prove your worth to the Fjell."

"Or else?"

"We return your power to the fjell."

"Which is done, how?"

Halvar's eyes met mine as a grinding noise sounded above our heads. Three crystalline stalactites jutted down from the ceiling. The pointed bits stopped mere inches from our skulls. Air rushed out of my lungs and I hunched over, hoping the massive piece of stone didn't skewer me like a kebab. "Death. Got it. Thanks."

An orb of water appeared above Halvar while Espen grabbed my hand and growled. "Don't you dare, Halvar."

The stalactite above my head dropped an inch lower, and I shuddered.

Halvar's gaze remained fixed on me. "Prove. Your. Worth."

"Nothing like a death threat and a challenge to get the blood pumping," I said.

Both of my guys moved to protest, but Halvar raised his hand, stopping them. "This is Fjell business and part of the Council's plan."

I peered at the men beside me. Both of their jaws were locked, their muscles jumping as they moved into positions like they were about to tackle Halvar. Part of me wanted to let them loose and see what happened. But the other part of me knew that Halvar, with his imposing stature and ability to create axes out of thin air, was the biggest threat in the room.

I reached out and rested my hands on Øyvin and Espen's elbows, drawing their attention. "It'll be fine. We can do this." I really fucking hoped we could. Halvar had thrown down a challenge, and I was going to meet it head-on in hopes he wouldn't take my head *off*.

Øyvin and Espen let out shaky breaths and nodded before refocusing on Halvar. The water ball, which Halvar hadn't even acknowledged, vanished.

Pulling my shoulders back and crossing my arms over my chest, I said, "Fine. I'll prove my trustworthiness and loyalty to the Fjell."

Halvar didn't move, but the stone icicles retreated and disappeared into the sky-blue ceiling as if they'd never existed.

I sucked in a breath and shook off the threat, catching the guys doing the same. "Now, who exactly do you want us to find?"

Halvar's gaze flicked to the side, and he noticeably swallowed a lump in his throat. "We seek to retrieve the heir of the Fjell Fae and return her to the throne."

All three of us flinched. *Heir?*

My jaw dropped, heading for the stone floor. I glanced between my fae, both of whom wore stunned expressions. At least they were as shocked as I was. I may not have known much Fjell Fae history, or fae history in general, but I'd never heard anyone mention a Fjell Fae Heir.

"Obviously you're not going to promote Nora after her betrayal. Long may she rot in the dungeon if you haven't already put one of those fancy icicles through her heart." I pointed to the ceiling where one such crystal stone spear had just been. "But I figured the Council would just make you king, Halvar, and be done with it."

Espen cleared his throat, and Øyvin jabbed his elbow into my side. I tilted away from his movement, the hit not painful but the message received. Time to shut up.

Silence settled over the room.

"Where is the heir?" Øyvin asked once Halvar no longer looked like he was about to drop a stalactite down on me again.

Halvar blinked and looked to Espen. "Alvdalen."

A chuckling noise escaped from Espen's throat and he tilted his head back with a smile. "Of course. *That*'s why you need me."

Halvar grunted in the affirmative.

I looked at Espen, my mouth pursed. "Care to explain what this *Alvdalen* is?" I asked, probably butchering the Norwegian. My language skills had significantly improved over the last few months, but my pro-nunciation could still use some fine-tuning. The main things I struggled with were the throatier words, the rolling Rs and those three extra letters in the Norwegian alphabet—one of which, æ, sounded like you were sticking your tongue out at the doctor's office.

Espen faced me, his eyes glittering with excitement. "My hometown."

My eyebrows met my hairline. "Your hometown?"

Espen's head bobbed, his grin growing as he turned back to Halvar. "You want someone who knows the area well."

Halvar nodded.

"I could just call my sister, Turi, and ask her to fetch your heir," Espen continued. "She knows just about everyone in town."

Halvar grimaced, and Espen's bubbly disposition popped. "Won't be that easy."

"And why not?" I asked.

"Because she is only known as the heir by one individual," he responded, but looked around the room as if struggling to find the right words. "That is to say, she's been in the care of an individual who is the only person in the town that knows her secret. The Council has failed to get in contact with her guardian. I'd go myself, but I cannot leave the fjell, not while my magic is tied to the mountain. I also wouldn't want to draw too much attention to them."

"Can I inform the Council of Elders of the heir?" Espen's eyebrows pinched together. "In a closed meeting of course."

Halvar nodded, light bouncing off his silver hair. "But only the Council. We don't want word getting out."

"Agreed. Thank you," Espen replied.

"Can you give us a name?" Øyvin asked, his voice firm and authoritative. "At least for the heir's guardian?"

"Vigdis Johansen is an old friend of the Fjell, and is the heir's guardian." Halvar glanced quickly at the throne behind him before adding, "I know this is asking a lot of you at such a fragile time for the fjord, but I would appreciate your assistance and cooperation. Mark it as a first request in our new alliance."

Øyvin nodded. "It would be my honor to assist you and the Council in this endeavor. I will, of course, have to inform the Fjord Council and receive their blessing, but considering the nature of the request, I don't believe there will be any resistance."

"Thank you," Halvar said with a barely there smile as if he hadn't threatened us all a few minutes ago. He reached into his back pocket and pulled out an envelope. "Please give Vigdis this. It explains why the Council sent you and that you mean the heir no harm."

I stepped forward and took the proffered letter from his extended hand. The beige-colored parchment was rough but lightweight, the envelope sealed with a glob of black wax. Part of me was desperate to peek inside, but Halvar had already explained its contents and it wasn't meant for me. So, I stuffed it into the inner pocket of my jacket and zipped it shut.

"We will make sure Vigdis gets the letter. But what's the heir's name?" I asked. "All this discussion about the heir's guardian is great, but it's the *heir* we need to find, not her."

"Aurora. A distant relative of Freija's." Tension radiated off Halvar, power wavering in the air around him reminding me just how powerful this fearsome fae was. "Give Vigdis the letter. She'll know what to do."

Halvar's sky-blue eyes bore into me and I didn't dare press further. We'd just have to find this Vigdis woman and hope she could fill us in a bit more.

"On behalf of the Forest Fae, we'd be honored to help," Espen said with a nod which Halvar returned in kind.

"How far away is Alvdalen?" I asked, choosing to ignore the threat for now and instead focus on the thrill of a new adventure bubbling up within me.

Espen shrugged. "Roughly a day's drive."

"Quick little road trip?" My voice rose, matching the excitement building in my veins as I looked between my guys.

Espen beamed at me. "Road trip." His hands flexed like he wanted to wrap me in a hug, but then remembered where we were and whose presence we were in. "I know someone we can borrow a car from."

I frowned. "And you didn't think to make such an offer last year when I needed to get back to my cruise ship?"

His smile morphed into a look that was definitely not meant for anyone else to see, and my insides heated at the sight. "I was selfish and wanted you to stay."

Well, if my heart had been pitter-pattering earlier this morning, it was now a full-on conga line with maracas.

With sneaky grins on our faces that promised a whole lot of *yoga* when we got home, the three of us spun for the exit and made it all of two steps before Halvar cleared his throat. Sliding to a halt and hoping the big guy just had a slight cough, I turned back to the Fjell Fae, the guys following suit.

"Lennie, you train with me today."

My mouth fell open and my stomach sank to my feet. *Satan help me.* "Ummm... I already trained today."

"Not with me you didn't," Halvar replied, then nodded to the guys. "You two are free to go. Lennie will be home for dinner."

I spun to Espen and Øyvin, my eyes wide, hands latching on to their jackets, hoping they could save me. Øyvin shrugged out of my hold and wandered off with a cocky grin plastered across his face, while Espen twisted his lips downward. "I'm sorry. You *do* need to train—"

"Not right now, I don't." My pulse ratcheted upward. I'd fully planned on taking a sexy mid-morning nap, and said plan now looked like it was drifting down the fjord.

Espen gave me a wistful smile while prying my fingers off his arm. "I'll make you mac and cheese for dinner."

Groaning, I stepped back and pulled my hair into a ponytail. "Fine, make it extra cheesy please."

"Of course." With a quick glance at Halvar, Espen lurched forward, planted a kiss on my temple, and then departed before he could get conscripted into anything else. *Smart man.*

I spun on my heels and faced Halvar.

He uncrossed his arms and rolled his broad shoulders. His muscles rippled, promising the Fjell Fae equivalent of leg day. "Are you ready?"

I whimpered at the sight, wishing Thor himself would appear and zap me into smithereens instead. "No."

3

ØYVIN

While Lennie was no doubt being destroyed by Halvar's training, I made my way to work beneath the surface of the fjord.

The biting cold water pressed against the air pocket I'd created around myself as I descended deeper. Crossing over abandoned fae homes built into the fjord bed and hidden between boulders—the piles of rocks and former protective shields now gone—I shook my head. Our people had unnecessarily suffered since Balder died, similar to the Fjell Fae. The grim side effects of our selfish and power-hungry former King's actions culminated in a need for those who lived in the deeper waters to relocate to shoreline caves, and a weaker wall against pollution. I grumbled as I zipped past a plastic bag, yet another piece of debris that'd need cleaning up. If I wasn't needed in chambers within the next five minutes, I'd slow to grab it, but as it was... I grit my teeth and pushed on.

The dark waters lightened as I descended toward the Fjord Palace. Glowing lights on either side of the entrance, courtesy of Valdemar, our own light-wielding Fjord Fae, beckoned me. The cavern-like entry with ornate carvings—consisting of aquatic creatures from ancient myth and reality—was guarded by my burliest soldiers, swimming around and scanning for any threats. I didn't expect any dangers in the foreseeable future, but as we'd lost our monarch and the power he'd wielded, we were all a little on edge. Like the Fjell, until our own heir took up the mantle as leader and received more powers from the ancestors, we were a weakened community.

Launching myself through the air pocket around the entrance, I landed with a dull thud against the stone floor, uniformed soldiers on my left and right greeting me with swift nods. My own air pocket dissolved on impact, the magic leaving me completely dry. Without faltering, I miraged my navy Fjord Fae uniform and shoulder-cape over my jacket and jeans, and strode toward the inner arteries of the palace, aiming for the council meeting room.

The council chamber bustled with a low hum of noise when I reached it, wood scraping against the stone floor as people took their seats at the long oak table in the center of the room. Magical light and flame-filled chandeliers lit the space, casting a flickering glow on the aquatic mural that adorned the entire length of the back wall. Mythological creatures, demons of the deep, and a giant sea-serpent with a bright-blue stone for an eye stretched across the stone surface, etched there by ancient hands. I found my chair to the right of the King's former seat, where our new chief advisor, Valdemar, prepared to preside over our meeting.

After Balder's demise, we scrambled to sort out our leadership. Valdemar was no stranger to the Fjord Fae Council, having served as the King's Chief Advisor several centuries ago. Thank the ancestors he'd agreed to take up the position once more.

White robes from a time long since passed draped over Valdemar's hunched form. His thin eyebrows pinched together as he clasped his wrinkled hands on the table in front of him. He turned to me as I sat, light bouncing off the few remaining white hairs on his head. "Do you bring good news or bad?"

I rolled my shoulders and pulled in my chair, before mimicking his hands' position. "Neutral, but politically good for us all, I believe."

A wizened smile spread across his lips. "I like to hear that." He clapped his hands together, the sound echoing around the room and garnering the other members' attention. "Shall we begin?"

Those who were still standing took their seats and all focus turned to Valdemar at the head of the table.

"Thank you all for being here," Valdemar started, his voice shaking slightly with age. "We have several matters to discuss, including an item brought forth by Øyvin. But we shall start, once more, with matters regarding the well-being of the monarchy."

"Have we heard anything else from the children?" I asked the assembled council, wondering if any of Balder's hoard of kids gave a damn about the fjord. It was well known that he'd slept around most of the Norwegian coastline, with his children of all ages now scattered around the world, some ignoring their magic, others living solely beneath the surface. But there was one I was most interested in: his heir, Reuven. Upon Balder's passing, he would've no doubt felt a shift in his magic. He'd need to return to Skolvik to take up the mantle as King and then receive whatever magic the ancestors were willing to re-bestow. Normally, Balder's magic would've been re-gifted to the heir... but, would the ancestors want to do so after everything that happened? Everything he'd stolen?

"All of the children have now been informed," Valdemar replied, regaining my attention. "We just got a message to the youngest, Siri in Scotland. She sends her regards and a few choice words about her late father that do not bear repeating."

I refrained from snorting as several members cleared their throats. Siri's attitude and personality wasn't dissimilar from Lennie's, and, whenever we'd been able to get in contact with her, she'd never minced her words. Clearly, nothing had changed.

Valdemar stirred in his seat. "And, most importantly, Reuven, the eldest, has finally expressed interest to return to the fjord with his wife."

Thank goodness. I'd never met Reuven. He was a century my senior and had been married off to a Fire Fae Princess in Iceland when he was just a boy in an effort by Balder to shore up *alliances.* Those alliances now took on a whole different meaning. In light of what he'd tried to do, and succeeded with in the case of both Queen Ragnhild of the Forest and Queen Freija of the Fjell, the deceased monarch had been amassing power and allegiance for a long time.

"Did Veigar send any messages about the alliance?" I asked, wondering if the Fire Fae King might pose a threat to us. At this rate, we needed to be cautious. And, from what I'd been told, caution was always wise when dealing with Veigar as he had an easily triggered temper. "He isn't concerned about sending his daughter across the North Sea?"

Valdemar shook his head and cupped his hands together on the table. "He sent no word. We shall await their arrival and see if there are any messages sent through Reuven."

I sighed. It was better than nothing. We'd been waiting for a response from Reuven for weeks, needing to know if he was going to take over as King and help maintain the well-being of the fjord and its inhabitants. His return was at least something to be grateful for.

"Does anyone have anything else to share with the Council regarding the monarchy?" Valdemar scanned the weathered faces around the table. When no one else said a word, he added, "Very well, Øyvin?"

All eyes swung to me.

"I have a request from the Fjell."

Valdemar waved his hand for me to proceed. "Go on."

I swallowed and straightened in my seat. "Halvar has requested that myself, the demi-fae, and Espen of the Forest, assist in locating the Fjell heir."

The entire room sucked in a breath, every council members' eyes widening. I couldn't blame them. I too had been shocked to hear that Freija had an heir that wasn't her traitorous sister. "I ask you for permission to take some time away from the fjord to assist with this search."

"Where will you be heading and for how long?" Idar, the fae to my right asked.

"Alvdalen. I don't know exactly how long—a couple of weeks at most."

"Why *you*?" Idar continued. "Or is this an effort to solidify an alliance with us?"

I hummed in agreement. I had no doubt Espen and Lennie could find the heir by themselves, but this was a good faith request after Balder's betrayal. That, and I wasn't entirely certain what would happen if someone denied Halvar what he wanted. From the tales and rumors I'd heard of his past, it would likely end in someone's early demise. His threat to Lennie further solidified those rumors and my resolve to make this happen without her getting hurt.

"It is indeed a request to solidify our alliance. One I think we'd be wise to take," I said.

Valdemar nodded and several other council members muttered their approval.

"If you all agree, I'll take a temporary leave of absence from my post here in the fjord, leaving Captain Sigurd in charge of operations and the wall." I glanced around the room, hoping I had their permission. We needed all the support we could get right now, and if helping Halvar find the Fjell heir would seal our alliance, then I'd do it.

"All those in favor, say aye," Valdemar stated. His sage stare took in every member of the assembled council.

A resounding response of "aye" came through. I relaxed in my seat, tension easing from my muscles.

"Any opposed? Hearing none. We, the Council, agree to this arrangement and wish you well on this endeavor, Øyvin." Valdemar smiled, his lips forming a curved line, no teeth visible. "If there are no further matters to discuss..." he let the sentence hang for a few seconds, but no one spoke up. "Then our meeting is adjourned. Have a good day."

I rose from my seat and pushed the chair back in, leaving it as I'd found it.

That had gone smoothly. Now all I needed to do was tackle the rest of my to-do list, including checking on the wall and temporarily promoting Sigurd. I chuckled to myself as I exited the council chambers and wandered down the smooth, stone hallway toward the main entrance, my cape fluttering around me. He'd find my becoming a Fjell errand boy very amusing.

As I reached the exit, I pressed my right hand to my left shoulder, removed my uniform mirage, and dove through the archway into the fjord.

4

LENNIE

I strolled behind Halvar into an empty cave, the ceiling of which rose to at least ten feet, the rough-hewn walls glinting in the light cast from the sconces around the space. Aside from those fixtures and the echo of our footsteps, the room sat eerily empty.

"Was this all a ploy to get me alone and kill me?" I asked, half-joking, half-serious, because being alone with Halvar was intimidating, to say the least.

He shook his head as he came to a halt and swept his arms behind his back in a militant pose I'd just seen my guys in—at ease, but most certainly in charge. "I know you've been training with Espen and Øyvin, but you need to finally start testing more of your Fjell powers. We need to know how much of my magic or Freija's magic you have. Plus, it would be useful to ascertain if you have any specialties."

"You mean like Torsten's light magic?" I glanced around the room at the fae in question's handy work, forever amazed at how he kept the lights on around here.

Halvar nodded. "That and any affinity, whether that might be healing, creating, smithing, and so on. Thankfully, you've been able to learn how to hide your ears, so we've got the basics out of the way."

I scoffed. That had been easier said than done and earned me the nickname of *The Streaking American* among the locals who'd witnessed—via their security cameras—one of my failed tests back in December. But, after some more trial and error, I'd eventually been able to shield my fae ears.

Halvar ignored my noise and spread his arms out wide. "This is the youngsters' training cave. One of the first things we Fjell Fae teach our young is how to create rocks and protect ourselves from cave-ins." He clasped his hands behind his back again like a general preparing his troops. I took a deep breath and focused on the lesson as he continued. "We cannot protect the fjell if we cannot protect ourselves. So, we learn how to withstand the pressure of the mountain, seal the cracks that form in the rock, and hold the stone ceilings above us should they start to fall."

He unclasped his hands and swept one in a gentle circle above his head before looking upward. I followed his gaze and startled at the faint trace of magic on the ceiling. Ebbing around and around like a translucent vortex was a circle of magic that pushed against the cavern above us, raising it ever so slightly. A small groan echoed through the chamber.

My mouth opened and closed as I struggled to understand the magnitude of what Halvar was asking of me. "You... You want me to move part of the mountain?"

"It'll be simple to start with, but you need to be able to do it again and again, which is where it becomes more of a challenge."

"Let's just lift a mountain for funsies. What could possibly go wrong?" I muttered then caught the serious expression Halvar wore. "Okie dokie."

"Focus on that well of warmth beneath your ribs, where your energy lies. Then urge it upward into a disk and push."

I did as I was told—which was rather miraculous, but I'd turned a new leaf since last autumn and was now into listening to authority figures... kind of. Channeling my thoughts toward the warm, swirling sensation within my sternum, I took a couple of deep breaths and raised my hands above my head. Pulsing energy swept up my arms toward the ceiling, searing through the lightning-shaped scar on my left arm—a result of obtaining Freija's magic when she died.

Resistance pressed against my power, reminding me I was lifting a damn mountain. I looked up and let out a slow, steady breath. A translucent, swirling mass had formed against the ceiling just like Halvar had done, and I let out a choked cough in surprise. "How was that so easy? Is it because I'm using my powers within the mountain? Or is it your presence?"

Halvar's nose wrinkled. "Now push upward," he said, his voice a soft command as he ignored my string of questions.

I pushed against that invisible opposition, willing my magic to move upward. A grinding noise echoed through the space and where my magic swirled, the cavern ceiling slowly rose.

A short laugh escaped me. "Well, I'll be damned."

I'd done it, and on the first try too. My guys would be so proud of me.

"Do that one hundred times."

My hands flopped back down to my sides. "Seriously?"

He nodded.

With a huff, I rolled my shoulders and bounced on my toes. How hard could it be?

"Again," Halvar commanded, hands gripped behind his back, not bothering to look in my direction where I panted. Exhaustion hung heavy across my limbs and a complaint sat at the end of my tongue, ready to be aimed at the stubborn troll who was accustomed to training soldiers, not demi-fae. Apparently, they were one and the same in Halvar's mind, and I was the lucky one to be stuck with him for a full-day torture session. We'd been at this for hours. He hadn't been kidding about lifting the ceiling a hundred times.

When we were finally done with that, he'd moved on to creating rocks from thin air, steadily getting them to increase in size. All I needed to do was picture a pebble and it would appear, then push my magic into it to make it larger. It was an easy process, willing them into being like my light balls, but at this point I wanted to hurl my little boulder collection at his head. Both my power and muscles were straining to keep up, even with the new demi-fae strength I'd obtained.

"Your bedside manner is shit by the way." I huffed, beads of sweat rolling down my temples. "Don't go into nursing when you decide to retire."

His lips twitched, which I'd learned meant I'd amused or annoyed him. I still wasn't entirely sure on which, but it was as much emotion as Halvar showed most days.

I collapsed to my butt on the cool, cave floor and wiped the perspiration from my forehead. "How the hell do young fae do this? Or are you training me differently than how you normally train youngsters?"

"Slightly different." Halvar rolled up his sleeves, and I gasped at the sight of lightning-shaped scars across both hands and forearms, exactly like mine.

The question that'd been lingering in the back of my mind for months burst forward, and I couldn't stop the words as they tumbled from my mouth. "Halvar, the scars. They're like the ones on the trees, aren't they? Like the ones on Nora's arms? Did Freija illegally transfer *all* her magic to you and me?"

His eyes bore into mine and he let out a slow breath through his nose. "Yes."

How one word could be laced with so much pain and grief was beyond me, but I felt it just the same.

I rested my elbows on top of my knees and hung my head, letting the reality of that confirmation settle over me. For weeks last year we'd been trying to find the culprit who was stealing magic from the mountain and areas around the fjord, illegally transferring it, not using the magic for its intended purpose—to protect the natural environment.

Now, after all we'd been through, Freija's last act had been an act of defiance. Her magic was supposed to go back to the earth, to the ancestors, where it would be handed over to her heir. Instead, she'd illegally transferred it to Halvar and me. *Fuck, he'd basically been a conduit that night.*

But, then again...

What if she hadn't transferred her magic to Halvar? Would he have been able to kill King Balder, the Fjord Fae behind all the chaos? Balder had a vendetta against the humans, and had been trying to amass power to do fuck knew what kind of damage to humankind. Along the way, he'd succeeded in killing not just Freija, but also the Queen of the Forest Fae, Ragnhild.

"Don't think too hard about it." Halvar's statement drew me from my spiraling thoughts and I looked back up at him where he stood as stoic as ever, his arms crossed over his chest.

"Does the Fjell Council know?" Had the Queen's former advisers been informed about what she'd done? Did her own people know what had actually happened in that throne room?

Halvar nodded.

"Well, shit," I mumbled, exhaustion creeping in as I mentally grappled with what that really meant. I'd had my suspicions, but to know for certain that Freija had illegally transferred all of her magic into Halvar, who couldn't take all of it and in turn transferred some to me, turning me into a demi-fae... it was a lot to process. The ramifications were huge. This was royal magic. Power that was to be wielded with great care. It meant I had a new responsibility with this magic that had been forced upon me. A responsibility not just to myself, but to the mountain this power was meant to protect. That pressure was borderline overwhelming, but I never backed down from a challenge. If anything, it filled me with a greater sense of motivation to prove myself to the Fjell and find their heir.

I rose to my feet, my thighs screaming at me and my arms hanging limp at my sides. With every movement, it felt like my muscles were being flayed apart and picked right off the bone. I grit my teeth and whimpered involuntarily, as a stray tear fell across my cheek. I could do this. I could train and use this power for good, for the well-being of the fjell.

I flicked my hands to shake off the pain and realization. Sparks flew away from me followed closely by a light clattering noise.

What the fuck?

Something glinted from across the room, and Halvar narrowed his gaze at the foreign object that hadn't been there a second ago. I lowered my hands as he traipsed over and picked it up.

Inching toward him, my pulse fluttered like a firefly in a corn field. "What is that?"

He threw what looked like an arrowhead into the air and caught it again, studying it closely. Had I made that?

He cast a look at me, his eyes slightly scrunched. "It's a change of plans."

5

LENNIE

Striding down the rocky hallway, glowing sconces along the walls lighting our way, we wound deeper and deeper into the mountain. Every muscle in my body screamed at me, my body begging for a nap, but Halvar had other ideas. My day of training wasn't over yet.

I yawned as my feet shuffled across the uneven ground. Tripping on my own damn foot, I wobbled before catching myself. "Any chance you could slow down? Some of us need time to bounce back and recover after the equivalent of a full-body Viking workout."

Halvar huffed. "You will be fine. Keep moving."

"Where exactly are we going?" I asked as we descended into the bowels of the mountain.

Halvar strode ahead of me, his long strides eating up the distance, and fellow Fjell Fae stepped aside to let him pass with respectful nods. "To my old workshop."

"Old work? You mean you had a job before you became *this*?" I waved my hand at his broad back, referring to his job as Queen Freija's Head Guard, now the Fjell's Head Guard.

"I was chosen for my raw strength and exceptional leadership skills a long time ago," he replied, not slowing down. "But my affinity lies with weapons, and that was where I started."

I snorted. "Let's not be too boastful, hey, big guy."

He didn't roll his eyes at me, but the sentiment was there, clear as day, in the way he shook his head... or clear as an unflappable Fjell Fae who wasn't a fan of my jokes.

A moment later, he turned a corner and headed inside a cavern that was slightly warmer than the rest. The magic within my sternum tingled, but I ignored the sensation as I took in my new surroundings, my eyebrows inching up my forehead.

All around the room, fae hammered and forged stone weapons and tools that looked heavier than a tractor. The cavernous place was filled with iron picks, axes, and a few swords while shields decorated the rocky walls. Orbs of light hung from the ceiling instead of the walls as they did in the rest of the fjell, lending the space a warm glow. It looked like a *ye olde* blacksmiths shop at a renaissance fair, but with one major difference—there wasn't a flaming hot forge. Instead, the fae, most of whom were wearing thick leather aprons over white blouses and black pants, used their magic to slowly carve the stone into weapons and sharpen them, one pass of their hands at a time. The mesmerizing display sent me into a trance-like state, and it wasn't until Halvar cleared his throat beside me that I regained my focus and opened my mouth.

"So, *this* is where you learned how to slice and dice?"

Halvar scrunched his brows and surveyed me like he had no idea what I was talking about.

"You know, I've seen you create an axe out of thin air and then use it to dismember a king. *Slice* and *dice*." I waved my hand in explanation and the air rippled and warmed around my palm.

Halvar's gaze cut to the motion, and the smiths in the room stilled, casting fearful looks in my direction.

I held my hands out in front of me, and didn't dare move in case I accidentally whacked someone with whatever magic I'd disturbed. "What just happened? Maybe bringing a baby fae into a room filled with sharp objects was a bad idea?" I'd never been super accident-prone, but as my time in Norway had shown, *shit* found me.

Narrowing his eyes at my outstretched palms, Halvar reached over and turned them both, examining them. "Hmmm."

"What's the verdict? Will I live or are they about to drop off?"

That one earned me an actual eye roll. Halvar straightened and looked out across the room. "Weapons down."

The smiths instantly set aside their work, several stepping back from their workbenches, their sharp, fear-filled gazes still locked on me.

"Care to explain what happened and why everyone is looking at me like I'm a live grenade?"

Halvar brushed his hand over his silvery beard. "You may have received some of my talents during the magic transfer."

I swallowed hard, and stared down at my hands, turning them over and then palm up again. The lightning scar on the back of my left hand glinted in the glow of the room, as if winking at me to say "bingo."

"You may be able to create weapons," Halvar said, drawing my gaze back up to his.

"So, I'm a demi-fae that can create stone... what, swords?" I peered around the room at the stone blades on the wall, the ones set aside on worktables—their sharp edges shining back at me. "Axes? Shields? Spears?"

Holy shit this was a lot to take in, especially after such an exhausting morning of training. I tightened my ponytail with both hands and every other Fjell Fae in the room, except Halvar, flinched. "Are they going to do that every time I move?"

Halvar tilted his head from one side and then the other, his lips downturned. He reached into his pants pocket and pulled out a stone... which, on closer inspection, as he held it up between his fingers, was the arrowhead I may have accidentally created earlier. "Let's test your magic."

I let out a long breath and rolled my shoulders. At this rate I wasn't sure I'd have any magic left in me to do more training.

"Could I ever deplete my magic?" I blurted. "Is that a thing? Or do I just naturally replenish? Basically, can I run out?"

"No you must stay here and finish training," Halvar replied and motioned for me to move to the corner of the room.

I moved to where he pointed, a secluded corner at the back of the room away from blades that were currently under construction, but beside a display of swords. "I'm not going to leave." At least, that wasn't the plan, and I doubted he'd actually let me run back to the boathouse until we'd finished training. "What I meant is, can my magic run out? Is there a finite amount of it?"

He leaned back, nodding slightly as my question sank in. "Ah, yes and no. As we do not know exactly how much magic you have, I cannot say anything for certain. But full fae can drain themselves and need time to replenish. It would take doing something drastic to warrant such a need though."

"Like..."

He tilted his head, thinking about it for a second. "Razing a battlefield for two days and two nights would do it."

"Do you speak from experience?" I asked, latching onto the word raze, and wondering, not for the first time, if Halvar had fought alongside

Vikings. I was desperate to find out how old he was, mostly to sate my own curiosity.

Halvar narrowed his eyes, opening his mouth to say something before swiftly shutting it again. With a twitch of his nose, he mumbled. "You'll have enough magic to see out today's training session."

"How can you—"

"Stand here, hold this." He corralled me into the corner of the room and dropped the arrowhead into my palm. I blinked and stared at the tiny rock shard as Halvar peered over his shoulder. "Brokkr."

"Yes, sir," a stout fae with a thick beard replied, his broad arms covered by a black shirt and pieces of leather that were probably some form of protective garb.

"You and your team may take the rest of the day off."

"Thank you, sir." And with that, the Fjell Fae smiths, who'd all been staring at me in fear and bewilderment, vacated the room, leaving me alone once more with Halvar.

I flipped the arrowhead a few times in my hand. "So, what exactly do you want me to do with this?"

Halvar stepped back, pulled down his shirt sleeves, hiding his forearms, before crossing his arms over his chest. He nodded. "You'll create a blade."

I snorted. "And you don't see any problem with that?" There were a plethora of ways this could go wrong, several of which ended up with me accidentally sawing off my own arm. Or perhaps that was a latent fear after seeing what Halvar had done to King Balder on the battlefield a few months ago?

"I'm here. You will be fine."

"If you say so."

"Focus on the piece of stone. Note its shape and picture it as a short blade. Once you have the image in mind, slide your free hand over your palm with the rock, like so." He did the motion himself, holding his palms so they faced each other, a small gap between them, and dragged the top hand across as if stroking a cat.

I did as requested and imagined a small, stabby blade in the palm of my hand. With a deep breath, I willed my magic to flood through my palms and flow into the shard, doing the same motion that Halvar had just shown me. The warmth of my magic spiraled down my arms and slowly but surely, a blade appeared—stretching from the tip of the arrowhead, forming the stone blade itself, then a small hilt and rounded pommel—just as I'd pictured it.

I let out an awed chuckle, moving the weapon from one hand to the other, testing its weight. My hand flexed around the handle, the stone heavy in my palm. I'd seen some of these weapons during the battle last year with Balder and witnessed Halvar forge an axe out of thin air. But, a couple of hours ago it'd never even dawned on me that I might be able to create and wield a stone sword of my own. "Well, damn."

Halvar nodded and swept his arms behind his back, clasping them there like he so often did. Apparently, I wasn't a threat even with a sharp object in my hand. Which, considering the beast of a man before me, was true.

"The more practice you have, the more blades and weapons you create, the stronger and sharper they will become," Halvar explained.

"How about lighter?" I asked, doing a bicep curl with it. My arm muscles ached, regret and pain washing through my limbs as I gently brought the sword back down to my side.

He shrugged. "Depends what you wield, but you're fae. You have the strength to brandish immensely heavy weapons without damage to your mortal form."

Huffing at his use of the word *mortal*, I cast my gaze around the room. I pointed with my blade at a broadsword hanging on the wall across the room, its knife-edge shining twice as bright as the one in my grasp. "So, one day, maybe even now, I'll be able to create things like that?"

"Yes. Perhaps not as sharp, but yes," Halvar replied. "I think we have ascertained your specialty."

"Safe to say I got some of your magic during the transfer."

Halvar nodded. "Yes, indeed. You have both the power of Fjell Fae royalty with Freija's light magic and my own smithing powers."

I smirked. "You have boy scout badges for those? Or perhaps an achievement pin?"

"We have a hat." His lips twitched slightly at the corners, and my mind whirled back to the baby hat joke I'd made when I'd first become a demi-fae.

"Seriously?"

"No."

"Did you just make a joke, big guy?"

"Also no. Try again."

I'd wear him down one day. I'd bet good money I didn't have that he had a knock-knock joke or a pun locked up somewhere in among all that broody beast-ness. "What do you want me to try now?"

He reached out and motioned toward himself, requesting the short blade I currently held. I passed it over, and he set it aside on the table beside us among the collection being stored there. Blades of all sizes and shapes, some curved like scimitars, others double ended. Brokkr and the smiths had quite the stash down here.

"I want you to make a sword," Halvar said, drawing my attention back to him and my eyebrows to my hairline.

"Are you sure?"

His dead-pan stare didn't falter.

"Okaaay." I focused on that well of energy again and pictured a broadsword like the ones I'd seen in movies: silver, sharp, and hefty. Like something that would've been wielded on battlefields during ancient times. "And I don't need starting material?" I asked, not daring to look at anything other than my own hands.

"No," Halvar replied.

Great. I let out a slow and steady breath as the warm tingling sensation of my magic worked its way down my arms and into my waiting palms. One held over the other, I pulled my hands apart horizontally, and watched in amazement as a piece of rock formed. Suspended mid-air between my palms, the blade in my mind appeared. However, instead of being made of metal, this one was solid stone. A glint of light emitted from the tip as it formed, startling me for a split second, and I grasped the pommel as it took shape in my right hand. The sword dropped slightly upon completion, but I didn't let it clatter to the floor.

"Well done," Halvar said, and I pointed the sword toward the glowing ceiling. Moving it up and down a couple times, the weight was surprisingly bearable.

"Not bad," I replied, assessing my work with a snicker. "But it's a little kinky."

Sure enough about three quarters of the way up the blade it curved slightly to the left. Probably from the light flicker that momentarily distracted me. Perhaps that'd even been some of my light magic trying to come out and play? Either way, my sword had a little bend in it.

Halvar quirked a single brow and shrugged. "Could be worse."

"Anything else I should know about creating swords?" I asked, unsure if this was a one and done lesson or if there was more to know.

"Creating? No. Wielding? Yes," Halvar replied.

I swiveled the sword to my side, pointing it downward so I didn't cause any damage to the room. There were a lot of things in here, especially the collections of shields, blades and daggers that were set aside on countertops to our left and mounted on the wall. I wouldn't earn myself any fans if I accidentally whacked something off the wall with my kinky sword.

"First rule of sword wielding—"

"Don't accidentally stab yourself," I interjected.

"Well, yes that is a good rule. Especially for you."

I laughed and popped my hip to one side. "I see my reputation precedes me."

Halvar let out a long-winded sigh. "It does. The first rule is to never accidentally injure yourself with your own blade. The second rule is to never, under any circumstances, abandon your sword. You do not want it used against you."

Sounded like solid advice to me. "And how exactly do I unwield,"—I waved my free hand at the sword grasped in my right—"a magical stone sword?"

Halvar straightened and rolled his shoulders. He didn't say a word, but instead slowly created a broadsword of his own, the end of the hilt formed into an ancient crown. *Show off.* But I couldn't deny, his ability was impressive. He raised the sword, the light catching on the sharp edges, the tip pointed upward. "To break down the sword, simply pull the magic back inside you. The sword is merely an extension of you and your powers." He brought his free hand down the side of the blade, close but not touching, and my mouth popped open in awe. The sword disintegrated, vanishing into thin air as Halvar drew the magic back inside him. While invisible, I could sense the magic flowing from the blade and into his open hand—returning home. Once the entire blade was gone, Halvar clasped his hands behind his back and nodded to me. "You try."

I pressed my lips together and widened my stance. Pointing the sword upward in front of me, I let my hand hover beside the blade, starting from the top and willing my magic to return to me. As my palm passed the tip, a spark of lightning shot out from the sword and into my left hand, singing up my scarred arm. I flinched and retracted my hand, shaking it out like I'd been stung by static. "What the hell was that?"

Halvar narrowed his eyes but motioned for me to continue.

I tried again. This time there were no sparks, but the air between my palm and the blade heated and pulsed like it was alive. I sucked in a breath, focusing intently on the sharp object. Little grains of stone broke off it, suspended in mid-air, then vanished. I kept my breathing steady as I worked my hand down the side of the sword until nothing remained. *Holy shit.* Had I really done that on the second attempt?

I looked to Halvar to see if I was correct in my assessment, that I'd done good, but the twitch of his nose betrayed nothing. "Not bad?" I asked, hoping for some sort of response.

He nodded slowly and brushed his hand across his silver beard. "Not bad."

Go me! I'd take that as a gold star from the big guy. Heck, that hadn't been as hard as wielding the light magic or as problematic as trying to shield my new fae ears. If I'd had the energy to do a victory dance, I would have. But following a day full of training, I was ready to go home, curl up on the sofa and take a nap.

"Anything else on the lesson plan for today or can I go home and have dinner?" I wasn't quite sure exactly what the time was, but we'd been training for hours and I wanted food—preferably the mac and cheese Espen mentioned earlier.

"That should be all." He motioned to the exit and I strode in that direction, taking one last look around the forge. It really was a spectacular space—the walls glowed orange from the lights in the ceiling, and each bench had a piece of work atop it in various stages of completion.

"You have any homework for me?" I couldn't quite believe the words that came out of my mouth, but seeing as I was a baby demi-fae, I imagined there'd be more training sessions with Halvar in my future. Anything I could do to prepare for those—even if it was just sleep and brace for torture—I'd do it.

"Perfect the process."

"That's it?"

"That's it," he said as we traipsed back up the tunnels toward the Fjell's main entrance. "Now, go find the Fjell heir."

6

LENNIE

My joints creaked, mimicking the sound of snow-heavy boughs around us. The waterproof material of my rain pants and jacket added a swishy percussion as Espen and I traipsed through the forest east of the village. Morning sunlight sprinkled over the hills, lighting our way as we hiked toward the Forest Fae's training location somewhere deep in the woods, away from any humans that might spot them.

"How much further?" I panted, my body sore after my training session with Halvar yesterday. I may have had new powers, but my twenty-eight-year-old body was still growing accustomed to the magic and my ability to endure more.

"Another mile." Espen squeezed my hand, both of us tromping through the snow that reached mid-calf in the deepest spots, the cold air biting at our cheeks. "Don't worry. The terrain will flatten out shortly."

Now there was a statement I longed to hear more of after moving to Norway. Aside from stunning scenery, the one thing this country could deliver on was steep inclines. Apparently on the south coast it was flatter, but here, along the jagged fjords that pierced the country's western flank, peaks and valleys reigned supreme.

I sucked in a breath and continued moving, Espen dutifully keeping pace beside me. "So, your talk with Bente went okay? Any issues with you taking time off?" I asked. I'd been too busy last night stuffing my face with cheesy pasta and then face-planting into bed to ask Espen about his day.

"Bente is the best." Espen nodded, the pom-pom on his green woolly hat wobbling. "She understood that I needed more time to settle family affairs"—our cover story for when he'd been poisoned last year—"and said to take all the time I needed. On one condition..."

"Which was?"

"That I return to work with them."

I couldn't blame Bente for making that request. Espen was great at his job and loved Skolvik. If the police station did an employee of the month thing, he'd probably win every time.

As we crested yet another hill atop a hill, Espen broke out his signature grin. "Almost there. Now, I know you don't like to take orders"—I scoffed because that was the damn truth, even though I'd been doing better lately—"but I'll advise you to stay near or beside me. Don't get drawn into anything. These are young Forest Fae soldiers training today. We don't want a wayward arrow hitting you."

I shuddered at the thought and memory of seeing one such arrow sticking out of King Balder's Chief Advisor-turned-crony Kjetil's head last year during the battle on the mountain. That sight had unfortunately been burned into my brain. I nodded firmly, willing to do anything to avoid a twig speared between my eyeballs. No need to become a plant pot.

"Good," he said. "Can't have you getting into more trouble."

"You're starting to sound like Øyvin."

Espen tugged my hand and pulled me to a stop. With a sneaky twinkle in his amber eyes, he pulled me toward him, spun me around, and dipped me. Pressing his lips to mine, I savored the warmth of his kiss before he righted me again. Standing nose to nose with the fae, my heart thrummed and the smell of moss and leather drifted over me, making me feel like I was home. "We both have a strong desire to protect you."

I bit my bottom lip and tried to hide a smile, but failed monumentally. "You mean to say I'm a naughty princess who likes to rebel and needs saving?"

Espen grinned, his long mop of hair brushing the tops of his eyebrows. "That's exactly what I'm saying... except the princess part." He swatted my behind, and I let out a small yelp, my hands instinctively flying back to protect my ass.

"Well, I promise to be on my best behavior, then," I replied and walked on, exaggerating the sway of my hips a little more and pretending to pick up my "skirts."

Five minutes later, muffled noises, like the sound of someone chopping wood underneath a blanket, met my ears and Espen nudged me with his elbow, nodding toward the tree line. "You go first. I'm shy," he whispered.

I spun on the spot, my arms windmilling from the momentum before I rested my hands on my hips. "Bullshit. You've never been shy a day of your life."

He rested his gloved hand against his chest and fluttered his lashes at me. "I'm shy on the inside."

I snorted, but pressed on. "Come on, Solbakke. I'm not buying your nonsense. Not one bit. You also told me not to leave your side."

"Just testing you," he snickered.

A couple more steps, and we entered a clearing full of Forest Fae in the middle of a massive snowball fight. Balls flew in all directions. One crashed with a splat against a tree trunk two feet from Espen's head. His eyes narrowed, searching the field, trying to ascertain who the launcher was.

"All clear! Back to training!" A feminine voice yelled from among the group and a split second later, Ylva jogged over to us. Her long blonde hair was split into two braids, and her white-and-green snowsuit blended seamlessly with our surroundings. She greeted us, and started saying something to Espen, but I was too enraptured by the Forest Fae soldiers to pay attention to her.

Some were heading back inside a small red-and-white cabin on the far side of the clearing, some were miraging the clothing they were wearing back to fatigues like Ylva's, and others picked up bows and arrows—aiming them at large mounds of snow in the distance.

"So, Lennie," Ylva started, dragging my attention away from her soldiers. "You've come to train with us today? Was Halvar too much for you?"

My brows pinched as I glared at Espen—that most certainly had not been the plan communicated to me this morning. "No to the former. Yes to the latter."

Espen chuckled with a quick shake of his head, and I looked between the two Forest Fae. "She's teasing you. We're just here to discuss what needs to happen while I'm gone and for you to see more of our world."

Well, thank fuck.

Ylva faced Espen and popped her hands on her hips. "So, what's this about you needing to put me in charge?"

"Halvar requested me, Lennie, and Øyvin retrieve an item of importance to the Fjell."

"Using you instead of his own to strengthen alliances."

Espen nodded. "And our destination is Alvdalen."

Ylva hummed like everything was finally clicking together in her head. "What's the motivation?"

"Aside from maintaining a good diplomatic relationship with the Fjell," Espen started and his eyes darkened, "he threatened Lennie."

"Why am I not surprised?"

I shrugged. "I don't even think a threat from Halvar makes me that special anymore. He threatens everyone. My ability to tie cherry stems with my tongue though? *That* is special."

Espen brushed a gloved hand over his mouth, and Ylva stared between the two of us, but I just grinned.

Talk turned to business, and my gaze drifted as Espen and Ylva discussed details and tasks of what needed to be done while he was away. Soldiers continued training. Some sparred with what looked like wooden swords, others appeared to be using tree roots as whips, while the marksmen continued volleying arrows at compacted snow dunes. They were like woodland sprites preparing for battle.

Ylva cleared her throat, drawing my focus back to her and Espen.

"Now, Espen." She crossed her arms and leaned back, quirking a brow in his direction. "How long has it been since you put in some serious training, or even participated in a sparring match?"

"Oh, snap." I laughed, adoring this woman and her combative nature.

Espen ignored me and raised his eyebrows at the woman who stood at least a foot shorter than him, but made up for it in sheer confidence. "Is that a challenge, Colonel?"

Ylva's chin tipped up, a hint of a smirk playing on her lips. "Are you up for the task, General? Or have you grown lax in your loved up haze?"

I blinked and straightened at the titles they used—choosing to ignore her use of the word *love*, too. "General? I've only ever heard people refer to you as Head Guard."

With a dramatic stage-whisper, Ylva said, "We did away with the official titles years ago, but they're fun to trot out from time to time."

I peered at Espen, curious to see how this would play out. My endlessly patient fae grinned, but shook his head as he motioned to the clearing. "Let's go then."

Ylva clenched her fist victoriously and spun. "Clear the field! Espen has agreed to a sparring match! It's high time we teach some of you more hand-to-hand combat strategies." She turned to me, her eyes wide with excitement. "It's been months since I last got him to teach a lesson. Now, we can really have some fun."

I smirked at her exuberance for battle and fighting. It was little wonder she'd been chosen as Espen's second.

"Stay with the class," Espen said. He widened his at me, conveying just how serious he was. "Whatever happens, don't leave the sidelines."

"What do you mean 'whatever happens?'" My voice pitched higher and my heart started to race. The memory of him convulsing on the floor in the mountain last year flashed through my mind. I couldn't bear the thought of him vulnerable or injured.

Espen rested his hands on my shoulders and offered me a reassuring look. "Ylva is the only one who has ever come close to besting me in battle thanks to her shrewd intellect and strategic thinking. Which is why I hired her as my second-in-command. However, I'm still the better of us."

I shook my head at his indefatigable confidence. "Could you actually get hurt, though?"

"Ancestors willing!" Ylva yelled from where she took up position on one side of the oval the fae were forming.

Espen scoffed and dropped his hands to his sides. "Ylva hasn't landed a blow in years."

"Yes, but it *has* happened," she said, stretching her arms where she waited. "It may have been five years ago, but you let down your guard and I got you in the ribs."

"I was drunk! It wasn't a fair fight."

"Well, let's hope you can hold your own today then."

I snickered at their friendly bickering. Espen turned back to me and planted a quick peck on my cheek. "I'll be fine. Just enjoy the show," he said with enough cockiness that my body flushed.

With a smirk on his lips and a flick of his eyebrows, Espen skipped backward onto the compacted snowy field. Murmurs broke out among the gathered Forest Fae soldiers, many of whom had pushed the snow into long mounds and were using them as makeshift benches. I popped a squat at the end of one, wiggling and molding the snow to my butt, and settled in to watch.

The two leaders started pacing at the opposite ends of the clearing, their eyes locked on each other's movements.

"Now, what is the main problem for a fae with destroyer powers in the winter?" Ylva asked the class, sounding more like a teacher using the Socratic Method on her students than someone who was currently in the ring.

"Avalanche," a fae two spots down from me shouted.

"Exactly." Ylva grinned like a cat that had trapped a mouse, and I let out a long-winded sigh. She'd known he would be at a loss during this exercise, which was probably why she'd asked for it in the first place.

Espen didn't look concerned though. In fact, the fae was grinning from ear to ear as if he was enjoying himself. He stretched his arms across him and behind him, like he was preparing for an eighties Jazzercise class. All he needed was the sweatband on his head and a unitard.

Without further preamble, Ylva crossed her arms in front of her before quickly bringing them down to her sides. Energy shimmered around her fists and two lightsaber-length sticks appeared in her hands, the wood polished smooth.

Espen rolled his eyes and several soldiers around me snickered.

"Sword please?" Espen commanded with a quick glance to his left.

A soldier scurried around and a second later, a sharp wooden blade that sparkled as if it had been reinforced with magic flew through the air. Without even looking, Espen caught it and spun it around a few times, assessing its weight.

"Thank you!" he said, never taking his eyes off Ylva. "Are you ready?"

She crouched and knocked her sticks together. "Are you?"

Espen narrowed his eyes at her taunt and launched.

They were a blur of sticks, arms, and swift feet. Espen brought down his blade aiming for Ylva's head, but she blocked its progress, crossing her thick batons and letting them take the hit rather than her. Their weapons had barely touched before they were moving again. Ylva swung for his legs with one stick while aiming upward with the other. Espen pirouetted out of her reach, coming up behind her. She spun on the spot, rising at the same time, and parried another blow from him.

I itched to have my camera, wanting to put it on rapid shutter speed and capture their mesmerizing movements. Especially Espen. I'd never seen him move like this before. For such a tall and built man, he moved like a feather on the wind. A very lethal feather that struck one of Ylva's sticks hard enough to send it flying.

Everyone nearby ducked as it flew over our heads and crashed against a tree with a *thwack*.

Espen chuckled and cocky energy rolled off him in waves, cresting over me and sending warmth down my spine as I watched.

The two in the ring continued their dance. Lunge, lunge, stab, sweep. Lunge, stab, sweep and spin. Dodging each other's blows or parrying them with ease, they kept at it. The sound of their weapons meeting ricocheted across the clearing, echoing off the tree line and the little red-and-white cabin.

I leaned over to the Forest Fae beside me, a short man with a dusting of freckles across his nose who looked too young to be a soldier. "Fifty Kroner says one of them taps out in the next five minutes."

The fae snorted just as Ylva flipped, lost her balance and landed on her back.

"Never mind," I said, refocusing on the clearing.

Espen was there in a heartbeat, sword at her throat, kicking away her remaining stick.

She slammed her fists into the snow beneath her. "Fuck it all."

Espen loomed over her, shook his head, retracted his sword, and extended his hand. She let out a long sigh and took his offer. He pulled her up and dusted the snow off her shoulders.

"Well, I tried," she said as the soldiers around me clapped.

"It was a valiant attempt," Espen said.

Ylva grumbled and huffed as the applause subsided.

With a smile, Espen faced the gathered soldiers. "My recommendation for you all is a minimum of three hours of yoga per week. It not only exercises the mind, but also the lungs and limbs. Improves flexibility too. So, when you need to move swiftly, your body is able to react accordingly." He ended his monologue with a namaste and bowed his head to his hands in prayer position.

I rose from my snowy seat and brushed my hands over my ass, removing any cold remnants as Espen gave the sword to a soldier and walked over.

Espen wiggled his eyebrows. "Did you like my moves?"

"Oh, I thoroughly enjoy your moves," I replied with a cheeky grin I couldn't keep at bay.

Espen slid his hand against my back, steering me toward the tree line and trail we'd taken to get up here.

"Don't get yourself killed while you're gone," Ylva yelled across the clearing, stopping us in our tracks. "I'm interested in a pay raise, not a promotion."

"I promise to bring back *lefse* and a couple extra Kroner for you," Espen replied.

"Deal!" She turned to me with a tiny salute. "Lennie, always a pleasure."

I waved. "Drinks at Fisken when we get back?"

"I'll get the first round." She smiled and bounced toward a group of marksmen lining up with their bows again.

I turned to Espen and shivered. My outerwear was good quality but not thick enough for the season, and I hadn't fully acclimated to Norwegian winters yet. "Can we head back home now? I'm getting cold."

A sneaky grin swept across his face. "Oh, I can think of many ways to warm you up. May take all afternoon to get through the list."

"Well, in that case, lead the way, General."

7

LENNIE

Tiny rays of early-morning sunlight peeked over the horizon and the lack of cloud cover made the air temperature colder than a witch's tit. I stepped out of our boathouse, bundled up in more layers than an ogre, ready for the long drive to Alvdalen. Espen and Øyvin had clearly had the same thought with their chunky sweaters and winter jackets shoved into the backseat of the vehicle.

I threw my duffel bag into the trunk of the dark-gray sedan, tucking it in beside Espen's. "So, whose car is this?"

Øyvin appeared beside me and put his pristine silver wheelie suitcase next to mine. "Oddvar's."

I bit my lip and took a deep breath through my nose, trying to remain calm. "You mean to tell me, that the little old man had a car this whole time? A car he could've used this past autumn to take me down fjord when I originally missed my cruise ship?"

Øyvin nodded and shut the trunk. "Yes, it's his son's—the supply boat captain. Rarely uses it, but he lets friends borrow it on occasion."

I inhaled in through my nose and out through my mouth, steadying my heart rate and mentally talking myself down from the looming expletive explosion that sat at the end of my tongue. It was fine. Oddvar had said most people would laugh at my misfortune and not help, which had certainly proved true. I just didn't realize that meant *him*, too. I hadn't been his friend that first day, but damn it, with all the coffee and sandwiches I bought at the man's café, surely that earned me the title of friend by now?

Øyvin walked away with a slick grin on his face, probably well aware of where my head was currently, and climbed into the front seat. I was about to protest when Espen sidled in front of me and placed his hands on my shoulders.

"One day, probably once you start working at the café this spring, Oddvar will consider you a friend," he said with a gentle smile, his hair in its usual unruly state, desperate to be pushed off his forehead. "And, as for Øyvin claiming the front seat, he's too tall to sit in the back for seven hours."

I sighed. He had a good point about both. Oddvar had graciously offered me a job at the café after my not-so-subtle request back in December, so that was a sign of good favor. But—

Hold up.

"Seven hours?" I shucked his palms off me and grabbed the front of his emerald sweater. "You said it was a long drive, but you failed to mention just *how* long last night."

He wrapped his fingers around mine, warming me, while also untangling my digits from his sweater. "We'll make a few stops along the way, but, because it's winter, we have to weave along the fjords before heading inland and take the long way around the mountains."

A whimper left my lips, and I deflated. Espen swept his arms around me, encasing me in a hug while backing me toward the car. He pressed a quick peck to my forehead. "I promise you a big lunch and some extra coffee at the halfway point."

He opened the door, and I let out an exasperated sigh as I clambered into the backseat. "Fine, but make it a really *big* coffee."

About thirty minutes outside of town, Espen pulled off the main road and started down a smaller side road, wending the car between the thick copse of trees on either side of us. The light dimmed slightly, but up ahead, it appeared a little brighter. He slowed as we reached the opening and drove us into the glade, snow and gravel crunching beneath the tires. My eyes bugged out at the sight before me.

A massive dark-wood church constructed in sections that grew smaller as it rose toward the sky sat in the middle of a snowy clearing filled with weather-worn tombstones. On some of the tallest spires sat rudimentary dragon heads, and on the very top one was a Christian cross. There were no other designs on the building, no runes or Nordic patterns. It looked as if Vikings had torn apart their boats and used the wood to erect a place of worship.

I gawked at the medieval looking building and whispered, "What is this place?"

"It's a Stave Church," Espen replied with a solemn tone as he parked in the little parking lot separated from the burial grounds by a small stone wall. "You can find them around coastal Norway. Some are from the Middle Ages, others are more recent builds."

"By 'more recent' he means the 1500s," Øyvin chimed in from the passenger seat, his shoulders set with tension.

I took a deep breath and let that number, that *age*, sink in. It was mind boggling, to say the least, and I wiped my hand across my face before staring back up at the ancient structure in front of me. "And how old is this one?"

Espen shut off the car and leaned back in his seat with a sigh. "Middle Ages."

"Did you bring me here to pray the trouble out of me, or to take me across the altar?" I wiggled my brows, catching Espen's gaze in the rearview mirror.

He rolled his lips, stifling a smile and the small chuckle that escaped, before shaking his head. "I stop here to leave some flowers every time I head North," he said, then opened the door and clambered out, not giving me further explanation.

I furrowed my brow and unbuckled my seatbelt, leaning forward to Øyvin. "Any idea what this is about?"

He let out a long breath and scratched his stubbled jaw. "This is where the Forest Fae Council used to meet."

I listened intently to Øyvin while Espen opened the trunk and grabbed the flowers he'd stashed in there. Closing it up again, he made his way into the graveyard, walking down a few rows before turning toward two gravestones and coming to a stop.

"Their council meetings were held here for decades," Øyvin continued, both of us watching the Forest Fae with his head bowed. "This is also where Queen Ragnhild and Espen's mentor, Mads, are buried."

My stomach sank, sadness easing through my limbs as I sat back in my seat. Trust me to make a crude joke at such a time, too. You'd think I'd learned my lesson by now, but nope. I reached for the door handle, then hesitated. Did Espen want me out there keeping him company? Would I be intruding?

Øyvin peered over his shoulder and gave me a short nod. "He won't mind."

"You sure?"

He nodded again.

"Okay, then." I opened the door, the smell of snow and pine drifting in the cold air. "Are you staying in here?"

Øyvin turned, facing forward once more, and grunted.

The change in his mood had me worried. But perhaps he didn't like graveyards? I myself wasn't exactly keen on them—the idea of lines of decomposing bodies had always given me the creeps—but this one was ancient and my Forest Fae was standing there looking morose. Maybe cemeteries reminded Øyvin of the brother he lost in the war down south twenty years ago, the battle that we now knew had been spearheaded by the late King Balder and which had led to the demise of the Forest Fae Queen and her Head Guard, too.

"I'll be right back," I muttered, leaving Øyvin in the warm car with his thoughts.

I staggered through the snow toward Espen, and the closer I got to the church, the further my mouth fell open. The doorway was tiny—even at five-foot-eight, I would have to hunch over to enter. The wood sides and tiled roof rose like the masts of a pirate ship. It was practically begging to be photographed, but my camera was in the car and now didn't feel like the right time.

Bracing against the chill, I wandered down the rows of gravestones, each marker more dilapidated than the next, with little tufts of snow adorning the top. Espen stood before two newer, light-gray stones, the bundle of flowers placed at the base of one and a single rose at the other. I stepped up beside him, and he glanced over, giving me a tender smile.

"So, you stop here every time to say hi?" My voice was soft and gentle as I gazed down at the two stones.

Ragnhild Thorleifson.

Mads Robertson.

Espen looked back at the graves. "I do."

The stones were simple, no dates listed, no other markers to reveal who they were or *what* they had been. The only exception was a small sky-blue stone embedded in a crown carved above Ragnhild's name—an indicator of her title and importance in the fae world that blended so seamlessly with our own.

"What was she like?" I asked, not sure if it was appropriate, but lacking anything else to say. Cool air wound around me and I fastened the zipper of my jacket up to my chin.

Espen let out a little scoff-like sound and bit his lower lip, holding back a smile. "She was the fiercest woman I've ever met. Kind and caring, but with a stoic facade that was rarely phased by anything."

I raised my brows, shoving my bare hands into my pockets. "More stoic than Halvar?"

"No one is more stoic than Halvar, but she was certainly a contender for the 'most unyielding' title." He tilted his head to one side, eyes not wavering from her gravestone.

"Sounds like my kinda Queen," I said. I'd always had a bit of a soft spot for the tough eggs. Including the one back in the fjell and the one currently in the car. I inched closer to Espen. "Are you okay?"

He nodded absentmindedly, then straightened up and turned toward me. "Quite all right. I just..." He let out a deep breath, his shoulders falling. "She would've been devastated to lose Queen Freija."

I couldn't blame him for feeling that way. The entire fjell and all the Forest Fae I'd run into at the funeral had been devastated at the loss of the Fjell Queen—her light snuffed out too soon.

"But," Espen continued, "Ranghild would've loved that you got some of Freija's magic. She'd have fun with that, train you till you cried."

I snickered. "She really does sound like Halvar. My poor arms are still sore from his training."

Espen laugh softly and reached for my hand. I pulled one out of my pocket and placed it in his. His palm was warm even in the cold weather, and he moved to leave. We walked side-by-side out of the graveyard toward the parking lot.

"She loved her people," Espen said, continuing his story about Ragnhild. "Always made sure to check in with everyone, knew everyone by name and their life's story. She was an exceptional leader." He tilted his head to the church at our backs. "We held our council meetings here for several decades before things eventually moved further inland and then to Alvdalen. She was able to encourage the nearby town to let a local fae—not that the humans knew what he was—become the caretaker and manager for the property. With him holding the keys, we were able to meet at night when the tourists and humans had gone to sleep and no one dared venture out here in the dark."

I glanced over my shoulder at the looming building and agreed with those humans. I wouldn't want to be wandering around here in the dark either. The church looked like something out of a Gothic or horror movie, all dark and gloomy wood with steeply pitched roofs and no windows. There was an ominous, almost creepy feeling about the place, too. Likely because of how extremely old the church was, and how many dead bodies lay buried around it. I shook off the goosebumps that settled across my skin and climbed back into the car.

Espen jumped back into the driver's seat and started the ignition. "You doing all right?" He asked Øyvin.

The Fjord Fae's eyes were shut tight, his chest rising and falling slowly. "Just taking a quick nap."

"Well, you can nap some more as we've still got six and a half hours to go," Espen replied as I buckled in. "While you do that, I'll listen to my audiobook. Aliens just landed and I need to know what happens next."

Øyvin let out a "mm-hmm" and said nothing more on the matter.

I leaned back in my seat with a groan, letting my head fall against the headrest with a small thump. Over six hours winding around fjords and mountains... part of me wanted to be awake and watch the scenery, the other part wanted to follow Øyvin and sleep.

After about thirty minutes staring out the window as we zigzagged along twisty roads, I decided Øyvin was on to something, and I settled in to sleep for as much of the journey as possible.

8

LENNIE

Around four hours into the drive, we stopped in a minuscule village and grabbed lunch. I'd gone for a reindeer stew which was delicious until Øyvin teased that I was eating Rudolph. Then I'd had to reason my way into finishing the dish. I'd eaten plenty of deer meat before—usually in the form of kielbasa sausages with eggs—but it took a moment for me to shake off the notion of eating a cute and innocent creature.

Øyvin finished his lunch before the rest of us—some sort of veggie sandwich—and ran to the outdoor sports store across the street, claiming he needed to grab something.

Once Espen and I finished eating, I sauntered out of the roadside café, my stomach full and satisfied. Another three hours on the road would be fine. I'd just take another nap, and, voilà, we'd be there.

As I reached the car with Espen, Øyvin ran back across the road, a massive brown paper bag in his hand. I furrowed my eyebrows. What on earth was that? The guys had lived here their entire lives, they were fully prepared for the weather and conditions. I on the other hand... *Oh no... Oh, please no...*

Stepping back and bumping into Espen, my smile vanished and my eyes widened. Øyvin caught the look and grinned as he stepped up by the car and pulled something out of the bag. A neon-orange winter jacket—hunting gear colors in most parts of the world—assaulted my eyeballs. Easily my least favorite color *ever*.

"Who is that for?" I asked, even though, deep down, I knew the answer.

Øyvin wiggled the piece of clothing, the rip-resistant material swishing as he did so. "You."

I shuddered and shook my head rapidly, while Espen desperately tried to contain his laughter behind me and failed miserably. I crossed my arms and pressed my lips together. "There's not a chance in hell I'm wearing that."

"Well, it's your size and will help us make sure you don't get lost," Øyvin countered, that grin still plastered across his annoyingly gorgeous lips.

"Ooooor." I raised my left hand and wiggled my fingers. Light bounced off the sparkling sapphire engagement ring. "You could just put a tracker in the ring?"

"This is cheaper."

Dropping my hand, I narrowed my eyes. "How do you know it's my size?"

That grin slowly turned into something more heated as he angled his head and leisurely ran his gaze down my body and then back up to my face. "Let's just say I'm well acquainted with your curves."

Heat flushed through me and I swayed on the spot under his heady stare, doing my damnedest not to cross my legs.

He stepped closer, leaning down to whisper in my ear. "Trust me, I'll take no pleasure in seeing you wear this." I swallowed hard before he continued. "But I'd rather not lose track of you on this trip."

How could he be such an endearing asshole?

He leaned back and shook the bag. "There's winter trousers in here, too."

I let out an exasperated sigh. "Of course there is."

Espen laughed and swatted my ass. "Get in the car, Lennie."

Øyvin shoved my new outerwear into my hands and gave me a wink before climbing into the passenger seat.

Shaking my head, I shoved the obnoxious jacket back into the paper bag with the matching pants and strode around to the other side of the car. Yanking on the door handle, I stutter-stepped when it failed to open. "For fuck's sake." My mouth curled into a scowl as Espen burst out laughing.

"Sorry." More snickers emanated from inside the vehicle as Espen pressed a button on his door and unlocked the car.

Waking up with an hour to go until we reached Alvdalen, I contented myself with watching the scenery. Trees were bedecked in white, their branches bowing under the weight, and tall orange sticks jutted up out of the snow on the side of the road, indicating where the lane ended. This far inland, the weather had morphed from glorious sunshine to overcast. It felt like the snow and sky were working together to cocoon me in a wintry blanket.

Espen was still behind the wheel, happy as can be, listening to his audiobook, which I hadn't really paid any attention to the entire drive. While I didn't want to stop his story-time, my mind spun with every mile we neared Alvdalen.

"Couple questions before we meet your family, if you have a moment," I said, and Espen quickly switched off the book before peering at me in the rearview mirror.

"Go ahead."

"Please remind me the names of everyone we're about to meet."

"Of course," he said, his bubbly demeanor seeming stronger as we closed in on his hometown. "I have two sisters, Ingrid and Turi. Ingrid is the oldest and she's married to Knut-Arne. They have three children; two girls and one boy. Turi is the middle sibling. She's not married, but does have a few cats that she treats like her children."

"And what are their jobs in the fae world?"

"Ingrid and Knut-Arne are gardeners. But they both work part-time so someone can be home with their youngest. Turi used to work with animals, mostly deer, but she is now the Mayor of Alvdalen."

"So, several members of the Solbakke family are in leadership roles," I said.

"Yes, I guess you're right. And Turi was selected to run our Forest Fae Council meetings when she took up the post as mayor. Always helpful to have someone working on the inside with the humans," he added as almost an afterthought.

"Just like working for the police station back in Skolvik?"

He smiled. "Exactly. Plus, I actually enjoy the work, especially my ranger duties."

He wasn't lying; aside from the chaos that had erupted last autumn, it was easy to see Espen truly enjoyed his job and cared about the people of Skolvik, both fae and human. The number of times he came home buzzing after a day of work was incalculable. It was as if the position gave him energy instead of sapping it from him. Then again, perhaps that was just Espen and his sunny demeanor?

"Anything else I should know about before I meet your family?" I asked, then quickly added, "Do they know about our... erm... impending legal marriage?" I was still mentally coming to terms with the fact that I would be marrying Espen so I could legally stay in Norway and remain close to the other Fjell Fae. I still hadn't told my family and couldn't figure out how to explain that it was for immigration purposes. My mother would be elated that I was getting married, but frustrated that there wouldn't be a ceremony or reception to plan.

"I may have mentioned it," Espen mumbled, and I straightened in my seat.

"Espen..."

"Okay, so I told them over the phone on Christmas Day while you were video calling your parents."

Of course he had.

However fast we were heading toward the inevitable label making—perhaps already had with my moving in with them—the three of us still hadn't said certain words out loud, or made any particular remarks that would be considered *defining the relationship*. Honest to hell, how could you define this? "Your family knows that it's paperwork, right? They know that Øyvin is in this too, even if we haven't made any definitions yet?"

"Yes, they know, and they're excited to meet you."

I glanced over at Øyvin who was still fast asleep, or more likely, pretending to nap while listening in on the conversation. Not much got past him. I doubted this conversation did either.

I also had a feeling we were driving straight toward definitions, and part of me warmed at the thought, while the other part was baffled. I hadn't been in a serious relationship in a long time, and hadn't felt the need for it. I was always traveling, too, which had not lent itself to anything steady. But, then, when I least expected it, this grumbly and bubbly pair came into my life and changed everything. I'd changed too. In so many ways. So, perhaps it was time to let down my guard a bit more and explore exactly where this *entanglement* would take me? I was obviously physically open to this trio. Maybe I was mentally too? Maybe I had been for a while and just hadn't recognized it yet.

"You still with us or did you fall asleep with your eyes open?" Espen said, regaining my attention.

I shook my head. "Yeah, I... Thank you for the run down. Let me know when we get into town."

I settled back in my seat and looked out the window. Maybe, just maybe, this was what people talked about when they said you found love when you least expected it.

9

LENNIE

I straightened as we drove into town, sweeping along snow-plowed roads into a small enclave of about twenty houses nestled at the head of a long lake, but set a ways back from the shoreline proper. Moonlight danced across the ice-covered lake, small snowbanks marking its edges. With a long-exposure and a tripod set-up, I could probably get a few good snaps of it, even in this lighting.

I stretched my arms to the sides and then above my head as best I could in the cramped backseat. "Does the lake have a name?"

"Big Long Lake," Espen replied, turning down another road.

I laughed, but when Espen didn't offer another name, I said, "Wait, you're serious?"

Espen nodded. "And the other lake nearby is Little Long Lake."

"Wow. Some people are not creative."

Espen grinned as we pulled into the short driveway of a dark-red house with white trim and a snow-covered roof. Wooden steps ran up to the front door and a large deck flanked the left side of the house surrounded by drifts of snow. It was a much smaller, simpler home than those in the US, but was well cared for—the driveway plowed, no chipped paint, and a warm glow emanated from the windows.

"We're here," Espen said with a beaming smile. He shut off the car and bounded out of the vehicle like he hadn't just driven for seven hours.

"Finally," Øyvin mumbled, unfurling himself as he got out, then stretching like a swimmer—waving his arms about and slapping himself on his back.

With a pasted on smile, and nerves fluttering like hummingbirds in my stomach, I unbuckled and followed their lead, heading toward the home. This was it. I was going to meet Espen's family. The most important people in his life. We reached the front step and I sucked in a lungful of cold air as Espen gently knocked on the door. Not waiting for a response, he pushed open the door and let us inside.

I was immediately assaulted by shrieks of laughter and tiny growls. Standing in the tiled and cluttered entryway, we removed our shoes and jackets, hanging the latter on crowded hooks full of colorful outerwear. Espen shook his head at the continued cacophony that escaped the living area and peered around the corner. Silence fell, followed swiftly by full on screams of delight.

"Uncle Espen!"

"Uncle Espy!"

Øyvin and I followed Espen through the archway into the living room that looked like something out of an IKEA catalog with toys strewn about the floor. Three small children launched themselves at Espen. Two girls, their brunette ringlets bouncing about their shoulders, wrapped their arms around Espen's, while a little boy who looked like a miniature version of my Forest Fae, locked his arms around Espen's knees.

"Uncle Espy," the boy said, his eyes wide as he beamed up at his uncle. "You can be a dragon with me."

"Nooo," the shorter girl butted in. "Uncle Espen is going to be the knight that kills the troll and saves the princess."

Øyvin scoffed, and I swatted him in the stomach. "Careful or I'll offer you up as the troll. Seems fitting don't you think?"

Øyvin scowled at me as the room fell silent. The trio of kids turned and stared at us like we were aliens straight out of Espen's audiobook. *Ah, I recognize that look.* We were strangers, and young kids weren't always fans of new people. That seemed to be the case with the girls, who hid slightly behind Espen, before starting up playtime again.

"Perhaps Uncle Espen and our guests would like to sit down and have something to drink?" a feminine voice said behind me, and I spun. In the whitewashed archway to a kitchen stood a woman with her brown hair tied up in the messiest of buns, flushed cheeks, and her eyes crinkling at the corners. If you'd put her in a line-up, I'd still know she was related to Espen solely for the clothes she wore: a rainbow striped sweater with a flower and toadstool broach, a yellow-pleated skirt, and black tights. The epitome of a ray of sunshine.

The kids continued playing, too caught up in the surprise arrival of their uncle, but I gave her a gentle smile. "Hi, I'm Lennie. This is Øyvin."

Her lips tilted up at one corner, happiness radiating from every part of her as she clasped her hands together at her chest. "I'm Ingrid. It is nice to finally meet you." Her brown eyes swept to Øyvin and she gave him a reverential nod like she knew exactly who he was. "Welcome to our home. I'm sorry for the ruckus, but when you have three under the age of ten, the volume is always set to high."

"Oh, I bet." I said, laughter lacing my tone, as the two girls tried to help Espen into a knight's costume with a sword and shield.

"May I see the ring?" Ingrid asked, her eyes widening.

I flinched slightly but proffered my left hand.

A gleeful smile spread across her lips as she took my fingers in hers, turning them for a closer look. The tear-shaped sapphire sparkled, light bouncing across its faceted surface.

I was slowly growing accustomed to wearing the silver band of intertwined vines and leaves, but every time someone asked to see the ring, it was a not-so-subtle reminder that I was in fact engaged. Even if it was just to keep me in Norway. Aside from family, the rest of the world couldn't know that though. If we were going to pull this off, I had to fake it and make everyone believe it was true. Operation Fake-Fae-gement was underway!

Ingrid released my hand. "It's beautiful."

Brushing a stray lock of hair behind my ear, I said, "Thank you, but it's just for immigration purposes, you know."

"Uh-huh," she replied, her voice flat and unbelieving as she turned toward the living room.

The little boy jumped off the arm of the sofa flapping his arms and yelling. "*Rawwwwr*! I will burn you alive!"

"Kristoffer, what have I said about jumping off the sofa?" Ingrid asked, her voice terse as she set her hands on her hips. Her lips moved differently from when she'd been talking directly to me. My forehead scrunched as I looked between her and the kids— *Ooooooh*. She'd been speaking English to me, but spoke Norwegian to the little ones.

"But Mamma," Kristoffer said in Norwegian, huffing and panting like she couldn't possibly understand. "I am the dragon. I must do dragon things."

"Well, do dragons like to eat?" Ingrid asked.

Kristoffer's eyes lit up and he gave his mother a look that universally conveyed, "Well duh." He sprinted for the kitchen, slip-sliding on the hardwood floors in his woolly socks.

Giving us a wide berth as he passed, and using his mother's legs as a shield, Kristoffer mumbled a "Hey."

Ingrid steered him toward the kitchen with a nudge. "This is Lennie and Øyvin, Uncle Espen's friends. Now, go wash your hands."

The kid shrugged and ran into the kitchen, swiftly followed by his sisters. Ingrid introduced them as they scuttled past. "Kristoffer, four. Kari, eight," she said, motioning toward the taller of the two girls. "And Katrine, six," she added, nodding toward the second. Both gave us shy waves as they passed, their pink tulle dresses swishing about their ankles.

Espen, meanwhile, groaned and panted, trying to remove a breast-plate that barely covered his left rib cage, without breaking it.

"With how long you've been in the Guard, brother, I'd thought you'd be more adept at removing armor," Ingrid said, a smile curling at her lips.

Espen laughed, finally able to wrangle the Velcro straps off himself and remove the fake armor. He gently threw the costume piece onto the well-worn couch. "They don't make them like they used to."

The remark earned a mumbled "True" from Øyvin.

I shook my head and turned to Ingrid. "You mentioned dinner?"

"Yes." She beamed and headed for the kitchen. "Follow me. Knut-Arne should be done with the steaks on the grill any minute."

"You grill in the winter?" I asked, my voice notching up a few octaves as I stumbled after her.

Ingrid nodded. "Rain, snow, sunshine. We grill whenever we want to here in Norway. If you let the weather dictate what you do, you'll never do anything."

I chuckled. That might be the most Norwegian sentence I'd ever heard.

The kitchen invited us with the warmth of a home-cooked meal. Pale yellow cabinets skirted the length of the room to my right, with white-washed ones running above them. Used cups sat beside the sink, waiting to be washed. We took our seats at a large pine table, the mismatched wood chairs scraping lightly against the tiled floor.

As my butt touched the checkered-cushion, the backdoor beside the fridge swung open, letting in a cold breeze and a large man with light-brown hair and a short beard. Snowflakes dappled his jacket-clad shoulders and a platter of grilled meat balanced on his broad, weathered hand.

"Welcome, welcome. I'm Knut-Arne." The rich timbre of his voice settled over the room as he nodded and turned to his brother-in-law. "Drive okay?"

Espen nodded in return. "Perfectly fine. Only ran into one brief snow shower, clear the rest of the way."

"Good, good, good," Knut-Arne muttered, setting the plate in the middle of the table and shucking off his jacket, hanging it over the back of his chair. The delectable smell of steak drifted through the room, and saliva gathered in my mouth.

"I heard you don't eat fish, Øyvin. So, I made sure we had steak instead," Knut-Arne said. He took a seat between his wife and eldest daughter, across from me, Øyvin and Espen. Kristoffer and Kari were at the ends of the table, with Kristoffer in a Tripp Trapp chair.

"Thank you," Øyvin replied, taking the dish of potatoes from Ingrid and helping himself before offering to help Kristoffer beside him.

Kristoffer quirked a single eyebrow. "You're a Fjord Fae. You don't eat fish because they're your friends?"

I choked on my own spit, covering the cough with my fist. *Damn.* Glad I hadn't taken a sip of water at that moment or it would've rushed out of my nose. Loud squawking aside, for making that remark, I liked the little kid.

"Kristoffer," Ingrid chided the boy who shrank at her admonishment. "We don't say things like that. Just because someone is from the Fjord Fae faction, doesn't mean they automatically don't eat fish. There are many Forest Fae and Fjell Fae that don't eat fish either. Apologize please."

"Sorry," Kristoffer muttered. Before Øyvin had a chance to say "apology accepted" the little guy shoveled a potato into his mouth.

I bit my bottom lip to stop the laughter bubbling up inside me and caught Espen doing the same. Øyvin merely shrugged and continued serving himself.

Dinner proceeded with congenial conversation while we devoured the delicious steak and potatoes with red cabbage and gravy. Ingrid agreed to share her gravy recipe with Øyvin, and Knut-Arne peppered Espen and I with questions about Skolvik.

I looked around the table, a sense of welcome and family washed over me—a feeling of ease and home. My heart fluttered. *This is going well.*

"I am The Darkness," Kristoffer mumbled, trying to get his voice to sound as grumbly as possible. "The Darkness is finished."

"The Darkness can wait until everyone is done with their dinner before he goes on rampaging," Ingrid said with a stern look in her son's direction.

"The Darkness wants freedom."

"You heard your mother," Knut-Arne piped in, and it took every ounce of my less-than-great resolve not to laugh out loud at the kid's antics. "You can wait five more minutes."

Kristoffer huffed and wrapped his little arms around himself, holding onto his shoulders like a bat.

Knut-Arne turned to Espen. "So, what *exactly* brings you to Alv-dalen?"

Ingrid bobbed her head beside him as she took another bite of her dinner.

"Well, we need to find someone and this was their last known location," Espen replied.

"A manhunt?" Knut-Arne asked. His eyes widened as he took a sip of water.

"Of a sort." Espen tilted his head from one side then the other before glancing at me and Øyvin, probably wondering how much he should divulge to his sister and brother-in-law. Plus, the kids were present. Little ears had a tendency to repeat things. "We need to find someone for the Fjell. Halvar thought we'd be the best for the job."

Ingrid elbowed her husband's side. "I told you Halvar was involved."

I set down my knife and fork on my plate and folded my hands in my lap. "You know Halvar?"

"Everyone knows *of* Halvar," Ingrid said. A truth that seemed to precede the stoic fae. While I still didn't know exactly how old Halvar was, he had an air of myth and legend around him. Clearly that reputation stretched this far inland, too. "So, you really can't tell us anything else? Not even *who* you're looking for?"

Espen let out a long sigh and rested his forearms against the table edge. "I shouldn't say until I've spoken to the Council. But I'm hoping Turi might be able to help us out. We're meeting her for lunch tomorrow."

"Ah, okay then." Ingrid conceded. "If there's anyone in this town that knows everyone by name, it's Turi. I'd say you fall into that category too, but..."

"Not this again," Espen laughed gently and his chair creaked as he leaned back.

"Don't blame me for wanting you closer."

"I'll consider moving back once enough time has passed. Too many humans are still alive from when I last lived here, even if they are predominantly in nursing homes."

"Fine."

Espen tilted his head toward his sister like he didn't believe she was "fine."

She set down her silverware and clasped her hands together against the edge of the table. "Just promise me this. While you're here, would you please join the kids and I for an afternoon of skating at the lake at the end of the week? I don't want to interrupt your work, but the girls have the day off school and we'd love to spend more time with you while you're in town."

Espen's shoulders slumped and he softened up, a gentle smile tugging at his lips. How could he possibly say no to that? While we needed to focus on our search, a few hours with his family wouldn't hurt.

Espen looked over my shoulder to Øyvin and then at me for confirmation. I nodded.

He turned back to his sister. "We'd love to."

Ingrid smiled from ear to ear, her mom-bun wobbling as she straightened in her seat. "Excellent."

Silence settled over us once more as we finished up our meal until Ingrid said, "Okay, Kristoffer, you may leave—"

Her son flew from his chair and barreled out of the kitchen, his arms spread wide. "The Darkness has been set free! *RAAAWR!*"

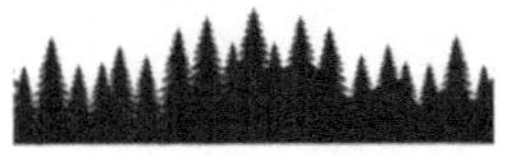

"We prepared the little cabin by the lake for you," Ingrid said after dinner, smiling at the three of us as we pulled on our jackets. Knut-Arne furrowed his brow and opened his mouth to say something, but was quickly shut down by his wife with a swat of her hand to his abdomen. She turned to me, adding, "The cabin was in Knut-Arne's family for years. We did some renovations, but it's relatively simple. If there are any problems, please let me know."

"Thank you," I said at the same time as the guys, and Ingrid gave me a toothy grin.

We tugged on our shoes, and said our goodbyes, drifting out the door as Ingrid turned to the living room and said, "Right, children. Time for bed!"

"Mamma, nooo."

"You cannot catch me!"

The door closed behind Øyvin. As we descended the front steps, I was instantly swept away to thoughts of my own nieces and how they never wanted to go to bed. Especially not after I'd visited. I might've had a bad habit of getting them riled up, but my brother Andrew always claimed they slept like logs when they finally got into bed.

The snick of a lock sounded and a door flew open. "The Darkness refuses! He cannot be locked away!" We turned in the driveway just in time to see Kristoffer barrel across the side-deck by the kitchen and launch himself like a flying squirrel into the snow drift, his father chasing after him.

"Do they need help?" I asked, laughing at the kid's hijinks.

Espen waved his hand. "No, Knut's got him."

Øyvin hummed to himself as he climbed into the front seat of Odd-var's sedan. "I like that kid."

Me too. I smiled up at the house. Unsurprisingly, I liked them all.

10

LENNIE

With the light of the full moon casting a white glow upon the area, we pulled up to the lakeside cabin surrounded by mounds of snow, much of which had been cleared aside to allow room to walk and park. With a little porch by the front door, and a dense woodland of pine trees on the right side of the house, the dark wooden building looked like something out of a wintry movie where the city girl fell for the small-town hero.

I got out of the car and stared at our surroundings, turning to the picturesque lake as the guys began to unload. Just like the big lake near Ingrid's house, this body of water—the Little Long Lake, as they called it—was frozen over, with a dusting of snow across it. Perched in the middle was a small island covered in snow and a variety of hibernating flora, including a few pines and some barren trees with dark bark.

I sighed at the beauty around me, breathing in the crystal clear air, wishing it was brighter so I could get out my new camera. But that could wait until tomorrow. The scenery would likely be even more spectacular in the daylight. I'd just have to sit tight until midday for the best lighting conditions due to Norway's short winter days.

"Are you coming inside?" Espen said.

I nodded and traipsed across the driveway, the snow crunching beneath my boots as I joined him and Øyvin on the porch. Espen pulled out a key and swiftly unlocked the door, pushing it open to let us in.

We stepped inside, and before I could take in the space, Espen instructed me to remove my outerwear. Shucking off our jackets and boots, we hung the former on the hooks by the door, and left the latter in the drip tray beneath them. Beside that was a bizarre contraption attached to the wall. It looked like an air-conditioning unit with four short but wide corrugated hose pipes coming off it.

Øyvin caught me staring at the machine. "It's a boot dryer. You put the hoses into your boots and it pumps hot air into them to dry them out."

"That's amazing."

He gave me a tiny lopsided grin. "Very useful after a long day in the snow."

Espen picked up our bags again and motioned for me to explore the cabin.

The interior of the tiny building was rugged and simple. Along the left wall were three large windows with cream-colored curtains facing the lake. That side of the open living space also boasted a small living room with a gingham-patterned sofa, and two worn and mismatched armchairs. Beyond that was a four person dining set and a minuscule kitchen with the smallest refrigerator I'd ever seen—barely counter height.

To the right of the entry were two more doors. I opened the first and found a small, tiled bathroom with a porthole-sized square window above the toilet. To the right was a slim shower with a glass door that probably wouldn't work for either of the guys as the showerhead was really low. I snickered at the mental visual of Øyvin trying to use the shower, and moved on to the next room.

I strode toward what must've been the bedroom, opened the door, and halted abruptly. There, in the middle of the room, flanked by two tiny nightstands, covered in a green-and-white checkered duvet, was a lone bed covered in rose petals and a white envelope placed in the middle. I let out a snort of laughter. "Espen, your sister's got jokes!"

The Forest Fae sidled up next to me and peered into the room. "Ah, yes, well..." His stumbling words were accompanied by a low grumble emanating from Øyvin's chest as he joined us in the doorway. I couldn't stop the laugh that bubbled out of me.

"Better see what the letter says," I said.

"Agreed." Espen strode into the room, dumped his bag in the corner beside a rickety dresser, and threw himself onto the large bed.

I brushed aside the red petals, snapped up the envelope addressed to: *the three of you*, and settled onto the bed beside the bubbly fae. Espen tucked his hands behind his head, and Øyvin leaned against the doorframe, his arms and ankles crossed. "Any guesses what might be inside?"

"Knowing my sister, it's probably something happy and sappy."

Another soft laugh escaped me. That was the exact vibe I got from Ingrid when we visited this evening. She clearly cared a lot about her brother and shared his bubbly enthusiasm.

I peeled open the envelope and pulled out the little card inside. It was a tourist postcard from Alvdalen with a deer and mountains on it, plus a little Norwegian flag in the shape of a heart. Turning it over, I found beautiful cursive handwriting that I'd never ever achieve no matter how long I lived.

Dear Espen, Øyvin, and Lennie —

Congratulations on your impending nuptials! We hope your time in Alvdalen is full of joy, laughter, and many happy memories. I've stocked the cupboards with some essentials, but you'll need to venture to the shops for bread and milk. If you need anything during your stay, please let us know.

Love,

Ingrid and Knut-Arne

A little note at the bottom in chicken-scratch style writing said, *The petals were your sister's idea. - KA*

Espen chuckled as he read over my shoulder.

Øyvin continued watching from the doorway.

"So…" I set the postcard and envelope on the bedside table to my right. "Any ideas on what we could do for the rest of the evening?" Sure, my back ached from being in the car all day and I was feeling all kinds of warm and cozy after spending time with family, but it wasn't quite bedtime yet.

Øyvin rolled his eyes as a hint of a smirk twisted his lips. "Do you always deviate to sex?"

Leaning back against the headboard, I crossed my arms and lifted my chest slightly. "You know I don't."

"If it isn't *yoga*," Espen said. "It's coffee, photography, what new dish you tried—"

"Or how best to annoy me," Øyvin chimed in. "Like rearranging the spice cabinet by regions or organizing my sheet music by the composer's place of birth."

I snickered. "See, you both know me so well." Pulling off my sweatshirt and throwing it toward Øyvin's face, I added, "So, is that a no on the sex?"

Øyvin caught my sweater and folded it up, setting it neatly atop the dresser. Looking over his shoulder with a heated gaze, he replied, "I never said that." He bent down and unlocked his fancy-schmancy suitcase, withdrawing his wash-bag. "But I'm going to take a shower."

"Boo!"

He didn't even bother to give me the middle finger, let alone say another word before strolling out of the bedroom and into the bathroom, shutting the door behind him. A moment later, the sound of running water met my ears.

Hadn't he showered this morning? I shrugged. Maybe he stank or maybe he just wanted to be close to water. Either way, his absence gave me two-thirds of the bed to spread out on.

"Thank goodness this bed is big enough for all three of us," I said.

Espen rolled onto his side and faced me, propping his head in his hand. "This is the old Mikkelsen cabin. You've seen how broad-shouldered Knut-Arne is. His side of the family are all like that. So, they had this custom-sized bed made. I believe you'd call it a King Size in America."

I nodded. It was definitely big enough to be classified as such.

Doing a full body stretch, I brushed my left hand past Espen. He caught my hand with his and brought it to his lips. Pressing a kiss to each knuckle, he took his time worshiping me as if paying his respects to a medieval queen, and brushed his thumb over the engagement ring.

My pulse sped up and heat washed through me, igniting every part of my body. It was such a simple gesture from Espen. Yet, with each touch of his lips against my skin, it felt like he was giving me unspoken promises or wishing upon a star.

I rolled onto my side and swept my free hand against his cheek.

He drew a breath and sunk his teeth into his bottom lip. His gaze turned molten as he rested his left palm against my waist and skimmed my curves.

A pleasurable shudder ran through me and my eyelashes fluttered.

The way he could draw me into such a comfortable state of bliss was breathtaking. It was as if he understood me and each of my foibles, and knew what I needed and when.

With a choked groan, he flipped us and settled over me, pressing his knee between my thighs. "I'm so glad you're here."

"Because if I wasn't, Halvar would kill me?"

Espen rested his forehead against mine. "Don't remind me. I'm glad you're here *in Alvdalen* so I can show you where I grew up and have you meet my sisters and family. It's been a very long time since I brought someone home... And, well, I'm glad it's you. I'm glad they get to meet you."

I cupped his face with my palms and stared into those gorgeous amber-colored eyes. Seeing him so happy did things to my insides that I couldn't quite comprehend. But I couldn't deny, his joy was infectious. I pressed a kiss to each corner of his mouth and felt his smile bloom.

"I'm glad to be here too," I said, my tone turning sultry. I brushed my palms down his chest, enjoying the pleasure-filled look that swept across his features. "Especially, *here.*"

He leaned in and peppered kisses up my neck, eliciting a throaty moan from me.

Rearing back, he knelt on the bed and raked his hand through his hair. "That's it."

"What?"

"Your moans. They're too much. I have to have you. Right now."

"Right now? While Øyvin is in the shower?"

Espen nodded rapidly.

Who was I to say no? I bit my bottom lip and raised my eyebrows once.

His smile brightened like it had gained wattage from my unspoken agreement.

Without waiting another second, we clambered off the bed and yanked off our clothes. Espen grabbed the bedcover and threw it off, sending it and the remaining rose petals to the floor. He snapped his fingers and pointed at the cleared bed. "Bridge pose. Now."

There was no stopping me from throwing myself back onto the bed and assuming the position, knees bent and my hips hoisted in the air.

Espen was on me a heartbeat later, his head buried between my thighs as his hands palmed my rear while helping me maintain the pose. His tongue lapped at my clit, teasing the bundle of nerves, and sending me into a panting mess. If he kept that up, I was going to combust in seconds.

As if reading my mind, Espen unlatched himself and smoothed his palms down my legs, moving them back onto the bed. I lay back down and straightened out, relishing the sweep of his hands. The care and attention he paid to every inch of my body—from my hips to my chest and everywhere in between—was like a sculptor studying their masterpiece in awe.

He leaned over me and, resting one hand beside my head, lined himself up and gently pushed in. A light moan left my lips and another shudder ran through me.

I wasn't going to last long. Not with the way his eyes melted into liquid caramel, or the way his fingers brushed my every bump and curve like they were made of the smoothest marble. Like I was his to worship and he'd do so forever.

I wouldn't stop him.

Our bodies pressed together and he rested his forehead against mine. "Lennie." His whispered words were like a prayer and secret. I swept my lips over his and breathed in the emotions I couldn't name as we rocked against each other.

Our kisses grew more passionate, and I wanted more of it. Needed more of him.

His thrusts sped up and I hooked my feet against his back, deepening each delicious stroke.

With a stuttered breath, a shock wave of pleasure ran through me, wrenching through every muscle. A deep groan from Espen danced with my euphoria and he fisted the bedsheets as he came.

Fuck, I was one lucky woman.

A smile twisted Espen's lips and his cheeks flushed.

I grinned, feeling the lingering ecstasy from the top of my head to the tips of my toes. Yeah, I was a very lucky woman.

Espen pulled out and settled beside me before brushing an errant hair off my forehead. "I will never tire of that."

I let out a deep breath. "Me neither."

He shuffled off the bed and returned with the duvet, crawling back in and throwing it over us. I snuggled up beside him and—

The shower shut off and I stilled. There wasn't a chance Øyvin would miss the scent of what we'd just done. Nor the clothes on the floor or the naked evidence beneath the covers.

The Fjord Fae vacated the bathroom and appeared in the doorway, his hair perfectly dry but mussed like he'd been caught in a windy field. His gray pajama pants hung low off his hips and the sight of his bare chest was enough to make me feel tingly again.

Espen completely ignored Øyvin, pretending to be fast asleep and like the scent that lingered in the room wasn't his doing.

Øyvin's nostrils flared, but his features didn't betray his thoughts as he climbed into bed, bringing his fresh linen scent with him. He turned away from me with a gentle huff and pulled the covers up to his neck. "I can't believe you two."

I flipped over and sidled up against him with a grin, planted a kiss between his shoulder blades, and fell asleep.

11

LENNIE

Sparkling in the dim rays of late-morning sunlight, the village of Alvdalen was tucked between rolling hillsides with snow-covered mountains looming in the distance. Similar in size to Skolvik, but hundreds of miles further inland, the small town had the same Nordic charm and bracing temperatures.

"I look like a hazard sign," I said as I zippered my awful neon-orange jacket over my chin, nestling into the puffer jacket for warmth. The whole ensemble clashed violently with my scarlet hat, but Øyvin was adamant that I wear the poofy get-up or I'd be left in the cabin.

"Accurate." Øyvin smirked and I slapped my hand into the middle of his rock-hard abs, likely hurting me more than I had my grumpy fae.

"This is the lovely main street through town." Espen waved both hands, gesturing as he walked backward like a college campus tour guide. We'd spent the morning unpacking and decided to do a quick tour of Alvdalen before meeting up with Espen's middle sister, Turi, during her lunch break. While it meant a slight delay in our search for Aurora, at least Øyvin and I would have a better understanding of the village layout. Plus, I'd never say no to having a look around a new town.

"The street is for pedestrians only," Espen added, pointing at the sign at the start of the road—a car with a slash through it.

We traipsed down the street, the snow shoveled into the middle creating a short divider between both sides of the wide lane. Stores of all types, constructed of vertical planks of wood, ran along what looked like a cobbled road beneath the thin layer of white. We passed several little coffee shops that reminded me of Oddvar's, a real estate office with photos of *eigenboligs* for sale in the area, and several clothing stores with window displays covered in colorful knitwear and boasting the Norwegian wool they used. I could practically smell the fibers and lanolin through the glass panes.

"And this," Espen said, his voice filled with awe. Drawing my attention away from a particularly bright, blue sweater with paw prints across the top third, I turned to where he pointed. "This is Alveskjegget."

Alvin did what? I shook my head. Apparently, my hearing magic didn't work on that word.

"What does... Al-vee-shegget... mean?" I asked, trying my best to pronounce the word that was emblazoned in big white letters above the dark wood exterior and heavy-looking double doors.

"It means," a male voice behind us started and we all spun to find a man with a long, thick red beard, piercing green eyes, and the countenance of a lumberjack... or perhaps it was the flannel-patterned jacket he was wearing that gave him the woodsy vibe. "The Elf Beard."

I stilled. Trying to keep my face from betraying how on the nose that name was.

"And it's my bar." The newcomer smiled before turning to Espen. "Good to see you back in town, Solbakke. You coming in for a drink? Care to share some news with me?"

Espen grinned and reached out a hand, giving the barkeep one of those bro greetings that was half handshake, half hug. "Felix, it's good to see you. We won't be stopping by this morning"—*boo*—"but we'll be at the council meeting."

My shoulders relaxed and I readjusted my stance, letting my hands fall to my sides. So, this guy, Felix, was a fae.

"Ah okay," Felix said. With a quick nod to Øyvin, he turned his attention to me. "Perhaps you could introduce me to your lovely friend here?"

Espen sidled up beside me, placing his palm on my lower back. "This is Lennie Martin. My fiancée."

Show time.

I smiled up at Espen before extending my hand to Felix. "It's nice to meet you."

"Well, damn. The rumors are true." Felix grasped my hand in his, gave it two firm shakes, and let go. "After all these years, Espen Solbakke is getting married. Have you set a date?"

Øyvin cleared his throat.

Espen curled his arm around me and tucked me into his side. Peering down at me with a hooded gaze, his lips kicked into a smirk that sent a tingle down my spine. "We're thinking late summer."

My breath hitched and my heart fluttered as I played along. Resting my gloved hand against his chest like a prom portrait, I stared up into his warm amber eyes. "Good time of year. Easier for family to travel and attend." What were the words coming out of my mouth? And why did they sound rational?

Espen's eyebrows rose as he tilted his head and brushed his free hand across my cheek, pushing aside a stray hair. A wave of comfort washed over me, and I involuntarily leaned into his touch. Why did this feel so good? Like sitting beneath a thick blanket on a cool summer evening by a bonfire.

"How wonderful," Felix said, pulling me out of whatever haze had settled over me.

I tried to blink it away, but it was useless. The cozy and comfortable sensation was glued to me, much like the Forest Fae at my side.

With a contented sound, Espen released me. "It truly is wonderful."

As I stepped back, wobbling at the loss of Espen's hold, a hand landed on my shoulder, steadying me. I glanced up at Øyvin and found a hint of a smile at the corner of his lips. Was he impressed by my acting? Or had he noticed how I practically melted like a popsicle under Espen's touch?

He gave no hint as we turned back to the lumberjack barkeep and my fiancé.

"Any update on our canine friends who paid a visit to the fjord recently?" Espen asked, glancing around at the few passersby that were more concerned with a sale across the street than the four of us.

Felix crossed his arms and shook his head. "Nothing more than what I already passed along."

"Well," Espen sighed and frowned. "Let me know if there are any shifts in power I need to be aware of. Or any more friends deciding to make trips to Skolvik."

"Of course. You have my word." Felix nodded firmly, moving toward the bar's front doors and setting a key in the lock. "But I'm sure your sister knows a thing or two as well."

Espen tilted his lips into a half smile. "Yes, but you have the more informal information that doesn't always reach her ears."

Felix wiggled his brows in a manner that relayed his status as Alvdalen's chief proprietor of Forest Fae gossip. And as owner of a bar named The Elf Beard, that would be fitting. I dared a quick glance at

Felix's beard and wondered just how many secrets had passed before it. Based on Espen's use of him as a confidant, I'd wager quite a lot.

Felix gestured over his shoulder to the bar at his back. "Are you sure you don't want to stop in for a quick beer?"

Yes! It was barely noon, but yes!

Espen shook his head. "No, but we'll see you later."

Boo!

"We need to pay a visit to Turi. She's expecting us."

"Welcome, welcome! Come in, come in," a woman with a long brown bob and a wide smile said as she ushered us inside the condo. Freckles brushed across her rosy cheeks and her eyes, the same amber-color as Espen's, beamed at us while we removed our outerwear.

"I'm Turi. It's so nice to finally meet you, Lennie." She swept forward and gave me a firm handshake, formal yet still informal. She instantly made me feel at home and like a long-lost friend, even though I'd barely stepped foot inside the tiled entryway. I could see how she'd won the mayoral election.

"It's nice to meet you, too," I replied, taking a look around as we stepped out of the hallway and into the main living area.

Turi's home was the top floor of a two-story split-house made of white-painted wood and black roof tiles. Where the exterior was a blank canvas, the interior was the polar opposite. Color was splattered across every surface, from the teal walls to the purple and gold furniture, it looked like a peacock had run amok with its feathers and covered everything with the shades of its plumage. Even the balls of yarn in a basket beside the sofa matched the color scheme.

I blinked, helping my eyes adjust to the brightness. A distinct smell of patchouli wafted through the space from a small diffuser on the cramped bookshelf, and a herd of cats, five in total, stalked around us as we wandered into the room. I tried my best not to accidentally step on any of them. "What are their names?"

"The white one is Frigg, the orange one is Thor, the black one is Fenrir, the gray-striped one is Ymir...and that,"—Turi pointed at the biggest one—"is my boy, Loki."

I glanced over at the behemoth of a cat perched like a gargoyle on a cat tree nestled behind a sofa by the window. Loki was the size of a bobcat, his big, black-and-gray fluffy coat sticking out in all directions like he'd just been electrocuted, his ears twitching as if he understood every word we said. "Is he a Maine Coon?" I asked, sitting down on the smaller velvet sofa in the living room as far away from the big cat as possible.

Turi shook her head. "He's a Norwegian Forest Cat. Usually a large breed, but I think Loki is double the average size."

No shit. That thing could probably fell a child or devour a chihuahua whole.

Øyvin sat beside me, while Espen took a spot on the other small sofa near Loki, a knick-knack covered coffee table wedged between us. It was a tight squeeze on the little couch, and Øyvin's knee brushed lightly against mine, sending a trill of warmth through me. I nudged him back, and the corner of his mouth quirked up minutely. Taking a deep breath, I glanced around the room just as the white cat plopped down on my lap and curled into a ball, making herself at home without further fanfare. Loki, though, wouldn't stop staring at me from across the room where he was perched on his cat tree behind Espen, his obnoxiously large tail swishing about below him. Even with Espen and his destroyer powers in the room with us, I got the sense that Loki the cat was the biggest predator. Especially as his gaze never broke from my face.

"Your cat is intimidating."

"Oh, Loki?" Turi said as she took a seat on a little pouf beside the coffee table and opened a tin of cookies. Golden-colored diamond shapes peeked out. *Sirupsnipper*, Espen's favorite. "He hates everyone except me."

"You don't say."

Loki may or may not have quirked an eyebrow at my remark. I couldn't be sure.

"Is he... domesticated?" I asked, wondering if I should be concerned for my well-being in his presence.

Turi tilted her head from one side to the other. "Kind of... he has a really great personality."

I cleared my throat. *Yeah, I'm not taking any chances with that one.*

"So," Turi started with a beaming smile as she extended her arm in my direction. "Let's see the ring."

I placed my fingers in Turi's outstretched hand. She tilted my digits in one direction, then the other, examining the silver branches and gorgeous stone on my finger. I swallowed hard, nervous but sure of the commitment I'd made. I didn't want to get tossed back across the Atlantic by the Norwegian equivalent of Customs and Immigration.

"Very pretty," she mumbled.

"Don't get all excited." Espen tilted his chin toward me. "It's for immigration purposes. So Lennie can stay in the country."

Turi released my fingers and looked between the three of us. "Uh-huh." Her mutter mirrored Ingrid's last night.

I bit my bottom lip to keep from smiling or making any sort of face. With this much attention on me, I didn't trust my facial features. I settled back on the sofa and stroked the cat in my lap.

"Fine. I'm just glad to see you happy." Turi huffed, raising a hand in defeat. She leaned forward. "Now, what exactly brings you home, brother? You weren't forthcoming on the phone."

Espen took a bite of a cookie before answering. "As I mentioned, Halvar sent us to retrieve someone. Her last known location was here in Alvdalen."

"Well, can you give me her name? I might know her." Turi snapped off half a cookie and shoved it in her mouth. I reached forward to grab one myself but the cat in my lap extended its claws into my thigh, hampering any further movement. I grumbled and sat back. The cat retracted her claws. *Little shit.*

Turi, noticing my plight, graciously proffered the cookie tin. I plucked out a *sirupsnippe* and thanked her.

"I know just about everyone in town," Turi continued.

Espen sighed and brushed his hand across his forehead. "I'm aware. Thought we'd meet with you prior to tonight's meeting to see what information you might have. Her name is Aurora. Last known to be living with Vigdis Johansen. Do you know her?"

Turi nodded, her brow furrowed in thought. "Vigdis passed a few years ago and she did have a daughter called Aurora. I, personally, haven't seen Aurora in a long time and don't think she lives here anymore."

That explained why no one at the fjell could get hold of Vigdis or Aurora. A huff escaped me between bites of my cookie. "Do you remember what she looks like?" I asked.

"She had very unique copper and silver hair. Usually wore it in a braid or two. Slight build. Pale skin." Turi nodded at me. "Perhaps a smidgen shorter than you."

"Do you know any of her contacts? Someone who might know where she's gone?" Espen asked gently as if to not fully disturb his sister's thoughts.

Turi bit her bottom lip before letting out a sigh and shaking her head. "For the life of me, I can't remember. The Council might know, especially Gunvor." She narrowed her gaze at her brother. "What exactly does Halvar need her for?"

Now it was Espen's turn to shake his head. "I think it would be better for us to discuss *that* at the Council meeting tonight. I want to share the information with everyone at the same time, avoid any grumbles from some of the council members that aren't exactly happy with my actions of late." Espen glanced at me, before turning back to his sister.

Turi let out a breath letting it create a raspberry noise with her lips. "Fine, you goody goody, quasi-rule follower."

"*Quasi?*... Oh, yeah, me." I was the exception. He'd told me about the fae. I really was a good influence on people.

Espen chuckled, while Øyvin remained silent, competing in some sort of staring competition with Loki. Had either of them blinked recently?

"You know me, sister. I always follow the rules."

Turi snort laughed. "Uh-huh. Like that time in '89 when you—"

"What about that wolf problem we discussed?" Espen raised his voice, cutting off his sister before she reached the good part of that sentence. I got the feeling he was talking about the wolves that attacked me a few months ago. He'd been less than pleased about that and promised to look into it. By the sounds of it, that hadn't entailed burying anyone alive... yet.

Turi stuck out her bottom lip, equally annoyed that she hadn't been able to throw a barb at her little brother. "Ah, yes, the wolves that came to Skolvik. I have a sneaking suspicion it might have been a few members of the pack. But when I asked Wilhelm, he outright denied any wrong-doing."

"And you believe him?" Espen leaned forward and rested his forearms on his knees.

"I have no other choice at the moment. He's the Alpha and we've..."—she took a deep breath—"we've had a wolf sighting recently among the humans."

All our eyes widened and the room grew silent save for the purring from the cat in my lap.

"What do you mean? Why didn't you inform me?" Espen pried, his usual bubbly persona vanishing and replaced by Head Guard Espen who was a lot more serious and diplomatic.

Turi brushed her hands through her hair, sweeping it back behind her ears—currently in their non-pointy state. "Because it happened two days ago and Town Hall has been on high-alert ever since. I myself went out last night to the location of the sighting to track any markings, but left without any evidence."

"Is it one of the Forest Fae?" I asked, unable to stop the words from slipping out.

Turi faced me and shook her head. "I can't be sure."

"Does this have anything to do with the dissent among the ranks Wilhelm was dealing with a while back? Or did a real wolf wander out of its protected area southeast of here?" Espen asked, and I was lost in the conversation once more, not entirely sure what was going on or what politics I was missing. Øyvin probably didn't know what was going on either, but he listened attentively all while continuing his staring match with Loki. At this rate, and with how tense his shoulders were, I was pretty sure Øyvin was protecting me from the cat.

Turi waved her hand and wobbled slightly on her purple pouf. "Likely the latter. As he mentioned in the council meeting way back when, Wilhelm got those skirmishes under control and we haven't seen any problems."

"Good," Espen answered, sounding like he wasn't a fan of whatever bullshit had happened with the wolves.

"Is there a problem if a wolf leaves its usual habitat?" I asked, still feeling a bit lost, but curious as to why a wolf sighting among the humans was an issue. Couldn't they just leave it be or coax it back home?

Espen turned to me, wrinkles lining his brow. "There's great debate among the Norwegian population and government on how to treat wolves. The Norwegian wolf is near extinction, listed as critically endangered, yet, the government still issues permits to kill and some people shoot them illegally if they are seen as a threat to livestock or towns. There are zones that the wolves are allowed to live in peacefully, but if any stray out of that area, there is a high chance they'll end up shot."

"That's awful," I muttered and stroked the cat in my lap for comfort. "And must make things difficult for the fae shifters."

Espen nodded and Turi chimed in. "A sighting by humans usually stirs the pot and incites violence. Pitchforks and guns style."

"Like in Beauty and the Beast? Where the villagers gather to take down the misunderstood creature?"

Turi pointed at me. "Exactly."

The whole thing sounded ridiculous. Why would anyone want to harm a creature that was trying to fend for itself? Especially an animal that was an endangered species. There had to be a way for farmers to protect their livestock and live peacefully with the apex predator.

"Worth bringing that up at tonight's meeting, too." Espen let out an extended sigh, drawing me from my thoughts.

"That's the plan," Turi replied then tilted her head to one side and clasped her hands over her knee, looking as innocent as her nieces and nephew. "Speaking of council meetings. You really should attend more in person."

Espen groaned and looked at the ceiling. "Not you, too."

"Ingrid's right, you know."

"Yes, but I'm needed in Skolvik for political purposes. We need to maintain strong relationships with the other factions, especially the Fjell. Queen Ragnhild was always adamant about that. So, calling in to our council meetings will have to do for now. You know I'd love to live close to you all, to spend our weekends together with the kids. But I have to take into consideration *all* Forest Fae's well-being."

I bit my lip to stifle a smile as Turi grumbled in reply. It was cute to see how much the Solbakke sisters cared about their brother.

"Fine, but you know Ingrid won't relent any time soon."

Espen sighed. "I know."

Beep, beep. Beep, beep.

Turi rose from her spot and tapped a button on her watch, stopping the beeping noise. All the cats ran over to her and brushed up against her legs. "Unfortunately, that's my alarm to get back to the office."

The three of us moved off the sofas, my lap now thoroughly covered in white cat hair. "We'll let you get back. Thank you for the cookies," Espen said, a smile returning to his face.

"Of course." Turi beamed back at him, looking happy to have her brother around. "I'll see you all at tonight's meeting." She turned to me, her hands clasped in front of her. "I look forward to spending time with you again, Lennie. Perhaps next time can be less work talk and more chats about Espen's most embarrassing stories."

"Oh, I would very much enjoy that," I replied with a grin of my own.

Espen snorted and brushed his hand through his hair.

We strode for the entryway, saying our goodbyes.

As we passed Loki, he hissed at Øyvin, and I let out a quick laugh. "Good kitty."

Øyvin grumbled and kept walking as if the cat were a mere nuisance and not likely to rip his face off. The cat was probably capable of the latter, and I'd pay whatever was left in my bank account to see it try. But I kept walking too, on the off chance Loki thought I would be a tasty snack.

"See you at nine o'clock," Turi said.

"See you then," Espen replied as we zipped up our jackets and finished pulling on our boots.

I shoved my hat onto my head and waved back at the cats. "Bye cats. Bye Loki."

The cat-beast squinted at me like he was a Norse god in hiding, waiting to be set loose and destroy everything. *Wrong move.*

Øyvin muttered, "Evil thing."

I sucked in a breath. I was now ninety percent certain that cat was Loki reincarnate and could fuck us up with a swipe of its claws. "Do you have a death wish?"

Espen laughed and the Fjord Fae grumbled as I pushed him out the door.

12

LENNIE

We strode into Alveskjegget late that night, the doors left unlocked for the meeting of the Forest Fae Council of Elders—the sign on the door marking that a private event was underway. Thick wood tables had been cleared and pushed together to create one large table beside the circular firepit in the middle of the space. The pit was full of smoldering embers that were starting to cool, but still lent a cozy, slightly smoky smell to the space. People—fae with their ears dutifully concealed, like myself—milled around chatting to one another, but silence quickly fell as the door bumped shut behind us.

Turi, who sat at the head of the long table, glanced between the individuals already present and our little trio. With a shrug, she turned to those gathering. "Shall we get started?"

Murmurs of agreement and head bobs came in response, and the fae—some visibly older with gray or white hair, and others with far fewer wrinkles—took up seats at the makeshift table.

Taking a spot near Turi between Espen and Øyvin, I pulled my chair in and rested my hands on my lap. Espen, to my left, brushed his fingers over my hand and started absentmindedly tracing the edge of my engagement ring. Warmth rushed through me at the innocent gesture and my heart did that fluttery thing again. Even as Espen's focus was on the room, with our hands hidden from view by the table, it kind of felt like we were sharing a secret.

"First thing on the agenda," Turi started, her voice resolute and confident, "is Wilhelm's request for more help this spring clearing the river that runs past pack lands." Espen's sister nodded at a lithe man with thick black hair that curled around his temple, eyebrows as dense as Tom Selleck's mustache, and a goatee straight out of the eighties.

Wilhelm gave her a terse nod in reply. "Indeed. We had this problem last year and I'd like to preempt it as much as possible. As soon as the snow melts, that runoff now sweeps closer to the pack cabins thanks to large debris from the woods upstream. We have enough hands to handle a good portion of it, but I could do with a few more on the team. I'm planning a work schedule to avoid too many questions from the locals." He said the last word with an ounce of disdain and I had flashbacks to a Fjord King gone loopy on power.

Several nods around the table drew my attention away from the shifter leader, and another fae—with wispy eyebrows that would give Oddvar's a run for his money—agreed to lend four fae from his stables to assist.

"Excellent. We also need to address the reforesting project northwest of Alvdalen," Turi said, surveying the assembled council. "There are several clearings scheduled for growth and input this spring."

I looked around too. Movement to my left caught my gaze, and I turned toward it. The man beside Wilhelm quickly peeked at me, then glanced away when he caught me staring back at him. His lips turned to a frown as he peered at me out of the corner of his eyes. My brow furrowed. There was something familiar about that slimy scowl.

I narrowed my eyes at Wilhelm and the guy beside him. "Were you the one who sent wolves to Skolvik?" I asked, interrupting whatever Turi was saying and knowing full well I was speaking out of turn. But, the more I looked at him, the more positive I was the man next to Wilhelm had attacked me last autumn.

Wilhelm turned to me slowly and tilted his head, wrinkling his nose as if I smelled like crap. "We have not sent fae to Skolvik."

I flexed my hands at my sides, feeling the attention of every single fae in the room, but ignoring the subsequent tingly warmth that crossed my shoulders. "I recognize that guy." I pointed to the fae at Wilhelm's side. "He and his friend attacked me. Then Halvar snapped one of their necks and told them to leave."

Wilhelm let out a diminutive chortle. "Your eyes must not work very well, *human*. None of my wolves have been anywhere near Halvar and the late Fjell Queen."

Liar, liar, tail on fire!

I leaned forward in my chair, bracing my arms against the table. "You're lying."

"You must've been seeing things," Wilhelm replied. "Humans tend to hallucinate and imagine wild fairytales to assuage their boredom."

I bit my lip. *This gas-lighting motherfucker.*

Øyvin squeezed my forearm as I started to rise from my seat, and Espen let out a shuddered breath like he too was trying to stop himself from ripping Wilhelm a new one.

Turi looked between us and Wilhelm, then clasped her hands in front of her. "Wilhelm, whose funeral pyre were you burning about three months ago? The one you requested a cover story for so the town didn't send out fire trucks."

Wilhelm cast his gaze toward Turi, who, impressively, didn't back down from the malice shot her way. "None of your business," he sneered.

She smiled like she'd won a game of chess. "Why did you send wolves to Skolvik?"

The entire room fell silent and I could almost hear the bubbles at the foamy top of people's beer bursting as I held my breath.

"To eliminate the threat to our existence after our secret was revealed," Wilhelm said, looking straight at me, and an instinctual chill ran down my spine.

Shit.

Øyvin and Espen shot to their feet and chaos ensued. Øyvin yanked me and my chair back. Moving in front of me, he clenched his fists and braced his legs, ready to attack anyone who dared try to touch me. Espen meanwhile, lunged forward grabbing Wilhelm's jacket with his fists, hauled him out of his seat, and glowered at the shifter fae. Snarls rent the air and Wilhelm's second tried to get between the two men, while Turi scrambled to pull Espen off the pack leader. As hard as they tried, the pair barely moved the two guys who looked ready to punch each other in the face.

Uproarious cries filled the air and fists hammered against the table as anger roiled through the gathered group. Shouts of *"We agreed with Espen to keep her close"* and *"She was helping with the investigation"* and *"You fool"* rang around the room, and I started to wonder if the bar was insulated to avoid humans overhearing disagreements if they walked by outside. One look at the unbothered barkeep reassured me that was likely the case, as Felix continued drying beer steins like nothing was amiss, soaking up every word that was uttered by the Council. *Smart man.*

Espen muttered something I couldn't hear through the calamity, and Wilhelm scrunched his face and grimaced. Finally, Espen let go of Wilhelm with a shove. The council members trying to break them apart stepped between them, doing their best to calm the two men. Turi tried to get her brother's attention by waving her hand in his face, but Espen and Wilhelm continued to stare at each other like they were imagining how to tear each other limb from limb.

My body flushed and I wriggled in my seat. I'd never had someone willing to actually fight for me like that before. If I was being completely honest with myself, it was kind of hot. I let out a long sigh turning my focus back to the table of council members.

All of them were either on their feet watching the commotion, or talking wildly, hands gesticulating like this whole thing was a big offense and needed further discussion. The lone council member who looked like she couldn't be bothered by the pissing match to her right was the old lady with long white hair at the end of the table.

With slow and gentle movements, she raised her frail hand to the full beer stein in front of her and gingerly lifted it to her lips. Sloshing only a little over the side, she took three large gulps, downing half the drink, before setting it back on the table with a thunk. My eyes bugged and I closed my mouth with my hand. She spotted me and gave me a gentle smile, her eyes crinkling at the corners, as she rose, leaning her hands against the smoothed out wood before her. "Silence," she muttered, her voice barely audible above the ruckus, but silence fell nonetheless. Everyone stilled, and the woman glanced around the room. "What has already passed cannot be altered. We must move forward with our discussions and"—she shot a glance at Wilhelm—"not act rashly. We are far stronger united than we are operating as lone wolves."

The wolfy remark earned her a sneer from Wilhelm and his friend, but I beamed at her blatant *"you idiot"* sentiment.

"Agreed, Gunvor." Turi extended her arms out wide, palms open. "Let's sit down and discuss matters with reason."

Nods flitted about the room, and once everyone had retaken their seats, Øyvin scooted me and my chair back into the table.

Espen dropped into his chair and clamped his hand down on my thigh, locking me in place. I brushed my palm over his hand, doing my best to calm him down and bring him back to his bubbly, happy self. Not that I didn't mind the guys' protective displays—my insides were still tingling from the rush of seeing them leap into action—but we had a job to do. We needed to find Aurora, and talking to the Council of Elders about our search was at the top of the to-do list.

"Now, what other matters did we have on the agenda for today? Brother, you want to go first?" Turi asked, smiling over at Espen with a look that said *"don't you fucking dare pull that shit again."*

Espen let out a long sigh, his shoulders relaxing as he squeezed my hand beneath the table. "Halvar, Head Guard for the Fjell Fae, asked for our assistance in locating a specific individual who allegedly resides in Alvdalen. We were informed that Aurora lived with the late Vigdis Johansen."

"Why are the Fjell Fae looking for her?" one of the fae elders asked, his thick brows meeting his non-existent hairline. "And why didn't they send one of their own?"

I slowly raised my hand. All eyes turned to me, and I did my best not to shrink back from their gazes. "Part Fjell Fae, right here."

Half the table glared at me, the other half looked at me like I was a science experiment, which wasn't wholly unwarranted all things considered.

"When Freija was dying, she transferred magic to Halvar and Lennie," Øyvin piped up, giving them what I considered a very vague explanation of the events from the night my whole life changed dramatically and I got myself a gnarly lightning tattoo up the length of my left arm. Then again, it was probably best that people didn't know the full details—that Halvar hadn't had the strength to contain all of Freija's magic plus his own and needed a vessel to transfer the excess to. Insert me, the vessel, and voilà: a demi-fae was born.

Wide eyes met Øyvin's remarks, and several of the council elders surveyed me with renewed interest. Wilhelm, on the other hand, scowled.

"As for the why," Espen jumped in, steering the conversation and attention away from me, which I greatly appreciated. "The individual in question is apparently the Heir of the Fjell."

Silence fell across the room. Even Felix the bartender stopped wiping down the bar top, unable to feign that he wasn't eavesdropping on the meeting. They must've paid him off to keep him quiet or something, because the guy had probably witnessed many meetings if they'd been gathering here for long.

Turi pressed her fist to her mouth. "Well, shit. Gunvor, have you heard anything from your cousin Vigdis's daughter?"

The old lady at the other end of the table tilted her head to one side, her long white hair falling over her shoulder. Her eyes narrowed before she let out a short sigh. "Aurora? No."

Damn.

"Do you know where she lives now?" I blurted before either Espen or Øyvin could throw their hands over my mouth. I had a mission after all, and I wanted to get this done without having Halvar split me in two. Failure was not an option.

Gunvor's dainty shoulders curved inward and she shook her head. "I haven't seen her in a couple years. She's about twenty years old by now, an adult. But I'll see what information I can find among Vigdis's things. Perhaps there is a clue as to where she moved."

My heart sank, but she gave the three of us a tentative smile, her lips curling up at one corner.

"Where are you staying? I can stop by with more information and perhaps tell you more about Aurora tomorrow?"

"The old Mikkelsen cabin by the lake," Espen replied.

I gave Gunvor a gentle smile. "That would be great. Thank you."

Gunvor's gaze softened as she took a final swig of her beer. Espen uttered his thanks and Øyvin nodded his head in the elder's direction. It wasn't much to go on, but it wasn't nothing. We needed all the information we could get on the heir.

Wilhelm cleared his throat, probably bored of the conversation.

"Wonderful," Turi piped up again, looking ready to steer the meeting on to the next agenda item. "The final thing we need to discuss this evening is a report from my office. Unfortunately, two days ago we received a call about a wolf sighting."

All eyes turned back to Wilhelm who didn't budge in his seat, but his second squirmed at the attention.

"We need to be cautious that our own wolf shifters aren't caught up in this and aren't the responsible party," Turi continued. "Wilhelm, is there anything we need to be aware of with the pack?"

The shifter sucked on his lips, and I wondered how big his canines were when he snapped into wolf form. Would he look like the saber-tooth tiger in *Ice Age* or a regular dog with a serious overbite?

"It must've been a non-fae wolf." Wilhelm brushed his fingers across his goatee.

"You're certain of that?" a fae elder asked, and Espen glowered at the wolf shifter.

Wilhelm swallowed hard and straightened in his seat. "Positive. My wolves wouldn't step out of line. They know the rules around staying hidden."

The questioning fae leaned against the table and everyone's attention remained locked on the conversation. "So, it's not that same problem you had a while ago? There aren't wolves that have gone rogue?"

Wilhelm snorted and crossed his arms. "You know how the young are these days—all wide-eyed and naive. As I said months ago, the problem was fixed and those wolves were brought to heel." He waved his hand, dismissing the problem.

I glanced at Gunvor, finding her beer stein completely empty and her head minutely shaking. Apparently I wasn't the only one at the table who disliked Wilhelm.

Espen fidgeted beside me, brushing his thumb over my ring again like it was helping him remain calm.

"Okay then," Turi said, her voice growing more stern. "I'll try to quell local fears by stating that it was just a wolf passing through. But, please... Have your wolves be extremely careful for the next few weeks until things die down. We can't have the humans sending out hunting parties again."

Wilhelm nodded, and more agreement peppered around the table with nods and hums.

Turi straightened up and clapped her hands together. "With that, our meeting is adjourned. I'll see you again in two weeks. Same time, same place. Don't forget to return your glasses to Felix at the bar."

We all rose from our seats, chairs scraping across the floorboards as people started saying their goodbyes and leaving.

"Shall we head home?" I glanced between my two fae, my chest warming slightly at the way they monitored our surroundings, like they were protecting me from attack. It was cute, really. I could kind of protect myself, but I'd never say no to someone willing to have my back—especially in a room full of magical beings.

Espen and Øyvin both gave me a nod before Espen waved to his sister. "We're leaving. Have a good night, and please don't tell Ingrid." He motioned to the spot where he'd launched at Wilhelm.

Turi's lips quirked into a grin and she shook her cell phone in the air. "Too late, brother."

Espen let out a low groan, and Øyvin snorted, nudging me in the back toward the door.

As we moved across the room, my eyes caught on Gunvor's long white hair, draping down to her low back. She gave me a quick smile when she spotted me staring.

I pressed up onto my tiptoes and leaned into Espen while prodding him in the ribs. "Who is she, exactly?"

He looked over his shoulder. "Ylva's mother. Her name is Gunvor Nygård."

She bowed her head ever so slightly in my direction, her eyes crinkling at the corners.

I returned the nod, thankful for her support earlier and wholly unsurprised that she was Ylva's mother. With that stoicism and knowing gaze, I should've clocked it as soon as I walked into the room. She was basically an ancient version of Ylva. A take-no-bullshit kind of lady.

"Is she friend or foe?" I asked, unsure of the politics between the council members or what their powers were.

"Definitely friend," Espen replied.

13

LENNIE

We'd just finished breakfast when a gentle knock sounded at the cabin door the next morning. "I'll get it," Espen said, jumping up and sprinting for the door, while Øyvin and I tidied up our bowls. The Fjord Fae set to work on washing them up, as I brushed my hands over my insulated leggings and wandered across the room to greet our visitor.

A gentle and slightly croaky voice sounded from the front door and I stopped mid-stride in the living room.

Gunvor stepped inside, guided by Espen who took a bread bin-sized box from her hands and offered her his elbow for support. She took it with a smile, the weight of time gifting her a collection of laugh lines that swept around the sides of her mouth. Her white hair was pulled back in a low ponytail, as if she'd grown frustrated with it getting in the way, and she wore a thick, emerald-green sweater that swamped her delicate frame.

"Good day to you all," she said as Espen guided her to the sofa and helped her sit.

I pulled up the sleeves of my navy-colored sweater. "Good morning, Gunvor. I'm Lennie—"

"I know, I know," she said with a wave of her hand.

"Did you find anything among Vigdis's things?" Espen asked, getting straight to the point and voicing my own query as he set down the teal box with flowers painted on the sides on the small, wooden coffee table pushing aside a tower of coasters to make room.

Gunvor smiled with her eyes, narrowing them so the skin at the corners crinkled in a knowing look that I'd seen Ylva do before too. "As mentioned last night, I thought I might be of assistance. I rummaged through some Vidgis's items and thought the contents of this box might prove helpful."

We all tilted our heads to take in her words, including Øyvin who'd finished up in the kitchen and leaned against the dining table. Espen and I stood watching her like she was from another world. Which, for me, I guessed she kind of was. Her ears were hidden by her hair, but even if I'd met Gunvor at the grocery store, I'd have thought she was from another planet. There was an ethereal aura when in her presence, and it had me fully ensnared.

"Sit, sit," she said, motioning to the sofa and the armchair around the coffee table. "Let us discuss what I do and don't know about the Fjell heir."

I slid in beside her on the couch, while Espen took the armchair, and Øyvin didn't move from his perch in the dining area.

"What can you tell us about your cousin Vigdis and the girl?" Espen asked, his remarks pointed but still diplomatically kind. This wasn't an interrogation down at the police station. This was a fact-finding mission with an elder as our primary source of information. Therefore, poise—which I'd never had much of—was necessary.

"Vigdis lived on the south coast for years. Three of my four girls moved down there to enjoy the warmer weather and spend time with her. Vigdis then moved back here, oh, about thirty years ago. Then she took in a ward about twenty years ago, saying it was the child of an old Fjell Fae friend from the south coast. The child's name was Aurora."

I sat straighter, hope filling my chest that we might find out more about our mystery girl.

"Vigdis passed a couple of years ago," Gunvor continued, nodding to the box on the table. "These are some of her things, letters, photos, the sort. Perhaps there are some clues in here that will help you locate Aurora."

"You didn't know her?" Øyvin asked, his arms and ankles crossed where he leaned, his cream knit sweater taut across his shoulders.

Gunvor shook her head. "Yes and no. I met Aurora several times, but she was a young girl with a strong sense of self. Aside from Vigdis, she had no interest in spending time with the adults, especially as she grew into her teenage years." She chuckled and patted her thigh. "Vigdis had her hands full with that one after she turned fourteen. Then when Vigdis passed, Aurora disappeared. And I wish,"—she let out a deep sigh, and cast her gaze over her shoulder toward the windows before turning back to us—"I should've stepped in. I should have protected her. But she was eighteen, an adult, and I always raised my girls to be independent by a young age. A woman has enough battles to face in this world and should be given the freedom to choose her own path. All four of my girls were raised as such, and they've all done well for themselves."

I stared at Gunvor as she wrung her hands together and visibly struggled to come to terms with the missing woman. "I should have guessed there was more to her story. That she wasn't merely an orphan as Vigdis once told me."

Growing more curious by the second, I reached out and lifted the lid from the box and set it aside. Inside was a small collection of envelopes secured into bundles with ribbons, a wooden wolf figurine, a few stacks of photographs, and a small green, leather notebook with an oak leaf embossed on the front. I picked that up first, while Espen carefully withdrew a stack of photos. Gunvor and Øyvin watched on in silence.

Inside the notebook were pages of doodles and curly script that I could barely read—in part because it was in Norwegian far more advanced than my current understanding, and also because it was the swirliest cursive I'd ever seen. The intricate drawings were plants, though, that was clear. Each part of the flora perfectly labeled. Near the back of the book, pressed between a tissue, was a bright-pink flower with a slight trumpet shape.

"Ah," Gunvor said softly, pointing at the delicate specimen. "Foxglove, much more common on the coast, and highly poisonous." Espen shuddered. "Vigdis was a botanist and scholar, tasked with researching the plants we Forest Fae are to protect."

After the number of run-ins we'd had with poisonous plants recently, I gently closed the book and set it back in the box. Couldn't be too careful, plus the little notebook clearly wasn't what we were looking for. What we desperately needed was more information about Aurora and where she might possibly have gone.

"Do you think Aurora may have gone south?" I asked Gunvor, while Espen continued thumbing through photos.

Gunvor shrugged. "In all honesty, she could be anywhere."

For fuck's sake. I hung my head and refrained from groaning.

Espen leaned forward and held out a photo toward us. The image was of a woman with vaguely familiar features to those of Gunvor, but the three women beside her would be a match for Gunvor if she had red hair.

"Vigdis and your other daughters?" Espen asked, and Gunvor nodded. I guessed Ylva had never introduced him to them... or perhaps they weren't close siblings.

Gunvor's smile radiated warmth and joy. "Yes, Ylva's older sisters... half-sisters. They inherited their father's, my first husband's, fiery red hair. Ylva, on the other hand, inherited my features and my second husband's penchant for strategy and battle."

Yeah, that tracked. I'd witnessed Ylva in battle against King Balder a few months ago. It was quite the sight to behold. Her recent skirmish with Espen on the training field outside Skolvik had been impressive too.

"And as her boss, I appreciate that skill set very much. She doesn't ever talk about her sisters, though," Espen said, handing the photo to Gunvor. She took the image and brushed her thumb across their faces as if she could magically stroke their cheeks. A pang of love hit my heart at the gesture, and a wave of homesickness and longing for my own family back in Ohio washed over me.

"There's a fifty year age gap between them," Gunvor said, jolting me out of my thoughts. *Fifty years?!* I knew fae had longer child-bearing cycles than humans, but it was still a jarring factoid that I couldn't entirely wrap my head around. With that said, the age gap between Gunvor's girls could explain why Espen didn't know Ylva's sisters.

I glanced at the woman beside me on the couch, trying to discern her age. Was she older than Halvar? Her appearance certainly would allude to that, but if I'd learned one thing while living among the fae, it was that appearances could be deceiving.

"Would they know where Aurora is?" Øyvin asked, drawing our attention back to the task at hand.

Gunvor shook her head and returned the photo to the box, setting it atop the stack that Espen had put back while she spoke. "I doubt they ever met."

"Do you have any other information about the girl?" Espen asked. "Her likes, dislikes. Anything she might've said in passing? Anything we should know about her?"

Gunvor took a deep breath and scooted back on the sofa, relaxing into the cushions and closing her eyes as if to think harder on the subject. The room fell silent as we gave her a second, the only noise coming from the hum of the tiny refrigerator in the kitchen. After another minute where I refrained from bouncing my knee in anticipation, opting instead to hold them in place with my hands, Gunvor spoke. "Aurora enjoyed the outdoors. She was rarely home when I visited Vigdis for coffee and cake. Vigdis always said she was outside in the forest playing with the neighborhood children, running around, building fortresses and the like."

That sounded very Norwegian and a damn sight different than the chalk drawings I'd made on sidewalks and basketball games with the neighbors during my childhood. Forest forts? Really?

"Aurora was never talkative and observed her surroundings with the keen eye of a hawk."

"Did she know she was a Fjell Fae?" I asked.

"I believe so. I don't recall Vigdis mentioning anything about Aurora's powers or affinity, but they did spend a lot of time outdoors together, observing and cataloging nature. Knowing Vigdis, she probably raised Aurora more like a Forest Fae than a Fjell Fae." Gunvor's shoulders rose and fell as she let out an extended sigh. "My first recommendation would be to check the forests around here. Or perhaps the villages to our south."

"Do you think she'd head toward Oslo?" Øyvin asked, arms still crossed over his chest and his eyes narrowed as if he were analyzing every word she said.

I turned back to Gunvor as she replied, "Many twenty-somethings head to the big city to see what's there. Some stay. Some come back. Seems to be the thing these days."

"We will keep that in mind," Espen said with a smile.

"Good. And on that note, I should let you get on with your search." She rose gingerly from her spot beside me and waved away my hand when I offered to help. "Just let me know what you find. I'm curious." She twitched her nose and wandered over to the door.

We agreed to keep her in the loop as she pulled on her boots and jacket, then waved her off as she headed out to her little Mini Cooper. My eyes bugged at the sight of the small car, but on closer inspection it had some beefy studded tires on it that no doubt would stop it from sliding around on the wintry roads.

Espen closed the door and we returned to the living room area. I threw myself back down onto the couch, tucking my feet underneath me for warmth.

"Well, whaddaya think?" I asked the room.

Both fae stood stock still, lost in their thoughts.

"If she's gone to Oslo, we don't stand a chance," Øyvin said.

"Agreed," Espen replied. "But based on what Gunvor said, I don't think Aurora would like Oslo. She preferred being outdoors and in the forests."

I pulled my hair into a ponytail. "What are you thinking?"

Espen brushed his hand across his short beard and let out a sigh. "I think we start canvassing the woods around here and work our way outward."

"As good a plan as any," Øyvin said.

"Agreed," I added.

Espen set his hands on his hips. "Let's get started then."

14

LENNIE

Rays of sun skittered across clear blue skies and a cold breeze wended around the hillsides. My cheeks smarted from the chill, but the sunshine made up for the sting, brightening what was turning into a frustrating day. After spending yesterday afternoon searching the woods around Alvdalen for the elusive Fjell heir, we'd resumed our search this morning.

"You sure you don't want to check the north side again?" I asked after lunch, clambering into the car. The *lefse*—a pastry with cinnamon, butter, and sugar—and a second coffee had been a delicious snack and I was ready to get back out there.

"No, I think we'd better pick up the pace and check the forest south of town," Espen said as he settled into the driver's seat.

Øyvin unzipped his navy jacket and clicked himself into the passenger seat with a deep sigh. The Fjord Fae was extra grumpy today, probably because our hunt was less straightforward than we'd hoped... Or maybe he'd woken up on the wrong side of the bed, so to speak. Either way, food had not improved his mood.

"Where to after the southern forest?" I asked as the engine hummed to life and Espen pulled out of our parking spot.

He took a moment to respond, focusing first on the road and getting us onto the main drag out of town. "Eastern hills. It would be deadly to hide in the western mountains at this time of year."

I twitched my nose. "What if she had a cabin there though?"

Espen shook his head. "Unlikely. Even those who do only venture up there for a long weekend or a week, at most. They're more holiday homes than permanent residences."

"And someone couldn't trespass and squat in one of these houses?"

"They'd be noticed pretty damn quick. The owners may not live in them, but Norwegians tend to visit their cabins regularly and throughout the year, not just seasonally."

"Duly noted," I replied, leaning back in my seat with a huff. Ingrid's statement about doing things no matter the weather conditions rang through my mind. Apparently that applied to cabin visits too.

The world flickered past in staccato images as I stared wistfully out the window. Red- and yellow-painted wood buildings with front steps cleared of snow preceded what I could only describe as fairytale woods. Hundreds of thin tree trunks shot out of the snowy ground, their leaves having abandoned them in the autumn. I wouldn't be surprised if this was where Norway got a lot of their folktales from. Stories of trolls, faeries, and creatures running between the trees, hiding from prying eyes, spreading their magic. I chuckled to myself, thinking of my own pointed ears. Perhaps the old storytellers had actually got that right?

I moved my lower seat belt off my abdomen, the pressure on my bladder growing uncomfortable.

We made a few more turns, the woods growing thicker, more pines blending in with the wispy barren trees. I squirmed in my seat, my bladder staging a protest complete with banners, flags, and chants of *"it's our time to go."* Squeezing my legs together, I tried to think about anything but running water...

Would Ohio beat Michigan this year? Dad would be elated if they did, as would Andrew and Jared.

Maybe my family would go to the game?

Did Norwegian's play American football or was it just soccer?

I still needed to edit the photos I'd taken of Skolvik on New Year's Eve and send a few to Mom. She'd love how the village sparkled under the glow of the fireworks.

We passed a frozen creek and my bladder screamed at me.

"Umm..." I said, interrupting the tranquil silence in the car. "Can we pull over somewhere?"

"We're almost there. You feeling sick?" Espen glanced into the rearview mirror, his eyebrows drawing together. "Staring at those trees is a bit like watching a flickering barcode."

He wasn't wrong, but... "No, it's not that." There wasn't any way to put this delicately, but I was rarely gentle with my words. "I need to pee."

Øyvin chuffed. "You didn't think to go before we left the café?"

"I did!" I exclaimed as Espen snickered and pulled over to the side of the road. "But having two large cups of coffee today may have been a mistake."

I could hear Øyvin's eye roll from the back seat.

Espen shut off the car and turned in his seat with a smile. "Hurry up, then."

"Thank you," I said as I rushed out of the car, accidentally slamming the door shut behind me.

I traipsed through the snowdrifts toward a thicket of snow-laden pine trees, the sound of my neon orange pants swishing together echoing around me. The cold air brushed my face and I was thankful it wasn't snowing today. Just the thought of a snow storm sent a shiver down my spine, and my legs tried to clamp together again. Because snow equals water and water equals...

Circling around briefly, I found a spot that was hidden from the road, beside a line of trees and a slightly larger mound of snow—probably a boulder or something hidden beneath the natural icing. It was as good a spot as any. I pulled down my pants and underwear, popped a squat, and angled my butt so I didn't piss on myself. A sigh of relief passed my lips at the release of pressure in my abdomen, feeling happier by the second. Peeing in the woods certainly wasn't ideal, but I'd left my pride at the café. Two large morning coffees had been a very big mistake.

A rustling sounded to my right, and I rolled my eyes as I let myself drip-dry a bit—the cold nipping at my butt and bits. "I'm not kink shaming, but golden showers are not something I want to experience or experiment with, guys," I said, hoping they weren't about to jump-scare me in such a vulnerable position.

"Disgusting," a female voice said, and my eyes went wide as I quickly yanked up my pants, doing my best not to stumble back into the yellow snow. I spun around, my heart in my throat, panic searing through my veins. A young woman wearing a thick white wool jacket with a deep hood leaned against a tree, her lips set in a firm grimace.

"Kind of rude to sneak up on someone while they're peeing." I scowled, eying up the newcomer. From her gray boots, to the white gloves she wore, her entire outfit was designed to blend in with the terrain, not stand out like my neon get-up.

She scoffed like I was the one in the wrong and shook her head.

A panting noise sounded from behind her, and she stepped aside, revealing a gray wolf with a shock of white across its face sweeping onto its chest and bright gray-blue eyes that bored into me. Perhaps it got a good look at my bare ass and thought I was a tasty snack?

It sneered.

Or not.

"What is this? You two Red Riding Hood and the Big Bad Wolf?" I asked, a mocking tone in my voice.

"No." The woman removed her hood, revealing a thick braid of copper-brown hair with streaks of silver in it, a delicate face fixed with a stern look, and eyes... I sucked in a breath. Her eyes were an unusual blend of gray-and-brown. A coloring I'd only seen on two others in my lifetime—one who was now in a rocky dungeon, the other passed away.

"What are you staring at?" The woman snarled, her attitude similar to someone else I'd come to know in recent months. She crossed her arms, braced her legs, and settled into a stoic posture fit for a queen.

Distant relative my ass, Halvar. I'd bet the limited funds in my bank account that this young woman was Aurora, the late-Fjell Queen's daughter. She looked exactly like Queen Freija—from the eyes, to the set of her lips and her genteel but strong stature. She matched Turi's visual description, too, and that keen look in her eye reminded me of what Gunvor had said: that Aurora observed her surroundings like a hawk.

"Any chance your name is Aurora?"

The woman squinted, her canine companion took a step toward me, and victory thundered in my chest as a smile tilted my lips.

"Nice to finally meet you."

The wolf lunged.

15

ESPEN

"What's taking her so long?" Øyvin ground out, his arms crossed as he leaned back in the passenger seat.

I shrugged and tapped my fingers on the steering wheel. "Perhaps she got more than she bargained for?"

My retort earned me a glare from my friend, and I snickered as I adjusted my wool hat. Lennie had gifted it to me for Christmas, and I really liked the green Nordic pattern and oversized pom-pom. Øyvin, who'd been gifted a navy-blue one, barely ever wore his. But, I saw the way it made Lennie smile every time I put it on, so I wore mine as much as possible. I liked seeing her happy, and I knew—deep, *deep* down—Øyvin did too. He just went about showing it in different ways, like protecting her when she didn't realize she needed protecting.

Sometimes I wondered if she even noticed his behavior. Just the other day he'd lingered behind her, hands loose, ready to pounce at Felix should the barkeep make a wrong move. Felix wasn't a threat to Lennie, but Øyvin hadn't known that at the time. He always put himself between Lennie and anything that might cause her harm—an admirable trait in my book.

"This is taking too long." Øyvin let out a huff of annoyance, his hand resting on the car door. "We should go find her."

I shook my head at him. "And watch her urinate? We don't need to see that."

"We've seen her naked." He yanked on the handle and pushed his door open. "Seeing her relieving herself, while unappealing, wouldn't be the worst thing in the world."

He clambered out of the car, stretched out his arms, and zippered up his jacket.

"Fair enough." I sighed and followed him into the deep snow, even though I'd argue that this was being a tad *too* overprotective.

We'd barely passed through the tree line when Øyvin stilled, then bolted forward, pushing through the snow that reached our calves in some spots. Sensing his panic, I sped up, sticking right behind him.

"Lennie!" Øyvin yelled as we came to a halt around a patch of sunken yellow snow. The only answer was a lump of ice falling off a nearby branch. He called again as I inspected the area.

The drifts around the boulder and tree line she'd stopped at had been trampled, like multiple people had been here. Some of the footprints were Lennie's based on the direction they'd come from—the same as us—but hers weren't the only ones. More worrisome were the paw prints that matched those of a large dog or even a wolf.

"We have a problem," I said, my voice barely a whisper.

Øyvin stomped over to me. "How bad?"

I pointed to the paw prints, and Øyvin's nostrils flared.

Tightening my jaw, I surveyed the traces of a squabble. Prints and downtrodden snow fanned out around the yellow-snow, with the largest grouping heading toward the woods. I moved and squatted around a pair of prints near some trees a few paces away from Lennie's marking.

Øyvin followed and passed me, tracking the prints further into the forest, moving swiftly through the snow.

Anger roiled within me, my pulse ticking upward as I clenched my fists. These were definitely wolf prints.

I trailed after Øyvin, taking in every aspect of our surroundings, monitoring for anything that might resemble our girl. Tall trees stood sentry guarding the peace of the land, drifts of snow-covered hibernating flora, and cathedral-like silence reigned.

"There are two sets of paw prints down here, and then the tracks change where they morph from canine to human." Øyvin pointed at markings shaped like large snow boots. They ran beside a smaller pair and the same wolf tracks from where Lennie stopped by the boulder.

Glancing back at the little clearing where all four individuals had met, my gut flipped over. "They took her. And she didn't scream?"

"She was probably too busy mouthing off," Øyvin said, and... Well, he had a point.

Øyvin grumbled and glared at the forest, like he wanted to boil everything within it with just a flick of his wrist. Which, knowing the fae, wasn't entirely out of the realm of possibility. His jaw ticked, hands balled into fists. "We let her out of our sight for five minutes and she lands herself in trouble."

"You have to admit," I said, trying to lighten the mood and hopefully get the Fjord Fae to pivot his focus away from simply killing everything to searching for our missing demi-fae. "It's rather on brand for her."

Øyvin huffed and pressed on through the woods.

Oh well, at least I tried.

We tracked the footprints about a kilometer from our starting point until they vanished, as if they'd been swept away by a phantom wind or tree branches. My head snapped upward, noting the markedly missing snow cover on the trees at the same time Øyvin spotted the oddity. "They've shaken the snow off all the trees from here onward to cover their tracks," I murmured, anger and annoyance skirting up my veins as I ground my teeth together.

Forget lightening the mood. I wanted my fiancée back.

Øyvin nodded and let out a deep sigh. "You think this was the shifter from the Council?"

That destructive power swarmed in my core, heating me from the inside out, begging to be unleashed. I nodded slowly, breathing hard through my nose. "Wilhelm."

16

LENNIE

I slowly opened my eyes, my head pounding from the hit I'd taken from hell knew what before I passed out. The dim light of my surroundings revealed dark wood walls like those in Espen's cabin, buckets and cleaning supplies shoved in one corner, and ratty curtains drawn over a small, square window. I was in a shed and... I shimmied on the seat, rope chafing against my wrists where they were tied to the back of the wooden chair.

Yup, kidnapped.

Thankfully, my clothes were still on and I didn't appear to have any injuries, but honest to hell, could I be more of a trouble magnet? My guys would have a complete conniption when they realized what happened. They'd probably go looking for me when Øyvin inevitably grew impatient and grumbly. And the only trace of me in that clearing was the yellow-stained snow—

The door to the little shed creaked open. Blinding light filtered in and I turned my face away, unable to properly shield my eyes from it. Footsteps pattered against the dusty floorboards and the door eventually swung shut with a gentle thud. I blinked, trying to see who my visitors were.

Aurora stood between two large wolves, both of which assessed me and my bindings from several paces away, careful not to get any closer as if *I* might actually be the threat here… which was ludicrous. Yes, I did have a good deal of power stored within me, but fuck if I knew how to use it all. They, on the other hand, had very large teeth that could definitely do some damage.

"If you're looking for a dentist, you've got the wrong woman. But I'd recommend flossing either way," I said to the brown-and-beige wolf as it stared at me. I didn't expect an answer, but Aurora snorted at my joke and the gray-and-white wolf beside her started to shift. Snapping and cracking noises rent the air and I watched with my stomach in my throat as the wolf transformed from canine to fae. He swiftly pressed his hand to his left shoulder, magically clothing himself before he could expose his family jewels.

Now, instead of one fae and two wolves, I had two fae and one wolf watching me closely. The white-haired male beside Aurora stepped forward, but she gently wrapped her fingers around his wrist. He glanced down at where she touched him, his black wool sweater preventing skin-to-skin contact. Their eyes met and he gave her a gentle nod before she turned her gaze on me again. "Why are you looking for me? Why are you asking around town for me?"

"Reasons," I replied, unsure if I should reveal her status as heir quite yet—did she even know?—or withhold some information in hopes it might buy the guys some more time to find me, or give me a chance to escape… somehow. Turning into puppy chow was not on my to-do list for the day.

I furrowed my brow. "How do you even know I've been looking for you?" That information had only been shared with the Forest Fae Council.

"We have our ways," the man next to Aurora grumbled with enough authority that I mentally marked him as some sort of leader.

"You mean you have an insider on the Council?"

Aurora shook her head, her braid falling off her shoulder and into the deep white hood on her back. "The Council has a traitor in their midst who isn't careful about who they share information with."

Well, fuck... but on the bright side. "That sucks, but either way. I've found you now. We should really get going."

The white-haired man took a step forward, his nose twitching into a snarl, and his eyes flashing silver. The latter happened so fast, I did a double take.

"Your eyes, they shimmered. Is that a normal Forest Fae thing?" I asked, recalling Espen's eyes doing that the day I'd first met—and punched—him.

"They only do that when a Forest Fae is flexing their power, showing off." Aurora turned to the guy, her jaw ticking. "Marius, let me handle this."

His nostrils flared, but he took a step back and straightened up.

"So, you're not like *Twilight* then? Oh no, wait, it was the vampires that sparkled. You're not a vampire too, are you?" Better to be safe than a blood bag. Like always, my tongue ran away from me the moment nerves and adrenaline kicked in and it was anyone's guess what came flying out.

Marius rolled his eyes and leaned against the door, crossing his arms and legs, his snow pants swishing where his ankles rubbed together. Aurora shook her head, while the wolf stared on quietly.

"Are you Team Jacob or Team Edward? Bet you're Team wolf, hey, Aurora?" I wiggled my brows at her suggestively before giving her a wink. "I myself was more of a Jacob fan, but now I think I'm more of a Daddy Charlie Swan fan. The facial hair, the quiet broody protective nature, and the uniform. Ugh, the uniform. Not to mention the wisdom that comes with age." I tilted my head to the side. "Now that I think about it, I guess I do have a thing for older men these days."

"Answer the questions," Aurora said, drawing me out of my thoughts of strolls along misty shores in the Pacific Northwest. "Why do you want me? Why are you looking for me?"

"So, your Council confidant didn't tell you everything? Didn't tell you *why* we were looking for you, just that we were looking?"

Her jaw tightened, and I nodded as I weighed my options. With no visible weapons on them, the trio didn't appear interested in hurting me. Or maybe they were and they wanted me to start talking before their torture session began. Either way, I was in a shitty situation. I could keep vocalizing my inner monologue and nervous thoughts, probably annoying the crap out of them and end up stuck here for days until my guys came to save me after I was beaten to within an inch of my life. Or... I could tell Aurora the truth, encourage her to come with me, see if I could broker an agreement without getting hurt. Neither one was ideal, but the latter might get us back to Skolvik quicker and save my neck from Halvar's axe or the myriad of weapons the Fjell Fae had stashed in the forge.

Oh well, here goes...

"We were sent to find you and bring you back to Skolvik," I said, leaving out some key details.

She huffed and set her hands on her hips in a pretty decent power pose. "I'm not going anywhere."

I admired her staunch tenacity—it would probably help her when she took up the throne— but I'd fucking found her and was *this* close to completing my mission and saving my neck from Halvar's guillotine. Finding and returning Aurora to the Fjell was my ticket to acceptance among the Fjell Fae. And I wasn't going to lose. No chance. Martin Family Rules: Wins only.

I clicked my tongue and tilted my head to one side. "I figured you might not want to, and Alvdalen is a beautiful place to live. But there are very good reasons for you to come with us."

"And those are?" Marius asked, his voice velvety smooth enough to be an audiobook narrator.

I let out a long sigh and tugged on my constraints again. Burning pain swept across the raw skin on my wrists and a wince slipped from my mouth. "You're needed by the Fjell Fae."

Aurora pursed her lips and looked over her shoulder at Marius, who in turn stared daggers at me. The wolf in the corner didn't move. It just watched, calmly monitoring the exchange, its ears twitching ever so often.

"And why is that?" Aurora asked, quirking a single brow.

Well, I could go with the blunt and honest truth... or divulge the information carefully, be respectful of the mountain I was about to dump on her head.

Fuck it.

"Based on your significant resemblance, your mother was the Queen of the Fjell. She died. Regicide by your aunt. Long story. And her Head Guard, Halvar, who I'm sure you've heard of, sent me to fetch you so you could take up the mantle, Little Miss Heir of the Fjell."

The room stilled, and Aurora dropped her arms to her sides.

Okay, maybe I could've offloaded a little better. Too late now.

Aurora's shoulders fell as she took a step backward, spinning to face Marius. He pressed his hand against the small of her back. "Rora," he mumbled, so quietly I could barely hear it. The wolf's brown eyes peered at the duo before swinging back to me and narrowing.

"True story, bro," I said, wholly unable to lighten the mood in the room, but here we were, details out in the open. Now all I needed was for them to untie me, and Aurora to come back to Skolvik. "I even have a letter that was meant for Vigdis, but you should probably have it. It's in my inner jacket pocket."

Aurora turned and stepped over to me. Unzippering my jacket, she pulled the material aside and located the pocket. Her breathing was calm and even as she pulled out the letter. I swallowed audibly as she stepped back and examined the small envelope.

"That should help explain," I said, hoping it was true. I had no idea what was written in there, but now didn't seem like the right time to say that.

Aurora slid her fingers beneath the flap of the envelope and popped the wax seal, withdrew a piece of thin parchment, and unfolded it. Her gaze flitted over the paper, before she huffed and said, "This doesn't explain anything."

I scrunched my eyebrows together. "What do you mean?"

"It says, 'It's time for the flower to come home. Thank you for everything. The trio can be trusted. H.'"

Yeah, I didn't understand the flower part either, but Halvar had meant the letter for Vigdis, and had said the guys and I were trustworthy. "It says you can trust me."

Aurora scoffed, turning her back on me again, and faced Marius.

Nervous energy skittered through me, my knees bouncing in anticipation as I watched them exchange an entire conversation without opening their mouths. A head shake here and a nod there. Yeah, these two were definitely an item. Aside from a couple of ear twitches, the wolf beside them didn't move, his eyes locked on me like he expected me to loosen my own restraints and bolt.

Just as I was about to start whistling the theme song for *Jeopardy*, Aurora glanced over her shoulder at me and shook her head. "You have the wrong person."

My brow furrowed. "I don't think so. You're a Fjell Fae, yes?"

She turned, narrowed her eyes, and gave me a single minute nod.

"You're about twenty years old and you were raised by Vigdis Johansen, right? Who took in her southern friend's daughter?"

Her fists opened and closed while the rest of Aurora's body remained still. I could practically hear the puzzle pieces clicking together in her head.

"Sorry to burst your bubble, sweet pea, but you're the Heir of the Fjell Fae."

"I—" Aurora shook her head and reached for the doorknob, yanking the door open. "You have the wrong person." She waltzed outside and slammed the door behind her.

Marius's nostrils flared and he let out an audible breath.

I quirked my eyebrow. "Something I said?"

Marius scowled and opened the door. "Nils," he said, and the wolf obediently trotted through the doorway.

"We'll be back to deal with you later," Marius grumbled, then swept from the room, locking the shed door behind him. *Fantastic.*

"Bring snacks when you do!" I yelled after them.

Tapping my fingers against the chair legs, I muttered, "Well, that went well."

Hopefully the guys were on their way.

17

ØYVIN

We barreled onto the compound where Wilhelm and his pack lived. The icy gravel road gave way to collections of wood cabins—some tucked away in the trees, others sitting side-by-side like row houses, trails cleared through the snow to each front step. Espen threw the car into park, and I was out of the vehicle before he shut the engine off. A big house, two stories with a sharply pitched roof, loomed over the tract we'd parked in and light streamed onto the shielded deck from two large front windows.

Scanning my surroundings for any threats, a tingling sensation ran up my spine. We were being watched. My pulse quickened, and I loosened my hands at my sides, ready to launch a boiling ball of water at anyone who crossed my path. Trust her to get herself kidnapped by a bunch of wolves. Here we were on a mission to find one woman and we'd lost ours in the process. Ancestors help me, when I got my hands on Trouble, I was tying her to my bed and never letting her out of my sight ever again.

Espen clambered out of the car and strode directly toward the main house. I followed him, uncaring of our stomping against the wooden stoop that further announced our presence. Espen knocked on the front door, but I pushed past him and went straight for the door knob. Unlocked, I strode inside the bright building and was immediately assaulted by the musty smell of wet dog and growls.

"Wilhelm!" Espen stepped in behind me and closed the door. "Wilhelm, we need to talk!"

Espen may have been in the mood for diplomacy, valiantly keeping his destructive powers under control, but I was ready to waterboard the fucker until he gave up Lennie's location.

A sneer sounded from my left and a dour-looking man I didn't recognize appeared from the living room. I grabbed him by the neck, slammed him against the wood-paneled wall, and hoisted him off his feet. A second later, water bubbled out of his mouth, and I growled, "Where is she?"

Saliva and water dripped over his chin, his eyes wide as his fingers clawed at my wrist.

"What the hell is going on here, Espen?" Wilhelm stepped out of the kitchen to our right. He pushed back his dark locks, narrowed his eyes, and raised his chin. Wilhelm's gaze cut to me. "Drop him."

Other men joined us in the hallway, the orange-colored hardwood floors marred by claw marks.

I tightened my grip. The man's pulse faded beneath my fingers.

"Drop him or I'll have my wolves shred you to pieces, Fjord Fae."

"I'll boil you all alive," I snarled, but let go of the blubbering mess in my hand. He dropped to the floor with a thud and crawled away, coughing and spluttering as he disappeared down the hallway.

Espen stepped between me and Wilhelm, blocking me from following through on the threat. "Where is she?" he asked through his teeth.

Wilhelm shook his head. "Who?"

"Lennie, of course." Espen slowly flexed his fingers at his sides. That action alone was a warning shot if I'd ever seen one, and Wilhelm was old enough to know how powerful Espen was. Now, we just had to inform him of how stupid he was for taking our woman.

Wilhelm chuckled and leaned against the staircase that bisected the building, crossing his arms. "You lost your human?"

"My fiancée is part fae," Espen replied.

"And what makes you think I have her?" Wilhelm raised a hand and gestured to the building around us.

"She was ambushed and we found wolf tracks in the snow."

"So? She could've easily been attacked by regular wolves. The locals haven't killed them all off yet."

I shook my head and sucked in a breath. We didn't have time for this. Espen may be playing good-cop and trying to keep his powers under wraps, but I was done being a polite statesman. I'd happily drown the whole house, starting with Wilhelm.

As if sensing my thoughts, Espen threw a brief glare at me over his shoulder, warning me to behave before twisting back to Wilhelm.

I let out a steady breath and relented. For now.

"The kidnappers covered their *boot-shaped* tracks after a while by removing the snowpack from the trees," Espen explained.

"I still don't understand why that means *I'm* suddenly to blame."

"You're the Alpha of the pack, and have previously sent wolves after Lennie," Espen supplied. I sidestepped, positioning myself so I could see both Wilhelm and Espen, and be able to launch myself past the Forest Fae if a fight broke out.

Wilhelm huffed like this was boring him and a waste of his time. Rolling up the sleeves of his shirt, he turned to the fae gathered in the living room to the left of the staircase. "Any of you steal a demi-fae recently?"

Eight fae peered over at us from where they stood against the walls, ready to defend their own. Some shook their heads, some snickered, and others snorted like we were idiots.

"You see." Wilhelm raised his hands in an innocent gesture. "Not mine."

Those weren't all the wolves in his pack, though. I'd bet the amount of fae in here barely scratched the surface of the numbers he had under his care. I jerked my head toward the front door. "What about the others who live on the compound?"

"They wouldn't disobey their Alpha."

"You sure about that?" Espen asked, his voice dropping and sounding like he was ready to tear the place apart. Perhaps he was teetering on the edge of composure, too.

"Positive, but..." Wilhelm let the word linger and sighed, watching us twitch as we waited for him to continue. "You might want to check with the junior pack."

"What?" we said in unison. Espen moved his hands to his hips, resting them there like he did when he wore his police utility belt.

"What happened, Wilhelm?" Espen asked. "You said all was well with the pack. Multiple times. Even when wolves tried to defect, you said you'd brought them in line. Was that a lie?"

Wilhelm grit his teeth and his shoulders dropped incrementally. "In the last year some of the youngsters did defect, claiming they didn't support our ways anymore. They formed their own pack and moved to an old campground near the river. About twenty-five strong, the eldest among them merely 30 years old. This rebellious behavior is just a phase they'll grow out of in time."

I clenched my fists as Espen took a deep breath. "So, you did lie. You lied to the Council repeatedly."

Wilhelm's nose wrinkled. "I did what I had to. The Council would have interfered in pack business if they found out."

"For good reason. We need to maintain harmony, Wilhelm, especially after Queen Ragnhild's demise."

"I have it under control." The Alpha shook his head. "Now, if I were you, I'd head over to the old southern campground and start asking questions there instead of shadowing my doorstep."

"Why should we trust you?" I asked, my voice filled with animosity and betraying the tension riding me.

Wilhelm snorted and glanced at Espen. "Because I'm the Alpha and have no reason to kidnap some silly—"

"Careful," Espen interjected and the building shook minutely, as if he was losing control and disturbing the soil beneath the foundation.

"—half-fae woman. If I were to cross paths with your problematic little thing. I wouldn't steal her. I'd kill her."

My blood boiled over.

I lunged, but Espen spun and caught me, pressing his hand to my chest before I could strangle the wolf leader.

"Don't," Espen said, and I backed down with a grumble. I threw his hand off my chest, but not before I caught the tremble there. He was struggling to contain his power.

Wilhelm straightened up and stepped closer, his pack fidgeting in anticipation. "Now, if you have no further business here, I'd like you to leave us in peace."

Nobody moved except the dust motes that caught in the light drifting out of the kitchen. The wind picked up outside and the wood building creaked, providing the only soundtrack to the tense showdown.

"Thank you for your time," Espen said like the goody-two-shoes that he was. "But if you go after her again, I will destroy you."

I smirked and peered around the room at the gathered shifters, letting them know I'd happily follow through on that threat too. Admittedly, it wasn't good diplomacy, but my patience ran out with this bastard the second he admitted to sending wolves after Lennie in Skolvik last year. Without another word, I grunted and turned for the exit, barely refraining from freezing them all to death.

"Is he lying?" I asked Espen once we were in the car and headed back down the long driveway, gravel and ice clinking against the sides of the vehicle.

He shook his head. "He'd make a bigger show of it if he was hiding her somewhere. No, I think he really wants to pin this on the junior pack."

"Did you know about this rift?" Espen was the Head Guard of the Forest Fae after all; he *should* know about these things.

Espen tilted his head from one side to the other as he steered us back onto the paved road that had been cleared of snow. The studded tires drummed against the ribbon of asphalt. "Yes, I was aware that there was dissent among the ranks, and that a group of fae had defected. But, like he said, and as mentioned in the meeting the other night; those wolves were brought back in and there were *supposedly* no more problems."

I tapped my fingers against my thighs, mimicking a rapid tune I played on the piano when frustrated and I needed to calm my thoughts.

"This will cause more internal instability, won't it?" I asked, my rational Head Guard mind taking over for a split-second, running through all the potential outcomes and scenarios their leadership would face.

Espen nodded with a grim expression.

Hopefully, something like this never happened to the Fjord Fae. We just needed our heir to return to Skolvik soon and we could avoid any potential political fallout.

Shaking off that horrible possibility, I asked, "Do you know where this southern campground is?"

Espen yanked off his hat and threw it over his shoulder into the back seat. "I know exactly where they are."

18

LENNIE

The only thing dustier than the shed I occupied was my wallet. The stiff wooden chair was growing more uncomfortable by the minute, and I was done with waiting around to be saved.

Now that Aurora and the others had left, I focused on picturing the blade I'd created with Halvar in the workshop and flailed my hands toward each other. If I could just bring my palms closer together, I might be able to replicate the magic I'd done so easily within the mountain. Heat flared in my left palm, tingles skipping down my scar, but nothing formed.

Tilting my head back, I let out a groan. Typical Lennie Martin luck. Thankfully, my captors didn't *seem* to want me dead, at least not based on my prior conversation with Marius and Aurora, but damn was I tired of sitting still. I grumbled just as the door to my shed-turned-prison swung open, and a bulb flickered on overhead, the light piercing the shadows.

"What are you doing?" A lightly-accented male voice asked as my eyes readjusted to the brightness and the door bumped shut.

"Flailing unsuccessfully," I muttered, taking him in. The young man had a long face, thick dark brows, and a quiet confidence that made his oversized sweatshirt look more like armor than a cozy piece of clothing. "You here to kill me?" Probably wise to double check in case my hunch was wrong.

He shook his head, but didn't approach. He lifted a paper bag clutched in his fist. "To feed you, actually."

I reared back in surprise. "Really?"

"Really."

"You're not going to poison me?"

"No."

"I thought this was a hostage situation. Isn't this where you give me some serum to make me spill all my secrets? Didn't you talk to Aurora and her beau?"

"I was in here." The newcomer nodded toward the corner by the door. "In wolf form. My name is Nils."

"Oh, so that was *you*! Ever consider wearing collars or something so the rest of us know who's who?"

Nils snorted, setting the brown paper bag on the floor. "That's funny."

"Thank you! I swear no one out here gets my jokes."

A warm and friendly laugh bubbled out of him. "Just don't say things like that around Marius. He's..." He thought for a second before answering. "Particular." He stepped closer, squatted beside my chair, and tapped at my wrist restraints. "Don't run away when I take these off."

"Hypothetically, what would happen if I did?"

"Hypothetically, at least five members of the pack are stationed nearby and would chase you. You wouldn't make it to the woods."

"Fair enough. Cardio isn't my thing anyway... At least not the running kind of cardio."

Nils giggled and blushed as he finished untying my hands and stepped back as I rose to my feet. Blood rushed from my butt to my toes, the same sensation I experienced whenever I got out of my seat after a long flight. I stretched out my fingers and twisted my wrists, enjoying the relief that swept through my limbs.

Nils passed me the bag and I pulled out a small wax-paper wrapped bread roll. Inside the *rundstykke*—as I'd learned they were called—was some cheese, salami, and butter. Not a well-rounded meal, but I wasn't going to complain. I'd been here for several hours and my stomach was starting to protest.

I paced back and forth taking a bite of the round snack. Now was as good a time as any to gather more information about what was going on around here. The Forest Fae may not have been my faction, but they were Espen's. And what was important to Espen, was important to me. Plus, as his fake fiancée I needed to keep up the show of care and affection—even if it was easy to do. I needed to know what was going on and I sure as fuck didn't believe I was held hostage only because I'd been asking around for Aurora. "Nils, my man. While I eat, why don't you tell me what's going on here."

Nils let out a long sigh and leaned against the wall beside a shovel and a rake, rubbing the heel of his palm across his brow. "It's a long story."

"I'm very busy, as you can see. The life of a bargaining chip is exhausting, let me tell you," I said, having had enough time with my thoughts to deduce why having me as a captive might help them get Espen's attention for something. If this was just about me asking around for Aurora, they'd have let me go by now, but as they hadn't... Well, it made sense that they had other reasons to keep me around.

The young shifter hung his head and confirmed my suspicion.

I waved my bread roll at him in a gesture to proceed.

Nils shoved his hands into the front pocket of his hoodie. "A few years ago, there were some problems with wolves again. A lot more sightings, and Wilhelm started to see them as a threat to our well-being as Forest Shifters. As our leader—"

"Your Alpha." I said, pulling on my knowledge from *Twilight*.

"Kind of. He's one of the stronger wolves in the pack, but ultimately, the Forest Fae Council of Elders could strip him of his leadership role. They decide among the candidates who is the better leader for the group, not us."

"That doesn't seem entirely democratic," I said between bites. "Or following any wolfish lore that I've heard of."

"Probably not, but the main goal is to protect nature and the existence of the fae. A leader should be able to do both those things with the faith and support from all members of the Forest Fae, not just the wolves."

"Fair enough."

"Anyway, as our leader, Wilhelm decided that killing the real wolves would help protect our secret and reduce the threat of humans accidentally killing one of our own should a real wolf stray too close to a village or cause a ruckus."

"That's not great," I said, taking another bite, crumbs falling from my lips.

"No, especially when they're almost extinct in this country."

"I heard about that. It sounds awful."

Nils nodded, his mouth turning down at the corners and those thick brows scrunching together. "The Norwegian Wolf has pretty much vanished. There are about 43 wolves remaining in Norway, and constant discussions in government about killing them all off."

My jaw hit the floor. I'd been shocked and saddened when Espen mentioned the wolves being almost extinct, but this was downright insane. "43? In the entire country? Are you serious?"

Nils grimaced again.

"Espen said they were critically endangered. I didn't realize how bad it was."

"A lot of them are inbred, too. So, if a parasite or virus infiltrates the packs, it'll wipe them all out." He snapped his fingers once.

Sadness swept over me as I took the last bite of my roll, brushing my hands off on my neon orange winter pants. How could people be so mean? How could a government actively support the eradication of animals like that? And how could Wilhelm support killing wolves when they were part of the forest he, as a fae, was supposed to protect? My stomach may have been quieted by food, but this new information didn't sit well with me.

"What are the Forest Fae and shifters doing about this? What about the Council?"

Nils's nose twitched and he rubbed a finger across it. "That's where our disagreements lie." He pushed off the wall, grabbing a water bottle from the front pocket of his hoodie, and passing it to me.

I thanked him and took a sip of the cool water as he continued. "The Council don't like the killings and would prefer to help the wolves. Marius challenged Wilhelm's leadership and position on the matter, claiming the need for harmony instead of violence. When Wilhelm laughed in his face and said he'd continue supporting the killing of real wolves, Marius defected, taking a group of us with him. We aren't many, only twenty-five strong at present, and mostly from the youngest generation of Forest Fae, but we all believe that the real wolves deserve to live their lives just as we do—free from harm."

Damn. I loved a good rebellion, and wholly agreed with this younger pack for standing up for their beliefs and sticking to the values of the Forest Fae.

"How many are there in Wilhelm's pack?" I asked.

"143. Most of which live in Alvdalen and the foothills west of town."

He motioned to the chair in the middle of the room, and I let out a long-winded sigh, handing back the water bottle.

"What has the Council said about all of this?" I reluctantly returned to my rickety perch. "Do they even know about your defection?" Based on what Wilhelm had said at the council meeting, I suspected the Council of Elders had no idea what was going on.

Nils's fingers barely brushed against me as he made swift work of retying my wrist bindings. "They don't know about us. We've tried to get messages to Council members, but haven't been successful."

"Do you have anyone on the Council to vouch for you other than Wilhelm? What about this insider that Aurora and Marius mentioned?"

"We have an insider with the senior pack and other local sources, but that's it." Nils stepped in front of me and surveyed his handy work while shaking his head.

"Well, I agree with you that those real wolves shouldn't be killed, and I'd support you, even call my fiancé and his sister, if you hadn't tied me up."

Nils's cheeks flushed with color as he swept his hand through his hair. "A good word with Espen would be helpful. We've tried reaching out to other members of the Council with nothing to show for it. We're hoping Espen might listen."

"I'm gonna be honest with you, buddy, kidnapping me will get his attention, but not in a good way." I tilted my head and raised my eyebrows at him. "In fact, demi-fae-napping me will probably lead to tense words and maybe some waterboarding by Øyvin. Fair warning for when they eventually show up."

Part of me was sad I'd miss it, stuck in here alone when they finally came to save me. Come to think of it, that was probably the horny part of me.

"Yeah, can't say I one hundred percent agreed with Marius and Aurora, but he needs to talk to Espen about some... erm... things. And you were asking around town for her and she was pretty adamant that we needed to find out what you wanted with her."

I scoffed. Could she be more of a pain in the ass? Probably. Best to tread carefully around that one.

"I need to get back." Nils added, heading for the door.

"Thank you for the information. I appreciate it and will talk to Espen." I wiggled my hands and winced, the rope scraping against my wrists once more. "Not too appreciative of the bracelets, though. They're cute and kind of kinky, but I'd have preferred diamonds. Resale value is much higher."

Nils laughed and tugged at the neck of his sweater as he wrapped one hand around the doorknob. "Noted. By the way, that color looks awful on you," he said with a nod toward my puffy getup.

I snickered at his boldness, but damn was he right. "Trust me, I wouldn't be in this if a Fjord Fae hadn't forced me to wear it." This neon orange shit was horrific. Hopefully the guys would rescue me soon so I could get out of it.

19

ØYVIN

The sun brushed beneath the horizon, drenching our surroundings in the pale blue light of dusk as we drove down the winding lane and pulled into a small clearing surrounded by pines and barren birch trees. It wouldn't be long before night settled in, and already too much time had passed since Lennie was taken.

We climbed out of the car, the campsite eerily quiet save for the burbling river nearby. The junior pack campground was located just outside of the village, tucked between two hillsides along a small river. With a copse of seven tiny buildings and some shelters where logs were stacked and stored for winter, the compound was minuscule compared to Wilhelm's.

Wolves appeared from buildings, several shifting into their fae form as they surrounded us.

"Where is Marius?" Espen asked, and I let him take the lead considering I was liable to start drowning people with the anger coursing through my veins like a lethal current. Killing any of these shifters, even Wilhelm's, wouldn't do well for inter-faction relations, especially right now with all we Fjord Fae had been through. I needed to keep a level head, but that was easier said than done when they'd taken what was mine.

A white-haired young man stepped out of a cabin to our right, followed swiftly by a brown-and-beige wolf who shifted beside him, jeans and a large sweater appearing on his lanky limbs.

"Espen, glad you finally made it." The white-haired one descended the front steps with a confident swagger. "Did you get my message?"

"Very clearly, Marius. Has she been harmed?" Espen asked, his voice cool and calm—the polar opposite of my thundering heart rate.

"She's alive and well."

I glanced around at the wolves and Forest Fae encircling us, watching for any tells or signs that they knew where Lennie was being held. Everyone's eyes remained locked on us, hands hung loose at sides, and feet were firmly planted, pointing toward the biggest threats—Espen and I.

"But," Marius added, "I need your help on the council with Wilhelm and for you to stop looking for Aurora. She doesn't want anything to do with Skolvik."

Adrenaline flushed through my body and I tensed. *Wait, Aurora?*

"And you thought kidnapping my fiancée would garner my support?" Espen asked, skipping right over the name of the woman we'd been sent here to find and focusing on the most important woman in our lives.

Marius shrugged. "Desperate times."

I could wring his desperate little neck—

"Well, you certainly got my attention," Espen said. "But I won't discuss any matters with you until she stands beside me."

Marius pulled his shoulders back and lifted his chin, blue eyes catching the last of the day's light. "I'll let her go, if you agree to throw your support behind our values on the Council."

This kid had some serious nerve.

Espen straightened and crossed his arms as he took a deep breath. "If you give me Lennie," he reiterated slowly, his voice dropping lower and lower with each word, "I'll discuss how we might proceed with your pack's concerns. Don't further test my patience, Marius."

Marius flared his nostrils and nodded to a small wooden shed near the forest to our left, a single bulb lighting the muddy front step. "Meet me back in the main house for that chat."

Espen and I moved before anyone said another word.

By the time we stomped onto the shed's front step, I could hear a feminine voice inside.

"That better be a dragon come to whisk me back to Skolvik! I'm done with my puppy playdate!"

I huffed and Espen snorted as I conjured a ball of water around the lock hanging from the door. Making sure the water had penetrated the locking mechanism, I turned my hand, willing the water to freeze and rapidly expand. The padlock shattered, pieces falling to the ground. Espen lurched forward and ripped the mangled metal from the door, tossing the scraps aside.

With a firm nudge from Espen's shoulder, the door creaked open. Inside the dry and dull storage shed was Lennie, tied to a chair.

Thank the ancestors.

"Hey!" She beamed at us, her eyes full of joy. Her hair hung limp around her face and her nose was rosy from the cold—the dusty and cluttered room was little warmer than the outdoors. "Fancy seeing you guys here. I have good news and bad news, which do you want first?"

"You don't want us to untie you first?" Espen asked as he stepped into the room and moved to undo the ropes holding her wrists against the chairback.

"We can multitask," Lennie responded with a half-shrug.

Her voice was like a balm to my frayed nerves and the tension in my muscles eased. I shook my head at her ridiculousness and scanned her for injuries.

Feet. Boots still on.

Legs. Fidgeting and moving without issue.

Wrists. Red and raw. I snarled.

Chest. Bundled in her jacket. Rising and falling normally.

Face. No bruises or marks. Just her damn mouth, pink cheeks, and eyebrows that were slightly more mismatched than normal thanks to a miscalculation with the tweezers last week.

I breathed a sigh of relief.

She was fine. Unharmed. Alive. And her sass hadn't got her torn to shreds.

I leaned my shoulder against the doorframe and crossed my arms, relief washing through me as the adrenaline started to subside. Letting out several steady breaths, I willed my pulse toward a more restful state, and my heart filled with a comforting warmth now that the three of us were reunited.

"Go on," I said, tilting my chin at her. "Good news first."

She smiled as Espen unbound one of her wrists. "I found Aurora!" She twisted her freed hand in circles, splaying and stretching her fingers.

"And the bad news?" I asked, bracing myself.

Espen untied the last rope and Lennie gingerly brushed her wrists where the fastenings had been. "She says we have the wrong person."

A low groan rumbled through my chest.

Espen cupped Lennie's wrists together in his hands. Pressing a gentle kiss to her fingers, he pushed his healing magic into her raw skin. A subtle silver light shone from his hands and, a moment later, the red marks on Lennie's wrists were gone. Thank fuck he was both Healer and Destroyer, because if I had to watch her get those healed by human methods, I'd drag that nearby river through the camp.

Lennie's eyes shot to me like she could hear my thoughts. She extricated herself from Espen's hold and wandered over. Pressing her hand against my chest just above my heart, she let out a long sigh. Her gaze flicked up and met mine. A loving tenderness crinkled the corners of her eyes a split second before a malicious smirk crossed her lips. "Relax your cheeks, Asshole. I'm fine."

This woman.

I pulled her into me and crashed my lips against hers. The shock of losing her, the desperate need to have her back, played over in my mind on a torturous loop. But she was fine, she was here, however troublesome that mouth of hers was. I threaded my hands into her hair, holding on to her as my tongue pressed her lips apart. She granted me passage with a faint whimper, and it took every ounce of the frayed control I had left not to haul her over my shoulder and drag her home. I never wanted to lose her. Never again.

She pulled back and swept her tongue across her bottom lip before straightening. "Oh, I almost forgot. There's a part three to the news."

"Good or bad?" I grumbled, sliding my hold to her sides.

"What else?" Espen asked.

"Aurora is totally Freija's daughter."

20

LENNIE

If there was ever a moment where I could knock down Øyvin and Espen at the same time, this was it. Both stared at me with blank gazes, trying to blink away the shocking news I'd just dumped at their feet.

"Are you sure?" Øyvin asked, uncertainty marring his voice.

"Pretty positive. She looks just like Freija, even has her eyes."

Øyvin grunted and waved his hand in front of his face. "The brown-and-gray ones?"

I nodded.

Espen didn't move, staring at the chair I'd been confined to for the better part of a day. "Espen?" I nudged him with my shoulder.

"Sorry," he said, raking his hand through his hair and brushing it off his temple. "I-I'm... Halvar said she was a distant relative."

"You know I'm not an expert on the man, but lying to protect the mountain and its interests doesn't seem out of the realm of possibility with Halvar."

Øyvin hummed in agreement as Espen nodded lightly. "Freija secretly had a daughter."

"Mind boggling, isn't it?" I said, having had more time to come to terms with the fact and actually met the woman herself.

Espen nodded slowly. "And certainly explains where Freija was twenty years ago when she couldn't come to the south to help Queen Ragnhild."

My eyes widened. I hadn't even thought of that. Freija had probably been giving birth, which was why she hadn't come to her friend's aid. My mind reeled back to something King Balder said while Halvar was interrogating him in the dungeons: "*Shame Freija couldn't have been by her dear friend's side during the skirmishes in the south twenty years ago. Where was she anyway?*" Had he known? Or did he suspect something? Halvar had certainly been quick to pivot the subject that day. But it did make sense.

"Aurora would've been targeted, wouldn't she?"

Espen straightened and brushed his hand across his short beard. "Yes, Queen Freija probably wanted to keep her hidden due to the unrest in the south and the target she'd have on her back as the heir."

"Is that common practice among the fae royals?" I asked.

"It varies based on the monarch, but it's more common with Fjord Fae and Forest Fae."

"Looks like we still have an heir to locate, though," Øyvin said from the doorway and glanced over his shoulder as voices sounded behind him. "Shall we go *chat* with Marius?"

A groan escaped me. I really didn't want to spend more time with the jerk who'd kidnapped me, but Espen took my hands in his and jumped in before I could complain. "Yes, we need to *discuss* certain matters with the young pup. Like the consequences of stealing what's ours."

Espen pulled me against his chest and sealed his mouth to mine. My knees shook and I melted into his hold, enjoying the possessiveness of his words and actions. He nipped at my lips and pressed himself against my curves, eliciting a subtle moan from me. If I didn't stop this, we'd end up naked on the shed floor.

Coming up for air, I found a satisfied smile on Espen's face. With a wink, he lightly tugged on my hand, coaxing me toward the door. I followed, my steps like those of someone who was drunk on something.

By the time Espen and I stepped out of my shed, Øyvin was halfway across the clearing, hurtling toward the only cabin with lights on.

Øyvin barreled up the front steps and booted the pack cabin door open. Yells sounded from inside as Espen and I passed through the front door and found Øyvin looming over Marius. The black-clad young wolf didn't back down from the monumental glare leveled at him, and if I wasn't annoyed about the kidnapping, I'd have been impressed.

"We need to talk, Marius," Espen growled beside me, squeezing my hand tighter.

Marius's eyes flicked to us as Nils shut the front door behind us. "Told you she hadn't been harmed."

A rumble sounded from Øyvin's chest, as Espen replied, "Which is the only reason I haven't already leveled your compound. Let's talk."

Marius stepped aside and motioned for us to join him in the living room next door.

We took up the three spots on the threadbare couch, the pillows sinking significantly beneath our weight. Marius's cabin was a mix between a frat house and a starter home. The living room furniture was mismatched or cobbled together, and maps of Norway were pinned to the wood walls with little green flags marking different locations on the eastern border with Sweden.

The three of us unzipped our jackets. While the guys left theirs on, I frantically removed my orange marshmallow container and stuffed it behind my back. Like stepping into an air-conditioned room during Ohio's hot summers, it was a relief to finally be out of the damn thing, even if it had kept me warm in the shed.

Espen perched on the edge of the sofa, staring daggers at Marius who took a seat in a lumpy armchair across from us and pushed up the sleeves of his black shirt. The young shifter waved several members of his pack out of the room. The only one who remained was Nils. He took up position by the door like the skinniest club bouncer I'd ever seen, hands clasped together in front of his crotch.

Espen clapped his hands together once, garnering the room's attention. "Let's get one thing clear, right away. If you or your wolves ever lay a hand on my wi—fiancée, ever again, I will bury you all alive. Do you understand?"

My brows scrunched at his almost slip up in title, but my body flushed at the protective display. Why was that hot and why did it make me want to jump him?

Marius blinked back at Espen but didn't move.

Øyvin raised his hand from where it rested on the armrest and a ball of water appeared in front of Nils's face, pressing against his mouth. His eyes widened in panic, his chest rapidly rising and falling.

I swatted Øyvin's rock-hard stomach. "Don't waterboard Nils. He fed me."

The water enveloped Nils's head and the young man swatted at the orb in vain.

"Fed you what?" Øyvin asked.

"*Rundstykke*. Not poison. Now stop. Aim that at the blond one."

The water disappeared and Nils gasped, bending over at his hips. He shook out his hair like a dog, sending water droplets across the wooden floor. A new sphere of water grew above Marius's head.

"Threat received," Marius said. "You can do away with the magic tricks, Håland. We won't touch her ever again."

Øyvin grumbled and lowered his hand. The orb disappeared, but not before letting a single droplet plop directly onto Marius's forehead.

He wiped it off and glared at all of us.

"So," Espen started, graciously pivoting before a fight broke out. "What exactly do you want to discuss? Gaining my support on the Council? Asking to make your pack official and separate from Wilhelm's?"

"More than that," Marius said.

"What do you mean?" Espen asked, his eyes narrowing on the young leader across from us.

"We'd like your backing and support for the harmonious life we've always lived and to refrain from killing the remaining natural wolves, as we Forest Fae are supposed to—"

Espen nodded.

"—But there's additional information you need to be aware of that might change things."

"Get on with it," Øyvin muttered as he leaned back and stretched his arm behind me. Setting his hand on my shoulder, he pulled me into him. Warmth radiated up my right side and I leaned further into the comfort of his unusual public display of affection as we waited for the shifter to respond.

Marius took a deep breath and brushed his thumb across his eyebrow. "Wilhelm is planning to defect from the Forest Fae."

Espen flinched beside me and Øyvin squeezed my shoulder. The room somehow grew quieter as the new information swirled around us in the dim lighting. Wilhelm leaving the Forest Fae couldn't be good, however much of a dick he was.

Espen leaned further forward and rested his elbows on his knees. Swallowing hard, he asked, "Where did you hear that?"

Marius planted his elbows on the armrests of his chair and laced his fingers together. "A rumor started spreading last spring. At first I thought nothing of it, but after a month of watching Wilhelm grow more frustrated with the Council and act outside of not just their guidance, but also our duties as Forest Fae to protect the environment and all creatures, I decided to gather my friends and defect."

"Sighting a disagreement on the wolf treatment as your reason," Espen added, earning a gentle nod from Marius.

"Which was also true. I mean, Wilhelm has been of that opinion for the past two years."

Espen hummed like this was something he was aware of or at least suspected.

"But if I'd started talking to the elders about his plans to defect," Marius continued, his blue eyes scanning Espen, "I'd more than likely end up face down in a shallow river."

Further evidence that Wilhelm thought of himself as and acted like some mafia don.

"Fair enough," Espen said, his amber eyes locked on the Junior Pack leader.

"I thought about calling you or perhaps getting a message to you through Turi, but I couldn't be sure it was safe. Then you came back into town, and... Well, an opportunity presented itself." Marius waved his hand toward me.

"Yes," Espen huffed. "Capturing my fiancée certainly caught my attention."

Marius's gaze latched onto the ring glinting in the low light on my left hand before moving back to Espen. "Like I said, desperate times."

While I was keeping up with most of their conversation, my chest tightened and questions swirled around my mind. The Forest Fae political system seemed democratic, but also not. It had been a monarchy at one point and then reconfigured to a council that had still existed under Queen Ragnhild's rule. It was all so different from how government and leadership worked in the US and other countries.

"I thought the Alpha was chosen by the Council?" I asked, unable to hold in the question any longer.

"They are. For this exact reason." Espen rose to his feet, his boots stomping across the floorboards as he paced. "It stops any one leader from gaining more power than the monarch, even if they too are a leader within the Forest Fae faction."

"Then why the hell was Wilhelm chosen? I think we can all agree the dude is a piece of shit."

Espen crossed his arms. "Because once upon a time, Queen Ragnhild trusted him and the Council agreed he was the strongest leader for the pack. Times have changed though."

"And so has Wilhelm," Marius interjected.

Øyvin listened intently. As Head Guard of the Fjord Fae this must've been a fascinating conversation for multiple reasons, the best of which was serious insight into the bubbling political unrest within the Forest Fae. Thank goodness we were all allies here. Then again, this was probably a prime example of something neither the Fjell Fae nor the Fjord Fae would want to happen to their factions. Øyvin's eyes roved over the Forest Fae in the room, watching their every move and taking in every morsel of information.

"Can you help us with the Council? Support us and alert them before things escalate?" Marius asked outright, looking to Espen for an answer. "They won't listen to me."

Espen brushed his palm across his short beard, his gaze locked in thought as he stared at nothing and everything in the room. I wanted to peer into his thoughts, see and hear what was going on in that mind of his. Espen strongly favored peaceful diplomacy—locking away his destructive powers—but how could he position himself in this situation without triggering backlash? I had an inkling on what side he might favor, and sincerely hoped I was right.

With a deep sigh, Espen halted in front of the sofa and looked over at the Junior Pack leader. "While I don't appreciate how you went about getting the information to me, I'm glad you finally did. Wilhelm defecting would cause immense upheaval and would set a precedent that wouldn't bode well for the Forest Fae, the resources we are meant to protect, and our allies." He glanced back at Øyvin and I, giving us both a gentle nod before turning back to Marius. "You have my support. I'll need to think about how we should proceed, but keep your phone on you and avoid Wilhelm and his pack unless I say otherwise."

Marius's shoulders slumped and he nodded. "Thank you."

A sense of relief swept through the room and me. Nils rested the back of his head against the door and let out a deep sigh.

It was sometimes hard to remember that Espen was a major leader and revered among the Forest Fae. To me, he was the bubbly ray of sunshine that brightened my days and snuggled me every night. But, I'd also be lying if I said that seeing him in his element wasn't eye-opening... and a huge turn on.

Silence grew and so did my impatience. I'd been sitting for hours today and wanted to get moving. We still had a mission to complete for Halvar.

"Any who." I dragged the word out as I bounced my knees. "Care to share where Aurora is? We could do with talking to her, too."

Marius turned to me and furrowed his brow. "She's not here."

"What do you mean?"

"She left before lunch. After what you said, she had zero interest in sticking around."

Øyvin leaned forward, resting his elbows on his thighs. "Where is she?" he grumbled, a commanding tone lacing his voice.

"She wouldn't tell me."

"Bullshit," I interjected. Those two were definitely an item. I highly doubted she went anywhere without him knowing. He may have been the Junior Pack leader, and only self- or internally-appointed as their Alpha, but this kid had alpha-male energy wrapped around him like a leather biker jacket. His black-on-black attire and confident disposition further solidified my assessment.

Marius tilted his head to one side and looked at me like I was crazy for calling him out. I could practically feel my guys trying to stifle their smiles. They were much more accustomed to my accusatory outbursts.

"I said bullshit," I added, doubling down when Marius didn't respond.

"Oh, I heard you."

"So?" I opened my hands in a serving motion, waiting for him to tell us more. "Where is she?"

Marius leaned back in his chair and wiped his hand over his chin. "She took her camping gear and said she'd be back in a week or so. I doubt she's gone too far, but she wouldn't tell me." A hint of frustration marred his voice, like he was annoyed with her for not telling him *and* us for causing this mess in the first place.

"We'll keep searching," Espen said, leaning his rear on the sofa's armrest, his ankles crossed. "But, I'm warning you now, Marius. We won't be leaving Alvdalen without her."

Marius snorted and smirked. Shaking his head, he replied, "You may have grown up here once upon a time, but Vigdis raised Aurora among these trees. Good luck finding her."

We stepped outside, re-bundled against the darkness and cold. With swift movements, we crossed the clearing to the parked car.

"Øyvin can you drive, please? I need to call Turi." Espen said, tousling his hair and looking more rattled than I'd ever seen him. But, the Fjord Fae nodded and took the keys from him.

We settled in the car, and I spread out in the back, buckling myself in while stretching across all three seats as best as I could. I'd been seated or standing all day long, and it felt like heaven to finally lie down, even if it was in the car.

Øyvin started the vehicle, and Espen had his phone to his ear. A heartbeat later he uttered, "Turi, we have a problem."

$$21$$

LENNIE

We lumbered into the cabin, shutting out the cold and dark. I pulled my fingers through my hair and groaned, glad to be back at our little home base. If someone had told me this morning that I'd be kidnapped by wolves, I'd have laughed in their face. What a freaking day.

Arms wrapped around my torso from behind, a soft sigh blowing my hair off my shoulder. I dropped my hands back down and twisted around. Espen's eyelids weighed heavily, his lips set in a soft line, and his hair mussed like he'd vigorously raked his hands through it.

"You okay?" I asked, brushing my palms up his jacketed arms and resting them on his shoulders.

He nodded. "I just... I need to..." His chest rose and fell. "I need to decompress. Eat something. Hold you."

I hugged and nuzzled into him. "You mean you need quiet time to process everything you've learned today?"

A smile slowly unfolded on his face. "You know me so well."

"Good thing I'm your fiancée then, isn't it?"

His smile turned into a beaming grin, like my words had turned it to full volume. "Very, very good." He brushed his thumb across my cheek and I couldn't stop myself from leaning into his touch. The tension from the day unraveled from my muscles and a weightlessness settled over me. I liked it here. In his arms where nothing and no one could get to me.

"It's my turn to cook dinner," he said. "Pasta okay?"

I nodded and tightened my arms around his torso. Pasta was always okay.

"Good." He pressed a gentle peck to my head, and I untangled myself from his hold. "Now go take a shower and I'll have food for you shortly after you're done."

He sauntered across the little living room and rounded into the tiny kitchen, aiming for the wooden cupboard filled with our groceries.

Wasting no more time, I shucked off my boots and hideous jacket and yanked off my snow pants as quickly as possible. Rolling my shoulders, I let out a satisfied sigh, happy to finally be out of my snow gear and inside a building that didn't smell like a garden shed.

"Are you all right?" Øyvin quirked his brow at me as he leaned against the wall by the front door, carefully monitoring my movements.

"Yeah." I grabbed the front collar of my shirt and lifted it to my nose. Bile rose in my throat. I smelled like my brothers' old gym bags when they got home from football practice. Dad had needed a hose to get the stench out of them. I apparently needed the same. "I just really want a hot shower and a ton of soap to remove *eau de puppy shed*."

Øyvin harumphed and tilted his chin toward the bathroom.

I didn't need further coaxing. That hot water and I had a date, and I wasn't even going to ask it to buy me dinner first. I sauntered into the little room with its cream-colored walls and white tiles, and flicked on the light. Nothing was getting between me and the suds this evening.

Øyvin stalked into the bathroom behind me. Without saying a word, he closed the door and settled against the tiny wood-and-stone vanity.

"I know you don't mind watching, but you're intruding on my date with this guy," I said as I turned on the water, grabbed a fresh towel out of the tiny cabinet, and set it atop the vanity beside Øyvin.

His eyes watched my every move. Those perfectly plush lips set in a firm line. "I'm not leaving," he said matter-of-factly.

"You're going to watch me shower?" Something inside me sparked at the thought, and I brushed my palms across my leggings.

"You need protecting," he replied and his gaze drifted to my legs before returning back to my face.

"I'm not going to get jumped while I'm in there." I pointed my thumb over my shoulder at the barely walk-in pantry-sized shower.

"I'm not taking my eyes off you."

"You really are an overprotective asshole." I huffed. "I've been around wet dogs all day. You sure you wanna be this close? I stink."

"Did they touch you?"

"What?" I pulled off my shirt and Øyvin's gaze momentarily dipped to my chest before resettling on my face.

"Did. They. Touch. You?"

Technically speaking I had been touched by a few of them, but not in the way he was asking about. "Only when they nabbed me in the woods. Marius grabbed my wrists and another hauled me by my feet. Don't remember much after that." I rubbed my hand across my temple. "Pretty sure Aurora was the one who clocked me over the head."

Øyvin's jaw tightened and it looked like he was about to break a tooth. *Okay, wrong answer.* This guy did not like losing control of anything in his life. Which extended to me too.

"There were no other touches, no tingly touches," I added, hoping it would calm him down and stop the muscle in his jaw twitching. "You know you and Espen are the only ones allowed to touch me like that."

"Do I?"

The steam in the room thickened, and I rolled my eyes at him. "Of course."

"Prove it."

My heart skipped a beat. "What?"

"Get in the shower, Lennie."

My body shuddered as I sucked in a heated breath. "Fine."

I peeled off my leggings slowly, hooking them over my feet and yanking off my thick woolly socks in the process. Pulling off my sports bra, I flicked it in his direction and, like the impressive ass that he was, he caught it with one hand, his eyes never straying from mine. *Fuck, why was that hot?*

"Keep going." He nodded, and I did as I was told—half caught in my own desire to wash, half swept away by the increasing pulsing between my thighs. I pulled off my underwear and tossed that at his face too. He caught it again, then stuffed it in his back pocket.

"You saving that for later?" I crossed my arms under my boobs, admittedly pushing them up to see if I could get any other reaction out of him.

He rolled his bottom lip between his teeth. "Get in the shower."

I flicked my brows at him and turned, giving him the full view of my ass, then opened the glass shower door, tested the water with my hand, and stepped inside. I let out a low and satisfied groan as hot water sluiced over my shoulders and down my body. Whoever invented showers needed to be knighted *and* made a saint, because this was bliss. Bliss that was made even more satisfying by the heady stare following my movements on the other side of the pane of glass.

I started with my hair, getting it all wet before washing it with both shampoo and conditioner. Then, I grabbed the bottle of soap, doling out a decent amount, and swept it across me. The suds clung to my skin as I moved my hands over my body in languorous strokes, enjoying the heat of the water, room, and Øyvin's gaze.

"Touch yourself," he commanded, and my toes curled, my breath stuttering.

Fog adhered to the shower door, creating a blurry scene of the room beyond and the man watching me like I was his dinner. A shudder ran through me at the thought of bringing myself to climax with him watching and my breaths shallowed.

I dipped my fingers over my stomach and down, reaching the apex of my thighs with a soft moan. Rubbing circles around the bundle of nerves, my eyes fluttered closed, the sensation between my legs building, the room steaming up quicker and quicker.

"Eyes on me, Trouble."

I looked into Øyvin's heated sapphire gaze, wholly aware of his hands gripping the sink so hard his knuckles turned white. I added more pressure from my fingers and let out a little whimper. Øyvin bit his bottom lip, his chest heaving, his breaths coming harder as he watched me. Increasing my pace, I reveled in the sensations fluttering through me and the need on the other side of the glass. The shower door swung open and I jumped back against the tile wall, my fingers stopping. Øyvin's eyes turned molten, his hair askew, the muscles in his arms jumping.

He stepped into the shower, pressing himself against me as the door shut behind him. We barely fit in here together. I was pretty sure his sweatpant-covered ass was plastered against the shower door. But I couldn't focus on that, the only thing registering with me right now was the butterflies in my stomach, the clenching between my thighs, and the man staring down at me like I was his anchor as water cascaded over us.

His hair, usually poking up slightly, fell across his forehead, undone by the water. He pressed his hands against the tiles on either side of my head. "Keep going."

I slipped my fingers back to my clit and slowly started massaging the sensitive mound. Sparks shuddered up and down my spine, as his breath brushed against my cheek.

My head dropped momentarily, but Øyvin pressed his thumb and forefinger against my chin, tilting it back up to look at him. "Once again, eyes on me, Trouble. And don't you dare stop." He rested his forehead against mine. "Fall apart for me."

My whole body shuddered at his words, the feeling of being protected yet vulnerable washing over me. The sensation of having this man, this creature, practically begging for my release invaded every nook of my mind. He'd lost control today. He'd lost me. And now he was reclaiming what was lost.

The tenderness between my thighs sparked like lightning, my fingers moving in faster and tighter circles as I chased my climax. Water swept across us, heating me from the outside in while the feeling of having him watch such an intimate moment warmed me from the inside out. It was all too much. I panted, desperate. Hungry. Wanting him to touch me, but knowing, if I asked, he'd refuse.

I fell apart with a cry and his lips were on mine, swallowing my moans, holding me upright with his own body. The brush of his wet cotton shirt against my nipples, the press of his length against me, plus the trembles of my orgasm—I never wanted this to end.

He pulled his lips from mine and nuzzled against my hair. "Don't ever run off again."

"I was kidnapped," I breathed and splayed my hands against his firm chest.

"Sentiment stands."

"You're such a demanding asshole."

He shut off the water and hitched my leg over his hip, rolling himself against me. "And you're rage-inducing trouble."

"We established that a while ago. Search your memory banks for a boat thief."

He grumbled and nipped at my ear. "Just be glad I'm feeling merciful and that lake outside is frozen over."

"You can't just throw me in the fjord or a body of water every time I annoy you."

"It's worked thus far."

"And yet"—I rolled my core against his erection—"I don't think you're annoyed with me right now."

His head tilted back and a low groan escaped his lips. A satisfied smirk grew on my face as he slowly released me and stepped out of the shower. Leaving the door open, he tossed my towel at me, and I caught it before it could land at the bottom of the shower stall. "Dry off, and come to bed."

The stubborn part of me wanted to counter him, but my head wasn't in charge at the moment. So, I followed him into the bedroom and settled for a sultry, "Yes, sir."

After watching him change and return his wet clothes to the bathroom—no doubt hanging them up to dry—I pulled on a clean pair of leggings and an oversized t-shirt from my bag, and crawled onto the bed beside Øyvin where he sat, propped up against the headboard. I snuggled in beside him and settled my leg over his. With a contented grumble, he pulled me into his side and held on like I might disappear.

"I'm okay," I whispered.

He squeezed me tighter and his eyes fluttered closed.

"I'm alive. Unharmed. And only made seventeen thousand wolf jokes while cooped up in that shed."

Øyvin's lips twisted into a smirk before straightening out as he sighed. "I don't ever want that to happen again."

I pressed my hand to his chest, and his heart thrummed beneath my palm. "Neither do I. That chair was as comfortable as a front row church pew."

Øyvin laughed softly as Espen's voice sounded through the cabin. "Dinner's ready!"

22

LENNIE

The next morning I found myself in an empty parking lot with Espen and Øyvin, ready to search for Aurora. The sun hid behind a thick layer of clouds as it rose above the horizon, lending a dull glow to our snowy surroundings. The cold air nipped at my cheeks and snot threatened to run from my nose.

Espen grabbed our borrowed skis and poles from the back of the car where we'd stuck them through the trunk and into the backseat to make room. He handed a set to Øyvin, then rested another pair against the back of the car, before turning to me with his signature smile plastered across his face. "You got your ski boots on?"

I lifted one foot and then the other, showing him the short-shafted white-and-blue boots I'd put on in the car when we first pulled in. They were a lot different from the downhill skiing boots I'd worn before, but we weren't doing downhill. Today we were cross-country skiing. The skis were thin and long compared to their curvier downhill counterparts, and the boots were shorter, narrower, and much lighter.

"Excellent. Cross-country skiing is a lot of fun. I promise," Espen said. He handed me the poles for balance, setting the skis in his hands down beside my feet, and kneeling before me. Not an unwelcome sight.

I clenched my gloved fingers around the poles, wanting to brush them through the floppy hair that poked out of Espen's hat.

He stalled and peered up at me through his lashes, his amber gaze warming like he could hear my thoughts. His lips curved up at one side, those soft cushions begging—

I cleared my throat and mentally shook off the tingling sensation. "So, do you think Aurora might have tucked herself away at the ranger cabin along this mountain trail?" I asked, confirming today's search activities and distracting myself from the handsome fae on his knees in front of me.

"Yes," Espen replied. "She might be camping as Marius suggested, but in these temperatures she'd need to be careful. Plus, the ranger cabin is rarely occupied and frequently used by skiers and hikers who need to seek shelter for whatever reason."

That seemed as good a hiding spot as any and worth looking into. Espen tapped my left foot with his hand. "Step forward and point your toe so I can click you into your ski." I curved my foot like a ballerina. He clutched my boot in his hand and pressed the toe of the shoe, which had some form of locking mechanism on it, to the boot-mount on the ski. The front of my shoe locked into place with a click.

He moved to the next foot and I repositioned some of my weight onto the poles. While Espen worked on the second boot, I glanced over at Øyvin with narrowed eyes as he clicked himself into his skis. He moved with ease in his navy-colored winter gear like he'd done this a thousand times.

"Let me guess, you're a professional skier because the snow is technically frozen flakes of water?"

He gave me a tiny smirk, his eyes glistening with humor. "No."

"No?" My voice rose several octaves, shocked by his confession.

"I'm a good skier because we live in Norway."

There it was. My lips fell into a firm line. I really should've heeded the phrase, "Norwegian's are born with skis on their feet," because it was apparently true for both fae and humans. Øyvin glided forward in swift movements, warming up and testing out the waxed underside of the skis.

Click.

"You're ready to go." Espen launched to his feet and planted a delicate kiss to the end of my cold nose. I slid one ski forward and then the other, hesitantly lifting my poles. The sensation was new, but not wholly unfamiliar after skiing trips in New England. These boots were like highly-engineered soccer cleats and only fastened at the front, letting the heel lift off the back instead of having the whole foot locked in. It was going to take some time to get used to. I rolled my shoulders, my orange jacket rustling with the motion and adding a soundtrack to my tingling nerves.

This was fine. We'd be venturing across mostly flat terrain, not hurtling down a hill at twenty miles-per-hour. The odds of falling on my face were low. Really, what could go wrong?

Click. Click.

I looked up at the sound and found Espen fastened into his skis, shimmying and ready to go. "Follow me!"

Trees weighed by snow lined the wide trail, some boughs so heavy they met the tops of the snow dunes. A peaceful calm wrapped around the three of us, only broken by our panted breaths and creaking branches.

It didn't take long for me to get the hang of cross-country skiing, but the first ten minutes of our journey were spent in my head thinking hard about the movements.

Slide one foot forward, move pole.

Slide other foot forward, move other pole.

Slide again.

Stay in Espen's tracks.

Don't hold up Øyvin—even if it would annoy him and bring a smile to my face.

After a little while, I grew confident enough in my coordination to strike up conversation.

"Okay, fill me in on some of the Forest Fae politics. I feel like I should probably know this stuff as the future wife-for-immigration-purposes of the Head Guard. How did the wolves come to be? Have the Forest Fae always had wolf shifters?"

"Good questions," Espen said with a quick grin over his shoulder, the pom-pom on his knit hat wobbling. "No, there haven't always been wolves among the Forest Fae. No one knows the full story—those who were there have all passed and when they were alive, none spoke of what happened."

"Sounds interesting," I mumbled, sliding one foot in front of the other. Øyvin let out a low grumble of agreement from behind me.

"It is," Espen replied. "It was about a thousand years ago. The King of the Forest Fae, Olaf, was concerned about deforestation, pelt hunting, and increasing population after the Viking era. He journeyed from the east where he resided at the time, back to Skolvik. Rumor has it he met with the Royals of the Fjell and Fjord. No one knows what was discussed or how it happened, but the soldiers who ventured west with King Olaf returned as wolf shifters."

"Well shit," I said. "That must have been a helluva pivot for those soldiers and probably their families. *Hey honey, I'm home and now I have a tail!* It's almost as wild as me becoming a demi-fae."

"Indeed." Espen nodded. "The men and women returned to their village, established their own settlement, and worked on their powers, learning how to shift and running around in their wolf forms protecting wildlife and defending the forests."

"And the rest is history?" I came to a stop at a split in the road and rested my hands on top of my ski poles. Espen stepped back beside me and pulled out a bottle of water, passing it to me for a swig—which I gladly took—before taking a sip of his own.

He set the bottle back in his pack and continued, "Wolves have been with us ever since. They've always had a seat on the council. They've always deferred to the monarch... Well, they did until we moved to a council-led governing system twenty years ago." Espen's voice faltered slightly at the reminder of the loss of his Queen and mentor in the southern battle. "Since then, Wilhelm has always been in concert with the Council of Elders."

"Until now," Øyvin said from where he stood on my other side.

"Until now," Espen reiterated.

"And no one knows exactly how the wolves were created? Was there a magic witch that cast a spell on them? Was it Heidi? No, never mind, she wouldn't be old enough. Not that I wouldn't put it past the Forest Fae Healer to pull some sort of witchy brouhaha. If there's any one fae that gives off crazy-witch-hidden-in-the-woods vibes, it's our dear friend Heidi."

Espen sighed, and rested his wrists atop his ski poles, matching my stance, his cheeks flushed from exercising in the cold. "The wolves never spoke of it. Stories over the years said they were sworn to secrecy by

King Olaf. Other tales said their new magic tied their tongues and didn't allow them to speak on the matter. At this point it's become more myth than history. But they're part of us: even with their shifter magic, they're fae. Never, at any point in time, have they been treated as lesser or unwelcome."

I liked that about the Forest Fae. I was slightly biased as Espen was the first to trust me, bringing me into their inner circle by telling me their secret, but it also seemed to be a trait that all Forest Fae shared; they were welcoming and caring. So, it was unsurprising that they'd accepted their own with open arms.

"Shall we continue on?" Espen said, pivoting the subject and drawing me out of my thoughts. "It's not far to the Ranger's cabin."

"Yeah, let's go." I readjusted the pole straps around my gloved wrists and slid toward the fork in the road. With a deep breath, I aimed for the road on the left that went downhill slightly and ignored the incline on the right.

"Um, Lennie." Espen cleared his throat. "Other road."

I glanced back over my shoulder and found him pointing to the hill on the right that wove into the trees.

I tilted my head and pouted. "Are you sure?"

Espen chuckled and skied up beside me. "Positive."

A groan befitting a toddler rumbled in my throat. I was totally going to end up on my ass... or face plant. Or both.

"Come on. It's only a slight incline." Espen nudged me with his elbow and gave me a salacious wink. "You can handle it with your new fae stamina."

I smirked and rolled my shoulders, feeling the pop of my joints and a spike of adrenaline. Both him and Øyvin really knew how to activate my competitive side. *Challenge accepted.*

The trees on either side of our narrow trail hung heavy with snow, some even leaning over the path and creating a quasi-tunnel, guiding us toward our destination. The cold air and lack of breeze gave the entire scenery a sense of stillness like that of a church. The quiet punctuated by my sharp breaths and the swish of our skis through the snow.

My hand-eye coordination was not cut out for cross-country skiing *up* a hillside. While I could physically handle the strain on my muscles thanks to an active lifestyle and whatever new fae juju I possessed, my ability to slide one ski forward in a vee shape, then the other, and use my poles to keep myself upright was a challenge. My skis wanted to go downhill, and, to be honest, so would I once we reached the cabin.

Thank goodness I'd left my camera back at the cabin, because odds were I was about to end up falling ass over tits at some point on these slippery skis. As if to prove my point, my left ski slipped backward and I wobbled. Plonking my ski pole hard enough into the snow to stop me from sliding downhill, I regained my balance.

"How much further?" I asked with a huff and set off again.

"Just over that hilltop," Espen replied from up ahead. I glanced toward where he pointed, a curve in the horizon maybe a couple hundred feet away, and relief washed through me. Not far to go at all.

A few moments later, I hauled myself over the final stretch and the trail flattened out, opening into a clearing. Surrounded by dense forest and mounds of snow was a weather-worn wood cabin. The roof was covered in snow, and icicles the length of my arm hung from the eaves. A tiny path was cleared in front of the cabin, but we all sank slightly as we neared the door, the snow here still deep and relatively untouched. Darkness seeped from the small windows and the only sign that anyone had been here recently was the distinct break in the icicles—someone had broken away the ones by the front door and tossed them into the snow.

Espen and Øyvin clicked out of their skis, using their poles to press the button on the housing mechanism. I followed suit, popped my boots off the skis, and leaned the equipment against the cabin wall beside Espen and Øyvin's.

Espen went for the door and stepped inside, Øyvin ushering me to follow as he took up the rear again.

Inside was... basic. An ancient wood-burning stove sat in the middle of the single room against the back wall. To my left was a thick wood table and chairs, plus a bookshelf with old Norwegian map books and novels with dusty, curled covers. On the right was the most uncomfortable looking sofa I'd ever seen and two chairs that looked like they could collapse if someone breathed wrong. I wasn't going to complain though—it was shelter and I had somewhere to sit down for a minute. I aimed for the wood couch that looked more like a bench and took a seat. The thin padding was practically non-existent as the hard surface pressed against my bright orange snow pants. Espen plopped down beside me and pulled my water bottle out of his backpack, handing it over to me. While I took several swigs, Øyvin perused the cabin for any recent signs of life.

"Anything?" I asked, as he opened the stove door and peered into the ash-covered fireplace.

He shook his head and shut the door, crossing to the other side of the room. "There are some footprints on the floorboards disturbing the dust, but they're all different sizes, which doesn't help us." Picking a random book from the shelf, he browsed the front and back cover. From my vantage point I could just make out a naked chest and a big, poofy skirt.

"To each their own," Øyvin muttered.

"Historical Romance not your thing?" I asked with a smirk. "Or does it feel weird to read about eras that you lived in that people now call *historical*?"

Espen laughed beside me, and Øyvin set the book firmly back on the shelf. "I prefer action and adventure books."

"And Espen, which of those books would you read?"

"Sci-fi and the maps," he said before taking a sip from his water bottle. "I've always enjoyed looking at maps."

Could he be more of a cute little park ranger nerd? Honest to hell, it was adorable. I nudged my knee against his and he nudged right back, giving me another smile. My heart pattered in a happy rhythm. He was so cute, caring, and outdoorsy. It was little wonder I was so attracted to him. The way he—

"Here," Øyvin said, and my gaze snapped back to him.

"What did you find?" I asked.

He pointed to the bookshelf. "There's one missing."

Espen and I returned our bottles to his backpack and crossed the room. Øyvin pointed to the empty spot on the shelf. Sure enough, a book had recently been removed. The tiny spot was dust free compared to the books and space around it.

I looked over the disheveled shelf. "And they can't have set aside the book elsewhere?"

"Mm-mm," Øyvin hummed. "There's a layer of dust on everything else except the floor and the sofa. The book has been taken."

Espen crossed his arms. "It could be anyone."

"True," I added, straightening and setting my hands on my hips. "But…"

"But…" Øyvin said.

"Grab your things and let's double check outside," Espen said. "It's only been twenty-four-ish hours since she left, and it didn't snow much last night. There's a chance it might've been her and there might still be some tracks outside." He hoisted his bag onto his back and buckled it at the waist.

I grabbed my gloves from the couch and followed the guys.

23

LENNIE

Stepping outside the cold air assaulted me once more, the chill grazing my cheeks as the snow crunched beneath our footfalls. I pulled the door shut behind me, double-checking that the old wood and metal had latched properly before turning to the task at hand: searching for signs of recent life.

Øyvin circled the perimeter while Espen kneeled in seemingly random spots. "What are you doing?" I asked as I tromped through the snow and stepped up beside the Forest Fae. He glanced back the way I came and then peered left into the pristine white clearing.

"Checking the height of the snow," he replied absentmindedly.

"Nothing around back," Øyvin muttered, and I flinched at his sudden reappearance.

"That's because they went this way." Espen gently swept his arm across the top of the snow in front of us, his thick, winter jacket rustling and removing a layer of powder. Beneath the newly fallen snow were indents the perfect shape and size of a human's stride and footwear.

I let out an impressed huff. "Note to self: if I ever misplace something, I'm asking you to find it. How'd you know what to look for?"

He set his hands on his hips and tilted his chin up slightly, then pointed to the tracks that aimed toward the tree line. "When the snow is compacted in these temperatures, it freezes in spots."

Øyvin crossed his arms and assessed the scene. "Remove the new layer that hasn't had time to melt in the sun and fuse with the tracks below. You're left with dips and can find a myriad of things beneath."

"So this is what they teach you in school in Norway. Snow 101. Or is it a fae thing?" Either way, their knowledge was impressive.

Neither deigned my genuine question and comedic brilliance with a response.

"Follow me." Espen strode in the direction of the tracks. Øyvin and I followed quietly, with our feet and shins traipsing and pushing through the snow that was knee-height in some spots.

My feet felt like they'd been introduced to a freezer and I mentally thanked Espen for talking me into wearing two pairs of socks this morning. Not only were the outer wool ones doing some serious work, but having the extra, thick cotton layer underneath was a blessing in disguise. Had it originally made the boots a tight fit? Yes. But the fact that my feet were only now getting cold, after hours outdoors... Yeah, I'd be adding more thick wool socks to my collection as soon as we got home.

We reached the edge of the forest, the thick pines and spindly, black-and-white birch trees standing sentry to the silent depths. Coming to a stop, Espen set his hands on his hips and shook his head. "They disappear." He motioned to the tracks. I peered further into the forest, hoping for something to leap out at me, but nothing snagged my attention. The dull gray day darkened the forest and the snow appeared untouched.

"Dead end," I muttered.

Espen nodded beside me, then sucked in a breath through his nose. His eyes widened, and both him and Øyvin spun on the spot, turning back toward the cabin.

I pivoted to see what had them tightening up like a wedgie and stilled at the sight before me.

Between us and the cabin stood a large wolf, its sharp eyes focused on us. Its brown-and-beige coat rippled on a phantom breeze, like it had just stopped moving but the fur hadn't got the memo. Muscled legs were entrenched in the snow, the white stuff brushing the underside of its belly. It tilted its head and assessed us, narrowing its eyes at me.

A pang of familiarity washed through me. "Hang on," I whispered. Brown-and-beige coat. Was this Nils, the guy who'd brought me lunch? Honestly, I wouldn't be surprised if Marius had sent someone to follow us. Who better than the guy who was clearly his second-in-command? "Nils?"

The canine tilted its head the other way like a curious puppy. I took a step toward it.

It didn't move.

Definitely was Nils.

I sauntered a little closer, a non-toothy smile blooming on my face to show that I wasn't going to hurt him. If he was going to follow us, he could do so in fae form. He didn't need to be all wolfy and hide from us. "Can you sniff Aurora around here? Do you think we're on the right track?"

Nils lifted his tail straight and up, like a dog spotting a friend.

"Lennie." Espen's voice wavered. I furrowed my brow and turned half-way, keeping one eye on the wolf and one on the Forest Fae. Espen's throat bobbed. "That isn't Nils."

"Yes, it is."

"No." He shook his head slowly. "It's not."

I set my hands on my hips and tilted my head. "And how do you know that? You barely met the guy... wolf."

Espen's gaze was securely on the canine close to me, and Øyvin didn't move a muscle, his limbs locked in place, hands hanging loose at his sides—his battle ready stance.

"Forest Fae shifters keep their eye color," Espen replied. "Only normal wolves have yellow eyes."

I glanced at the wolf and flinched. Shiny yellow eyes blinked back at me.

Shit.

The wolf took a tentative step forward, and I shrunk back, eyes wide and my stomach in my throat.

"Don't turn your back on it," Espen said, his voice calm and low. "Don't run."

Him and Øyvin appeared on either side of me, Espen to my right, Øyvin to my left, their arms spread out wide. The wolf slunk backward, its ears and lips twitching.

My chest rose and fell as I tried my best to remain calm and not spin around and high-tail it out of here. Just my luck to land myself in another shitty situation.

"Fuck," Øyvin grumbled and my head snapped toward movement to my left.

Another, smaller wolf, with a reddish-tinged beige coat appeared from behind the cabin, blood smeared around its mouth, blocking our path to warmth and safety.

"A female," Espen said. "Less to worry about, but still as dangerous as Not-Nils here. Based on the blood, there must be a kill site nearby, which is going to make them more aggressive than normal."

"Fuck," Øyvin said again, his voice rumbling softly. "Another one."

Espen and I followed his gaze to the right and another wolf with a beige-and-gray coat appeared from the tree line.

"What do we do?" I asked as my body started to tremble. To the wolves I probably looked like a shaking orange marshmallow. "Espen?"

If there was any one of us who'd know what to do in this situation, it would be him. As part-police officer, part-ranger, and 100 percent Forest Fae, he'd know.

"Here's the plan. Act aggressively, use your magic to scare them. They're currently trying to protect their kill, but if we present ourselves as the biggest predator, they'll start to back down. Whatever you do, don't hurt them."

I nodded, entirely on board with the plan and uninterested in causing the creatures harm. "Got it."

Espen reached over slowly and brushed his hand down my arm. "Øyvin, flank me and take on these two males. Lennie, go for the female. Whatever you do, don't turn your back on them."

Swallowing hard, I nodded once more. I was well aware that I was completely out of my element here. The wolves continued staring at us, snarling as their tails barely wavered.

"Ready?" Espen asked.

Øyvin settled into a fighting stance and called forth a ball of water in each hand. The liquid magic swished around and looked like tiny waves curving in on each other. "Ready."

"On the count of three," Espen muttered, and I nodded minutely as I swallowed the large lump that had formed in my throat. My heart pounded in my chest, hopefully not loud enough for the wolf to hear, and I pulled on my power. The magic prickled and tickled as it swept down my arms and appeared in my hands in the form of two shiny balls of light.

"Three..." Espen started.

"Two..."

"One..."

The guys veered away from me and Øyvin volleyed orbs of water at the wolves' feet. I raised my arms above my head, making myself look as big and scary as possible—light shimmering in my palms.

The largest wolf, Not-Nils, followed Espen, pivoting away from me. My guys focused on their targets, using their fae magic to scare the animals.

The smaller wolf approached me, pulling her lips back and showing off a row of sharp, red-tipped teeth. Gloria Gaynor's *I Will Survive* started playing in my head and I belted out the lyrics as I launched my first ball of light to the right of the wolf. She dodged to the side away from the light and shook, her fur bristling. I threw the other ball, still singing at the top of my lungs. The sound was atrocious, but if it got the wolf back into the woods and me safely home, then these hills would be alive with my cringe-worthy singing voice.

My wolf darted back and forth to the left of the cabin, carving a trench in the snow between the building and the tree line. I twisted my body, following her movements like some form of dance, careful not to show her my back.

"She's herding you!" Espen yelled and I stopped singing.

"Stun her, Lennie," Øyvin commanded. "Don't kill."

I shook my head. "I'm not going to hurt her."

"Use your royal light magic and spook her!" Øyvin roared. "Now!"

Stun only. I pulled on my power once more, willing that swirling mass in my sternum forward. Tendrils of magic swept through me, sparking down my arms. I could do this. Careful to keep the wolf in front of me, I inhaled deeply, curved my hands toward each other, and formed a large magic ball of light that sparked gently.

The wolf stopped her strategic pacing and stared at the crackling light.

Mimicking Øyvin, I launched the light toward the snow around the wolf's paws. It crashed into the cold powder, snowy spray flying all over the canine and the magic disintegrated. The wolf shuffled backward, spun around, and loped into the forest.

I let out a shuddered breath and shook out my hands as my pulse pounded in my ears.

Øyvin and Espen continued dancing around the other two wolves. Espen's yells were incoherent as he waved a barren branch around him, corralling Not-Nils toward the tree line. Oversized snowballs littered the clearing between Øyvin and the other snarling wolf.

A howl sounded from the woods, echoing through the valley and snow fell from boughs of surrounding trees. The two remaining wolves' ears twitched, and a second later they ran toward the forest and the noise. Whichever wolf had made that howl had called back their pack.

Thank fuck.

Espen tossed aside his big stick and both he and Øyvin came running over, their steps muffled by the snow.

I hunched over and rested my hands on my knees, my panted breaths fogging in front of me. "You know… There have been way too many traumatic incidents on this vacation."

Øyvin crossed his arms and snorted. "You're no longer on vacation, Trouble. This is just your life."

An erratic laugh escaped me as Espen brushed his hand over my back like he needed to reassure himself that I was there and in one piece. "Why do you have to be right?" I smiled and straightened.

Espen wrapped his arms around me, pulling me into his warmth, and Øyvin quirked his lips. "You're getting better though."

"Huh?"

"Your light magic," Øyvin said. "That last ball wasn't merely light. I saw it sparking. You could've stunned the wolf with that."

I'd certainly felt the slight difference when creating that bit of magic compared to the normal magic I used to form light balls. I'd put the stun intention behind it too. But still... My brow creased. "How do you know? How is that even possible?"

"I've seen Balder use it in the past. Don't ask why or how."

I got the distinct feeling he was referring to battles best left to history.

"Me too," Espen said, taking a step back and dropping his hands to his hips. "But with Queen Ragnhild, not Balder."

I let out a high-pitched humph. "Well, look at me leveling up. Torsten and Halvar are going to be so proud."

The guys snickered as I raised my hand, extending my pointer finger toward the sky. "And I'll concede. That wasn't Nils."

"No, shit," Espen replied with a laugh.

Collapsing onto my butt, the snow catching my fall, I rested my arms on my knees and stared up at the guys. Adrenaline rushed out of my system, leaving me buzzing but exhausted.

Another day, another gratefully missed opportunity to become puppy kibble. *I should start keeping track at this rate.*

I looked out toward where the wolves had disappeared into the forest and then to the trails we'd first followed across the clearing, now scuffed up by our canine encounter. "Any chance those wolves were coaxed over here by Aurora? Could she have used them as a distraction?"

Espen shook his head and followed my gaze. "Highly unlikely. If—as seems to be the case—she is truly affiliated with Marius's new pack, which wants to protect the wolves, I doubt she'd plant a kill site this close to humans."

"You're probably right. But if she were a wolf, could she voodoo communicate with the real wolves and encourage them in this direction?"

Espen shrugged. "I mean, we don't know who her father is. He might've been a shifter. But even Forest Fae wolves can't mind-speak like they do in movies or books. Aside from howling and barking, their communication is instinctual and non-verbal, which doesn't exactly lend itself to messages of 'go exactly here and antagonize these people.'"

"Fair enough."

"We're all okay, though," Espen said, rolling his shoulders and brushing his hands across his arms as if to remove invisible lint or anxiety from his limbs. "That's the most important thing."

Øyvin inhaled audibly and nodded.

I had a bad track record with hikes now. Almost dying when I fell through the bridge last year, getting ganged up on by Forest Fae shifters and then saved by Halvar, and being herded by real wolves this year. I really was a walking target.

It hadn't always been like this. Growing up and post-college, I was always careful when setting out on a hike. I always wore the proper attire and shoes, and never went hiking without a substantial first-aid kit and huge bottle of water. But after several months in Norway, all that preparation was useless. At this point, it felt like the wilderness was out to get me. "Perhaps, in the future, we should teach me more about Norwegian wildlife before hiking."

"I'm going to agree with that," Espen conceded.

Øyvin huffed. "But who steps *toward* a wolf?"

I pointed to myself. "Apparently this dumbass."

He rolled his eyes.

"You can't entirely blame me though. It made sense for Marius to send a wolf to follow us, and that wolf looked exactly like Nils."

Øyvin shook his head like I was being ridiculous. "At least you're cute."

My skin warmed at his backhanded compliment. "I have my moments," I countered, my voice coming out more sultry than planned. Cold nipped at my butt through my neon snow pants, and I rose to my feet with a helping hand from Espen. Planting my hands on my hips, I started a heated staring competition with Øyvin. His sapphire gaze darkened and he didn't blink.

"Unless you two wish to give snow sex a go"—my eyes widened at Espen's statement—"I suggest we head home for the day and take a break from the search."

While I wouldn't mind some adventurous yoga, hypothermia was a thing, and I couldn't have their dicks freezing. I liked that part of their bodies too much to lose. Plus, I was exhausted and could do with a nap. "Let's table that idea for spring. I'm thinking a rainy day instead of snow." Why just kiss in the rain when you could go all the way?

"Deal," they both muttered.

Espen looped his arm through mine and steered us back toward the cabin where our skis rested against the wall beside the front door. "I'll call Turi when we get back to the car. The Mayor's Office should know there's been another wolf sighting this close to town."

"You think the locals will make a ruckus about it?"

He shook his head. "As long as Turi makes sure the information gets out correctly, the right departments are informed, and the news outlets don't make a huge deal out of it, we should be fine. It was only a sighting"—I scoffed at his belittlement of the canines and the magical Argentinian tango I'd just performed in an effort to protect my back—"and no one was injured or bit. The humans get worked up when livestock or people are hurt."

Understandable. For the Forest Fae's sake and the wolves, I hoped things didn't get chaotic. Hopefully, Turi could keep the town calm.

"Come on." Espen grabbed my skis and handed them to me. "Let's go home and have some coffee. Then we can have a fun family day tomorrow before refocusing on our search for Aurora."

"Family day?" Øyvin said from my other side, voicing the same question that rang through my head. I didn't remember scheduling a family day. But perhaps I was too caught up in the whole hounded-by-wolves thing that my memory was failing me.

Espen beamed from ear to ear. "Family day. We promised Ingrid that we'd join her and the kids for an afternoon."

Oh, yeah. She'd mentioned that at dinner the other night. While it wasn't exactly staying on mission to find Aurora, I wouldn't say no to spending more time with Espen's family.

"But first," Espen said. "We need to ski back down that hill."

I whimpered. "What could possibly go wrong?"

Espen brushed his gloved hand over my cold cheek and stared into my eyes with both joy and laughter. "Just point your toes together and sit on your butt if you start to go too fast."

I'd give it a go, but I'd probably end up scooting down the hillside. "Can do, but it's on you if I hurt my butt."

Øyvin grabbed his skis and turned to me. "We'll kiss it and make it better if you do."

I smiled. "Well, in that case."

24

LENNIE

Our morning was spent searching the western forests for Aurora, and this time the guys didn't let me out of their sight. We searched high and low, peered through windows of vacated cabins, and considered going door to door asking villagers if they'd seen the woman. But our efforts were frustratingly fruitless. There was no sign of the heir anywhere. It was like she'd donned an invisibility cloak or camouflaged herself as a rock in the endless scenery of white and gray.

By mid-day we abandoned our search and headed for the lake to spend the afternoon with Ingrid and the kids. Our agenda: ice skating.

The sun's rays glittered across the frozen lake framed by white snow drifts from where the local residents had cleared it. The aptly named "Big Long Lake" was exactly that—surrounded on three sides by dense forest and hills, the body of water stretched for at least a mile and was longer than it was wide. We pulled into the small parking lot that abutted a beach and boat landing area, finding Ingrid and the kids already setting up camp at a wooden picnic table by the shore.

Shrieks of laughter met my ears as I clambered out of the car, my borrowed skates firmly in hand. All three kids were donning their ice-skates, even four-year-old Kristoffer.

"Glad you could join us!" Ingrid smiled and propped her hands on her hips, letting out a quick breath like she'd been busy all morning and hadn't taken a break. Which, considering she was a mother of three under ten, I didn't doubt was the case. Her hair was piled on top of her head again and she was bundled up in bright yellow outerwear paired with a knit headband that shielded her ears from the cold.

"Are you hungry?" she asked. "I brought lunch, too."

"Oooo," Espen and I muttered at the same time, while Øyvin nodded and politely thanked Ingrid.

Øyvin took a seat at the picnic table, hoisting his legs over and under the wooden structure with ease. I perched on the edge of the same bench and Espen stood by his sister, his legs spread into a triangle and his arms crossed over his chest as he surveyed the lake and watched the kids.

"The kids are so excited to have you here today," Ingrid said as she pulled a thermos from her backpack and a square paper bag.

"Pretty sure that excitement is solely for Espen," I replied. All three kids tried to coax Espen out onto the ice, appealing to him with pirouettes and, in Kristoffer's case, *fast* movements and karate chops.

"That may be true, but it's still nice to have all three of you here." She retrieved a napkin from her backpack and then pulled a small tortilla from the paper bag on the table, setting the latter atop the former.

Espen laughed at his nieces and nephew, the sound warming something within me and settling somewhere near my heart. I glanced over my shoulder and found Øyvin quirking his lips into a gentle lopsided smile that didn't quite meet his eyes. He caught me looking and his mouth dipped back into a line as he clasped his hands on the table and looked back over the lake.

I hoped he was okay. He hadn't been his usual grumbly self this morning. Ever since we crawled out of bed, he'd shut down a bit. It wasn't too alarming, but... I needed to keep an eye on him. Something was up.

Out of the corner of my eye I caught Ingrid spearing something in the thermos with a fork and—

"Did you just put a hot dog in a tortilla?" I asked and turned my attention back to the Solbakke sibling. I'd seen some interesting dishes on my past travels, but this was a new one.

Ingrid chuckled, her eyes creasing at the corners, but continued preparing the "meal."

"It's not a tortilla," she said, a beaming smile sweeping across her lips as she squirted ketchup onto the hot dog and rolled it up. She wandered over to her eldest daughter and handed the hot-dog-burrito she'd just put together to Katrine, who took a huge bite and skated off with it. "It's called sausage in *lompe*."

I shook my head at that last word and pressed at my ear, hoping the tap-tap would get my magical translation juju to work. Ingrid noticed the movement, and Espen must've told her what Nora had done to my hearing, because she added, "Ah, there isn't a good direct translation for the word. But the tortilla"—she retrieved another from the paper bag on the table and waved it about gently—"is actually a soft potato flatbread. The humans, and we, commonly have them as snacks or part of meals. Some people even have eating competitions on Norway's National Day to see how many they can eat with sausages."

Kristoffer appeared next to me as if out of thin air, still somehow wearing his skates—which couldn't have been good for them or safe for him. "I eat five thousand."

"Five whole thousand?" I asked and Ingrid translated for me since the kid didn't know English and my Norwegian wasn't great yet.

Kristoffer nodded, pursing his lips and narrowing his eyes like an old man. "It is serious business. Big competition."

"I bet. And did you win this competition recently?" Ingrid translated for me once more.

"The Darkness always wins."

I snorted and clapped my hand over my mouth to stop from laughing in the kid's face.

Espen stepped up beside me, placing his hand on my shoulder. "The Darkness had four hot dogs in *lompe* last *Seventeenth of May* and proceeded to vomit on his uncle an hour later."

Kristoffer stuck his tongue out at Espen, plucked a hot dog and *lompe* out of Ingrid's hand, and scampered off. Ingrid scolded him in Norwegian as he swept back onto the ice.

She turned back to me with a smile and a wobble of the mom-bun on her head. "Would you like one?"

"Yes, please." It was a little unusual, but I wasn't going to say no to warm food when we were outside in the cold. Storing cooked hot dogs in a thermos for a picnic or a hike was a genius idea I would be implementing in future.

Ingrid handed me my lunch and I took a bite, pleasantly surprised by the taste. And hey, I'd also found another food made of potatoes. That was definitely a win.

The guys practically inhaled theirs and a few minutes later Espen was shucking on his borrowed skates and encouraging me and Øyvin to put ours on. I yanked the white skates on and laced them up over my ankles, glad that Knut-Arne's family cabin came fully stocked with every kind of outdoor equipment a Norwegian might ever need.

"You ready to head out onto the ice, Trouble?" Øyvin asked.

It'd been a long time since I'd skated and that had been at a pop-up rink in my hometown for the holiday season eons ago before I moved to Massachusetts for college. "As long as you help me not fall on my ah—" I stopped myself before I swore around kids. "Butt. Fall on my butt."

Øyvin flicked his brows. "That can be arranged."

I narrowed my gaze. "Why do I get the feeling you mean me on my butt can be *arranged*?"

He smirked and pulled me to my feet, helping me over to the lake's edge. Meanwhile, Espen had bolted after the kiddos, a complete natural on skates. Because, of course, my Forest Fae was good at skating. Was there anything outdoorsy he wasn't good at? Or indoors for that matter?

I peered back to Ingrid before stepping onto the ice. "Aren't you joining us?"

She shook her head and waved her hand before crossing her arms, her yellow jacket scrunching with the motion. "Oh no. I've fallen one too many times and I bruise far more easily at my age."

I raised my hand. "Fair enough." I wasn't going to counter her 200-plus years of knowledge and experience.

Øyvin tugged lightly on my wrist. "Come on. Stop stalling."

"Don't be an Ass—"

"Uh-uh," he tutted.

I pursed my lips and let him lead me onto the crystal clear ice scarred with crisscrossing lines where people had already carved it up with their skates.

Øyvin dropped my hands and I slid one foot outward then the other, forming a tiny vee with my movements. My steps stuttered and I held my arms out to maintain some semblance of balance. Turning in a wide circle, pride bubbled within me as I completed an ungraceful yet princessy pirouette. Flailing but upright was better than ass down on the ice. So, slow and steady was the way to go.

Øyvin glided up beside me and caught my hands in his. I grasped his fingers, holding on tightly as he steered me across the lake, his strides smooth and even, like he'd been doing this his entire life.

He skated like he was water personified and I couldn't look away. Øyvin near his natural element really was a sight to see. His hair fluttered in the wind, sunlight caught on the stubble across his jaw, and his legs moved in a steady rhythm. He gave me a lopsided grin that turned evil as he sped up and let go of my hands, launching me back toward the shore where the girls were twirling around Espen, their mother watching on from land. An undignified squeak left my lips as I flapped across the ice.

"Look at you!" Espen beamed, holding his arms out wide.

I mimicked his movement but wobbled and thought better of it—which earned me a few giggles from shore.

I rounded back toward the middle of the lake, then drifted closer to shore, enjoying the freedom and feel of gliding across the frozen water. The cool air whipped against my cheeks and the sun shone down on the ice, making every inch sparkle like a blue, crystal vase. More families joined us on the lake. Fae or human, I couldn't tell the difference, but within minutes, Ingrid was striking up conversation with some other moms and the girls were chatting away with other kids.

Spinning around, a smile on my face, I searched for Øyvin. He stood further from the shoreline, barely moving, watching the goings-on with a solemn face. Hmmm. Something wasn't right with my grumpy fae. He'd been in this funk ever since we arrived in Alvdalen, and it was worse today.

Maybe he was worried about being so far from the fjord? His actions and comments when I first met him would certainly allude to that, but...

that didn't feel right. He'd willingly agreed to this trip. Accepted the mission from Halvar to find the Fjell Heir. So, it had to be something else.

I skated over to him, finally feeling like I was getting into a rhythm that wasn't going to earn me a bruised butt by the evening.

"You okay?" I asked as I bumped into Øyvin. He wrapped his arms around me, letting my momentum move us back slightly.

His hooded gaze met mine. "Yes."

"Mm-hmm." I didn't believe him for a second. Here I'd given him ample opportunity to laugh at me today and make grumbly little remarks that I'd come to find endearing, and he hadn't taken the chance at all. "I call bullshit."

He shook his head and brushed his hands down my back, peering over me. I followed his line of sight and landed on the families having fun... *oh*. It dawned on me like being doused in cold water. Family. Øyvin was missing his family. The loves and lives he'd lost over the years. And here we were gallivanting around with such a young family with their lives ahead of them, centuries if they were lucky.

"You miss your family," I said, not a question but airing what was written across his face.

Øyvin nodded. "My brother and I used to skate together when we were young boys. He was exceptionally fast and I could never keep up."

A tiny smile twisted my lips as I imagined a small and frustrated blond-haired boy trying to chase after another, their skates cutting up the ice. "Even as the older brother?" I asked, and his pensive gaze dropped to mine.

Mired in thought, he replied with a nod. "Peder, like many Fjord Fae, loved being on the water. Whenever the lakes froze over, he was the first on the ice. We'd make courses out of branches and race each other for hours."

My heart clenched on Øyvin's behalf. Of course being out here today would stir up memories. Memories he was clearly caught up in as he stared off into the distance, lost in a trance.

I slid in closer and brushed my hands up his arms. His sapphire eyes locked on mine, and he let out a heavy breath. "Lennie."

I pressed my palms to his chest and pushed lightly. "Skate with me."

He needed a distraction. A happy memory to pull him from the mental spiral he was winding down.

With a hint of warmth in his eyes and a twitch of his lips, he placed his hands atop mine on his chest and drifted backward. Controlling our movements, Øyvin turned us around in a wide circle. The wind curled around my cheeks, chilling my flushed skin, and the sun shone over us as we glided across the frozen lake.

We passed Espen and the girls, all three of whom smiled at us as they spun in ever faster pirouettes. The girls' brown curls flew around their faces, their scarves whipping in the breeze as they giggled and laughed with their uncle. Before we drifted away, Espen gave me a quick wink, and I gave him a gentle smile in return.

Øyvin moved his hands, placing them on the small of my back, and my lips parted into a wider smile as I returned my gaze to him. Unwavering, we swirled around and around, carving large circles and infinity symbols into the ice. After a few moments, he drew me closer into his embrace, holding me against his broad chest. I let out a satisfied hum and wrapped my arms around his back, still never breaking eye contact. It was the most intimate moment we'd had out in public. And yet, it felt like we were locked away in our own little cocoon where nothing and no one could touch us. In his arms, I felt protected and at home. Nothing could break us as long as we held on to each other. I pressed my head against his chest. His heart beat in a rapid but steady rhythm.

He swept his hand up my back, neck, and cupped my head. "This," he muttered so quietly I could barely hear him. "I like this."

"I like this, too," I whispered back and squeezed him a little tighter. I was acutely aware of every spot where our bodies touched, warmth radiating through me. I didn't want to let go. In fact, realization settled over me like a warm blanket on a cold day: I would never want to let go of this, of what we had together. I'd always been a bit of an ostrich with my emotions, dunking my head into the sand when things got uncomfortable or I didn't know how to respond. But with the swell of feelings coursing through me, the pitter-patter of my heartbeat, and the strength of the man holding me as we glided across the ice, I wanted to respond. To tell him just how much I liked this.

"Ø-Øyvin," I faltered, my throat thick with emotion.

"Hmmm." He tilted my head up until our eyes met again. His pupils were dilated, his lips slightly parted.

"I-I..." My voice trembled and I took a deep breath.

Bubbles of laughter emitted from the girls near the shore and a cracking sound rent the air.

I turned toward the noise, looking past Øyvin's shoulder, and stilled, my stomach flipping into my throat. Kristoffer was out in the middle of the lake. The cracking grew louder, and before anyone could move, Kristoffer's eyes went wide and he dropped through the ice.

25

LENNIE

I screamed, people on shore screamed, and the cry of despair that could only ever be emitted by a mother losing a child struck through the air like lightning.

Øyvin pushed me back toward the edge of the lake, yelled at Espen to get everyone off the ice, and barreled toward the spot where Kristoffer had disappeared.

Shaking and sucking in sharp breaths, I slid toward land, all the while casting glances over my shoulder.

Øyvin dove into the water, crashing through the broken shards of ice like they were butter and he was a hot knife.

My lungs stopped working and time stood still as I reached the shore and wobbled to the picnic table. Maybe an hour passed, or maybe it was just seconds, but time stopped as we all watched the jagged ice and waited for them to appear.

Two heads breached the surface, and the gathered crowd let out a collective sigh of relief. Ingrid whimpered and her daughters cried, tears streaming down their faces.

Øyvin slid Kristoffer onto the ice and gingerly pulled himself out of the frigid water, his hair plastered to his forehead, his jaw locked.

Espen made a move to head back onto the ice, but even at that distance, Øyvin caught his movement and raised his hand. Espen stopped immediately and let out a shuddered breath. I slipped my hand into his and squeezed. He squeezed back, keeping his eyes locked on the duo that slowly crossed the lake.

Øyvin cradled the young boy in his arms. Kristoffer's shaking subsided the closer they got to shore.

My stomach was in my throat, adrenaline coursing through my system. I wobbled and remembered I still had my skates on. Stepping briskly over to the picnic table, I exchanged them for my boots. Espen did the same, but never took his eyes off his nephew.

As Øyvin and Kristoffer crossed onto land, Ingrid bolted to them and brushed her hand over her son's cheek.

Kristoffer's lips were blue, his skin as pale as a starched sheet, but he was alive and moving.

"Help him," Ingrid said, her voice thick with worry.

Droplets ran down Øyvin's face and clung to his outerwear, some appearing to freeze. "I am," he replied, glancing around us.

I followed his gaze. *Shit.* Humans. They'd gathered around in their worry, and Øyvin couldn't use the full strength of his magic to wick the water off the boy. He must have subtly used some already as Kristoffer wasn't shivering.

Espen nudged his sister. "To the car. Now."

Øyvin moved straight past the gawking crowd and headed for the parking lot. Ingrid and the girls followed swiftly behind him, mentioning which car was hers. All the while, Øyvin never loosened his hold on the whimpering boy.

"Can you do anything?" I asked Espen as we rushed behind the others.

"Not fully. Not until we get home," he said, his brows drawn together and his focus never wavering from Kristoffer.

Ingrid yanked open the back door to the mini-van, and the girls shuffled inside without being asked, having already removed their skates while Øyvin crossed the lake.

We all came to a stop outside the vehicle.

"I've wicked away as much water as I could," Øyvin said. "Get him in the car and I can get the rest." He looked around at the people behind us who'd gathered along the shoreline, several of which were parents stopping their kids from returning to the ice or holding their hands over their mouths in terror.

Tears streamed down Ingrid's reddened cheeks as she gulped down controlled breaths and stepped aside for him. Øyvin deposited the shell-shocked boy into his car seat and stepped back. Espen immediately swooped in. We needed his healer fae skills to check the boy for any injuries.

"It's okay," Espen said, his voice calm and soft as his hands hovered over Kristoffer, moving from his little legs upward. "Øyvin, a moment?"

Øyvin and I moved in a heartbeat, our backs to the rest of the world, shielding Kristoffer from onlookers. Øyvin reached over and rested his hand on Kristoffer's shaking shoulder. A moment later his clothes were completely dry and his hair had lightened to its normal brown color instead of the inky drenched state.

"Thank you," Ingrid muttered, her hand clutched to her chest.

"No injuries, but he's not out of the woods yet. He's still too cold." Espen turned to his sister. "Drive out of here swiftly, pretend you're rushing to the hospital, but head home instead. We'll meet you there and I can heal any other lingering effects."

She nodded and didn't hesitate. We stepped out of her way and she slid the mini-van door shut and bolted around to the driver's seat. We ran back to the picnic table and grabbed our things, throwing them into Ingrid's forgotten backpack. By the time we got back to the car, Ingrid was long gone.

We pulled up at Ingrid's house, launched ourselves out of the car, and barreled through the front door.

"In here." Ingrid's voice drifted into the hallway from the living room and we rapidly shucked off our boots. Espen moved so fast he practically floated, his focus locked on helping his nephew, and he was beside him in a heartbeat.

Boots and outerwear deposited in the hallway, Øyvin and I joined the gathered fae in the living room. Kristoffer lay on the sofa with a blanket thrown over his lower half, his head nestled against a plump pillow in Ingrid's lap. The girls were on the other side of the room next to their overflowing toy baskets playing with some dolls while pretending not to pay attention to the grown-ups. Espen kneeled beside the boy and rested his hands over him, assessing Kristoffer with his magic.

"No external injuries," he muttered. Rubbing his hands together he did another pass of the kid's head. His fingers splayed as he used his healing powers. "Stay still for me."

The little boy nodded.

I glanced over my shoulder and found Øyvin still in the archway to the living room, surveying the scene, his lips in a firm line. He crossed his arms, shoulders curved inwards.

Taking a step backward, I leaned into him and whispered, "You doing okay?"

He let out a low hum, but made no other reply.

"Are you hurt?" I asked, unsure if he'd even admit it if he was.

He shook his head.

Footsteps thundered outside and a moment later the front door swung open and closed. "Where is my boy?" Knut-Arne yelled, his voice shaking. He didn't bother removing his shoes, and dollops of snow followed him into the living room. Øyvin discreetly waved his right hand, and the little puddles disappeared behind the distressed father.

Espen peered up at his brother-in-law. "He's going to be all right," he said as he brushed his hands through Kristoffer's hair and rose to his feet. "I've eased some of the aches in his legs from the ice and a couple bruises, but he will be fine once the shock subsides."

Knut-Arne brushed his light-brown beard with one hand and patted Espen on the back with the other. "Thank you, brother."

"Of course," Espen replied. "But it's Øyvin who deserves the thanks. He dove in."

Øyvin clenched his jaw as the entire room turned to look at him.

"Thank you," Knut-Arne said. "Thank you for saving my boy."

Øyvin nodded once, tension strung through his brow and limbs.

Knut-Arne and Ingrid switched spots on the couch, and she strode over to us with Espen at her side. "I think we need coffee. Follow me." She strode into the kitchen and none of us disagreed.

The kitchen counters were covered with thermoses, lunch bags, and dishes that had been left out to dry on tea-towels. Light streamed through the bank of windows on the opposite side of the room, dappling the centralized pine table in a soft glow. The three of us pulled out a chair each and sat down while Ingrid rolled up the sleeves of her striped sweater and busied herself making a pot of coffee. Part of me wanted to ask if she needed any help, but the other part recognized a woman who needed to distract herself from the chaos and shock of the day.

At the head of the table, with Øyvin and I on either side of him, Espen set his elbows down and leaned forward, brushing his hands across his face and through his hair. Øyvin stared at the table, tracing the lines and knots in the wood with his finger.

My heart clenched seeing them like this. But the way they'd both handled the near-tragedy, how they'd sprung into action, had pride welling inside me. My breath stuttered as I looked between the two of them. One so kind and caring, never wanting harm to come to anyone yet capable of immense amounts of destruction. The other calm and reserved, but ferociously protective of the fjord and... me.

I leaned back in my chair, the wood biting against my shoulder blades, and pushed up my sleeves as my mouth fell open into an *o* shape. All I wanted to do was hold onto these two men, squeeze them with every fiber of my being, protect them in turn and never let go. *Shit.* I brushed my hands across my cheeks. I was totally, irrevocably, falling in love with them. Probably had been for some time.

Staring down at the shimmering ring on my left hand, I let out a long winded, but contented, sigh. This thing between us had been brewing for a while. Well before they got me the highly personalized ring for our *immigration purposes* engagement. While that had been fake, nothing about our actions around each other or how we went about our lives together was fake. It was like a pot of coffee, slowly percolating into the perfect brew.

I wrung my hands together before crossing my legs and shoving them between my thighs. Turning my gaze back to the guys, I found them both deep in thought, their heads hanging heavy. I looked between the two of them. Øyvin had always challenged me, put me in my place or egged me on. Not out of spite—well, at least once we got to know each other beyond names and snide remarks—but out of a desire to broaden my perspective. Espen, on the other hand, had always made me smile, made me feel young and giddy. But, at the core of both relationships and what all three of us had together was a prevailing sentiment that I couldn't ignore anymore: love.

Fuck me sideways, I'd totally fallen in love with two fae men.

Ingrid brought over a steaming pot of coffee and three small white mugs, setting them on the table between the three of us. "Drink up. I'll be in the other room."

We nodded and thanked her before she swept back into the living room.

Espen poured out three servings and passed out the cups. I took mine with a murmured thank you and pressed the rim to my lips, my hand shaking as I did so.

"You all right, Lennie?" Espen asked, and Øyvin's gaze shot from the table to mine, his brow momentarily furrowing. I wanted to smooth those lines off his forehead with my fingers, and cup Espen's jaw. Ease their troubles...

Yeah, I had it bad.

"I'm okay."

26

LENNIE

We drove home in silence, all three of us emotionally exhausted and lost in our own thoughts. Espen pulled into the driveway and as Øyvin and I climbed out, he moved slower, trailing behind us as we climbed the stairs to the porch and front door.

"Are you coming?" I tilted my head to one side as keys jingled and Øyvin unlocked the door and stepped inside.

Espen rolled his shoulders, stared at me, then shook his head.

"Is everything all right?"

He pressed his lips together and straightened. "No, but it will be."

I started at his remark. "What do you mean?"

"I have something to take care of." He gingerly lifted his hand and pointed at me. "You head inside, keep Øyvin company. I'll be back in a couple of hours." He took three long strides and was on the step in front of me before I could blink. Grabbing my hand, he squeezed it lightly and pulled it against his chest.

"You promise?"

His eyes crinkled at the corners and a gentle smile crossed his lips before he pressed them to mine. "I promise."

After shedding my outer layers and boots, I leaned against the bedroom doorframe, my arms crossed over my chest. Øyvin sat on the edge of the bed, his hair rumpled, shoulders curved, and his head hung heavy as if a depressive cloud had settled over him.

He looked through the doorway and into the entryway behind me. "Where's Espen?"

"He said he had something to deal with."

"Did he elaborate?"

I shook my head.

Øyvin nodded solemnly, turning his gaze back to his hands as he wrung them, leaning his forearms against his thighs. I'd never seen him so encumbered and wracked with emotions. Even in the mountain after I'd been attacked by the wolves, he hadn't shown this level of emotion.

"Are you doing okay?" I asked.

He sighed and didn't reply.

"Kristoffer is all right. You saved him."

Øyvin ran his hand through his hair and took a deep breath. "I keep seeing his little face drop through the ice. It's running on repeat."

"And you saved him. Øyvin, look at me." His head rose slowly and his eyes met mine. Pain and fear and torment filled his dark-blue gaze like a never-ending ocean. "You saved that little boy today. You saved Katrine and Kari's brother."

I knew I'd hit the nail on the head while we were out on the ice before Kristoffer had fallen through. All this happy family stuff was a reminder to Øyvin of the family he once had that no longer existed. Long years and a life well-lived had taken his parents, but his brother was killed in the battle twenty years ago, the same battle that took the lives of Queen Ragnhild and Espen's mentor, Mads. So, it came as no surprise that the events of the day were taking a toll on Øyvin. It was little wonder he needed some time to grieve again.

"You saved him," I reiterated.

"And Espen healed him."

"He did. Do you need some healing, too?" I shuffled across the room to stand in front of him. It sounded silly, but I wanted to help him in any way I could.

He gave me a deadpanned look.

"Yeah, I know I don't have healing magic like the all-powerful and mighty ball of sunshine that's probably perusing the cheese aisle right now trying to decide between a Gouda and a blue—"

"Whoever eats that moldy stuff is mad."

"Another thing we can agree on."

"Is he actually at the grocery store?"

I shook my head. "I have no idea, but see how that distracted you? And... is that a smile?"

It most definitely was not and he emphasized that fact by scowling even further.

I put my hands on my hips and settled into a confident power pose. "Look, I'm not the sunshine in this sandwich situation we have going on here."

"You're the pain in the ass that sits in the middle."

"Exactly. But I can bring a smile to your face or make you feel a bit better." Without giving him a warning, I moved forward and straddled him, doing my best to distract him from his fidgeting. Perhaps my tits in his face would help divert his attention.

He stared up at me, and I swallowed a breath. He looked so fragile, so hurt. An urge to protect him swelled within me, the same feeling I'd had sitting at Ingrid's kitchen table.

"Am I about to get Serious-Lennie?" he asked.

"That you are." I wrapped my hands behind his neck, resting my forearms on his broad shoulders. "Brace yourself, honey."

He settled his hands against my waist, gently squeezing my curves, and I took a deep breath before diving in.

"You did everything you could today and succeeded in saving the life of a little boy. None of us could've done what you did. Not even Espen. He may have been able to break through that ice, but who knows how much damage he would have done and there is a good chance that he could have accidentally hurt Kristoffer in his panic to get to him. *You*, on the other hand, knew exactly what to do. And the Mikkelsens are going to be forever grateful for you. I know I am."

I cupped his cheeks and brought his attention back up to my face, lest he decide to burrow and hide in my boobs. He could do that later. "You can't save and protect everyone."

He bristled, but I didn't stop. I didn't let go.

"You may not even be able to save me some day."

"Don't say that."

I warmed at his words, but didn't let them stop me. He needed to hear this. He needed to be reminded before his mind spiraled even further. "You may not have been able to save your brother all those years ago"—he flinched, and I sank deeper into him, bringing my hands to his shoulders and holding him tight—"but in the past few months you've saved countless lives, helped save the fjord from a dick of a king, and saved a little boy. You do so much for this world, and your *family*."

"I don't—"

I pressed my finger to his lips. "Yes, you do have a family. The Fjord Fae look to you as a leader and care about you, members of the Forest and Fjell Fae care about you, and most importantly, I care about you. We are your family. Especially, Espen and I."

It was true. Every word, every syllable. This man was cared for, whether he realized it or not. He was a protector of the Fjord, and I didn't doubt for one second that its inhabitants wouldn't protect him in turn. They'd rise from the waters and come to his aid, not because he was their Head Guard, but because they valued him and the work he did for them.

Øyvin took a deep breath. "You're right." Before I could do a victory dance and bask in the sound of those words, he spun and flipped me onto my back, laying me on the bed with his hands on either side of my head, his hips between my thighs. "And I care about you, too."

I pulled my hands down the expanse of his chest, enjoying the way his abdomen tensed under my touch. "Look at us."

His gaze bored into mine, the weight of the moment settling in the room, and that smell of clean linen washed off him, even though he hadn't showered since this morning. The thought of showering pulled my focus to a couple of days ago when he'd watched me shower. The way he'd made me feel then and the way he made me feel now, looking down at me like I was breakable or might run away, had my throat tightening and my adrenaline running a million miles per hour.

He leaned over me and settled us further back onto the bed before skimming his nose up the side of my neck. Goosebumps skittered down my arms in response, but my newfound emotions, feelings, and truths needed to be released.

"Not to break the moment," I said, hoping to hell this was going to come out the way I wanted. This was brand new territory for me, but it felt right. It felt like home. He had to know. "But I was thinking..."

He tilted his head to one side and huffed. "Always dangerous."

"Maybe," I muttered, but highly doubted it. "But you should know…"

His eyes roved over my face, taking in every detail.

"However much of an asshole you are," I said, garnering a faint smirk, "I'm pretty damn sure I've fallen in love with you."

He pressed his forehead to mine and breathed us in. The world around us fell away and in that moment there was only me and Øyvin, the steady thrum of our heartbeats, and the truth. He brushed his thumb across my bottom lip and let out a sigh. "I didn't stand a chance."

I swallowed the lump in my throat and my heart skipped two beats.

"More than that," he whispered. "You've ruined me."

I let out a shuddered gasp, my lips brushing over his. He pulled back ever so slightly, not giving in to the kiss I desperately wanted to share with him.

"I've never been good with this sort of thing, but I've fallen so hard, I couldn't ever possibly love another," he admitted and then crashed his lips against mine. I melted into his hold, my hands raking into his hair, desperate to have our bodies closer, to say how I felt with actions alone. Because, and I couldn't quite believe it had happened. I'd fallen for him. This grumpy, dedicated, and protective Asshole had stolen part of my heart.

A second later, clothes flew to the floor and Øyvin guided me back onto the bed. I lay down on the soft sheets and he settled on his knees between my legs. A delicious shudder ran through me as he brushed his palms over my breasts and continued down. He caressed my curves like a god worshiping his own creation, marveling at every peak and valley.

I clutched at the bedlinen, my toes curling.

He took his time exploring me, like this was the first chance he'd had to see me naked and at his mercy. His eyes hooded and the warmth of his body enveloped mine like an invisible embrace.

How did I get so lucky? He was beautiful. Utterly stunning. Photographs could never do him justice.

That usual push and pull between us was momentarily gone, and in its place was something solid, something intangible yet clearly defined. A mutual respect, care, and love.

He notched himself at my entrance and planted his hands on either side of my head.

I reached out and wrapped my fingers around his forearms, feeling the taught muscles there.

With a sweet smile on his face, Øyvin slowly sank into me, and I let out a soft moan.

He leaned forward and nuzzled underneath my ear. "I love that, too."

"What?"

"Those little noises you make. The sounds that escape when we're together."

All I could do was nod as we explored each other with our hands and Øyvin pushed inside me with languorous and passionate strokes. My body quivered and my lungs expanded, desperate for more of everything. For more of him.

"*Fuck*, Øyvin."

"You can take it," he said, keeping a gentle but steady pace that would unravel me.

As if he could tell I was already on the precipice, he thrust deeper, harder. His breaths mingled with my own as my focus narrowed in on us. Just us. The press of our bodies together, the heat flaring in his eyes, and my fingers digging into his shoulder muscles—holding on to what

I could have for a lifetime. Sparks shot through me and Øyvin's breath stuttered as we fell apart together.

We came down from our high and Øyvin pulled out, rolled off me, and tucked me into his side. I felt like the most precious thing in the world, more valuable than his fjord... I felt like his.

"I never want this feeling to end," I said, unable to stop the words from tumbling out of my mouth as I rested my palm against his bare chest.

Øyvin squeezed me tighter and brushed his hand through my rumpled hair. "It won't. I'll make sure of it."

My heart pulsed hard. He didn't mean the post-orgasm bliss. He meant us. The challenging, supportive, and protective love we shared. I'd do everything I could to safeguard this too. Forever.

"I love you, Lennie."

I tilted my head to meet his gaze. "Are you getting emotional on me?"

A smile grew on his face. "Are you?"

With a chuckle, I pressed my lips to his in a tender kiss and lost myself in the comforting joy that hummed through my entire body.

27

ESPEN

After sending a quick text to Turi and Gunvor asking them to meet me at Turi's apartment, I hopped in the car and left Lennie and Øyvin at the cabin to rest and talk through their feelings. No one had missed the moment they'd shared on the ice today, least of all me. While they annoyed and challenged each other, deep down they truly cared for each other.

I was happy for them. I'd always be happy when she was happy. And I liked the dynamic between the three of us. I may have been the one engaged to her for immigration purposes, but we were a trio. Even though Lennie still hadn't put any definitions on us, I could feel our connection in my bones and see it in her actions. Those emotional barriers she'd erected were slowly but surely crumbling, and I was confident she'd realize soon enough how deeply Øyvin and I both cared for her. She was it for me—for Øyvin too.

Smiling to myself, I turned down the road toward Turi's house and refocused my thoughts to the matter at hand. The Forest Fae had an internal threat and today was a reminder that time was precious. This wolf problem needed fixing immediately. Wilhelm defecting would cause major upheaval in the delicate balance we'd established with the Council after the demise of Queen Ragnhild. I'd sworn an oath to serve and protect the Forest Fae, and that included trouble from within.

I pulled into my sister's driveway, Gunvor's little Mini Cooper already parked up.

Without bothering to ring the doorbell, I knocked once and let myself in. I was instantly assaulted by the smell of cats and whatever herbaceous thing Turi was burning somewhere.

"We're in here!" my sister's voice called from the depths of her living room. I pulled off my boots and hung up my jacket, stuffing my hat into the pocket, and headed toward the chattering noise of two women.

"How's Kristoffer?" Turi asked when I was barely two steps into the eclectic candle-lit room. "Ingrid called me and told me what happened."

I threw myself down on the vacant velvet sofa, narrowly avoiding Loki the cat, who hissed at me and sauntered to the kitchen. "He'll be fine. Still a little shell-shocked, but physically all right."

"Thank the ancestors Øyvin was there." Turi leaned forward and poured steaming hot coffee into an emerald-colored mug and passed it to me.

Nodding in agreement, I accepted the drink and took a gulp before setting it on the coffee table. If not for Øyvin, the outcome would've been monumentally different.

Gunvor sat forward, her black-and-white poncho a stark contrast to the bright mug in her hand, and tapped Turi's thigh. "The little ones bounce back quickly, and he's young enough that the memory will ease and fade with time."

I certainly hoped that was the case for him, because the memory of him disappearing under the ice was burned into my brain. No doubt it would play on repeat for years to come.

I shook my head, ready to pivot the topic as Turi's white cat walked into my lap, kneaded my thigh, and curled into a ball. "I have news about Wilhelm and the pack."

"What is it that was so urgent?" Gunvor asked, and Turi took a sip of her drink, already aware of what had transpired as I'd called her after finding Lennie the other day.

I let out a long breath, the weight of the problem in front of me making my shoulders sag. "According to Marius, Wilhelm has plans to defect from the Forest Fae."

Gunvor blinked twice and took another sip of her coffee before gently setting it on the table between us. "Well…" She folded her delicate hands in her lap. "The man has always been a challenge. Even when he was a boy, he tried to bend rules to fit his purpose."

I brushed my hand across my mouth, stifling a laugh, but coming away with a smile nonetheless. Sometimes it was easy to forget just how old Gunvor was. While her outward appearance portrayed her as a sprightly, albeit petite, octogenarian, she was actually several centuries my senior.

"How do we go forward with the Council now that we know this?" Turi asked. "Can we call a vote of no confidence in his position as Alpha? Do we even have grounds for removal?"

"He sent wolves after your fiancée. I'd call that grounds enough." Gunvor nodded to me, and I wholeheartedly agreed. I knew there'd be consequences for me telling Lennie about the fae, but I never in my wildest dreams thought she'd be attacked by wolves because of me.

"I agree," I said. "The Council was angry with me after I told Lennie about the fae, but agreed that keeping her close during the investigation into illegal magic transfers was important. Wilhelm should never have acted alone and sent his wolves after her. Knowing him, he probably meant to come for me too, but I just so happened to be poisoned at the time, unconscious at Heidi's place in the woods."

Turi pursed her lips, her usual tell when she was thinking hard about some kind of puzzle. "There's never been a vote of no confidence for the Alpha position."

Gunvor shook her head, her long, white ponytail sliding across her shoulder.

"If we call a vote of no confidence, it has to be swift," I said.

"Agreed," Gunvor added.

Turi straightened. "And we need the votes lined up beforehand—"

"Plus security measures in place," I interrupted Turi, and both women nodded. "We can't have Wilhelm lashing out. I need to call in some of the local soldiers to hang out at Alveskjegget during the vote, and perhaps send a couple to stake out the pack compound, just in case."

Gunvor sucked in a long breath, before slowly letting it out and relaxing her shoulders. "The votes shouldn't be too difficult to obtain, but I fear we may have some convincing to do."

With twelve people on the council, including myself and the two women in the room, we'd need to convince another four council members to support the motion if we wanted it to pass.

Turi leaned back against the sofa and brushed her hands through her hair, the brown locks matching the color of my own. "Jan has never been a fan of Wilhelm's. We shouldn't have any trouble there."

"Hanne dislikes conflict, but I think I can bring her around to vote in favor of removal." Gunvor stared off toward the fireplace where embers smoldered, keeping the entire room cocooned in a cozy warmth. "And Frøydis should support us too, especially after the debacle a couple of years ago."

Turi nodded, but I couldn't remember what happened at the event they were referring to. Either way, we had a couple more votes easily secured, and only needed one or two more.

"Can you talk to some of the others?" I asked Gunvor. She was the eldest member of the Council, and a majority of the members looked to her as a bellwether on things. If she could sway more council members, we'd have enough votes to remove Wilhelm from his post.

She nodded. "I'll see what I can do."

"Thank you," I replied with a solemn smile. "Let's see if we can get this done as swiftly as possible. I don't want him to get suspicious, nor enact whatever plans he might have in the next few days."

Turi poured herself another cup of coffee. "In the meantime, do we need to discuss his replacement?"

"Good point. We need someone the council can trust and who has all the wolves' best interest at heart, fae or otherwise." I stroked the cat in my lap and its purrs hummed against my thigh. Biting my bottom lip, I grimaced and glanced over at my sister. "I have a suggestion, but you might not like it."

She narrowed her eyes. "What are you thinking?"

28

LENNIE

"Looks like I missed something," a low voice said.

Shucking off the covers from my post-coital nap, I blinked away dregs of sleep to find Espen leaning against the bedroom doorframe, his arms crossed and a smirk on his lips.

"Good times befell the kingdom." I yawned and stretched my hands over my head.

Øyvin grumbled and buried his face in his pillow where he lay beside me.

"Glad to hear it." Espen smiled, his eyes crinkling. "Would the kingdom like to go get something to eat? It's already past dinner time."

Øyvin shook his head and threw the duvet over himself, cocooning his entire body under the warm covers.

I, on the other hand, was starving. "Are you thinking take-out or grabbing something from the store?" I asked as I slipped from the bed and searched my duffel bag for a pair of clean underwear.

Espen cleared his throat. "Let's visit the shops and pick up something we could cook here. Wear layers, we're walking."

"Sounds good to me." I put my bra on and grabbed a clean, long-sleeved shirt. "You figure out the thing that needed sorting?"

He nodded, pursing his lips. "Yes, everything's good. A plan is in place."

"Hmmm," I mumbled and grabbed a pair of jeans from my bag. "Do I want to know?"

"It's to do with Wilhelm."

I bristled and grimaced as I buttoned my pants. "Just get rid of the slimy fuck."

"That's the goal."

Pulling on my white-and-blue Nordic knit sweater, I flipped my hair out of its confines and set my hands on my hips. "Great. Now, food?"

"Let's go."

We walked about two miles through the snow to the nearest grocery store that, when compared to American supermarkets, was more the size of a convenience store. But it had everything we needed, from potatoes and green beans, to some frozen meatballs that'd be easy to throw together when we got home. With our bags in hand, we made the short trek back to the cabin under the dull glow of the moon that tried to pierce the cloud cover.

Tall street lamps cast golden rays onto the snowy road and the air hinted at the chilly night to come as we strolled home. Barely a single person was out on the roads, and those that had ventured out for the evening, were securely ensconced in the warmth of their cars. The exhausted part of me wished we'd taken the car into the village, the other part of me—the part of me that was slowly melting and had developed serious feelings for the Forest Fae holding my hand in his—didn't mind at all.

I glanced over at Espen carrying our bag of groceries, taking in his dark locks that poked out from beneath his green bobble hat, and I couldn't hold back the smile that swept across my lips.

"What?" he asked, grinning back at me. "Do I have something on my face?"

I shook my head and looked forward again, my body warming under his gaze. Damn, I had it bad. Every time I looked at him a wave of contentment settled over me. Not in a *"I need him to survive"* kind of way—although, with my track record, that might be true. But in a *"I want him by my side"* manner. This perfect ray of sunshine, with his caring heart, his beaming smile, and hugs that could melt a snowman, had broken my defenses completely.

Snow crunched beneath my boots and Espen tugged on my hand, spinning me in a perfect pirouette and wrapping me into his arms. "Out with it, Lennie. What has you thinking and smiling like that?"

I let out a strangled breath and pressed my back against his front as we continued walking. If he ever gained the ability to read my mind, I'd be in serious trouble... Then again, that look he'd had in his eyes told me he probably already knew exactly what was going on in my head. Or at the very least assumed it was something dirty, and seven times out of ten that would be correct.

"I'm thinking about you."

He nuzzled against my neck. "Are you, now?" he whispered, and his warm breath sent a shiver down my spine.

"Mm-hmm."

"Dirty things?" There it was.

I snickered. "More like happy things."

"Care to elaborate?" He tightened his hold on me as we turned down the road that would lead us out of town and toward the little cabin.

Spinning in his arms, I walked backwards, fully trusting that Espen wouldn't let me fall on my butt. I could do this. I could be vulnerable with him. Today was the most openly emotional I'd been in a long time. Even with my old exes and dalliances, I'd never been so forthright with my emotions—which was in part why some of those relationships hadn't lasted very long. Or perhaps those relationships weren't *meant to be*? I took a deep breath, the cold air tickling my throat. "I was thinking about how we met, and how you've somehow broken down my defenses, and wormed your sunny little ass into my heart."

Espen bit his bottom lip as if that could stop his beaming smile. The corners of his eyes crinkled as the Forest Fae moved us closer to the edge of the road and stopped. Creating a small divot in the snow with his gloved hand, he put down the groceries in the waist-high snowbank. The lamp above us lit our surroundings, from the pine trees behind it to the little driveways on the other side of the road. But all I could focus on was the man in front of me.

"Well, that's excellent," Espen said. "I'm glad to hear my plan worked."

My eyes bugged. "Your what?!"

He snickered and flicked his eyebrows. "Once upon a hill in Skolvik, I met a woman—"

"Who better have been me." *Hello Jealousy, welcome to the party.*

"—who *bewitched* me with every fiber of her being." He held one hand against my back keeping my trembling body upright, while pressing the other to his chest as if he were about to recite Shakespeare. "That day I vowed to myself that I would win her heart."

Yeah, this was definitely veering Bard-like.

"Even if she was to leave my fair kingdom in a week's time."

Houston, we have Full Bard.

Smiling at his ridiculousness, I said, "Long story short: you saw something you wanted?"

"Yes, I did. And I did everything I could, even revealed my fae secret, to entice her without forcing her hand."

I narrowed my eyes. "*Everything* you could? Like getting me alone in your cabin on a Friday night for a game of cards? Seducing me with forest yoga? Or making a bridge a little rickety to engineer a hero moment?"

Espen sucked in a breath and shuddered. "Definitely not that. Seeing you fall through that bridge took ten years off my life."

I chuckled. Almost falling into that ravine had given me a few more gray hairs.

"So, what was it then? What caught your attention?" I pried, stepping into his embrace once more. He wrapped his arms around me completely and pressed our bodies firmly together.

"It was love at first punch."

My heart stuttered. "Seriously?" That was novel. I hadn't meant to punch him, it was a knee-jerk defensive reaction to having him appear so close behind me.

"I *bullshit* you not," he replied with a sly grin. "It's not every day that a Forest Fae is punched by a human. I dare say you were the first."

A tiny snowflake settled on the edge of his woolly hat, its spokes caught in the wisps of yarn. Another alighted on my cheek and Espen swept it off with his thumb. The rays from the moon had disappeared behind the clouds, the street lamp above us now our main light source. We stood there in the silence, our eyes locked on each other, our breaths intermingling, as more snowflakes drifted down around us. It was like we were stuck in our own little snow globe where nothing could touch us, and if shaken, we'd weather the blizzard together. My heart hammered in my chest, a rhythm that had started up a long time ago, but that I'd only deigned to fully recognize this afternoon while we sat in his sister's kitchen.

Espen swallowed audibly and cradled my head in his hands. "You're the best thing that has ever happened to me."

My heart officially melted and I couldn't stop myself, I pressed my lips against his, wrapping my arms around his neck. A warmth that felt like home swept through me. There would be no more denying this. No more ignoring my own feelings. No more bottling them up or hiding in the proverbial sand. I was in love with Øyvin *and* Espen, and I felt more alive today than any before.

Espen pulled back, his eyes blown wide. "You're pure chaos, Lennie Martin, but I love every part of your storm."

I bit my bottom lip, letting his words sink in, before admitting, "I love you too, Sunshine."

If I thought I'd seen Espen's biggest smile, I was wrong. The grin that swept across his lips in that moment was the broadest and happiest smile I'd ever witnessed from my bubbly fae, and I was glad to be the one to put it there. He kissed me once more and dipped me for good measure. If anyone drove past us right now, they'd think we were some love-sick teenagers... and they'd only be partially wrong.

"Love at first punch, hey?" I said as Espen righted me.

He nodded as snowflakes flitted around us. "Love at first punch."

29

LENNIE

After dinner that night, I sauntered into our bedroom and started pulling off my clothes. It'd been a long, eventful day and I was ready for bed, even if my brain wouldn't shut off. Thoughts of the day ran rampant.

The bedside lamp emitted a soft glow that danced across the wood-paneled room, and the rumpled bed invited me toward its warmth. Wearing nothing more than my underwear, my bra abandoned on top of the dresser, I scrambled into the king-sized bed and pulled the fluffy duvet up to my chin.

Caught up in my own thoughts and the soft sheets, I barely noticed Espen and Øyvin coming into the room. The men I'd exchanged *I love yous* with today. I shook my head at the surprise of my own actions.

Taking a deep breath and letting it out slowly, I let my shoulders drop. They both loved me.

We'd reached the point of no return.

It was label making time.

Scrambling from beneath the covers, I sat up and looked at the fae crawling into bed on either side of me. Was it rude to stop them going to sleep? Yes, but if I didn't get this off my chest now, I'd never actually do it. *No time like the present.*

I slipped from beneath the duvet and crept to the end of the bed where I turned to face the two of them. "We need to have *the* talk."

Øyvin's eyes were already locked on me, and Espen stretched his arms above his head as a cheeky grin settled across his face. The cold air in the room brushed against my skin, and I shivered. Only wearing underwear to bed was fine when you were sandwiched between two guys, but outside of that little cocoon of warmth... Well, my nipples were putting on a full Broadway show.

"Now, Lennie," Espen said, his voice husky as he leaned back onto the plump pillows. "When two people care about each other very much—"

I waved my hand at him just as Øyvin snorted, propped himself against the headboard, and crossed his arms. I motioned between the three of us. "We're not only two people. We're three... and fae. That doesn't exactly make things simple."

"How isn't it simple?" Espen asked and Øyvin tilted his head in a way that said the exact same thing.

"Cover your tits or neither of us will be able to focus," Øyvin grumbled, pointedly staring at my eyes.

I crossed my arms over my boobs, and continued. "There's three of us. Do you..." I tried to form the words, but it was like my entire vocabulary had drifted out the window looking for a more hospitable location. "You both like me, yes?"

They both nodded, while Espen mumbled something that sounded like "and more."

"Do you like each other?" My voice lifted at the end of the question. We hadn't ever fully discussed *their* relationship. We'd just sort of started cohabitating and orbiting around each other.

Øyvin shook his head, and Espen scrunched his face together before responding. "We both love *you*, and are okay with sharing you, and spending more time around each other isn't necessarily a negative."

My shoulders relaxed again, and I looked to Øyvin. "And you agree with this?"

"Not in as many words, but yes. He isn't wholly annoying to be around and I trust he'll protect you."

"So, you'd be okay with me calling you both my partners, but you won't use that term for each other?"

They shared a look and returned their focus to me. "Exactly," Espen replied with a gentle smile.

"And are you all right with me using those terms in public?" My eyes landed on Øyvin knowing full well that Espen wouldn't have a problem with it.

He took a deep breath before nodding, and I let out a sigh of relief.

"And let's not forget," Espen added. "You're technically my fiancée."

I hadn't forgotten. Not at all. In fact, that gorgeous silver ring with the blue tear-shaped sapphire sparkled on my hand every day—a constant reminder of what I'd agreed to. And, ironically, where things were truly heading for us. I think, in that moment at Christmas when they'd given me the ring, deep in the recesses of my refuse-to-acknowledge-or-rock-the-boat mind, I'd known this would develop into something more. Into something I didn't want to let go of. Truth be told, I was obsessed with both of them and the thought of spending however many years I had on this earth without them rattled me.

"You are my fiancé," I responded to Espen, who adjusted the duvet around his waist with a gentle smile on his lips. "You both are." Espen's grin widened, and I turned to Øyvin. What did he think of all this? What thoughts were swimming through that mind of his?

He crossed his arms over his bare pecks, rolled his bottom lip between his teeth, and gave me a single nod.

"Thank fuck," I said on an exasperated sigh. Adrenaline coursed through my veins and my hands shook as I raked my fingers through my hair, pushing it away from my forehead. That went better than expected, but there was one more thing I wanted to address.

I took another quick breath. "And... So... We're getting married not just for immigration purposes. This isn't fake. We're doing it because we love each other?"

Espen bit his bottom lip. "Yes. Now how about you remove your underwear, assume bridge pose, and let Øyvin and I have our way with you?"

"You are exceptionally good at pivoting a conversation."

Espen beamed. "Is that a yes to sex?"

"Always."

"Fantastic," Espen said and jumped out of bed.

Øyvin raised his hand and gave me a come-hither motion with my two favorite fingers of his.

Crawling across the bed to him, my body lit up from head to toe under his heady stare. Butterflies swept through me at the prospect of having them both, especially after everything we'd said today.

Øyvin made a turn motion and I spun, settling back against his bare chest where he leaned against the headboard.

Espen swept his hand through his hair, and a wave of heat brushed across my bare skin under his gaze. "Pull those off and touch her," he commanded.

Øyvin obliged, and with a little maneuvering, we got my underwear off. He nipped at my ear and pressed his hand down my stomach before reaching the apex of my thighs. My clit ached to be touched and my breasts hung heavy, my nipples erect and begging for attention. As if hearing my own thoughts, Øyvin moved his free hand to my boob and cupped it, taking the weight of it in his broad palm. I whimpered and let out a moan at the sensation plus the pleasure he wrung from me with his fingers drawing circles around my clit.

My skin tingled and my mind cleared of all thoughts under his ministrations and the heady stare from Espen who stood at the end of the bed watching. A plea sat at the edge of my lips, desperate for Espen to join in. "Please," I whimpered. "More."

Espen gave me a sly grin, removed his boxers, and sidled onto the bed. He was already hard, and watching him fist himself drew me closer to the precipice of my orgasm. Øyvin must've sensed the roaring inferno that threatened to overwhelm me. He cupped his palm against my bundle of nerves and pushed two fingers inside. I gasped and rocked my hips forward as Espen settled between them, pressing our legs into a wider vee with his hands. "Fuck you're wet," he growled.

I couldn't do anything but whimper and writhe, needing more from both of them.

Øyvin removed his fingers and returned them to my clit, painting lazy circles around the tender bundle. Espen settled in closer and grasped my legs, holding them just above the knee and opening me up completely to him. He licked his bottom lip, his gaze locked on my core. Releasing me for a split second, he notched himself at my entrance, planted his hands on the bed, and slowly slid inside. Tiny sparks zipped up and down my spine and Øyvin let out a low rumble behind me, his warm chest rising and falling with the motion. My skin heated and Espen pulled back before pushing in again. Back and forth he went while Øyvin continued touching me, the two of them eliciting whimpers and moans from me as I climbed toward my undoing. My breaths came harder, Øyvin squeezed my breast and nibbled at my ear, and Espen pumped in a steady rhythm that a few moments later had me cascading through waves of pleasure. My body convulsed and Espen pulled out, his chest heaving.

"Switch," Øyvin said, his voice husky and teetering on the limit of control. Something he clung to so valiantly, but I was desperate to watch him lose in the bedroom.

We were a tangle of limbs as the guys moved around, repositioning but somehow still keeping me between them. I had no idea what they wanted to do with me next, but I honestly didn't care. I was a trembling mess, blissed out on pleasure and ready for more if they wanted it. Based on the hungry looks in their eyes that was a solid yes.

I settled on my hands and knees, my rear toward Øyvin as Espen rested his head on the pillows at the top of the bed.

Øyvin trailed his fingertips down the line of my spine then smacked his hand across my ass. "I think I'll take this now."

Fucking finally.

His hand cracked across my rear again and I couldn't help myself. I wiggled my ass in his face, taunting him. It earned me yet another smack, but I relished in the heat that bloomed across my skin.

"You think you can take both of us, Trouble?"

The thought of having both of them inside me sent shivers through my body, and I let out a throaty and strained, "Yes."

Øyvin leaned over me, warmth washing across my back, as he tangled his fingers in my hair and pulled my head gently to one side. "Slide forward and take him first," he commanded, his breath skittering across my cheek. I glanced up at the heat-filled amber eyes before me and swallowed hard. Øyvin lifted his weight off me and released his grasp on my hair. I shuffled forward over the sheets and straddled Espen, pressing my palms against his firm chest.

"You ready?" I asked.

Espen nodded and pressed his dick against my entrance. "There's a bottle of lube in the bedside table," he announced to the room and slid home with a groan. "Not that I need it for this part of you."

He really didn't. I was soaking wet and desperate for what was to come. I rocked forward and back, taking every inch of him and savoring every brush of my clit against his pelvis. Espen's fingers dug into my hips, urging me to slow our pace, and I obliged with a reluctant huff.

The bed dipped and I peered over my shoulder. Øyvin squirted a heavy amount of lube into his hand and tossed aside the bottle, letting it land on the floor with a dull thud.

Øyvin's free hand was on my back once more, this time coaxing me forward and bending me over, pressing my chest against Espen's. He quirked his dark brows and gave me a salacious grin before sweeping his mouth across mine. His tongue slid between my lips and possessed me, taking my breath away.

At the same moment, Øyvin swept the lube in his hand down between my cheeks, spreading it around in preparation. It was cold against my heated skin and I shuddered at the sensation, which only seemed to make them happier as satisfied noises filled the room.

I barely moved against Espen when Øyvin pressed his fingertip to my asshole.

"You ready?" he asked.

My lips broke away from Espen's and I let out a breathy response. "Yes. Please."

Øyvin gently pushed through that first tight ring. *Damn.* I moaned as he stretched me wider, adding another lube-slicked finger to prepare me for his cock. The slow way he toyed with me, driving in and out, had sweat beading across every inch of my skin, my nipples rubbing against Espen's hard chest beneath me. I needed more. I needed everything.

"Øyvin, please," I begged.

His free hand grasped my ass cheek, sending sumptuous pain through my rear as he pulled his knuckles out of me.

He nudged his tip inside me and let out the sexiest groan I'd ever heard. "Fuck."

I relaxed my body against Espen, letting Øyvin control our movements. He took the invitation and pressed another inch of his thick length into my ass. My legs shook and my heart pounded. I wouldn't last long like this. Øyvin moved and pushed in further, dragging an incoherent noise from my mouth. I definitely wasn't going to last long.

The fullness of having them both inside me was insane. Something I'd dreamed about. *Why the hell hadn't we done this sooner?*

Espen wrapped his arms over my back and Øyvin grasped my hips, steadying me, as he slowly began thrusting back and forth. Espen moved beneath me, demanding more from my soaking core, and it was all I could do to maintain my own sanity. I wanted this bliss to last forever.

Tension spiraled within me, building with each thrust from below and behind. In and out. In and out. Deeper, and deeper, and deeper. Espen's ragged breaths brushed over my ear as Øyvin dug his fingers into my curves. His shallow thrusts drove me wild and I bucked against them. A minute later, a heady symphony rocked me with a toe curling crescendo as my orgasm tore through every nerve.

Fuck indeed.

I pressed my forehead against Espen's and watched him come undone beneath me. His cock twitched inside me as he let out a sexy groan.

Øyvin was right behind him with sharp exhales punctuating the room. He pushed forward one final time and shuddered, his thighs slick against the backs of mine.

Spent and blissed out, I collapsed forward onto Espen, letting Øyvin fall out of me.

He flipped over onto the bed beside us, lying on his back with his arm bent behind his head. "Fuck," Øyvin muttered again.

With the little breath that remained in my lungs, I had the audacity to say, "I told you I'd never had any complaints."

He shook his head and lightly smacked my ass again.

I jolted at the searing sensation, my skin raw and sensitive. My core pulsed, happy and sated.

Espen wriggled slightly and slipped out of me, but didn't move me from where I rested against his chest. He delivered a gentle kiss to the bridge of my nose, then another against my lips. "That was..." he drifted off.

"Sensational. Fan-fucking-tastic—"

"Definitely happening again," Øyvin finished for us.

He was right. There was no way in hell I wasn't doing that again.

And we had a lifetime and then some to do it. Together.

30

ESPEN

Late the next morning, well after the sun had risen above the horizon, I donned my winter gear and slipped out of the cabin as quietly as possible, trying not to wake up Lennie and Øyvin.

The three of us would continue our search for Aurora this afternoon, but first I needed to have a chat with Wilhelm about his behavior. As Head Guard of the Forest Fae, he was my problem to deal with. Wilhelm's actions—disregarding the wishes of his junior members, attempting to kill the love of my life, planning to defect, and causing chaos with his beliefs on the wild wolves—were a problem. A problem that would explode in our faces if something wasn't done about it.

I climbed into the car and texted Turi that our plan was in motion, then left a voicemail with Gunvor, asking her to stop by the cabin in half an hour so we could follow up on the number of votes we had to remove Wilhelm as pack Alpha. She quickly replied, saying was waiting to hear from one last council member.

With those messages sent, and a quick "go" message to my local soldiers on stand-by, I started the car and set off for the senior wolf pack compound on the north side of town.

I parked in the middle of the compound, the headlight beams bouncing across the front porch of the rugged main house where Wilhelm resided and held court. I didn't need to honk the horn or alert them to my presence—they had guards half a kilometer back, all of which were hidden in the trees and had, no doubt, called ahead to warn Wilhelm of my arrival.

Wolves appeared from behind buildings and Forest Fae alighted their doorsteps as I got out of the car, stepping toward the main house. Their hooded stares were like an ice storm, frosty and unforgiving, filled with animosity I'd never experienced from them before.

I stopped halfway between my car and the house, careful not to get too close. I was ten times more powerful than Wilhelm and the other wolves here, but I didn't want to hurt anyone. Plus, the winter months put me at a disadvantage—avalanches and ice fall were a serious consequence should I decide to tap into my destroyer powers.

The front door opened and my gaze snapped to it. Wilhem stepped out of the main lodge, his heavy boots thudding against the wooden porch that wrapped around the building, brown eyes focused on me. He reached the top step of the deck and crossed his arms, standing his ground.

"To what do we owe the pleasure, General Solbakke?" Wilhelm's lips curled around the words as if they left a sour taste in his mouth. The use of my rarely used title told me he'd been alerted to my Forest Fae soldiers at the end of the driveway, and maybe even the ones I'd asked to stand watch at the north end of his compound in the woods.

I crossed my arms too and braced my feet in the snow. "I'm here on official business."

"Out with it kid," he huffed, and several chuffs from the other wolves present echoed around the clearing. Lennie was right, this guy had become a piece of shit.

"Concerns about your leadership have been brought to my attention and—"

His brows met his hairline. "With *my* leadership? Who was it that told a human of our existence?"

I ignored the jab, refusing to let him get a rise out of me. "We have a duty to uphold, Wilhelm, and you've been reneging on your oath to protect the Forest Fae and all wolves."

He sneered, but I didn't back down. Energy coursed through my limbs, pushing at me, begging me to be released against this would-be tyrant. "Are you planning to defect from the Forest Fae?"

His lips quirked to one side. "Planning? We've already started."

Shit. "When?"

He raised his hands in a motion that said *look around*. My eyes flicked over the scene—snow, ice, wolves at attention. Their gazes locked on me, paws steeled in the snow. *His* wolves.

I shook my head slightly. He'd already rallied his forces and turned them against the rest of the Forest Fae. And at this time of year...

"The timing of it all. You did this during the autumn and winter, knowing full well I couldn't retaliate, didn't you?" I asked, aware of exactly how much Wilhelm disliked me, as so many others did for the destructive powers I held. It was why Queen Ragnhild had kept me close when she found out about my powers. I was cognizant of her intentions, but, as like-minded individuals, we established a good friendship and bond that lasted until her final day.

Wilhelm's shoulders and head bristled. "Everything is always about you, isn't it Espen?" he spat. "I did it because the Council has never prioritized the wolves." A lie—they were an important part of our faction and always treated as such. "I sent those wolves to Skolvik because you were incapable of protecting us the moment you revealed our secret to a human. Exposing our world—"

"I was protecting our world, both fae *and* humans! You don't think I know what would've happened to Lennie if she spoke of what she saw, what she photographed?" Some bastard would've killed her. Probably Halvar, but even members of my own faction weren't fans of our secret getting out.

Wilhelm clenched his fists at his sides, the knobbly knuckles paling. "You were a love sick fool."

"That may be the case, but I would never do anything to jeopardize the well-being of my people. By telling her and keeping her close, I've been protecting her ever since. Protecting her from idiots like you who follow the old ways and simply kill the problem, the same way you are with the natural wolves."

Wilhelm tutted. "Even in your two-hundreds, you're still so young and naive."

"And at your age, you still cannot fathom another way of living." I shook my head. This was going off the rails. "We have a duty to protect the forest and the creatures that reside within them, Wilhelm. Human, fae, and all others. Or have you forgotten that?"

"I take care of my pack."

I scoffed, sounding a bit like Lennie. "By foregoing your sworn purpose in this world? By ostracizing those who disagree with you?"

"They don't know what it's—"

I raised my hand for him to stop and miraculously he did. "Spare me." I'd heard this before and understood that the shifters had their own struggles to contend with. We'd eased their burdens countless times over the years, helped each other where we could. But we needed to keep working together, be one cohesive unit of Forest Fae. His actions threatened that precious harmony. "I'm already on my last thread of patience with you for what you tried to do to Lennie."

"Would've got away with it too if it hadn't been for that oaf from the mountain."

Ancestors, I wish he'd said that in Halvar's presence, then I'd no longer have to deal with him.

My power swirled in my sternum as I took another deep yogic breath, letting it fill every part of my lungs and chest. "Here's what's going to happen."

"No." Wilhelm descended the porch steps to the snowy, circular driveway. "Here's what *my* pack will—"

"You're no king."

His eyes widened and nostrils flared. "And neither are you."

He strode forward, raising his hand toward my throat. I stepped back and something zinged past Wilhelm's head, stopping him in his tracks. A stony blade impaled the doorframe behind Wilhelm with a dull twang, and a firm and unforgiving feminine voice behind me said, "Back away from my fiancé."

31

LENNIE

Well, that knife hadn't gone exactly where I wanted, but hey, I'd successfully created and thrown a stone weapon. Halvar would be so proud.

Wilhelm snarled, his dark, beady eyes narrowing.

"Try me puppy dog, and we'll see who ends up with severed balls." I stepped up beside Espen. He looked down at me, his eyes wide and a tiny smile lingering on his lips. Shocked or turned on, I couldn't tell.

The second Gunvor and I had pulled up and spotted the two arguing, I'd been on high alert. When Wilhelm lunged toward Espen, looking ready to transform into his wolf, I fucking lost it. No way in hell was he laying a hand on my man.

Wilhelm took three steps back and the wolves and fae around us relaxed. The pack leader raised his chin and exposed his throat. "What's going on?"

Espen opened his mouth to speak, but Gunvor appeared on his other side and rested her hand against his shoulder. "I can take it from here."

Espen nodded, and I looked on in bewilderment at the elder fae. Gunvor clued me in on what their plan was on the drive over, and while I was slightly disappointed that Espen hadn't shared all the information with me, I also understood. He wanted to get this sorted as quickly as possible without putting me or any innocent bystanders in harm's way.

Gunvor strolled toward Wilhelm, her tiny lithe frame practically floating over the snow, coming to a stop a few paces before him.

"Wilhelm." She clasped her gloved hands in front of her, reminding me of some kind of ancient pixie as she stared down the pack leader. Espen was quiet, his gaze flicking between Wilhelm and the wolves around us, same as mine. "Your presence has been requested at an emergency council meeting tomorrow."

Wilhelm tilted his head to the side, scrunching his nose. "To discuss what, exactly?"

Wolves on our left stepped forward, and the magic in my sternum swirled, wanting to protect Gunvor.

Lightning fast, she waved her hand over her head and roots erupted up from the ground. Reaching high above our heads, some taller than the buildings, the roots clunked against each other and wove themselves together into an impenetrable lattice that encircled the three of us, plus Wilhelm. Wolves howled and paced outside, their eyes focused on us. One wolf prepared to lunge but Wilhelm barked a no at him and the canine slunk away into the trees surrounding the clearing.

My eyes widened as I took in our confines. Gunvor definitely didn't need protecting.

She held her hands together at her waist, her puffy jacket swishing with the movement. "We need to discuss the matter that was brought up at the last council meeting regarding the wolves you sent to Skolvik and—"

"You mean the pack member who didn't return because he was *murdered*?" Wilhelm's voice rose at the end of the sentence, more anger seeping into his tone.

Gunvor didn't rise to his bait. "We are greatly concerned with the leadership you've shown and will be holding a vote of no confidence. Consider yourself summoned."

"And if I refuse to attend?"

She shrugged. "Then you'll be unable to argue your case and the odds of your replacement increase significantly."

"You can't do that." He took a step toward Gunvor, and Espen and I took a half-step forward. Fae crept out of the large cabin behind Wilhelm, providing him some sort of macho back up. But still, Gunvor, the Galadriel of the Forest Fae, creator of root-cages, and consummate badass, didn't so much as flinch. She reminded me of a willow tree, with broad vine-like branches that moved with the wind like nature's wind-chime. Whenever I'd photographed one, I'd always marveled at how you could see through the branches to the thick and wizened trunk at the center—wholly unyielding.

"The Council has the authority to appoint and remove all Forest Fae Alphas," Gunvor said. "You know the rules."

I really wanted to learn more about these rules and more about the inner-workings of the pack. They didn't operate like the ones I'd seen in movies, where the strongest was the Alpha and that usually ran in a family. No, no. These puppies did things differently. Fascinating shit. Perhaps I could attend tomorrow's meeting and bring popcorn?

"We meet at Alveskjegget tomorrow at nine o'clock. Attend, don't attend. It's up to you. You have been summoned." Gunvor peered over her shoulder and looked directly at us. "I think we're done here. Unless there is something else that needs to be conveyed?" She raised a single eyebrow at Espen.

Espen straightened and his voice took on a firmer tone as he looked to Wilhelm. "As you're no doubt already aware, Forest Fae soldiers have been stationed around the compound."

Wilhelm brushed a hand across his wrinkled and rugged cheeks, wiping down his chin.

"They'll remain there for a few days," Espen continued. "You and your pack aren't prisoners—"

Wilhelm scoffed.

"—but we have put measures in place to stop you from leaving the area until the meeting. And safeguards to protect the wolves and villagers from any retaliation."

"Do you really think me so callous and cruel?"

"Previously? No. Now? Yes," Espen replied without hesitation.

"You're kind of a dick," I added.

The root barriers around us slowly receded back into the disturbed snow and earth. My jaw hung open in awe of Gunvor and her powers. What exactly was her job with the Forest Fae? Or had once been? I highly doubted she was a botanist like her cousin Vigdis. Maybe she was a bit more like Ylva, a warrior defending her people? Either way, I was developing a girl crush on the woman.

Once the tendrils returned to their winter slumber beneath the snowy driveway, the three of us headed back to our cars.

Espen opened Gunvor's car door for her. "The votes?" he asked, his voice barely a whisper.

Gunvor nodded. "We have them. More than enough."

Espen's shoulders slumped. "Thank you."

She patted his arm and climbed into her car.

"Thanks for the ride over," I said before she departed.

"Of course. I'll see you both tomorrow at the meeting."

I was silent in the car with Espen until we'd passed the last snow-laden trees of the compound driveway and reached the main road. I twisted in my seat to face him.

"So, this is what you've been planning?"

Espen looked at me briefly before turning his gaze back to the windshield and nodded. "I wanted to take care of this myself. Keep as many people from harm as possible. Including you. Wilhelm's already had wolves nipping at you, I didn't want that to happen again."

"Fair enough. I suspected as much, but I'm not wholly human anymore. I have balls of light and stone knives at my disposal now."

He nodded. "I know you're stronger than you were last year, but I don't trust him around you. Please believe me when I say, keeping this from you was more about protecting you from his hatred than purposefully leaving you out. But, I'm sorry if you felt excluded. That was not my intent."

I melted in my seat, my heart pattering happily. "It's okay, I get it. I would probably do the same. For the record, Øyvin would've come too if he could've folded himself into Gunvor's Mini-Cooper." I really wished he'd tried. It would've been hilarious. Instead he took one look at the vehicle that was primarily meant for two people, huffed, and sauntered back inside. I'd even offered to strap him to the roof, but he'd grumbled and slammed the door, leaving us ladies to head over to the compound by ourselves.

Espen laughed softly.

I set my hand on his thigh, and he placed his atop it, brushing small circles over my knuckles with his thumb.

"I have to say though... Super impressed by your throwing knife," he said, pivoting the conversation with a sly smile in my direction. "I like that you swooped in to protect me."

My cheeks flushed. "It was pretty hot, wasn't it?"

"You have no idea. I very much appreciated the fiancé line, too." He lifted my hand to his lips and pressed a soft kiss to the back of it. My whole body warmed at his simple touch and I slumped in my seat.

Here he was, my ray of sunshine. My fiancé who could level battlefields and heal flora and creatures. A man that had me worried one minute and proud the next. Someone I'd defend at all costs.

"Please know that if we weren't in Oddvar's car right now, I'd ask you to pull over and show me just how much you enjoyed my heroics."

His grin turned wicked. "Oh, I already considered it." He flicked his gaze to mine. "But, fucking you in your future boss's car might not be wise. I'd never be able to keep a straight face and order coffee from him again."

A snort bubbled out of me. "Same."

"Let's get home and have a snack instead," Espen said. "Then we can continue searching for Aurora."

He was right. We needed to focus on our mission. "Deal."

32

LENNIE

After an eventful morning handling the wolf situation, Espen, Øyvin and I spent the remaining daylight hours searching the neighboring village for any sign of Aurora. From snow laden parks, to a World War Two-era bomb shelter dug into the hillside, the thick metal door covered in bright graffiti. No matter where we looked, there was no sign of the Fjell heir. So, we returned to the cozy cabin, started a fire in the fireplace, and made a plan for tomorrow's search over dinner—a trip to the town of Lillehammer, home of the 1994 Olympics and, according to Espen, a decent number of campgrounds.

As we washed and put our clean plates away, my phone rang. I glanced at the caller ID and smiled, heading into the living room area and taking up position by the window to accept the call.

"Torsten! Hey, buddy! How's the mountain?"

"Not good," a gruff voice that definitely wasn't Torsten's replied, and my whole body tensed at the words.

Shit.

"Who is it?" Espen whispered behind me.

I twisted and mouthed, "Halvar."

His eyes widened. "You need—"

I shook my head. I could handle a phone call with the big guy... probably. Espen took the hint and sauntered toward the bathroom, just as Øyvin wandered into the bedroom, the sound of the bed groaning under his weight meeting my ears.

"Are you there?" Halvar grumbled.

"Yes, here." I spun back to the window, a narrow slip of glass visible between the pair of cream-colored curtains. "What's wrong?"

"Find Aurora and get back as quickly as possible," Halvar said, his voice tense and laced with an ounce of panic.

"Forgive the bluntness"—he scoffed—"but are you aware that Aurora is not a *distant relative* and possibly Freija's daughter?" It hadn't been fully confirmed, but the young woman was a match for the late-Queen. "She even has her unique, gray-and-brown eyes."

Silence hung heavy across the line, like the world was holding its breath to hear what the beast from the mountain had to say.

A deep and long sigh met my ear. "She is Freija's." A statement, not a question.

"Why didn't you tell us?" I pushed the curtain further aside before peering across the lake. Something on the island moved, but I refocused my attention on the phone call. Probably just the wind.

"Because the fewer people that know the better," Halvar replied. "Her safety and the fjell's safety are at stake here, and I won't have either jeopardized."

My stomach lurched at the underlying threat, and I sucked in a breath between my teeth—which was a grave mistake.

"Tell me what happened," Halvar ground out, and part of me, the part that had never done well with orders or authority figures, wanted to hang up on the guy.

"About the whole *safety* thing..."

"Tell me. Now."

"We may have lost her." A rumble of anger started up, so I quickly pulled the pin on the proverbial grenade. "She kind of ran away after I pulled the *who's your mommy* card."

Heavy breathing thrummed against my ear and I scrunched up my face, bracing for impact. "Find her and get back before the end of the week. Or else..."

"Or else, what?" *I really should have duct tape on standby for my mouth.* No wonder Øyvin was always slapping his palm across my loose lips.

Halvar sucked in a breath. "The fjell needs her and *you* back here immediately."

I reared back. "Me?"

"We have cave-ins, mirages, and entrances crumbling around us. There is only so much my magic can do. What I have of Freija's magic—the main source for keeping those entrances shielded but open—clearly isn't enough."

"Isn't enough? Espen said you and the guards had closed some of the entrances to hide them. That you'd used your magic to create those cave-ins."

"Some, not all. The royal fjell magic was never meant to stray too far from the mountain. I didn't realize that would extend to *you* having her magic, too."

I pressed my fingers to my temple. "What *exactly* do you mean, big guy?"

"Majority of those cave-ins weren't controlled. Parts of the mountain are growing weak. A fissure we have been monitoring grows by the day. We need both you and I here to protect the fjell."

"But I went back to the US for Thanksgiving and nothing happened. I was gone for a week and thousands of miles away. A literal ocean and some cornfields away."

He sighed. "There were cave-ins while you were away. The Council and I attributed those to Freija's demise. It would appear that we were wrong."

I swallowed hard. "Well shit."

"Get back as fast as you can." He hung up, and I let my hand and the phone fall away from my ear, unease creeping across my limbs.

My thoughts ran a mile a minute, flitting between everything he'd said and back again. If what Halvar said was true—and I wasn't going to question the likely-ancient being's logic—then he needed me and my new magic back at the fjell ASAP. Plus Aurora, of course.

I huffed and brushed my palm across my mouth and chin. Trust me to land myself in yet another chaotic situation and have the well-being of an entire hidden community resting upon my shoulders.

Something moved on the island across the lake again and my head snapped to attention. Narrowing my eyes, I tried to discern what it was, but it was a bit too far away to distinguish whether it was an animal, human, or just a tree swaying in the wind. My gut yelled at me and my curiosity peaked, so I sprinted across the room and grabbed my new DSLR camera from its bag. Turning it on, I ran back to the window and lined up a couple quick shots.

The lens clicked twice, and I peered at the screen. Nothing unusual. Just a snow-covered island, with rocks and trees dotting the slightly mounded surface. The glow from the moon reflected off the snow, providing a decent, but not ideal, light source.

Popping my hip and settling my weight to one side, I zoomed in on the image and scanned it for any other sign of life. I could've sworn I saw something moving out—

I sucked in a breath. In the middle of the second picture, slightly obscured by a thin birch tree, was a white-and-gray figure—too tall to be a rock and too curvy to be a tree. A line of copper peeked out of a white hood-like shape...

"Have you been hiding right under our noses?" I whispered to myself.

It couldn't be her. Could it? No, it was probably just a trick of the light. At this hour and with only the delicate blue glow of moonlight for clarity, my mind was likely playing tricks on me. It wouldn't be wise to head outdoors in the dark and cold right now. I'd wait until sunrise to have a better look.

33

LENNIE

I opened my eyes. What if it *was* Aurora?

There was zero fucking chance I was waiting any longer. With my eyes having adjusted to the dark bedroom, I gently removed Espen's hand from my abdomen, nudged Øyvin's foot aside, and wiggled to the end of the bed like a worm. Slipping from beneath the covers, I crossed the room and grabbed my clothes. I was much less likely to bump into something in the hallway while pulling them on. So, I tiptoed across the floorboards, hoping they wouldn't creak, and snuck toward the door.

With a quick look over my shoulder to make sure my guys were still sleeping, I let out a soft sigh of relief and slunk into the hallway.

Once dressed, I peeked at my phone. *Six in the freaking morning?* It was way too early to be up, and yet, I'd barely slept. Thoughts of my island photo and the potential Fjell heir had haunted me every minute. If that was her and she moved before dawn, I'd be kicking myself... and dead as soon as Halvar found out.

I had to take charge and be a little secretive this morning. I had to check on this hunch by myself. How embarrassing would it be if it wasn't her and instead was a weird branch? No, I couldn't tell my guys. If I was wrong, they'd never let it go. Especially Øyvin.

Whatever I found on that island, there wasn't a chance in hell I was making the long drive back to Skolvik empty-handed. I had to prove myself to the Fjell Fae Council. And, while I usually wasn't one for obeying orders or any sort of authority figure, Halvar, admittedly, scared me enough to spur me into action. That and with Fjell Fae magic now coursing through me, I felt an obligation to the place and its people.

I moved to close the bedroom door completely and Espen stirred. He peeped out from beneath the covers, narrowing his sleepy eyes at me.

"Can't sleep. Going outside for some fresh air," I whispered.

He nodded and yawned before turning and hitching the covers back over his face.

I didn't like partially lying to him, but I had a hunch, and I wanted to follow it through. The guys would yell at me for it, but the mountain was struggling and needed me back, so we didn't have time for dilly-dallying.

I pulled on my jacket, snow pants, boots and gloves. Stepping outside into the chilly morning air, the sun's rays barely peeked over the horizon, and the snow twinkled in the soft glow from the porch light.

I needed to find Aurora... today.

If yesterday's photo was anything to go by, I knew where to look.

In the middle of the frozen lake, the little island sat peacefully, covered in a thin blanket of snow. There had been no signs of life over there last night, not even a puff of smoke from a fire, but I could've sworn I saw movement among the skinny trees during my call with Halvar.

I took a deep breath and assessed my options, which were, rather unfortunately, limited to one. I had to cross the frozen lake.

A shudder ran across my skin at the thought. It was stupid. Extremely stupid. But, today I was getting shit done. Curiosity may have killed cats, but I was a demi-fae. Huge difference... I hoped.

I traipsed around the edge of the lake, moving further and further away from the cabin and honed in on a spot that looked like the shortest distance from shore to isle. The entire time I cast looks over my shoulder, making sure I wasn't being followed. Øyvin would lose his ever loving mind if he saw what I was about to do... and would probably mutter something about me constantly finding trouble. Which wasn't wrong, but wasn't helpful. I was taking initiative, being a leader. Had I failed to loop in my team? Yes. Had all our other ventures proved unsuccessful? Also, yes. This was more of a potentially embarrassing, ask for forgiveness later kind of thing. I should know, I was well versed in those.

I reached the edge of the lake where I would cross and knelt down in the snow to inspect the ice. It appeared thick from multiple angles, but as we'd seen on the other lake, the ice could be deceptive. With that in mind, I straightened up and took a deep breath, checking in on my powers. Warmth swirled in my sternum—present and awake. If things went awry, I couldn't use water magic, but I could at least blast my way back through the ice with rocks.

Sending a prayer down to the devil in hopes I wouldn't be meeting him today, I crept slowly onto the ice, sliding one foot forward and then the other, the frozen water holding my weight. *Thank fuck.* I shimmied further along, one step at a time, listening carefully for any creaks from the ice. Hearing none, I kept moving. If the guys looked out of the cabin window right now... Well, I'd probably get my ass handed to me and not in the pleasurable way I'd prefer.

Crack.

My heart jumped into my throat and my gaze snapped to my feet. The ice had splintered like a spider-web with sharp tendrils, but only under my left foot.

"Fuck."

I swallowed hard and gently scooted my right foot forward. The ice creaked like an old wooden door, but didn't crack further. Sliding my left foot again, I let out a sigh of relief. That was too close and probably too much weight on one spot.

"Maybe I should distribute my weight more?" I crouched and moved onto my hands and knees. The ice beneath me remained silent, my blurry reflection staring back at me. "Yeah, that feels safer."

With a deep breath, I started to shuffle across the frozen lake.

About halfway across, my arms began to tremble. The tension in my body put pressure on my muscles, but I didn't dare relax. "Nicely done, Martin," I muttered to myself, voicing my thoughts in hopes that my mind wouldn't drift to images of falling through. "What would your mother say? *Evelyn Martin, how dare you put your life at risk... again! I taught you better than that.* Yes, I know, Mom. You did. I'm sorry. Can I introduce you to my two partners?"

My mind drifted back to her meeting them last year at her house. The look on her face when she'd seen Espen and Øyvin looming over me was priceless. And most definitely had her internally doing a happy dance in hopes that I might marry one of them. "Well, Mom, I am marrying them... or at least one of them."

Had I told her yet? If not, note to self.

I scooted forward, getting closer to my destination, my gloved hands splayed over the glassy surface.

"But there's more too." This part I could never tell her. "I'm actually part fae now, and in order to keep me safe and the magic close to the mountain, I need to become a permanent resident of Norway. Marrying Espen is the easiest way to do that."

Saying it out loud sounded as crazy as it was.

I peered toward the shore, and my lips twitched into a quick smile. I had roughly a quarter of the distance remaining as my mind drifted back to my fake conversation with my mom.

"*Do you even love him?* Yes, I do love him. No, it's not just for immigration purposes... At least, not anymore." I shook my head and chuckled, willing myself to keep moving over the ice. "Look at me, talking to myself to distract from the fact I'm a few inches away from death. What a way to start the day."

With a soft breeze and the stillness of a church keeping me company, it took another ten minutes, but I eventually made it to the other side and threw myself onto the snowy shore. Flopping onto my back, I stared up at the sky and took a moment to catch my breath. The sun peeked over the horizon, casting my surroundings in a light-blue glow.

My heart beat hard and fast, like a camera stuck on rapid shutter speed, as I took several steadying breaths. "That was stupid."

"Agreed," a feminine voice said.

34

LENNIE

I scrambled to my knees, finding Aurora leaning against a tree, arms crossed and her braided hair resting over her shoulder. Her lips were pursed and her eyes watched me closely, like an owl visually dissecting their prey.

"We need to talk," I wheezed. Had I tried holding my breath across parts of the lake?

"There's a land bridge on the other side of the island by the way."

My shoulders slumped and I hung my head in defeat. "Fucking hell."

"I was hoping you'd fall through."

"Rude!"

Aurora shrugged and walked off, muttering, "Entertainment."

I clambered to my feet and shot after the fae as quickly as I could, lifting my feet extra high to step through the calf-deep snow. Aurora's white jacket and pants blended seamlessly with the natural surroundings. If she put her hood up, I could easily lose her again. I couldn't have that. Halvar would probably sacrifice me to some Fjell Fae gods that I'd yet to learn about or their ancestors that bestowed magic. Or maybe he'd present me on some sort of rocky platter saying, "Apologies but this one is faulty. You should probably take her powers back and redistribute them elsewhere. In fact, please do." I shook off the thought and pushed aside a snow-covered branch, refocusing on the task at hand.

"I know you don't want to come back with us, Aurora, but the Fjell needs you."

She scoffed and pressed deeper onto the little island.

"The car is that way." I pointed behind us, doing my best to follow her. Boulders the size of tiny houses inhabited the middle of the isle along with a dense copse of tree trunks, their branches empty for the winter, save for the pines. Everything was covered in a layer of snow and the entire scene looked like a beignet doused in icing sugar.

"I never said I was going back with you."

"Did you not hear the part about the Fjell needing you?"

Reaching a clearing in the middle of the island where the mainland and our cabin wasn't visible, Aurora spun on me. Her eyes flared, full of rage and annoyance. "No one has ever asked if I care. *I* do not need the fjell now, and I never have before."

"Are you sure?" I turned around, pointing at her little campsite. A small gas camping stove, the size of a coffee-press, sat outside a pale gray one-man tent that looked like an oversized butterfly cocoon, and a few logs were scattered around the tamped down snow, likely used as little chairs. "This setup is great and all, but looks kind of cold."

My breath caught in my throat as it dawned on me. *Oh, shit.* "Do you have a home? Have you been homeless since Vigdis died? I thought you lived with Marius and the young wolves?"

She sneered and crossed her arms, popping her hip. Damn, the sass on this one. She was giving me a run for my money with that attitude. "I have a home. But someone has been hunting me, so my home is no longer safe until they leave." She waved her hand as if to *shoo* me. "Please do."

I matched her stance. "I'm not leaving here without you."

"Then you'll be here a while, because I'm not going anywhere."

Was this what it was like to try and reason with me? Damn. I felt bad for everyone who'd ever tried to make me do anything.

"Look here," I started. "All I'm saying is, you are needed by people who you may not know, nor even care about."

She squinted and tilted her head. *Good, she's listening.*

"When your mother died she illegally transferred her magic to Halvar and, by extension, me. I don't know the ins and outs of the Fjell Fae magic or royals or, shit, even the full extent of whatever magic I have in here." I tapped my chest.

"Sounds like a *you* problem."

I took a deep breath and tried to quell the frustration that arose within me. "It is. But *you* are the heir, not me. Your presence is needed by the Fjell Fae Council and the residents of the mountain, to accept or reject whatever their proposal is. From the brief history I know, there's some form of ceremony for the heir, and the royal power will be recycled by the ancestors and bestowed upon the new monarch. But since Freija didn't die with her magic, things might have changed a bit, so who the fuck knows now. My point is, Halvar and the Council need you. I have to bring you back with me."

"You have the wrong person," Aurora said.

"Why do you think that?"

"Heirs are powerful. I'm not."

I let out a sigh, my breath fogging in front of me. "Heirs are granted more power when they ascend to the throne." Fuck, I hoped Nora hadn't been lying about that history lesson.

Aurora held out her palm and let out a steady breath. Slowly but surely a gray pebble formed in her hand. "See?"

"That just reinforces that you're a Fjell Fae, chickadee."

Aurora grimaced and threw the rock aside. "That's the extent of it."

"Size isn't everything," I said, glad that my guys couldn't hear those words coming from my mouth.

"Really?" Aurora tilted her head to one side, her voice filled with sarcasm. "Royals have decent power and skills from what I've been told—"

"And you're without *any* impressive skills?"

She took a step back and shrugged. "You have the wrong person. I'm not who you think I am."

I readjusted my hat. This was like arguing with a tree. No, not a tree, a stump. "Look, if you don't come back with me, I may very well be killed and the mountain is already falling apart."

She blinked and a flicker of concern washed over her face. "Falling apart?"

"I don't know the full extent, but there have been cave-ins, cracks, and the like. The fjell is home to hundreds of fae and it's crumbling without the royal magic to keep it intact."

She opened her mouth and paused, her eyebrows drawing together. "People are losing their homes?

"Like I said, I don't know everything, but I do know they need their heir." Hope bubbled within me. "Please, come back with us. We have cookies."

Aurora shook her head and took another step backward. "Don't ever become a diplomat."

My bubble of hope popped, and I grumbled like Øyvin as I paced a few steps before turning to her. "Just come back to Skolvik. Talk to the Council. Hear them out. That's all I ask."

She set her hands on her hips.

"Please."

Those brown-and-gray eyes, the same as her mother's, studied me intently as she tilted her head to one side. Did she think like her mother? Was she considerate and kind in nature? Hopefully she at least had some of the late Queen's traits. That she might see reason and come to the fjell and speak to the Council.

Aurora's lips hooked into a grimace, and panic welled inside me. This wasn't working. I needed to do something. I peered around frantically, coming up empty handed. *Wait a second...* My gaze flicked to my hands. My magic! I could show her.

"I'm pretty sure this shit"—I formed a ball of light in my palms and motioned it forward, letting the glowing and swirling orb float between us—"was meant for you."

"Don't use that magic on me." Aurora stepped forward and swatted it away. The ball disintegrated at her touch, the magic fizzling out. "I'm not going to Skolvik."

My shoulders slumped, but an idea popped into my head. I cursed myself for my own brilliant, but troublesome, thinking. If this went wrong, I'd end up with my head on a stone tableau. Or my ass. Or both. *Please work.*

"Go long," I said and backed up, preparing a sparking ball of light in my hand. Specifically, an orb that could stun, like the one I'd shot toward the wolf. I pushed the intention into the ball that formed, hoping it would work. My stance matched that of a quarterback, my arms bent, hands hiked up as if I was preparing to launch a football into the end-zone. Aurora stepped backward, her eyes wide like I was crazy—which wasn't untrue.

Taking a deep breath, I pulled my arm back. "Ready?"

She shook her head, brows pinching together.

I launched the ball toward her face. She dipped left, narrowly avoiding it, which I was expecting. I swung my tingling left arm and sent a second curved shot that came at her from the side. Before she could figure out what I was up to, the new orb hit her smack-dab across the face and sent her to the ground with a thud.

Yes!

She didn't move.

Shit.

I ran over and bent down in the snow beside her. The light ball hadn't burned her, but her cheek and temple were both red, like a big ol' shiner was going to form in the next few hours. I winced at the sight, then stuck my palm in front of her nose and mouth.

"Please don't be dead."

Warm air brushed across my fingers, and I tilted my head back in relief.

Was this whole plan utterly ludicrous? Yes.

Had it worked though? Also, yes.

I didn't like taking away Aurora's choice—she really should be able to have her decisions respected—but right now the fjell was falling apart, I needed to prove myself, and I'd seen what Halvar could do when he was angry. So, she was coming back to Skolvik, no matter what. All I had to do was figure out how to get her off the island.

I surveyed my surroundings: trees, snow, Aurora's small camp with tent and—

My eyes widened. *Her tent!*

Stepping over her prone form, I raced to the small tent. I tugged the zipper and pushed aside the fabric. There, on the floor, was a gray-and-navy sleeping bag and thin camping mattress. *Jackpot.* I grabbed both and ran back over to Aurora. She still lay in the snow, which probably wasn't good for her health, but that was the least of my worries right now.

I sized up both the mattress and the sleeping bag. Which would be easier to slide her back to the cabin in? The mattress was lightweight, but there weren't any straps to hold her in place. The sleeping bag though... That could contain her and I could scrunch the material in my hands more easily than the flimsy mattress. I flung the latter aside and stepped up beside Aurora.

Grabbing her by the feet, I shoved them into the bag first then pulled it underneath her, sheathing her in it. She didn't make a noise, but her chest still rose and fell. Hopefully she hadn't hit her head, but Espen could heal her, surely. Problem for future Lennie.

With Aurora securely inside the sleeping bag, I hooked the top end around my fists and started dragging the bag toward the land bridge she'd mentioned that was indeed right behind us. Snow covered the thin spit of earth, trampled and frozen enough to let me easily walk on the surface.

Aurora didn't stir, her face poking out of the hole at the top of the bag near my hands, the "foot" end sliding along in the snow. She wasn't extremely heavy, but I'd be in trouble without the bag.

I heaved the Fjell Fae heir across the little bridge and set out for the cabin, hoping she didn't wake up until I could enact part two of my plan: shove her into the car and drive.

I looked over my shoulder at her and chuckled, recalling how she'd kidnapped me recently. "Payback's a bitch in orange."

35

ESPEN

Subtle rays of golden sunlight kissed the window in the bedroom, alighting on my features and bringing a smile to my face. Today was the day we'd remove Wilhelm as pack Alpha and the three of us could continue our search for Aurora in peace.

"She bolted!" a grumbly voice yelled in my ear. I snorted and rolled onto my back. "Lennie's gone missing."

With a sigh, I opened my eyes. Øyvin hovered above me, his gaze wide and blond hair a mess. "She woke up early and went for a walk," I replied, my voice hoarse with sleep.

"I know. I was half-awake, too." He waved his hand toward the window. "She's not out there though."

My pulse quickened and I pulled the covers away from my face. "What?"

"I can't see her anywhere."

Shit.

I jumped out of bed, swaying slightly on my feet as I grabbed my socks and a pair of winter trousers. Øyvin threw a t-shirt at me. He was already fully dressed, jacket on and boots fastened, ready to go. I tugged on my clothes and grabbed my sweater off the floor before moving out into the living room. Øyvin ripped open the curtains, and the wintry lake vista came into view.

"See. Nowhere!" he exclaimed, panic lacing his tone. Panic that slowly infected me too.

I pulled my sweater on and stepped up to the window, scanning the scenery. White on white on white with specks of green and the light-blue of the frozen lake was all I could see. I let out a long breath and put my hands on my hips, assessing the situation—

Orange. A dot of orange came into view on the far side of the lake, and I pointed toward it.

Øyvin stepped up beside me and narrowed his eyes. "That troublesome little..."

"I told you she went on a walk." I turned away from the window and aimed for the kitchen. She'd want coffee this early in the morning, and so did I. "Coffee?"

Øyvin grunted and took up a vigil by the window, his boots still on and his jacket securely fastened at his neck. I took his grunt as a yes and set to work on preparing the coffee, making sure I added some creamer stuff into Lennie's and a huge heap of sugar.

"Espen," the Fjord Fae said after a few minutes, that panicked tone still stuck in his throat. "What is she doing?"

"Walking," I replied, not bothering to look up from my coffee making.

"Espen, she's dragging something."

The spoon fell out of my hand and clattered on the countertop. "What?" I abandoned the drinks in the kitchen and waltzed back to the window to see what he was talking about. Sure enough, just over halfway around the lake, Lennie dragged some sort of bag behind her, straining a little with the weight and the snow. I squinted. "What is that?"

Øyvin inhaled sharply. "It's a fucking sleeping bag." He spun on his heels and stormed out the front door.

My eyes widened. He was right. I shot for the cabin entrance, throwing on my jacket and boots, rushing outside into the cold.

Øyvin stilled by the lake edge, watching Lennie in awe, his eyes about to pop out of his head. I stepped up beside him and took in the frenzy headed toward us.

"Get in the car!" Lennie yelled as she tromped closer. "Get in the car!" She started sprinting—running as best she could with the heavy sleeping bag and the snow boots she wore, making surprising progress.

"What have you done?" Øyvin growled as she ran straight past us toward the car.

"Go get our shit, and get in the car," she bit out, hauling— *Oh, no.*

"Lennie, is that Aurora?" I asked, shock weighing down my limbs and inhibiting any movement. *Halvar is going to kill us.* There would be no more forest hikes, no more morning coffee dates at Oddvar's, and, most sadly, no more *yoga.* We were doomed.

Lennie panted as she set down the sleeping bag with the person in it, the latter's eyes firmly shut, her chest moving lightly.

Lennie gave us a shaky two thumbs up. "Yes. I got shit done."

I brushed my hand across my beard while Øyvin stewed beside me, his eyes no doubt boring a hole into Lennie's chest. "Sometimes I think you're more trouble than you're worth," he ground out.

"Your cock believes otherwise," she replied, then clapped her hands together. "Chop chop. Let's go." And with that she disappeared inside, probably going to grab her stuff and the keys.

Øyvin stomped after her, crossing the threshold with a growl, just as a rustling sounded from the sleeping bag. Aurora groaned and lifted her head. Our eyes met and her gaze widened. I sucked in a sharp breath, and, before she could extract herself from her cocoon, I called forth my power and pulled the roots that lined the gravel driveway toward us. The tendrils shook off their snow cover, snapped in places, and swiftly wrapped around her from shoulders to feet. I wasn't a tree-speaker like Gunvor—able to command trees—but I had some control over the roots thanks to my destroyer powers. Unfortunately, the roots would probably need healing after I was done with them.

"You piece of shit," Aurora spat and wriggled to no avail—the thick tendrils tightening around her upper body.

This was definitely Aurora. Lennie was right, she shared quite a few of her mother's traits, including those marble-like eyes.

I sighed and crossed my arms, my shoulders still tense beneath my jacket. "This goes against a lot of my personal rules and code of ethics."

"Then why are you helping?" Aurora seethed, giving me a familiar glare that I couldn't quite place. I shook off the eerie sensation that rippled across my body at the sight. "Let me guess, you love her, would do anything for her."

I shrugged. "Yes, yes I would."

"Pussy." Aurora kicked her legs like a puppy trying to get out of being held.

I tightened her bindings and frowned. "Behave."

Aurora's responding grimace was the equivalent of a middle finger. I opened my mouth to speak, but Lennie and Øyvin stepped out of the cabin with our bags, the latter with his shiny silver suitcase in one hand and my duffel in the other. He pointed the keys toward the car and unlocked it, the lights on the little passenger car blinking.

Lennie yanked the front door shut and made it all of two steps before a ringing noise filled the morning silence. We all stopped, glancing at each other. Lennie grumbled and dropped her bag on the front deck, unzipping her jacket and grabbing her phone out of the internal breast pocket.

"Andrew," she said, answering the call. "Is someone dying? Mom and Dad okay? Kind of early to be calling."

I let out a breath and turned my focus to the angry heir still stuck in her sleeping bag. Øyvin shoved our belongings into the boot and came over to help me with our other cargo.

Coaxing the roots off her, I let them fall into the snow. Aurora growled and wriggled incessantly as I grabbed her feet and Øyvin opened the door to the backseat before lifting her at the shoulders. While we worked on loading the unhappy Fjell Fae into the car, Lennie scurried and loaded her duffel bag into the boot while trying to get her eldest brother off the phone.

"This really isn't a good time," she muttered, slightly out of breath. "Yeah, yeah, sure." She pulled the phone away from her ear and covered the end. "Shotgun," she said and put the phone back to her ear.

Øyvin grumbled and closed the door to the backseat. I shut my side and clambered in behind the wheel. I was definitely going to miss today's council meeting, which was unfortunate, but even without my vote, we had a majority of the council members to support our motion to remove Wilhelm as Alpha. Part of me—the vengeful Lennie's fiancé part—wished I could've been there to witness his downfall though.

Øyvin made an attempt to get into the front passenger seat, but Lennie grabbed his arm and yanked him back. Shaking her head, she mouthed, "Calling shotgun means I get the front seat. She will kill me. You get in there." She pointed at the back, before returning to her call. "No, no, I'm fine. Sorry, Andrew. Yeah, totally, but I really need to go. I'll talk to you soon."

She hung up and swung herself into the seat that Øyvin had tried to claim. His jaw tightened, but he relented and climbed into the back, moving the sleeping bag bound Fjell Fae to a seated position so he could fit.

"Right," I said, trying to pierce the tension in the car with some positivity. "Are we ready to go?"

A single yes sounded among a low hum of displeasure.

Øyvin leaned between the two front seats, grabbed the handle between Lennie's legs and yanked her seat forward, giving himself more leg room. He slumped back in his spot, all scrunched up still, and threw on his seatbelt. "Now, I'm ready."

"Is the child-lock on?" Lennie asked, her cheeks slightly flushed as she turned to check on the two in the back.

They both grumbled, sounding wholly unamused.

She beamed. "Great. Let's go home."

36

LENNIE

I sat at the small, circular dining table in the boathouse finishing up my oatmeal with cinnamon and sugar. Øyvin sat across from me drinking his coffee, his shoulders relaxed as he gazed toward the kitchen window. We arrived back in Skolvik late last night and chose to wait until this morning to return Aurora to the fjell. To make sleeping arrangements easier and protect our precious cargo from bolting, we'd split up, sending Espen and Aurora to his cabin for the night.

So, it was just me, Øyvin, and the water lapping against the building's stilted foundation this morning. The curtains were drawn to keep in the warmth, and my duffel bag was still downstairs beside the piano, much to Øyvin's annoyance.

"Are you going to join us at the mountain or do you need to head below the surface?" I asked before eating another spoonful of my breakfast.

Øyvin set his coffee on the table between us and leaned back in his chair, brushing a hand through his hair. "Thought I'd see this through before—"

Ring, ring, ring.

We both straightened, and Øyvin pulled his phone out of his pocket.

Ring, ring, ring.

His eyes narrowed momentarily as he read the name, then answered the call and brought the device to his ear. "Yes?"

Muffled words breached our contented silence. I started to mouth "who is it" as Øyvin rose to his feet, the chair scraping across the hardwood floor. His brow furrowed and he marched toward the sofa, resting his free hand on the back of it. His grasp tightened, knuckles paling, and I gulped down the last mouthful of my meal. I gingerly returned my spoon to the now empty bowl, careful not to disturb his call. What on earth had him tensing like the roof was about to cave in?

"How long?" he asked. Whatever the answer was had him pivoting toward the front door. He pressed his phone between his ear and shoulder, holding it in place while he pulled on his boots. "Have they been informed?" He didn't even give me a backward glance as he grabbed his jacket and strode out the door.

I leaned back in my chair and crossed my arms. *What the hell is going on?*

Not wanting to be kept out of the loop, I stood, placed my bowl in the dishwasher, and headed over to the entryway. While it wasn't my responsibility to know everything as a non-member of the Fjord Fae, a nervous energy rode me hard today, low-grade adrenaline coursing through my limbs. And color me curious, but early morning tense phone calls never bode well.

I pressed my side against the front door and sporadic words met my ears. "Fjord... Ceremony... Heir..."

Heir?

My brow furrowed as silence grew again, Øyvin no doubt listening intently to the call. Jittery interest and concern rushed through me. I needed to know what was happening.

Without waiting another second, I yanked on my boots and grabbed my jacket off the hook. Øyvin's voice subsided, footfalls tapping against the dock that wrapped around one side of the boathouse. He was moving to the fjord side of the building.

Purposefully avoiding wearing my orange snow pants and opting for only insulated leggings instead today, I pulled on my jacket and gloves, threw my hat on, and headed out into the cool morning.

Øyvin stood with his back against the red boathouse beside the boat garage door, his phone nowhere to be seen as he stared across the fjord. The tall, snowy pines and gray waters sat dormant beneath a dull glow, the sun not bothering to grace us with her presence today. Øyvin watched the scene closely with his hands in his front pockets, like something was about to breach the surface. The picture of him and the fjord in front of us sent a shiver of anxiety down my spine.

"What's wrong?"

Øyvin pursed his lips and shook his head.

I rolled my eyes. *Love it when he's verbose.*

Stepping beside him, I settled against the wall and pulled my hat down over my ears to hide from the cold breeze that swept across the fjord. "Is there a Fjord heir?" I asked. Based on what I'd overheard, it sounded like a spawn of Balder was about to rise from the depths and wreak havoc on our little village.

Øyvin nodded, and I drew in a sharp breath. "His name is Reuven."

Well, shit. "Anything like his dad?"

Øyvin shrugged. "I've never met him in person, but from what I gather, he's a shade of his father—has some of his temper but not the entire brutish personality."

"This Reuven doesn't live around here, then?"

He shook his head and glanced down at me. "He lives in Iceland. Has for quite some time after a betrothal that now has more meaning than we first thought."

"Sounds dramatic."

Øyvin looked back across the fjord and sighed. "Story for another time, but let's just say Reuven didn't have a choice in the matter."

Another heir with their choices taken from them. My chest tightened and I toed the planks beneath me. I was to blame for taking away Aurora's choice, bringing her to Skolvik against her wishes. My stomach churned at the thought. Yeah, I'd made a mistake—one that would likely save me from a beheading, but it still didn't sit right with me. I'd apologize at some point, but first we needed to head up the mountain and introduce her to the Council.

As if thinking of them magically produced them, light footfalls thumped against the dock and Espen and Aurora waltzed around the corner of the boathouse.

"Good morning." Espen beamed and hopped over to me, planting a kiss on my cold cheek. He was in his thick green winter jacket, with the hat I'd given him for Christmas firmly on his head, wisps of his unruly brown hair peeking out across his forehead. "You sleep all right?"

I nodded toward Øyvin. "Yeah. He didn't bite."

"I was too tired," the Fjord Fae groused and honed in on Aurora. She locked eyes with him and didn't blink, didn't move. She stood there, tendrils of her silver-and-brown braided hair whipping around her, the white jacket tightened around her chin shielding her from the chilly air drifting down the fjord. I sucked in a breath between my teeth—her right cheek was still a little pink from where my stunning magic had smacked her yesterday. Yeah, I really had a lot to apologize for.

"Did *you* sleep okay?" I asked Espen. Hopefully he hadn't had any problems with Aurora.

"Yes, but..."

My eyes widened at his remark. "But what?" Why was there never a dull moment in life? Could a woman never have five minutes of peace?

"Wilhelm was removed from the Forest Fae Council of Elders last night."

"That's great news!"

"Agreed, but that's not all."

Nope, apparently there wasn't any peace for an almost twenty-nine-year-old demi-fae. I let out a long sigh and wiped my fingers across my brow. "What now?"

"Wilhelm disappeared. Ran off with a bunch of his pack according to Turi. Evaded my soldiers."

Of course he did. "That can't be a good sign. But at least he's out of everyone's hair."

Espen shrugged while Øyvin let out a low grumble of agreement.

"Who's pack Alpha?" Aurora piped up, reminding us that she was still here and hadn't bolted herself.

Espen turned to face her. "Marius. Gunvor sponsored him and the Council agreed to test his skills and appoint him Alpha."

Aurora let out a long-winded sigh, shoulders relaxing. "Well, good. Now, can we get this over with?"

"Do you promise not to run off while we walk over to the mountain?" I asked. "Are you being agreeable today?"

Aurora shrugged. "I'm already here. You have the wrong person, and I'd like to get through this without being tied up again or threatened."

Espen cleared his throat. "I also promised to drive her back to Alvdalen if she decides not to stay."

I swatted his arm. "Why'd you do that? She's the heir."

His face creased and he raised his hands above his head. "I'm trying to keep the peace here."

Øyvin let out a single grunt, and I couldn't argue with my bubbly fiancé. While I may disagree with offering her passage, Aurora was mellower today and didn't look like she wanted to rip my face off.

"Fine," I muttered and set my hands on my hips. "Want to get going then?"

All three fae nodded.

We traipsed through the snow-laden village. Frost painted the corners of the windows we passed and our breath fogged before us. I waved to Oddvar through the window of the café as we passed, the elder villager preparing for the day's customers, some of whom already graced the tables within the establishment.

The trail on the north side of the village rose into the dense forest, the snow cushioning our steps as we strode out of town toward the nearest entrance to the fjell—one of the side entrances I'd learned about over Christmas. We passed snow-covered rocks, treetops dusted with a layer of powder, and frozen brooks, the ice undulating where it had been locked in place by the cold. It wasn't long before we reached our destination and my mouth fell open.

"Well, shit," I muttered as we stilled at the entrance to the mountain. This was what Halvar had been talking about on our phone call a couple of days ago.

A mound of stones covered in a light layer of snow blocked the magical entry to the fjell.

Espen brushed snow off the nearest boulder. "We'll have to try the main entrance further down."

"Use your magic," Øyvin said to me with a raised brow.

"What?"

He rolled his eyes. "Press your magic into that."

I looked around, my eyes wide. "It's the middle of the day, and we're not that far from town. Now doesn't seem like the best time to be testing my demi-fae powers."

Espen stepped aside and Øyvin crowded me, forcing me to take a couple of steps backward until my butt bumped against the rockfall. "Try."

Damn did he know how to activate that Martin family competitiveness within me. I rolled my shoulders and grumbled before turning to face my adversary. The magic in my sternum swirled, like it could tell it was home and where it was needed.

I pressed my gloved hand against the nearest boulder. Magic zipped down my left arm, winding its way down the lightning-shaped scar and through my palm. I willed the stone to budge, pictured it rolling aside like the ones they used as doors in the dungeons. The rock grumbled and groaned as it moved minutely to the left, setting off a ripple effect. The stones around it shuddered, and I immediately removed my hand, withdrawing my power. "Maybe not," I muttered as I shuffled back toward the others.

Øyvin pressed his thumb and forefinger against my lower back, steadying me. "At least we know you can move a couple tons of stone."

"Uh-huh." While I'd almost caused another rock slide that could've injured us, he was right. I had moved the stones with ease. Was it enough to get us inside? No. But it was *something*. A bubble of pride grew within me, warming me from the inside out.

"Good attempt." Espen's eyes crinkled at the corner as he extended his hand to me. "Shall we head for the main entrance? See if that one is open?"

"Yes, but first"—I looked at Aurora and nodded over my shoulder—"give it a go."

"You've already seen the extent of my Fjell powers," she replied.

"Sure, but now you're right next to the mountain. It might help."

Aurora grumbled and shook her head.

She pressed her hand against the rock closest to her and a second later it budged... by a quarter of an inch and settled back into its position like it couldn't be bothered to get out of its comfortable spot.

My eyes widened and I glanced at Espen and Øyvin. The former pinched his lips together, while the latter wore an unreadable blank face. Their gazes met mine though, and their eyes betrayed them—uncertainty.

"Well..." Espen straightened and gave Aurora a smile. "Not every fae perfects their skills early in life. I'm sure with a bit of time you'll be moving mountains!"

If there was ever a time to appreciate Espen's ability to pivot a conversation or lighten the mood, now was it.

Aurora stuffed her hands in her jacket pockets and stepped back. "Told you."

"It'll be fine," I said, sounding more like I was trying to convince myself than her.

She rolled her eyes and strode away, Espen following and then pulling up beside her as they headed back down the trail. "Come along, this way to the main entrance," the bubbly fae said.

I peered after them, my steps faltering as I followed Øyvin along the snowy trail. This wasn't good. What if she was right and I'd nabbed the wrong person? Everything I'd been told and seen had led me to believe she was the heir, but... My stomach churned and visions of the guys calling my parents to inform them of my untimely demise filled my mind.

As Espen and Aurora traipsed ahead, I pulled on Øyvin's sleeve and brought him to a stop. "How common is the name Aurora in Norway?"

His forehead creased. "Not uncommon."

"Shit."

"What are you thinking?"

"Maybe we *do* have the wrong person."

Øyvin shook his head. "She does look like Queen Freija, but..."

"But?"

"There's only one way to find out, and Espen and I won't let Halvar kill you."

I squeezed his forearm. "Promise?"

He smiled. "Promise."

Thankfully, the main entrance was miraged like a cliff-face with no rock slide in sight. When we pressed against the rocky facade, the magic granted us entry and let us slip behind the illusion.

The temperature inside the rugged mountain tunnel was slightly warmer than that outside, so I pulled off my hat and gloves, shoving them into my jacket pocket. Espen did the same, while Aurora lowered the oversized hood of her white jacket, and Øyvin ran his hand through his blond hair.

"Where's Halvar?" I asked the two soldiers guarding the entry.

Their short capes, attached at one shoulder, fluttered around their waists and both nodded to Espen and Øyvin. The one to my right turned his gaze on me. "Council chambers. He's in their daily meeting."

"Excellent." I strode forward, Espen on my heels and Aurora between him and Øyvin. Without discussing it, we fell into a protective formation, our treasure secured between us. While I still owed her an apology, that would have to wait until after we spoke to Halvar.

We wound our way through the rough stone tunnels dotted with magical sconces every few yards, passing fae who nodded in greeting before staring at Aurora. It had only been a handful of months since I first stepped inside these meandering passages, but I now recognized them and knew where I was going... or maybe that was my new magic guiding me? Either way, it wasn't long before the four of us stepped through the blue quartz-like stone archway into the throne room.

Guards spun to attention, their gazes honing in on us—the only other beings in the room. A pang of emotion ripped through me at the sight of the empty throne and I glanced over my shoulder at Aurora. She scanned the space, taking in the glassy sky-blue walls and the crystal facets around the seat of power. Who knew what was going through her head right now, but the time had come to deliver her to Halvar and the Council as requested.

I aimed for the door to the left of the throne. I'd never been through it, but I'd witnessed Halvar and Queen Freija use it countless times.

A guard stood vigil outside the arched door that was fastened to the mountain. I strode toward it and he stammered, moving to block me from the doorway. Raising my hand to knock, he reached for my wrist. One grumble from Øyvin had the soldier rethinking his priorities and he stepped back.

"We were sent on a mission by the Council," I said, hoping I could calm down the soldier. "They're expecting us." *Kind of.*

He narrowed his eyes, then shrugged as if to say it was my funeral. Which it might honestly be, but I was also doing as requested. So, the Council couldn't be too annoyed by my interrupting their meeting.

I knocked, and instead of waiting for a reply, pushed open the wooden door.

The walls inside were slate-gray but veins of the sky-blue stone in the throne room cleaved through them like a mangled spiderweb. Light orbs hung from the ceiling and flickered from sconces on either side of the doors—of which there were two more on the other side of the room. Eleven council members, including the light-wielding Fjell Fae, Torsten, sat around a large stone slab in the center of the room.

All eyes spun to me, and I felt Halvar's annoyance from the head of the table before I caught his tightened glare.

Clasping my hands together in front of me and rocking on the balls of my feet, I announced, "Delivery."

37

LENNIE

"You found her in one piece, I presume?" Halvar said as he rose from his chair and strode across the room.

"That I did. Vigdis has unfortunately passed, but Aurora is alive and breathing steadily," I reassured the big guy towering over me in his black shirt, equally dark pants with a bajillion pockets, and a stone sword hanging from a belt cinched at his hips.

"Good." He peered over his shoulder. "Shall we move this to the throne room?"

Nods flitted around behind him and chairs scraped across the floor.

He motioned for me to return to the throne room and I did as requested, backing up a few steps before turning to the trio I'd arrived with. Aurora stood between Espen and Øyvin. Her eyes widened and she swallowed hard as she took in the beast of a man behind me.

Øyvin nudged her and all four of us moved into the middle of the room. It felt like I was about to give a PowerPoint presentation, but instead of a slide show, I was presenting the heir to the Fjell Fae Council. No pressure. Maybe the guys and I should've set up a safeword if something went wrong? A cue that it was time to run. Like papaya or tripod or sexy trolls. I bit my lip. Too late now.

The council members filed out behind Halvar with Torsten bringing up the rear and closing the door behind him with a dull thud. The group fanned out on the left side of the room, some taking a seat on the bench carved into the blue stone wall, while others remained standing. All of them had their eyes locked on the four of us.

Halvar took up position in front of the throne, like a de facto king. But having spent some quality time with the fae in recent weeks, I knew he hadn't claimed that seat. He'd protect it until his dying day, though. His sky-blue eyes honed in on me, Espen, and Øyvin, stopping on each of us in turn. "Thank you for your work. I speak for the Council when I say we are most grateful for your assistance in the retrieval of the heir. Should your factions ever need anything from the Fjell, know that we are amenable." The council members nodded in agreement.

"If you'd please." Halvar raised his hand and motioned to the right side of the room. The three of us slipped to the side, and Aurora made a move to join us—

"Aurora Johansen," Halvar said, his voice echoing around the chamber, and Aurora stopped in her tracks. "My name is Halvar. Welcome to Skolvik."

She turned back to the center of the room and let out a long sigh. Anxiety zipped through me, wondering how this was going to unfold. I shook my hands out hoping to dispel some of the jitters, but there was no use. We were all about to witness a conversation that was unlikely to end well considering her prior thoughts on returning to the fjell.

I looked between Aurora and Halvar. Halvar and Aurora. Then again. *Wait a second.*

My head whipped from one Fjell Fae to the other. Their shoulders were set back like soldiers, their sharp chins slightly raised, their noses a smidgen crooked, and silver hair...

My eyes widened and my pulse thrashed.

"Oh, Halvar…" I let out a long, quiet whistle. "You naughty, naughty boy."

The man himself didn't hear me or chose not to acknowledge me. Nor did he make any remarks about the tittering that rose from the council members and soldiers, their heads flitting between Halvar and the heir. I wasn't the only one who'd noticed.

Espen let out a chuckle while Øyvin quietly mumbled, "Shit."

Now there was no doubt in my mind that we had the right person. Her magic may not have been strong—likely untrained as Espen had touched on during our trek here—but *this* Aurora was a thousand percent the woman we'd been sent to find.

She was a perfect combination of Queen Freija and Halvar.

I didn't know why I hadn't noticed it until now. But seeing them in the same room, facing each other, there was zero doubt in my mind. Aurora was Halvar's daughter, too.

Halvar's gaze washed slowly across the room, bringing the murmuring to a close. He turned back to Aurora and clasped his hands behind him. "You've been made aware of your status as the heir of the Fjell?"

Aurora looked at me before turning her gaze to Halvar. "Yes, I was *bluntly* informed."

"Way to throw me under the bus," I whisper-yelled. I'd done what I needed to do. With minor regrets, but still. We'd found her and she was here. Mission accomplished.

Halvar let that information sink in, his body language betraying none of his thoughts before he continued. "Did Vigdis Johansen ever inform you who your mother was?"

My body tensed and I swallowed hard as my heart clenched at the use of the past tense. I reached out to Espen and Øyvin on either side of me for comfort. Espen gave my hand a gentle squeeze while Øyvin brushed the back of his hand against mine in a reassuring gesture.

"She did not," Aurora answered, regaining my full attention.

Halvar blinked at the response and several council members tilted their heads in surprise.

"What did she tell you of your parents?" Halvar asked.

Aurora crossed her arms, her expression pinched with tension, her tone flat and succinct. "That she didn't know who my father was, but that my mother was an old friend of hers. The two women met centuries ago while she lived on the south coast. Vigdis mentioned that the woman asked for help and requested her guardianship. She never said anything else."

"Did you ever ask about your mother?"

"A couple of times when I was very young."

"And what do you recall of those conversations?" Halvar leaned into the questioning, digging for information from the young woman.

"Not much. She said I looked just like her and that my mother was a Fjell Fae."

"She never mentioned anything else?"

Aurora shook her head.

"Did she ever teach you any specific magic uses?" In other words, what powers did Aurora have? Damn, Halvar really was a good soldier and inquirer.

"Vigdis was a botanist. While she taught me some basics, they were limited to Forest Fae magic which I cannot wield and what little under-standing she had of the Fjell."

"So no affinities were cultivated?"

"None of note."

"Expand upon that... please?" Halvar asked with a nod.

"I whittle and I'm good with knives, but aside from being fast and able to call forth tiny pebbles, there isn't much important."

A line formed between Halvar's eyebrows and several members of the Council brushed their hands across their chins. Sounded to me like she hadn't had the right people to train her fjell powers. No doubt Halvar and the others were thinking the same.

Halvar lowered his head slightly. "Thank you for sharing."

The room fell still, tiny dust motes swirling around in the white-and-blue glow reflecting off the walls. Halvar turned his face to the Council and appeared to have a non-verbal conversation with them all. Nods flitted between several members before Halvar straightened again and faced Aurora who still stood alone in the center of the room.

"Aurora Johansen, daughter of the Fjell, heir of Freija, child of mine."

A collective gasp zipped around the room, and Aurora's eyebrows hit her hairline.

The cat was definitely out of the bag now.

"Based on your story and the evidence presented, the Fjell Fae Council recognizes you as the heir and formally requests your ascent to the throne." Halvar's voice never wavered. "While we don't know what magic the ancestors may grant you considering Queen Freija's actions during her last moments, you are the heir of the Fjell. Do you accept your position as monarch?"

This was it, the moment we'd been waiting for. The moment we'd been working toward. Would she opt to stay, deal with whatever magic nonsense needed to happen for her to become Queen? Would the ancestors bestow royal magic to her? Did she already have some? Or...

"No," Aurora said, her voice echoing through the chamber.

Several strangled breaths emitted from the council members, and I winced.

Halvar didn't budge.

"I have a family in Alvdalen." Aurora straightened and unfurled her arms, setting her hands on her hips. "That is where I belong."

I wanted to argue for her to stay, wanted to convince her to change her mind, but Gunvor's voice popped into my head—a reminder of her parenting strategy and choices. *A woman should be given the freedom to choose her own path.* Regardless of who her parents were, Aurora deserved the right to make her own choices in life. Part of me felt guilty for bringing her here under duress—I'd forced her hand and I shouldn't have. The other part of me was glad to help the Fjell Fae, even if it hadn't gone according to plan.

The beast of the mountain watched his daughter with emotionless features, his eyes locked on her, betraying none of the thoughts likely running through his mind. This probably wasn't the family reunion he was expecting. But I'd seen the way he broke when he held the dying Freija in his arms. To see their child before him must be difficult, and to hear her rejection of his request, even more so.

He swallowed, rolled his shoulders, and clasped his hands behind his back again. "If that is your choice—"

"It is," Aurora said firmly, not backing down from the pressure.

"—then we shall honor your decision."

Aurora brushed her braid off her shoulder and muttered a "thank you" as Torsten stepped up beside Halvar, his eyes wide with panic.

"What does this mean for the Fjell? We can't go on like this. We need a royal and their power to maintain the integrity of our home."

"I'm well aware of the consequences," Halvar replied, swiping his hand across his short beard before casting his gaze toward me.

I flinched at the attention and squirmed on the spot when Torsten looked over, too.

Halvar narrowed his eyes. "Perhaps our future lies elsewhere."

Ah, fuck.

"We must consider our other options," a Fjell Fae council member announced from the other side of the room. His wizened stare locked on me before flitting back to Halvar.

Double fuck.

I clenched my fists together and Espen nudged my shoulder with his. "It'll be okay."

I wasn't so sure about that, but the gnawing anxiety in my stomach didn't last long. Heavy footfalls sounded from the hallway, growing louder and louder by the second. All eyes turned to the entry, and Halvar brought his whispered conversation with Torsten to a close.

Øyvin went ramrod straight beside me and muttered, "He's here."

"He, who?" I peered toward the entrance and took a few steps away from my guys to get a better look.

Aurora spun on the spot, turning her back to the throne, and stumbled backward three paces.

A pair of Fjell Fae soldiers strode into the room, blue-caped Fjord Fae soldiers hot on their heels. A contingent of Fjord Fae breached the archway and broke aside, revealing the two individuals they were guarding, just as Øyvin replied, "Reuven."

38

LENNIE

Air left my lungs as I took in the newcomers, and, more specifically the man in the middle. His dirty blond hair was buzzed short, a scar cleaved his right eyebrow ending at the top of his cheek, and a smattering of stubble graced his chin. If you'd put him in a line-up and asked me to pick out King Balder's son, I'd pick this guy. And it wasn't because of the light-blue eyes or the oval face shape he'd inherited, but the cunning gaze and countenance. This man looked like he'd weathered centuries and could withstand several more.

"Seems like I'm not the only heir to return to Skolvik today," Reuven said as he strolled further into the room, his gaze briefly lingering on Aurora.

I peered over my shoulder and looked up at my Fjord Fae. Øyvin bowed and Reuven returned the gesture with a nod and slanted smile.

Soldiers around the room followed Øyvin's lead, bowing to the Fjord Fae heir. Torsten stepped back among the other council members, all of whom watched on with rapt attention.

"Reuven," Halvar said, his voice like rolling rocks as he nodded toward the royal.

The Fjord Fae heir's short blue cape fluttered around his waist, the underside covered in intricate silver swirls and aquatic creatures, some of which I didn't recognize, including a snake-like animal.

"Halvar. It's been some time." A shrewd note laced Reuven's every word, like he was picking each with care.

"Indeed. Might I welcome you both to the fjell. I don't believe your wife has ever had the fortune of a visit."

Reuven shook his head and motioned to the woman at the back of the room. "May I introduce my wife, Salka Veigarsdóttir."

A tall woman hung back by the entrance. She wore a long beige tunic-style dress with a swirling Nordic pattern down the front, and her onyx hair was bound into a crown braid that wrapped around her head, small tendrils floating down around her pointed ears. Definitely fae, and that notion was hammered home when our eyes met across the room and I flinched. They were pitch black. Completely and utterly black with no whites. It was as if she only had pupils. My body and instincts screamed at me to be wary, my magic swirling faster within my sternum like a warning.

"The Council and I weren't sure you'd be taking up your position as heir."

"You killed my father, Halvar," Reuven said with a single mocking laugh. "You don't expect me to come home after that?"

"I'd expect you not to take several months."

I tilted my head toward Øyvin and mouthed, "New boss?" He nodded once and turned his eyes warily back to the woman, his hands open at his sides in what to some might look like a relaxed state, but I'd seen Øyvin in battle and been around him for long enough to recognize that as one of his ready positions. He didn't think Reuven was a threat, but *she* was. Why?

"As you know, my wife cannot travel via aircraft or among humans as freely as the rest of us," Reuven drawled, his deep voice resonating throughout the chamber.

I looked to Espen and mouthed, "why?"

His eyes were wide and he swallowed hard before mouthing back. "Fire."

Every ounce of oxygen in my lungs disappeared and my stomach sank to my feet. *Fire Fae?*

I needed to hit pause on this show, turn to my guys, and immediately ask for a full fae history lesson. Classes 101, 202, 300. Hell, throw me into the deep end and give me PhD level classes on the fae, because I was seriously lacking in knowledge. Fire fae? We're they kidding? What'd they do, control lava or some shit? Wield balls of fire?

One look at the woman standing at the back of the room would say so. She was, for lack of a better term, other-worldly.

"What brings you here today, Reuven?" Halvar asked, sounding very much like the leader he was.

Reuven opened his mouth to speak as howls sounded down the hall, followed by yells from men and women.

Time slowed and everyone stilled, myself included, like air had been sucked out of the room and replaced by terror.

A moment later a wolf appeared in the archway, the azure-hued light of the room catching the blood stains on his fur. His brown eyes locked on me and his lips pulled back from his teeth. Tremors ran through my body and I gulped down air. Before the creature could move, the Fjell soldiers guarding the entrance had rocks levitating over his head, waiting for orders to crush the invader.

Reuven swept to one side, taking Salka's hand, his own soldiers crowding around him with orbs of water swirling in their grasp. Øyvin did the same, while Espen...

Anger rolled off the Forest Fae in waves as he moved closer, positioning himself between me and the wolf.

Swallowing my fear, I slid in front of Halvar and Aurora, drawing on the magic within me, the need to protect coursing through my veins. The lights in the room flickered, matching the rhythm of my hammering heart as if the fjell and I were one. I placed my forearms against each other, holding them diagonally, and pulled my hands apart. By the time my right arm was fully extended, magic shooting and prickling across the scar on my left, a short stone sword appeared in my hand, light-magic bouncing off the tip of the blade. A shearing noise sounded behind me, and I chanced a quick glance over my shoulder. Halvar had drawn his sword and pressed his daughter behind him.

"Do not threaten the Fjell," Halvar grumbled.

The wolf snarled and launched toward Espen.

Fjell Fae rocks crushed its head and cracked its spine, the snapping noise ricocheting off the walls. Water balls washed over its thick brown fur, drenching it from nose to tail as it collapsed to the floor and froze.

This wasn't good. My chest heaved and my magic swirled in my sternum, begging to be released.

"What have you brought to our door, Espen Solbakke?" Halvar growled, sheathing his sword.

I stepped toward Espen as he turned around, his eyes wide with shock and anger.

"I never imagined he'd bring his fight and animosity to Skolvik. Run away to lick his wounds, certainly, but Wilhelm has never had a death wish."

I looked between Espen and the dead animal. Was that wolf Wilhelm? Or one of his cronies?

"That's exactly what'll happen if I get my hands on him," Halvar bit out.

I shivered at the threat, glinting sparks shooting from the tip of my blade where it hung in my hand at my side.

"I'm sorry for any injuries that may have occurred to Fjell Fae," Espen said. He shouldn't have been the one apologizing, but I understood where his mind was. Wilhelm's removal from the Council of Elders was spurred on by his actions, and he was feeling the guilt of its result. "But I don't think he's after your heir."

"The timing is suspicious," Halvar groused and several council members nodded in agreement.

"It's unfortunate. But I think they're after me and Lennie."

"And what of you?" One of the council members asked, pointing to Reuven, their wispy brows reaching their salt-and-pepper hairline.

"Don't worry." Reuven moved his focus from the council member to Halvar. "I'm not here to kill your heir or your friends. Quite the opposite." He squeezed his wife's hand.

"How can we be assured of that?" Halvar asked, nodding to Salka. "You're aligned with Veigar's house."

Reuven's eyes crinkled, his scar twitching with the movement. "I will always prioritize the well-being of the fjord."

Howls rent the air once more and fae around us stiffened. My heart hammered against my ribs. There were more of them?

"Fjord Fae, time to go!" Reuven announced, heading toward the exit. "Øyvin, you're with me."

I stared at Øyvin, my eyes wide. He hesitated for a second, looking between his new monarch and me, his brow creased. "Permission to stay and assist our new alliance, sir?"

Air caught in my throat. He'd always prioritized the fjord. And while this was, in a way, helping the fjord, I got the distinct feeling he'd just put me first.

Reuven narrowed his gaze at Øyvin and tilted his head to one side. With a nod, he said, "Report to my chambers when the threat is eliminated." With another nod to Halvar and the Fjell Council, the incoming Fjord king and his fiery queen swept from the room in a crowd of billowing blue capes.

Fjell soldiers entered the room after them and bolted toward us, or more specifically, Halvar. I stepped out of their way, but still somehow ended up on the fringes of the group of twenty-plus in their gray Fjell Fae uniforms. "Orders, sir."

Halvar raised his chin and his nostrils flared. "Find the weakened entrance and seal it. No one out. No one in."

"Yes, sir!" They shouted in unison.

"They harm one of us, they harm all of us." Halvar's gaze swept across the gathered soldiers and he raised his stone sword above his head. "Hunt them down."

39

LENNIE

Chaos erupted in the throne room. Soldiers running to and fro, growls echoing down hallways. The tunnels and entrances must've been severely troubled if the wolves could sneak into the mountain unnoticed.

I used my magic to collapse my stone sword, amazingly getting it to disappear on the first try.

"Espen, I want you here with me," Halvar announced through the bustling noise of soldiers and commanders growing around us as more people barreled into the room.

Espen tightened his jaw and shoulders, readying to protest.

"You know these creatures better than anyone else here," Halvar said with an unyielding tone. "You stay with me."

Espen let out a long breath. "Of course."

There was more to it than just Espen knowing the wolves. It was no doubt wise to keep him nearby should he get angered, lose control, and let loose his destructive powers within the mountain. The consequences of which would be disastrous. If he could level a battlefield, he could probably bring down the mountain.

"Torsten," Halvar turned to the light magic wielding Fjell Fae. "Take Aurora, Lennie, and Øyvin into the tunnels. Keep moving, head for you-know-where."

"Of course." Torsten nodded, already turning for the council chamber door. "Follow me."

Espen caught me by the arm before I could take a step and pulled me into his embrace. The smell of leather and moss settled over me as Espen scanned every inch of my face, like he was committing it to memory. He pressed a gentle kiss to my temple before muttering, "Stay safe. Come back to me in one piece."

I brushed my palms across his chest, feeling the steady thrum of his heartbeat beneath my fingers. This wasn't a goodbye. I wouldn't let it be. Yet, my heart clenched and a lump formed in my throat. "I'll be okay," I said, unwelcome anxiety trembling through my words.

"Come on, Trouble." Øyvin placed his hand on my shoulder. "We need to move."

I stepped out of Espen's arms, already missing the warmth and comfort I'd always found there.

"Keep her safe," Espen said.

"Always," Øyvin replied, tugging me by the elbow. I acquiesced and sucked in a breath, pulling on all my courage to get through this new shitstorm. After taking one final glance at Espen, who strode over to Halvar and other fae who appeared to be commanders or some sort of leaders, I walked away with Øyvin.

"Let's get one thing straight," I muttered as we hurried after Torsten and Aurora who were already at the large wooden door. "I can take care of myself."

Øyvin's lips quirked into a tiny smirk. "That's usually the problem."

I swatted his ass.

His eyes flared.

"Come on, then." I wiggled my brows, mentally distracting myself from the chaos unfurling around us.

Torsten opened the door to the council chamber and ushered us through. The stone slab table rested like a dragon in the middle of the room, chairs strewn around it, and dust motes dancing in the glow from the magical lights.

"This way." Torsten circled the table to one of the doors on the other side of the space. He pressed against the exit, the wood groaning on its black iron hinges, and cool air blew across my cheeks. "We need to head down. Keep you two safe."

"You two?" I asked, my voice notched with confusion. "There are three of us."

Torsten turned to me, his thick brows pinching together. "I have no doubt Øyvin can defend himself. Probably drown the wolves with a snap of his fingers."

Øyvin's lips tipped down at the corners and he bobbed his head.

"But our priority," Torsten continued. "The Fjell's priority is you two." He pointed to me and Aurora.

Aurora waved her hand as if to say "can we get this over with?" She no doubt just wanted to go home, and I couldn't blame her.

"Fine," I replied and brushed my hand across my forehead. "Let's keep moving."

All four of us strode through the doorway—Torsten taking the lead, accompanied by Aurora, me, and then Øyvin who closed the door behind us.

We followed Torsten down winding tunnels I'd never seen before. They looked similar to all the others I'd been through—gray stone walls and magically lit sconces every few feet—but this one was slightly different, darker. Or maybe it was the fact that as soon as Øyvin passed a light, Torsten twisted his right hand and snuffed it. The darkness at our backs sent a shiver down my spine and the anxiety that'd been riding me earlier, poked at me once more.

We descended deeper and deeper, passing intersections and divergences, never slowing, but always turning out the lights behind us. Fjell Fae scurried into their apartments, several motioning for us to join them, but Torsten waved them off with a grateful nod.

"Where exactly are you taking us?" I asked, careful not to trip over my own feet.

"Somewhere safe," Torsten replied.

"That isn't exactly reassuring," I said as Øyvin grumbled, "More details, Torsten."

A sigh sounded from up ahead. "This is one way to the tombs."

"Dead people? Really? That better not be a sign of things to come."

Aurora snorted, sounding like she agreed.

Torsten cast a look over his uniformed shoulder, his tawny man bun bobbing with the movement. "There's a safe room of sorts down there. Very few individuals have ever been granted access."

"And it's defended?" Øyvin asked, hot on my tail.

"Near impenetrable," Torsten replied as we swept left, into another tunnel.

I was about to open my mouth and ask about the defenses when a howl sounded up ahead. Tiny shards of stone sprinkled across mine and Aurora's heads and we all sucked in an audible breath.

Øyvin pushed past Aurora and I as we brushed the debris off our jackets.

The guys slowly moved forward, balls of light and water forming in their respective hands.

A cracking noise reverberated around us and unwelcome flashbacks from the frozen lake flitted through my mind. Kristoffer's little face as he fell—

Before I could grasp what was happening, Aurora yanked my arm, pulling me back five steps.

The horrific noise grew louder and a table-sized rock came crashing down. Then another. Separating us from the guys.

The next second my vision swam with Øyvin's fear-stricken face disappearing behind boulders and chunks of the mountain. "Len—" His roar was cut short and my heart felt like it exploded into a million pieces.

Where Torsten and Øyvin had stood was a wall of boulders, the largest of which were tall enough to reach my waist.

No. No no no no no no no...

"Øyvin!" My scream ripped through my lungs and echoed through the tunnel. I sucked in a lungful of dusty air and coughed it all back up. "*Øyvin!*"

I couldn't lose him. We'd only just defined our relationship, shared I Love Yous. When I pictured the rest of my life, he was in it, standing beside me. Challenging me. Calling me Trouble with that irresistible tiny smirk curling his lips. Holding me in the quiet moments when we needed each other.

My heart clenched and my hands trembled as I brushed them through my hair, tangling them in the debris-covered strands.

I stepped back and back and back. This couldn't be happening. I blinked once, twice, three times... but the rockfall remained. I'd lost him. At the start of our story, our picture coming into focus, it had come to a crashing halt and blurred. A tear fell across my cheek and I swatted it away as I swallowed the need to cry. To mourn. The three of us, together, had formed not just a bond, but a family. A unit I'd believed to be unstoppable, with men I never wanted to lose.

I can't lose him.

Something touched my shoulder and I flinched, throwing my hand up to bat—

"It's just me," Aurora said. "Breathe."

I nodded and pulled in air through my nose, then sputtered. "Are you okay?"

"Mm-hmm."

The lump in my throat swelled and I looked back at the mound of rock that blocked the tunnel ahead. "We—"

"Lennie!"

My eyes widened and I whimpered at the sound. "Did you hear that?"

"Yes, I did," Aurora replied.

"LENNIE!"

Holy fuck. He was alive.

I scrambled toward the rocks, moving toward the sound of his voice.

"Lennie, up here!"

Following the noise, I pinpointed what he was talking about. In the top right corner of the rockfall was a tiny opening, no larger than a coffee mug. Light streamed through it, sending a subtle ray into the dim and dusty tunnel.

I clambered up onto the bottom boulders, careful with my foot placement. "Øyvin, I'm here." Pressing up onto my tiptoes, my fingers clawing for purchase... I couldn't see. My heart burst. I couldn't reach.

"Are you all right?" Øyvin asked, his voice clearer now that I was close to the gap.

"Yeah. You?"

"Dusty, but fine."

I snorted as another tear fell down my face. "There's an age joke in there somewhere, but I think I'll save it for later."

A chortle sounded from the other side and I wasn't sure if it was from Torsten or Øyvin. "Is Torsten dead?"

"No, he's fine," Øyvin replied. "But I need you to focus. Torsten doesn't have usual Fjell powers. So, he can't move the rocks. We need you to carefully start dismantling the blockade. Can you do that?"

His voice was like a balm to my frayed nerves, slowly easing the shock out of my system. He was fine. He was alive. We were okay.

"Lennie, we need you."

I nodded vigorously. "Yeah, yeah, I can do it."

I would do it. To save him. To save us. To get us to the hiding place Torsten had mentioned.

"Lennie... Trouble. I believe in you."

A scoff shook free from my throat as I climbed down to the dust-ridden floor. "I never thought I'd hear those words from your mouth."

"Enjoy the moment," he replied.

"Will do. Now, please step as far back as possible. I don't want to crush anyone."

"Do it."

I stepped away from the mound of rocks and twisted to Aurora. "You may want to scoot back."

She shuffled backward without any complaint.

Raising my hands, I focused on the top rocks in the barricade. I inhaled deeply and focused on the power in my chest, willing it forward and down my arms as I raised my hands. Aiming my palms at that top rock, I gently pushed my magic toward it and pulled it back. The power latched onto the stone with ease, like a hand reaching out and plucking it. A satisfied squeak left me as the stone moved through the air and I set it down to one side.

I was fucking doing this.

Repeating the movement like a Tai Chi practice, pushing and pulling, picking up one rock after another and moving them aside. Slowly but surely, the opening at the top widened and—

A howl brought my magic to a stop and I dropped my hands. The rock in mid-air came crashing down.

I rushed toward the right side of the barricade and yelled up at the gap, "Øyvin! What's happening over there?"

Please don't be a wolf. Please don't be a wolf. Please don't be a wolf.

"We've got company," he replied.

Fuck.

"Stay there. We'll get through these and come to you…" A beat of silence broke his sentence. "Torsten says it'll take at least ten minutes to get there. Don't move!"

All I wanted to do was rip down this wall. But if they were busy fighting wolves and not focusing on potentially tumbling rocks, then I could get someone hurt. And I couldn't have that. So, for the gazillionth time since moving to Norway, I did as requested. "Don't die!"

The only reply was growls and grunts.

I shuffled back and turned to Aurora.

"We stay here and wait," I said, sounding like Halvar commanding a soldier. Which was some character growth I had not been expecting when I crawled out of bed that morning.

Aurora nodded and brushed her hands over her arms, removing more dust from her now less-than-white jacket.

I glanced around the dim tunnel-turned-cavern we were in. Rock walls surrounded us on all but one side and the single orb-filled sconce flickered like a candle. "Let's get some more light in here."

Holding my trembling hands out in front of me, I called upon my magic, picturing the light we needed. Faster than I'd ever done before, power prickled through me and flooded between my palms, forming a ball of light that crackled and swirled like lightning. All I needed to do was place it into one of the sconces along the wall and keep—

A skittering noise sounded from deeper within the tunnel and my head whipped in its direction.

A light padding of footsteps met my ears.

We weren't alone.

Aurora moved into a defensive position, hands loose at her sides. I followed suit, switching the orb of light to my right hand. My jaw tightened, my knees locked, and my pulse raced. A moment later, the shadows at the end of the tunnel shifted, revealing a big, black wolf.

40

LENNIE

Dust and detritus skittered around us, and the wall of boulders loomed at our backs. My breathing hitched and my stomach filled my throat again. Aurora panted beside me as neither of us dared to move—unable to escape the figure blocking our path.

The shadow shifted off its haunches and a cracking noise sounded as it transformed, straightened, and stepped into the last vestiges of light.

My heart stopped.

"No one will save you this time, human," Wilhelm said in his human form, his top lip curled into a snarl.

He wasn't wrong. Halvar couldn't save me now, neither could Espen or Øyvin. Aurora and I were quite literally stuck between rocks and an angry puppy with very big teeth. But... unlike the last time I'd been cornered by two of his goons, this time I had my own tricks up my sleeve. And dammit, I wasn't going down without a fight.

I raised my ball of light to the ceiling, swept my leg behind me and braced for impact as I called forth my power and formed it into a short sword. "Here's the thing," I started, willing my light magic to skitter across the stone sword in my hands and pointing the tip in his direction.

"I don't need saving." Totally did, but now was *not* the time to dwell on my never-ending unfortunate circumstances.

"Neither do I." Aurora crouched and pulled twin knives from her boots.

Sisterly pride swelled within me as I added, "We can take care of ourselves."

Wilhelm huffed. "That's the problem with you youngsters. You're too naive, too gullible."

What a dick.

"Says the fallen Alpha who couldn't unite his own pack, who wants to stand against his own kind and defect. Tell me, Assface, what kind of leader refuses to listen to his people? His family?" Aurora sucked in a breath, but I didn't hold back. The proverbial gloves were off. "Why the power trip? Mommy drop you on your head when you were a baby? Or no, let me guess, your wife got tired of sucking your cock and you now retaliate by belittling others?"

A low growl ricocheted off the stone walls around us. I tightened my hold on my sword. Yeah, that last one may have taken it too far. Wilhelm apparently agreed as he snapped and crackled back into a wolf. Those wolves last year had scared me, but Wilhelm in his wolf form was straight-up terrifying. Broad paws stomped against the floor, large canines protruded from his jaw, and his thick black coat danced with the shadows.

With a gut-clenching snarl, he lunged.

Wilhelm's maw opened wide as he launched himself through the air, aiming toward my legs. Aurora moved out of the way and I twisted to the right, bringing down my sword to act as a shield and parry away his sharp teeth. He dodged at the last second, narrowly avoiding my blade.

I stepped back, readjusted my position, and braced for his next move.

He spun on us, a low grumble emanating from his chest.

This wasn't good. We couldn't outrun him. Those tunnels wouldn't save us. We had to fight him.

Aurora moved to stab him, but was swatted aside by his large head. Wilhelm growled, saliva dripping from his lips, and refocused his attention on me. He leaned back on his haunches again and I raised my sword, instinctively angling it at his head. I could do this. I had to do this or he'd kill me and probably Aurora too. I winced as he neared, closing my eyes for a millisecond. Which was a grave mistake...

Agonizing pain ripped through my left leg and all the air in my lungs escaped as I dropped my sword and let out an almighty scream. Fire seared my calf as I collapsed onto the cold stone floor, dust and debris clouding around me. I cast my gaze across the tunnel. Wilhelm stood between me and Aurora. His lips pulled back from his teeth and he spat out blood and bits of—

My stomach roiled and I glanced down at my leg, or what remained of it behind the flesh that had been torn to pieces and the blood pooling around me. That was another mistake. Bile rose in my throat but I swallowed it down. I couldn't puke now.

My power swirled within my chest, buffeting against my insides like it could tell I'd been wounded and was panicking on my behalf. I twisted onto my side and leaned on my forearms, panting and groaning through the agony. My vision faded in and out like an old TV turning on and off.

Wilhelm turned slowly, his paw pads featherlight on the floor. This fae wasn't just a shifter, he was some sort of phantom wolf—even if he wasn't spectral. As he set his sights on Aurora, my nerves sparked and the top of my head tingled.

"Come on, Wilhelm," Aurora goaded, settling into a crouched stance, a knife in each hand. In her dusty white coat, she was the light to his dark. "Try your best."

The wolf responded by hurtling toward her, tilting his head and stretching his jaw wide. But Aurora was fucking fast. She dipped and rolled beneath him as he soared over her head. She extended her arms, the twin knives in her clutches sliced into Wilhelm's hind legs and came away scarlet. They both spun and faced each other once more, Wilhelm stuttering his steps. I, on the other hand, couldn't move, I couldn't do a damn thing but watch—my sight growing hazier by the second.

Beads of sweat dappled my forehead as I panted and balled my hands into fists. My magic swirled within me once more, reminding me of its presence, but what the hell could I do? The pain in my leg... Fuck, it hurt. Would I bleed out? Could I? What if— No, don't go there. Would they— *Goddamn, this mind-numbing pain.*

Wilhelm lunged again and Aurora spun in a pirouette befitting a ballerina. She let out a wince as his sharp claw nicked her arm, but she was still standing, participating in this battle that could only end in death or severe injury. I couldn't let that happen though. My breaths grew harder, in and out through my nose, and I ignored the smell of copper in the air.

With his back to me, Wilhelm howled, the noise bouncing and echoing off the stone tunnel around us. Even the magic light I'd created flickered at the sound. He lunged again, and, in a split second, he had her on her back, landing with a thud and groan. Her knives flew from her hands, skittering across the floor and out of reach.

He raised his head and bayed like a beast that had caught its prey.

My heart stopped. Power burned through me and I aimed my trembling hand toward them.

He opened his jaw and went for her neck.

Not today, Satan. Lightning power surged through me, arching my spine as it flew from my palm. The ball of crackling light crashed against his back and wrapped around him like a vice. Wilhelm yowled and collapsed on top of Aurora.

Aurora's screams echoed around us.

My screams joined hers as the power flowed out of me, burning and searing, wholly uncontrolled, but protecting. Doing what it was sworn to do, what I needed to do: protect the fae of the fjell.

My vision blurred and my head throbbed as I dropped my hand to the stone floor. The magic vanished, my eyes shut, and everything went dark. *Please be okay...*

I couldn't feel my left calf anymore. There was only pain as exhaustion took over and delirium set in. All I wanted was my guys. I wanted to curl up in bed with Espen and Øyvin, their arms around me, holding me together. Maybe even a hot cup of coffee from Oddvar's on the bedside table for me to sip on. Yeah, that sounded... That sounded... Fantastic...

41

ØYVIN

After dispatching a trio of wolves, we careened through the tunnels. Blood and dust stained our clothes as Torsten launched orbs of light ahead of us, illuminating our path.

"Down here." Torsten pointed left and I followed his instruction.

Eerie silence rang through the tunnel and the smell of copper singed my nostrils, panic filling my veins. If someone had hurt her, I'd boil them alive and then hand them over to Espen for a brutal burial.

We rounded the corner and my footsteps faltered at the sight before me, my world shattering.

No.

Lennie lay on the floor, her eyes shut, hair splayed around her like a halo, and blood pooling around the lower half of her body.

"Lennie!" I stumbled forward and crashed to my knees, ignoring the sting of pain.

"Shit," Torsten said, scrambling past me. I peered over my shoulder and found Aurora lying by the cave-in, trapped by a large black wolf splayed over her. Torsten's muscles strained as he hauled the singed, dead animal off Aurora. She appeared unharmed, but Lennie...

I looked down at her and my breath stuttered.

Head. Fine.

Chest. Rising and falling in shallow but consistent movements.

Legs… I grit my teeth together and pulled in air through my nose. Her left leg was mangled, torn apart.

"Lennie," I said. "Lennie. Wake up."

She groaned, and I leaned in, brushing my hand across her cheek. I couldn't lose her. She was everything I'd never dared to dream of. Mine. My family.

"Lennie."

"Nibbled," she mumbled.

I huffed. Of course she'd try to make a joke while barely conscious.

Drawing on my magic, I formed a swirling orb of water between my palms. "This will sting."

I didn't want to cause her more pain, but I had to do it. If I didn't, she'd bleed out or get infected.

She hummed. Her eyes still shut. "Bumble bee…"

Shaking my head at her delirious muttering, I tensed and moved the ball of water over her leg. Settling it around—

Lennie's eyes flew open and her fingers scraped against the rocky ground. "HOLY MOTHER FUCKING SHIT BALLS!"

"I need to keep it clean until we get you to a healer." The water would act as a bandage of sorts. It wouldn't stop the bleeding, but would slow it and keep the gnarly wound clean until we could get help. I wasn't a healer by any means, but I'd seen injured soldiers and knew the signs. With how pale she was, we didn't have much time.

"I'm going to pick you up now."

She moved her head in a motion that was neither nod nor shake, but somewhere in between.

"This might hurt too, but we need to get you upstairs."

A sly smile twisted her lips, eyes fluttering closed, and her body went limp. Unconsciousness wasn't a good sign either.

I hoisted her into my arms, carrying her like a princess—her legs hanging over the side. She was going to destroy me if we didn't get to a healer strong enough to save her.

I glanced over my shoulder. The black wolf lay at Aurora and Torsten's feet, their jackets covered in dust and blood. Red stains marred Aurora's wrists as she wiped two bloody knives on her thighs before returning them to hidden holsters in her tall boots. Torsten's bun had come undone, his blondish hair hanging around his clavicles in stark contrast to his gray Fjell Fae uniform. He looked like he'd seen a ghost.

With a nod to the dead wolf, I asked, "Who was that?"

Aurora swallowed. "Wilhelm."

I should've known. Anger roiled within me like a tidal wave ready to destroy everything in its path. At least the mongrel was dead.

"You grab the wolf. I've got Lennie," I commanded.

Torsten nodded. "Of course."

I strode behind the others as they carried the wolf back through the re-lit tunnels. Aurora held onto the rear legs, while Torsten carried the wolf's front legs. The canine dangled between them like a pig on a spit roast. After a minute of walking as quickly as possible, Aurora said, "We're lucky he didn't rip off her leg."

I grunted. "Thank you for stopping him."

She peered over her shoulder. "That wasn't me. She's the one who killed Wilhelm."

What?

Lennie's lips were lightly parted, drawing faint breaths. Her eyes shut, lashes brushing the tops of her cheeks. She looked so harmless like this. Incapable of killing, but... I didn't doubt for a second that she'd tear anyone apart if they threatened something she cared about. It was one of the many things I loved about her.

"How?" I asked.

Aurora kept her focus forward again. "Royal fae magic. Don't know how it works, but it looked like he was being electrocuted from the inside out."

Torsten stutter-stepped and jostled the wolf. "Say that again."

"Zapped from the inside out."

"Wow," he replied and kept moving.

Wow, indeed. I furrowed my brow. I'd only ever heard of monarchs using that type of power. The fact that she'd used it was unfathomable.

"Almost there," Torsten said, interrupting my thoughts.

We rounded yet another corner and the pale blue stone of the throne room entrance came into view, the jagged pieces glinting in the light from the wall sconces. Voices echoed out of the chamber as we darted closer and closer, Wilhelm probably leaving a bloody Hansel and Gretel style trail all the way behind us.

Stepping into the throne room, the space quieted immediately, all eyes trained on us.

42

LENNIE

As I came to again, chatter around us stopped along with the jostling. The crystalline blue of the throne room ceiling blinked down at me and I sucked in a deep breath as my vision blurred at the edges.

A strangled whimper sounded from my left and drew my attention. Espen stumbled over from the dais, his eyes wide, face pale, and the corners of his lips turned down.

"She needs you. Now," Øyvin said, his voice thick with emotion.

Espen nodded as a thump and gasps sounded elsewhere in the room, but my eyes were locked with my fiancé's. He brushed his hand through my hair. "Lay her down over here. Quickly."

The room spun as Øyvin turned, and I clamped my eyes shut until I felt the stone floor against my back.

Hands settled around my knee and I chanced a quick look down. Øyvin removed the layer of water with a grimace, the deep red liquid slowly vanishing into thin air.

"Hold her still," a blurry Espen commanded from where he crouched, and Øyvin knelt beside me, grabbing my wrists. He moved my arms upward and positioned them like football goalposts, elbows bent at a ninety-degree angle.

"I'm sorry, Lennie," Espen said. "This is going to hurt."

Everything felt numb. Whatever Espen was about to do couldn't possibly be that bad, so I mumbled a "mm-hmm" in reply. He'd just magic it better like Heidi did with that Forest Fae soldier last year. I furrowed my brows, trying to remember how that'd gone. There'd been lots of blood... and did two fae hold the man down?

Øyvin tightened his hold on my wrists. "Eyes on me, Trouble."

"That was so much hotter when we were in the shower."

He smirked.

With a feather light touch, Espen assessed the wound and took a deep breath. A soft glow appeared near Espen and fiery pain shot down my calf, a scream ripping from my lips as I bucked. It was like flames themselves wrapped around my leg, burning and knitting the wound shut.

Øyvin leaned down and pressed his forehead to mine. "Keep still." His words were a balm but that was the last thing I wanted to do right now. I wanted to wriggle free of the searing sensation weaving across my leg. I wanted to kick Espen's hands off me, remove them from my knee and ankle—stop the fire incinerating my leg.

Espen gulped like it pained him to see me like this. "A little bit longer."

A tear fell across my right cheek, shortly followed by another on the left. The only thing visible through my watery gaze was an anguished Fjord Fae—his lips locked in a grimace, brow creased.

The burning sensation spiked and I whimpered in response, but didn't move. I wanted this to be over. I wanted to curl up in a ball with my guys on either side of me in a world where a wolf hadn't taken a bite out of my leg and ruined my favorite fuzzy leggings.

"Almost there," Espen panted.

I wanted to go home to the boathouse. I wanted five fucking minutes of peace where trouble wasn't breaking down the door. I wanted the pain to go away and leave me alone.

Øyvin nudged my nose with his, the motion sending another stream of tears to the stone floor. He glanced over his shoulder and a moment later, released my wrists, his lips curving into a gentle smile and the corner of his eyes crinkling. "Well done," he mouthed, sitting back on his haunches.

I wrapped my arms around my torso, giving myself a hug.

Espen appeared on my left and brushed his hand over my head. He swallowed hard and cleared his throat. "Don't ever get injured like that again."

With panted breath and my vision clearing of the dizzying haze and unshed tears, I nodded. There wasn't a chance in hell I'd ever go toe to toe with a wolf again. Suffering one gnarly bite was more than enough, thank you very much.

The throbbing pain slowly eased to an uncomfortable pulse that matched the exhaustion weighing down the rest of my body. "How bad was it?" I asked, my voice raspy.

"Let's just say I'm glad you got here when you did."

I grimaced.

Espen extended his bloodied hands in Øyvin's direction and he swiftly wrapped water around them. A split second later, the pinkish liquid vanished, leaving Espen's hands clean. The Forest Fae looked to Øyvin and asked, "How'd it happen anyway?"

"Tunnel caved in between us. Wolves found us. Took Torsten and I ten minutes of running through other routes to get to Lennie and Aurora."

"Thank fuck you did." Espen brushed hairs off my forehead with his fingertips.

I leaned into his touch and chanced a look at my leg. The skin was red raw and warped in places as if Espen's magic had wrapped and twisted it shut. Several red lines puckered together, overlapping in multiple locations like a diamond-patterned tapestry. "That's going to leave a scar, isn't it?"

Espen sighed. "Yeah..."

Fantastic.

"My entire left side is getting scarred," I huffed. "What, with the lightning one on my arm and now my leg being used as a chew toy."

"Well..." Espen nodded. "That seems to be the—"

"Oh my god," I gasped and smacked their arms. "I could be like Phantom, but instead of the opera, I'd be the phantom of the fjell. With shields for my scars and a mask. Do either of you have a mask kink?"

Snorts sounded around me.

"I think she's gone into shock," Øyvin said.

"I think she's coming out of it actually." Espen tried to hold back a smile, but failed spectacularly. "Will you sing opera, too?"

"I could try."

"Please don't," Øyvin grunted and crossed his arms.

Movement by my feet caught my attention and Trygve—the head Fjell Fae healer—came running over, his apron flapping around his knees, his white blouse sleeves shoddily rolled up above his elbows. "Miss Lennie," he gasped, taking in my scarred leg.

"Another day, another injury, Trygve. You know me."

"Indeed." He cleared his throat. "But you are in good hands."

"I am. Any chance you have some of that fancy scar salve lying around?" The stuff he'd given me for my arm was bottled bliss and had cooled the skin nicely. Hopefully it would work for my leg too.

"I'll see if I can find some once I'm done tending to the others."

"Thank you."

Espen smiled. "We might need a bucket, Trygve."

"I will see to it and have someone bring it to you. Now, I must check on my other patients. I'm glad to see you're doing well." He nodded to all of us and departed in a swirl of herbaceous smells.

As Trygve left, he was replaced by a set of crossed arms, pursed lips, and a braid on the verge of giving up. Aurora glanced at my leg. "You'll live?"

"Looks like it."

She hummed and made to move away—

"Aurora, wait." Now was as good a time as any to apologize. She wouldn't have been put in harm's way if I hadn't ignored her wishes and brought her to Skolvik.

She stopped and blinked at me.

"I owe you an apology." I'd done wrong and needed to own up to that shit... even if it had saved me from being beheaded by Halvar. "I shouldn't have kidnapped you and brought you here without your consent. I regret it, and I'm sorry."

Aurora sucked in a breath and stared at the ceiling. Sweat settled at the nape of my neck. I'd never wanted her to get hurt or put her life at risk. I'd never meant for her to get caught in the crossfire of Wilhelm's anger and wrath. All I'd wanted was to bring the heir home and facilitate a peaceful conversation between her and the Fjell Council.

"I don't forgive you," she replied. "This isn't my home, nor will it ever be. But... I can see why you did it. Halvar looks like he might have a temper-tantrum if things don't go according to plan."

I snorted and bit my bottom lip. That was something we could definitely agree on.

"But, I'm not faultless," she added. "I'm sorry I kidnapped you first."

"I guess we're even then?"

"Let's call it a truce."

"I can work with that."

"Are your boyfriends going to agree?" She raised a single brow and looked between the two fae who were doing their best to pretend they weren't listening to the conversation.

"They'll do as they're told," I laughed in reply.

She wandered off with a chuckle, and I leaned onto my elbows as the guys rose to their feet on either side of me. While she hadn't forgiven me, that interaction went better than expected.

I scanned the room. On the far side of the space, triage stations had been set up with healers flitting between three stations where injured soldiers and Fjell Fae lay on the ground. Trygve flapped between them all, doling out bottles to healers and pressing magic into patients. By the archway—

My breath hitched. To the left of the entryway was a lump of black fur, unmoving but guarded by three soldiers.

Wilhelm.

I swallowed hard and my pulse thrummed. I'd done that.

Staring up at the stubble coating Øyvin's jaw, I whispered, "Is he... dead?"

The guys crouched beside me again, and Espen rested his hand against my upper back, holding me upright.

Øyvin took a deep breath and nodded.

My chest tightened, my lungs constricting as if they'd been bound by barbed wire. "Shit. I didn't mean… I don't know how…"

All I'd wanted was to protect Aurora, protect the fjell.

Øyvin's gaze met mine. "You did what you needed to do to protect yourself and Aurora."

"He's right," Espen added.

"Yeah, but I hadn't meant to kill him." It was an instinctual reaction. I barely felt in control—blinded by pain and the need to protect.

"Whatever magic you used, you did the right thing," Øyvin said.

Espen brushed circles with his hand between my shoulder blades, easing the tension in my muscles. "He wasn't going to stop until he'd removed you from the board in payback for me telling you about us and for having him removed from the Forest Fae Council of Elders."

I sighed and accepted the reality. I'd killed a creature, and while it would take some time to come to terms with, Espen was right. Wilhelm wouldn't have stopped until he got his revenge.

"We all know you're Espen's weakness," Øyvin said, and my gaze flitted between my two guys. "Hurting you, hurts him."

"And you," I mumbled.

Øyvin nodded, his elbows resting on his knees and his hands clasped together. "And me."

He was right. By falling in love with each other we'd forged not only a loving bond, but something that others could target. We'd become each other's weakness, but I wouldn't change that. We were stronger together. The three of us were one unstoppable unit—a trio forged of three fae factions.

They were mine and I was theirs.

The room fell silent and we all looked toward the throne where Halvar took up position in front of the glacial looking chair.

"The wolves have been routed and run out of the mountain. My thanks to you all," Halvar said, his voice booming through the room, grabbing the attention of injured and healers alike. "If you are able, please make your way to the Great Room. The Council has some announcements to make."

That sounded ominous.

Halvar's gaze flicked to me. I gave him a quick salute which earned me a sharp nod in return before he strode from the room with a cadre of soldiers at his back and members of the Council following suit.

I looked to Espen as he brushed his hand through his beard. He'd been with the council and Halvar during all of this. "Do you know anything about this?"

He shook his head, dashing my hopes. "No idea." He looked down at me with a creased brow. "Do you think you can stand and walk to the other room?"

I shrugged. "Worth a try."

I was exhausted and in need of a nap, but I wanted to know what these announcements were.

Rolling onto my right side, I pushed my hands against the floor, lifting myself into an upright position. The room didn't spin and the pain in my leg had subsided to a dull burn, the movement not making anything worse. So, I pivoted my right leg underneath me and rose, keeping most of my weight on my right foot. Espen and Øyvin remained on either side of me, their hands out in front of them ready to catch me should I wobble and fall.

With a deep breath, I settled more weight onto my left leg and the twisting, burning sensation grew worse, but it was more like a bad leg cramp than the absolute agony I'd been in while Espen healed it.

"I've got this," I said, mentally cheering myself on. "Let's go."

Espen looped my arm through his. "Are you sure?"

"Yeah. What's the worst thing that could happen? I've already been bitten by a wolf today."

43

LENNIE

We wandered into the great room, the same ballroom where Freija's birthday party had been held last fall. Fae in all manner of attire, from the gray Fjell Fae uniform, to the traditional looking dresses, to shirts and jeans, were assembled around the cavernous, pale gray room, all looking toward the little platform at the far end where the band had once played.

Sconces lit the curved stone walls, and several orbs of light hung high above our heads as Torsten conjured and launched a few more from near the dais. A low hum of chatter echoed through the chamber, buzzing in anticipation of whatever the Council had to announce.

Halvar stepped up to the edge of the platform, the council members assembled behind him. "Espen Solbakke, Head Guard of the Forest Fae, Lennie Martin and Aurora Johansen, will you step forward please?"

Ah, fuck.

The crowd parted and let us through, forming a large circle around us.

Halvar stared at the fae on my right. "Espen. Members of your faction were killed in our tunnels today, including the pack Alpha. We have an alliance, but I must know, in front of our council and residents of the mountain, was this an official attack?"

Espen sighed, his hands clasped behind his back in a diplomatic posture. "It was not. Wilhem was removed from his post as pack Alpha yesterday by the Forest Fae Council and acted alone."

Murmurs swept through the room as Halvar gave Espen a quick nod.

"Speaking on behalf of the Council, our alliance remains," Espen added. "Wilhelm's actions were neither condoned nor sanctioned by our Council of Elders. You have our sincere apologies for the havoc he has wreaked upon your families."

My heart fractured hearing his words. Of course Wilhelm was wholly to blame for this shit show, but Espen in his role as Head Guard had to make reassurances to his friends.

A Fjell council member shuffled forward a few steps, their frame so much shorter than Halvar. "The wolves have been removed to an anti-chamber of the throne room."

"What *exactly* happened to Wilhelm?" Espen asked with a quick glance to me and Aurora who twitched minutely on the spot. "I was preoccupied when Torsten and Aurora brought him in."

Yeah, stitching me up. We hadn't exactly had time to mention all the details of our run in with the snappy puppy.

"That is why the two of you were called forward too," Halvar said with a nod to me and Aurora. "Perhaps you would care to enlighten us all on what happened?"

I peered over at Aurora. Quirking a single eyebrow, she waved her hand in a motion that said *go ahead.*

I rolled my eyes and took a deep breath. Best to give everyone the Cliff Notes version of today's events. "We were cornered by Wilhelm in his wolf form after a cave in. He attacked, and we retaliated in self-defense, me with my powers and Aurora with her knives. She, like someone else I know"—I gave Halvar a pointed look—"sliced and diced our assailant, and I launched... erm... lightning or royal magic at him when he lunged for her."

Halvar's beard twitched and, in a blink-and-you-miss-it moment, I could've sworn I saw a hint of a smile.

He turned to his daughter. "You were the one who cut his thighs, thereby slowing his movements?"

"Aurora here is apparently good with knives," I chimed in.

She shrugged. "I whittle."

A snort escaped me. "That was a damn sight more than whittling. You carved up the guy's junk."

Another shrug from Aurora was met by winces from the assembled crowd.

"Lennie was compromised. She needed help."

"Thank you," Espen whispered from my other side, and Aurora's lips twisted into a wry smile from my left. "As an act of self-defense," he added, his voice carrying through the large space so everyone could hear, "these actions will not be held against them by the Council of Elders."

"Thank you," Halvar replied.

"The bodies may be claimed and removed from the fjell," a dark-haired council member to Halvar's right said. "We ask that you do so as swiftly as possible."

Espen nodded. "I'll have them removed today."

"Good." Halvar turned his gaze to me. "Aurora, thank you for helping protect the mountain. You and Espen are dismissed."

What? No, they couldn't leave me up here. My heart raced as I stared at the hundreds of people watching. I'd done as requested and brought the heir home to the mountain, but I'd inadvertently brought back some stray dogs too. Dogs with big teeth that had—based on the injuries I'd seen in the throne room and the words spoken by Halvar and Espen—severely injured and killed Fjell Fae. Their families and Halvar were no doubt upset about that turn of events, even if it wasn't my fault that people got injured.

I reached for Espen's arm and he gave my hand a quick squeeze. "It's all right," he said with a soft smile. "He won't harm you. I won't let him."

The former was debatable.

Espen lifted my fingers off his forearm and kissed my hand before retreating back into the surrounding circle, joining Øyvin and Aurora.

I swallowed the massive lump in my throat and looked back at the dais, taking in the figures standing there. This did not bode well for me.

Halvar straightened, his voice projecting across the cavernous room. "As Freija's royal magic is now split between both of us"—gasps broke out in the crowd—"and you're a demi-fae with both Fjell Fae magic and that of a royal, the Council has deemed you of great importance. Indeed, the mountain itself was unwell with you away." My heart beat faster than a camera on sport mode and I caught people nodding out of the corner of my eye.

"With the heir having respectfully declined to take the throne," Halvar continued, "it is the Council's opinion that another leadership system be put in place. One that will be council led, should the Fjell Fae deem it so. Council members have been discussing this option with residents for the past few weeks. So, Fjell Fae, how do you vote?"

The room rumbled with movement and murmurs, and the gathered masses settled onto one knee, bowing their heads.

My jaw fell open and I looked around at their version of democracy. Nobody objected. Several hundred fae took a knee, choosing this new governing system. The only people who remained standing were Øyvin, Espen, and Aurora.

"The people have spoken," Halvar boomed and raised his arms.

The crowd rose to their feet once more, their gazes flitting between me and the folks on the dais.

"Now that's settled..." Halvar locked his gaze with mine and raised a single eyebrow.

My heart hammered in my chest and I sucked in a breath. *Oh shit, oh shit, oh shit...*

"Lennie Martin, demi-fae, resident of Skolvik, we offer you the position of Deputy Head Guard, a role that has not been filled for centuries, but is befitting of your powers and importance to the Fjell."

Fuck me. This was their plan B? Create a council-led government and add me to their roster? Had they met me? Chaos-incarnate over here.

Crossing my arms, I narrowed my eyes at Halvar. "What exactly does that entail?"

"You have now proved your worth and willingness to protect us. So, you will be an official member of the Fjell Fae Council, serve as a commander, and swear an oath to protect all Fjell Fae."

My eyes widened at the gargantuan weight of those tasks. That was a lot of responsibility. Hundreds of fae watched me like a deer caught in the proverbial headlights as I looked around, the *Jeopardy* theme song playing in my head. *No pressure.* Rolling my shoulders, I took a deep breath in an attempt to calm my pounding heart.

Here I was, standing before a community of fae, having been asked to take up a position of authority. How ironic. I'd never done well with authority figures and now they were asking me to be one. How did that Shakespeare quote go? Something about thrusting greatness?

I looked between Halvar and the assembled council members. "Are you sure about this?"

They all nodded.

Halvar tilted his head but withheld any sign of emotion from his facial features. "Are you rejecting the position?"

Was I rejecting their offer? With everything that had happened recently I knew they needed Freija's power—now my power—near the mountain to keep things stable and protected. That degree of tying me down to something was new and novel, definitely forcing me to remain in Skolvik. Then again...

I peered over my shoulder to my guys at the edge of the circle around me. One a grumpy and protective asshole. The other a bubbly ray of sunshine that cared deeply for everyone around him. I'd already committed to them. I'd even committed to a part-time job at Oddvar's this summer. In so many ways, I was already part of this community. Already swept up in the magic of this world. And I loved those two fae... would be marrying them, not just for immigration purposes.

I had no intention of going anywhere else. I'd traveled all over the world, from the dizzying tops of Machu Picchu, to the crystal waters of Croatia. I'd seen so much... And, yet, this right here, being tied to this place was so much more important than the freedom to see the world.

This was my new home. And it needed protecting.

Using these powers for good, to help the people of the fjell and the surrounding fjord region felt right. I may have started by taking photos of the landscape, but now I had the ability to protect it from harm. To protect these people and their secret. To protect my new family.

I wrung my hands and rubbed my right thumb over my engagement ring.

It wasn't a hard decision.

"Do I get a badge?"

The council scrunched their faces in confusion and Halvar rolled his eyes.

"No, but I'll get you a hat," Halvar replied.

I smiled at our inside joke. "Deal."

44

LENNIE

A few weeks later, the house was quiet, with both Espen and Øyvin called in to work—the former back at his job with the local police station, and the latter beneath the surface of the fjord. With the boathouse to myself, I'd planned a quiet evening with the TV. Grabbing a hot mug of cocoa and wearing my comfiest sweatpants and sweater, I settled on the couch beneath a blanket.

While flicking through the movie options for the third time, my phone dinged, signaling the arrival of a text. Setting aside my drink with a huff, I swiped my phone off the coffee table, unlocked it, and checked to see who it was from. The guys and I didn't usually text much while they were working—I was trying to be respectful of their time and work—but every so often I'd get cute little messages from Espen telling me that he missed me. Those always sent my heart fluttering and sometimes devolved into something akin to sexting. So, my pulse was racing when I opened the text and found...

Andrew: Incoming!

I shook my head and furrowed my brow at the odd message in the group chat with my three older brothers. What the fuck was he talking about?

Lennie: Incoming, what?

Ryan: Funny! That wasn't a knock-knock joke.

Jared: lol

What the hell was going on? And what sort of inside joke were they sharing? Had I missed something? I started typing out a reply when a knock sounded at the front door, followed by a peeling ring from a doorbell I didn't know we had.

Wrenching the warm blanket off my legs, I flung my phone onto the sofa. I'd deal with my brothers once I'd dealt with whoever had stopped by.

Wandering across to the little foyer, I narrowly avoided tripping over the pile of shoes. They annoyed the shit out of Øyvin, but at least the snow boots were in a tray so they didn't leave puddles on the wood floors.

I opened the door and my stomach fell to the floor, my eyes bugging out of my head. There, on the doorstep, beaming from ear to ear, were all three of my older brothers with duffel bags slung over their shoulders.

"What the fuck?" The words slipped from my mouth on a long exhale as my two worlds collided.

"Language, Lennie," Andrew said, his blond hair in complete disarray compared to his usual coif.

"You gonna let us in or what?" Jared asked, his dark brown hair half-hidden by a wool beanie.

"H-how did... How did you get out here?" None of them answered my question as they pushed in, not interested in waiting in the cold a moment longer, and dumped their stuff beside the shoes. I shut the door behind them, then spun and fell against it. All feeling in my knees started to disappear as two of them failed to remove their boots, leaving gritty blobs of water in their wake. Øyvin was going to have a conniption. "*Why* are you here?"

Jared scoffed and headed straight for the refrigerator, hunting for snacks like this was our parents' house.

Andrew pulled off his shoes and set them neatly beside his bag, while Ryan popped a squat on the piano bench, stretching his arms as if he was preparing for a workout.

"What are you talking about, Lennie? I called you weeks ago and you agreed to a sibling ski vacation," Andrew explained, before surveying the living quarters with his hands on his hips.

"No, you didn't," I countered. When had I'd last spoken to my brother? Surely, I would've remembered if I'd spoken to him.

"You did sound busy, may have even said as much given how you practically rushed through the call, but you agreed to the last-minute trip."

"I don't..." I trailed off as a tiny light bulb went off, shattering inside my brain as I recalled when we'd last spoken. I'd been trying to bundle Aurora into the car in Alvdalen and attempting to make a hasty getaway before she could escape. I pressed my palm across my forehead and groaned. I *had* agreed to the trip.

"Well, no take-backs as we're here how," Andrew said, his voice as warm as his brotherly smiles.

I pushed my hair behind my ears and straightened up. He was right. They were here now. In my house. In Norway. Where I lived with two fae. What could possibly go wrong?

Jared wandered past me and took a bite out of an apple before throwing himself onto the sofa, his long arms and legs spreading out in exhaustion. "Nice ears by the way, didn't realize it was Halloween."

My heart stopped beating and I gingerly brushed my hand over my right ear. Fuck me sideways, my ears were out!

"It's... uh... it's..." I swallowed hard, desperately trying to come up with an excuse. I flipped my hair back over my ears and blurted, "Øyvin has a fairy kink."

"Gross!"

"Evelyn!"

"Wow." Jared waved his apple in the air, the core already visible on one side. "I did *not* need to hear that."

"You three are the ones who just showed up unannounced! What if I was in a compromising position?" I set my hands on my hips, my breathing steadying even though my heart was racing a mile a minute. *Sorry, Øyvin. Hope that bus didn't hurt too much after I threw you under it. Beep, beep.*

Andrew shook his head and pinched the bridge of his nose. "Technically not unannounced. We spoke about this weeks ago. How could you forget?"

"More importantly," Ryan piped up, narrowing his eyes at me. "Where are your Vikings? We better *not* have interrupted something."

"They're at work for a little while longer," I explained.

"Can you please take those off, then?" Jared pointed his apple at my head. "We don't need a reminder that our baby sister has—"

Ryan made a gagging noise, cutting him off. "Don't say it."

"Fine." I lifted my hands in the air. "Just... nobody move."

I scurried past the kitchen to the bathroom and slammed the door shut behind me. I'd have to make this quick, pretend I was removing prosthetics. Focusing on the magic swirling in my core, I pulled on some of it and pictured a magical hat being placed over my head, hiding away the pointy bits. My reflection in the bathroom mirror morphed as the power hid the evidence of my new demi-fae-ness. I was glad for all the ear training we'd done over Christmas and the time since then that I'd had to perfect the magic. While it was by no means easy, it came to me a lot quicker than it used to. And right now, I was grateful for that.

Ears hidden, I yanked open the bathroom door and strode through the kitchen area, finding my brothers where I'd left them. Miraculously, they'd all listened when I'd asked them not to move.

"Okay," I said, coming to a stop between the kitchen space and the sofa that marked the start of the living room area. Time to triage. "Let's figure this out, shall we?"

"By the way, Jennifer's pregnant. You're going to be an aunt again," Jared announced nonchalantly before taking another bite of his apple.

"That's wonder— Hang on. You left your *pregnant* wife at home alone?!" My emotions swung from elated to WTF in under two seconds. Jared was the most introverted of all the Martin siblings, and as kind and caring as Andrew was, but sometimes I wondered what went on in that head of his.

"It's only for a week." He waved the apple core. "She'll be fine."

My brain caught on his words, my heart careening to a stop. "You're here for a week?"

"Yes," Andrew said. He glanced around the room with his brow furrowed like he was analyzing the space for safety concerns. Typical father of two behavior. "Although, when you agreed to let us stay, I thought you actually had room. This looks like a one-bedroom. We can find a hotel," he added, clearly not having done his usual degree of research before booking this trip.

"Not possible. The main lodge is closed for the season," I countered.

Andrew furrowed his brow and brushed his hand across his chin. "Really?"

"Yes, really. Skolvik isn't a skiing town. Except for this one guy that skis through the village every day wearing a tight bodysuit that hugs all the wrong places. We cater to summer cruises and hikers out here."

"Any rentals then?" Andrew asked.

I nodded. "A friend might have room for you."

"Great."

I hung my head and ran my palms across my temples. Damn me for not paying attention on the phone. Now I'd have to call in another favor with Solveig and hope she had room at her house.

I let out a long sigh and straightened up. "You've all gone mad. You've become a dunce who leaves his *pregnant* wife for a week-long vacation." I pointed to Jared before motioning to Andrew. "And you've suddenly gone lax on your planning and follow-up."

Andrew beamed. "I'm trying to be spontaneous."

I ignored him with a shake of my head and turned to Ryan who was smirking by the piano. "And, let me guess, you're here for the booze?"

His smug grin widened. "I've heard Aquavit is amazing."

"Trust me." I huffed, stroking my hand across my neck, memories of fire-breathing invading my mind. "It's not."

"Don't worry, Lennie," Andrew started, his usual calm voice easing my nerves. "We'll figure out a place to crash and have a great week together."

I was about to remark on how there was too much testosterone in the house, when the front door opened.

Øyvin stepped in—thankfully wearing his usual jeans and cream-knit sweater and not his uniform—his eyes wide and a bewildered look plastered across his features. My brothers, on the other hand, were being childish little kink-shamers who needed to keep their damn mouths shut. Which was wishful thinking, especially with Ryan present, but still, a woman could hope. All three looked like they were struggling to keep it together—with Andrew pursing his lips, Ryan investigating the music sheet on the piano, and Jared snickering into a throw pillow.

"What's going on?" Øyvin asked, his voice straining to not vault into a higher volume as he turned to me. "Why are your brothers here?"

"Hi..." I said with a smile, clasping my hands behind my back. "Welcome home. Here's the deal—"

"She fucked up," Ryan interjected, and I gave him the middle finger in response just as the front door swung open again.

"Ah, hello guys. A family reunion I see," Espen said as he walked into the boathouse and shucked off his shoes and police jacket. He looked at me, his amber-colored eyes full of warmth and joy. "Why didn't you tell us they were coming?"

I shook my hands above my head. "I didn't know!"

"Well, this does provide the perfect opportunity to go out to dinner and properly celebrate with your family." Espen pointed to the engagement ring on my finger and hell broke loose.

All three brothers gasped, their eyes bugging out of their heads.

"Evelyn, are you engaged?"

"Are you pregnant, too?" Jared asked just as Ryan said, "Who's the daddy?"

I gave them both a deadpanned look and rolled my eyes. "I'm *not* pregnant," I retorted, withholding the fact that I was currently on my period.

"Why didn't you tell us you were engaged? Or is this recent?" Andrew crossed his arms before sucking in a breath. "Have you told Mom and Dad?"

Espen bit his bottom lip and did his best not to laugh, while Øyvin tilted his head and narrowed his eyes at me.

I wiped my hands across my cheeks, wishing I could turn back the clock by thirty minutes and hide underneath the blanket on the sofa. I'd spent the past few weeks since the attack on the mountain trying to figure out how to tell my family about the engagement. This was decidedly *not* the family video call I'd had in mind.

"I can explain."

EPILOGUE

Halvar

She had her eyes.

I never thought I'd see them again.

Never thought I'd see our daughter after delivering her to Alvdalen all those years ago.

It was a safety measure, a way to ensure no one tried to take her or kill her. She was our weakness. The one thing that truly spoke of our bond, our love, our union, and it broke our hearts that she was safer away from us. Aside from Lennie's magic, this young lady was the only piece of Freija that remained on earth.

She had her mother's eyes, and I couldn't look away. "Thank you for joining me. I have something I'd like to show you before you leave."

"Sure." Aurora shrugged, peering around the council chambers like this wasn't a burden on her time.

After the debacle with the wolves, she'd agreed to stay for a week to learn more about her own powers. So far, she spent her days training with my soldiers and her nights at Espen's cabin, which he'd kindly offered to her for the duration of her stay. While I knew she didn't want to stay with us in the fjell, I was glad she wanted to take some time to train with us. If anything, it would keep her safe over in Alvdalen.

I nodded and motioned her to follow me into the tunnels skirting past the Royal chambers, residences, and deeper into the mountain.

"There is something you need to see as a royal—"

"I don't want—"

"I know," I said, interrupting her by raising my hand, too. She'd made her choice, and just because we were related by blood didn't mean I was her family. If she wanted a relationship with me, she was welcome to it, but I had no illusions on who her true family was. She belonged with the pack of Forest Fae, if that's where she was happiest. I wouldn't come between her and them. "But, as a Fjell Fae of royal lineage you have a right to know this information."

"Sounds ominous," she muttered, strolling beside me.

I tried not to roll my eyes.

"Where are we going exactly?"

"The royal tombs."

She screeched to a halt. "I don't want to visit my mother." Her voice was flat and the look in her eyes was one of caution.

"We will walk past her." The words stung in my mouth, and I lowered my voice. "What I need to show you lies beyond the tombs."

"All right." She shrugged again, looking more like she wanted to get this over with and back to her friends and family. I couldn't blame her, but she had a right to know, and I wasn't going to be the one to withhold this from her. I'd withheld enough from her already in her twenty years. And, most importantly, Freija would've wanted to share this with her one day.

We continued further into the mountain. The temperature dropped the deeper we went, the rugged stone walls turning from light-gray to dark. Sconces dotted the tunnel walls every few meters, lighting our way. Fjell Fae of all kinds passed us, nodding to me and staring at Aurora with confusion and curiosity. No doubt talking about her resemblance to her mother. If only Aurora had had a chance to know her mother. But Freija had been right to hide the pregnancy with a magical mirage gifted from the ancestors, and then keep our child hidden away. After the battle during her birth, we both knew it was safer to do so.

"What do you know of the fjell and fae history?" I asked, hoping her guardian had at least taught her something about us even if it was generalizations.

"The basics. Fjell Fae protect the mountains, hold them upright, can create rocks," she rattled off, having done the latter all week with my soldiers.

"And fae history?"

"Is this a lesson or is there a reason for all the questions?"

Ancestors help me, she was definitely mine.

I clasped my hands behind my back and ignored her remark. "You likely know that Skolvik is considered the birthplace of the Fae."

She huffed and nodded, the light catching on her shiny hair. "Yeah, that old rumor."

I let out a long sigh as we turned into the cool and dry anti-chamber to the tombs. Swallowing hard, I continued. "It's not a rumor. It is a fact."

Her eyes widened and she let out a surprised little noise.

At that moment two guards stepped forward, their gray Fjell Fae uniform capes fluttering around their elbows. "Sir," they both said with a nod, resting their hands on the stone swords slung from the belts at their hips.

"At ease."

They did as they were commanded, adjusting their feet slightly and taking up the triangular position, hands behind their backs. Aurora, meanwhile, remained quiet and observant, her gaze flitting over everything.

We passed the soldiers and entered the royal tomb, separated from the other tombs that lay on the other side of the hallway, through the stone mirage sealing it off. Twenty past monarchs, and their family members that had been deemed worthy of such a burial, lay in neat rows. Each stone tomb had an effigy atop it with the fae's likeness. As we wandered through, I kept my eyes off the most recent addition to my right. Hands clenched behind my back, I aimed for the rear of the cavern-like room, where thick pillars of stone had been carved out of the mountain, seemingly holding it aloft.

Reaching the back of the space, we drew to a stop before a wall covered in a carving of a large mountain, its peak dusted with snow, and stars all around it. At the base were swirls of water and on either side was a large tree with branches so long they reached out onto the adjoining walls like vines snaking around the room. Beside the roots of the tree on the right was a carving of a wolf, baying at the starry sky. The canine was added to the mural about a thousand years ago when the Forest Fae King Olaf had paid a visit and asked for help.

With Aurora off to the side behind me, I placed my palm against the center of the mountain, pressing my power into it and requesting entrance. Silvery light spread through the carving, bringing it to life, waking it up.

A small gasp sounded behind me, but I didn't turn nor move my hand until the magic had filled every single line and crevice of the picture. When every part of the mural glowed, a grinding noise filled the cool air and the mountain part of the etching pivoted inward like a door.

I stepped through first and Aurora hesitantly followed, her footsteps light against the quartz-stone floor.

"What is this place?" Her eyes widened as she peered around the room in awe.

The space glowed like the inside of an iceberg, the blues and whites shimmering as if lights moved within the walls. Glossy pillars held the ceiling, while the walls looked similar to the history cave we had elsewhere in the mountain. Unlike that room, though, the carvings in here were far older and of a time that hadn't existed for eons on this earth.

"While the Fjord Fae and Forest Fae have the waters and forests to protect from pollution and harm," I explained, "we, the Fjell Fae, have yet another obligation. We are sworn not only to protect the mountain and its inhabitants, but to protect this, The Temple of the Fae. The birthplace of our kind." Only those with royal magic or head guards had access to the temple. While select soldiers and the Council knew of its existence, it was purposefully a small number of people in order to protect the space from threats.

Aurora's eyebrows rose to meet her hairline. "And you're sharing this with me?"

I took a deep breath and swallowed the lump in my throat. "Because your mother would've wanted you to know." It was true. While Freija hadn't spoken of her much, she longed for the day when she could share the mountain's secrets with our daughter. "And I'm curious to see how the ancestors will react to you declining your title."

She stilled, but didn't flinch at my words. "What do you mean by that?"

"I mean, this is where you would have come to receive your powers once you accepted your place as Queen of the Fjell." That time she flinched. "I do not recall ever having an heir decline, so I'm curious to see what will happen."

I nodded to the plinth at the back of the room. Aurora's gaze drifted to it warily. The sky-blue quartz pedestal rose from the matching stone at our feet reaching the height of a tall table. Nothing sat atop the small square surface which was chipped at three corners, but the glossy piece was carved with intricate swirls and designs that were far older than I. It was a language that hadn't been spoken in over a millennium, maybe even two.

"When an heir..." My throat tightened. I couldn't say the words, couldn't mention the loss of the monarch. "When a Fjell heir takes the throne, part of the private ceremony is to come here and receive the magic of the prior monarch, bestowed from the ancestors. From what I've been told by those I've served, in what information they have told me"—her mother told me everything—"the heir comes here and receives all the magic that their predecessor had, plus anything that might be required at the time."

Aurora huffed and crossed her arms. "And this only applies to the Fjell, not Fjord, Fire, or Forest monarchs?"

I shook my head. "We do not know for sure. I assume there is a similar process... unless there's something they're not telling me." It wouldn't be surprising if the past monarchs had kept information to themselves. Those three corner chunks of the pedestal had been missing from the fjell forever, and it was long suspected that the other factions each had a piece. "What I do know is that this cave and the magic contained herein was our birthplace and a location monarchs have visited in the past for greater assistance from the ancestors."

"So, you want to use me as a test subject?" Aurora asked.

"There have been a lot of firsts in this mountain recently. My hope is that it hasn't thrown off the delicate balance of magic."

"And how exactly are we supposed to find out?"

I nodded at the pedestal. "You place your palm on that."

She snorted and shook her head like I'd lost my mind.

"It won't hurt you..." I hoped.

"Put *your* hand on it then."

I grit my teeth and crossed my arms, taking a step back from the whole situation. "I'm not the heir."

She blinked twice. "You've done it before, haven't you?"

Pursing my lips, I let out a huff through my nose. She was right. I had. Freija had snuck me down here one night, testing my patience and teasing me. Then she challenged me to do it. I'd argued, she'd rolled her eyes, next thing I knew I'd smacked my hand atop the podium. The thing zapped me and I'd pulled back my palm only to find a red mark in the middle of it, as if the ancestors were scolding me for touching something I was merely sworn to protect, not interact with.

"You did, didn't you?" Aurora's lips curled into a smile and my heart clenched. She had her mother's smile, too. One that looked like she was hiding a secret and wouldn't dare share it with you unless you could guess it correctly.

"I did," I conceded. "It merely zapped me."

"And you think shoving your daughter's hand on there is going to do something different?"

"You're Freija's daughter, too. I doubt the ancestors will harm you."

"Are you sure about that?"

No. But I'd destroy anything that harmed this girl. "Try it and see."

She rolled her eyes once more, but stepped up to the plinth. The lights within the walls swirled, as if the magic within them watched us. Taking a deep breath, she stretched her hand over the pedestal and gingerly set it down.

All the oxygen in my lungs stopped moving, waiting to see what would happen. The shimmering lights in the wall picked up speed, like glitter running in circles around us. Silence grew, her eyes narrowed, and my heart beat like I was on a damn battlefield, ready to strike at a moment's notice.

Aurora slowly removed her hand from the top and flexed her fingers.

"Anything?" I asked.

She furrowed her brow and shook her head. "Nothing. Absolutely nothing at all."

I sighed and brushed my hand over my beard. I was worried that might happen. It further solidified mine and the Fjell Council's theory.

"Great. So, the ancestors are okay with me staying in Alvdalen." It was both a question and a statement.

"It would seem so. But it certainly matches my theory."

She gave me a look as if to say, *"which is?"*

"Freija illegally transferred *all* her magic into me"—I tilted my head briefly to one side—"some of which went to Lennie. Which means, there is none of her magic to be gifted on to you. Not until Lennie and I die, and the magic returns to the ancestors for redistribution." Which I had no plans to do any time soon. There was only one fae remaining on this planet that could potentially overpower me, and thankfully, he lived on an island over a thousand kilometers away.

"Okay." Aurora gave me a blank look, and I shook my head. She was as verbose as I was at her age.

"Thank you for coming down here and trying, though," I replied.

"Sure."

"Let me escort you back to the entrance. I'm sure your pack is anxious for your return to Alvdalen." I motioned toward the exit and she followed without any hesitation. "Promise me you will never tell anyone about what you have seen today."

She nodded. "I promise. And yeah, Marius doesn't like me being away from the pack for too long," she replied as we walked past Kings and Queens, ancestors that she'd never learned about and probably never would.

"And this... Marius..." I couldn't believe the words about to come out of my mouth, but I couldn't stop them either. "Is he your... partner?"

She grew quiet, but her breathing stuttered as we passed the tomb guards. "It's... complicated."

I sighed. It always was.

"Halvar..." she muttered and I reduced my pace as we wound further into the tunnels.

"Yes?"

She stopped and turned, her eyebrows drawn together. "Why exactly did she hide me?"

"To keep you from harm."

"I guessed as much."

"Heirs are born with targets on their heads," I said. "You were born during a tumultuous time. War had been brewing in the south and Freija's best friend, Queen Ragnhild, died in the ensuing battle. Freija feared that unrest would come to Skolvik. With everything that has occurred over the past two decades, I'm glad you were safe in Alvdalen."

"Now that I and more people know about"—she waved at herself and then me—"will that target increase?"

I certainly hoped not, but we would always need to be careful. "Word will no doubt spread, but if you keep a low profile and continue practicing your magic, you should remain unharmed."

Her head bobbed and she pursed her lips.

As we were on the subject matter of future plans, I cleared my throat and motioned between us. "How do you wish to proceed?"

She shrugged and twitched her nose. "I appreciate knowing who you are and who she was. But my life isn't here."

"Agreed."

"So, I'm going to head home to Alvdalen."

I straightened. "I accept that. But, if you ever need anything—whether it be a safe haven or a legion to route your enemies—you may always call on us."

A snort escaped from her and her lips quivered into a momentary smile. "Thank you."

With a nod, I took two more steps down the tunnel.

"One more question," Aurora said. I came to a stop once more and faced her. "Lennie stunned me when she kidnapped me and blasted Wilhelm to death."

I grimaced at the tidbit Lennie had no doubt purposefully left out of her tales of searching for Aurora.

"How much Royal Fjell Fae power does she have?" Aurora asked.

My jaw tensed. I was hoping nobody else had noticed. Torsten had spotted it the first day they'd trained together. It wasn't surprising that Lennie's magic was strong since it came from Freija, but it had shocked the light-wielding fae. I'd noticed it when she'd drawn that sword in the forge and again in the throne room, power sparking and dancing across the blade. Then there was the death blow she'd delivered to the wolf—a tactic I'd only ever seen monarchs use in war. I doubted Lennie fully understood what was happening or what she was doing.

My lungs expanded and I exhaled the truth. "More than she knows."

REVIEW

Thank you for reading! I hope you enjoyed Lennie's story. If you did, please consider leaving a review on Amazon, Goodreads, or social media!

Reviews are extremely helpful for indie authors, and I'd greatly appreciate your support!

Best wishes,
Elle

THANK YOU

Thank you for reading! I hope you enjoyed the story and that kind-of cliff-hanger wasn't too brutal lol. This one took me a long time to write, but I'm so happy with how Lennie's story is unfolding and can't believe there's only one book remaining in the trilogy. I hope you stick around for the badassery that's about to go down in book three!

To Riley Jo: Thank you for being the best beta-reader a woman could ask for! Your feedback is always so insightful, and your friendship and support are so appreciated.

To Rosie: My Queen of Typos! Thank you for covering my ass on spellchecks and those bloody hyphens! Lol. I'm so glad to call you my friend.

To Aimee: Goddess of Punctuation and Chaos! In the words of DJ Khaled, "Another one." Thank you for all your feedback and support on this author journey.

To Carl: There are no words for the amount of gratitude I have for you. Thank you for holding me in the dark. I love you.

To River: Thank you for exiting the puppy stage and being the cutest little floof that has ever graced the streets of Boston.

To my readers and supporters: THANK YOU. THANK YOU. THANK YOU FOR READING. Please know that if I ever have the chance to meet you I person, I will hug the ever-loving shit out of you. (Or give you a fist bump if hugs aren't your thing.) Thank you for supporting me as I continue this journey and dream.

About the Author

Hey! I'm Elle Thrasher, an author of romantic fantasy books.

My books are filled with relatable heroines, swoon-worthy heroes, lots of laughs, and locations that will give you wanderlust.

While I'm originally from the UK, and lived in Norway for seven years too, I now live in the US with my husband and one very fluffy dog. When I'm not writing, I can usually be found drinking a cup of tea, staring at my never-ending tbr, or taking a joke waaaaay too far.

Follow me on <u>Instagram</u> for updates and don't forget to sign up for my <u>newsletter</u> to receive behind-the-scenes info, bonus material, and details about upcoming books!

www.ellethrasher.com

ALSO BY ELLE THRASHER

The Cerulean Lazulum Series

(Romantic Suspense/Urban Fantasy)

Cavendish

Hawke

The Nordic Fae Series

(Romantic Fantasy)

The Fae of the Fjord

Christmas on the Fjord (Novella)

The Fae of the Forest

The Fae of the Fjell